JN316615

STUDIES IN CHAUCER'S WORDS
AND
HIS NARRATIVES

STUDIES IN CHAUCER'S WORDS
AND
HIS NARRATIVES

AKIYUKI JIMURA

"The word moot cosyn be to the werking."

KEISUISHA
Hiroshima, Japan
2005

First published on 1st December, 2005

The financial help for the publication of this book is provided by Japan Society for the Promotion of Science, as a Grant-in-Aid (No.175137) for Publication of Scientific Research Results.

Jimura, Akiyuki, 1952-
    Studies in Chaucer's Words and his Narratives / Akiyuki Jimura
    Includes bibliographical references and index
    ISBN 4-87440-903-2 C3098

Copyright © 2005 Akiyuki Jimura

All rights reserved. No part of this publication may be reproduced, stored in a retrieval system, or transmitted, in any form, or by any means, electronic, mechanical, photocopying, recording or otherwise, without the prior permission in writing of Keisuisha Publishing Company.

Published in Japan by
Keisuisha Co., Ltd., 1-4 Komachi, Naka-ku, Hiroshima 730-0041

Printed in Japan

PREFACE

This book is based upon my doctoral dissertation by which I received a doctorate in literature at the Graduate School of Letters, Hiroshima University on the 21st of October, 2002. This consists of four chapters: Chapter 1 Analysis of Textual Structure, Chapter 2 Dialects, Chapter 3 Collocations, and Chapter 4 Grammar. Conclusion has been attached to these chapters as concluding remarks of this book. I would like to hope that this little book will contribute to English philological studies of Chaucer's works.

My personal acknowledgements are too many for the completion of this book.

First of all, it is with deep gratitude that I acknowledge the supervision given by the members of the Dissertation Committee in the Graduate School of Letters, Hiroshima University. The members were Yasunari Ueda, Professor of Linguistics, Graduate School of Letters, Toshiro Tanaka, Professor of English Philology, Graduate School of Letters, Kensuke Ueki, Professor of English Literature, Graduate School of Letters, Toshiyuki Takeshima, Professor of Linguistics, Graduate School of Letters and Yoshiyuki Nakao, Professor of English Education, Graduate School of Education. Tadao Kubouchi, Professor Emeritus at Tokyo University, evaluated my thesis as an external examiner.

I have to state my sincere acknowledgement of my respected professors: Michio Masui, the late professor of Hiroshima University, who had been a perpetual source of inspiration to me. Michio Kawai, Professor Emeritus at Hiroshima University, introduced me to a number of grammatical and philological studies of the English language. Hisashi Takahashi, Professor Emeritus at Hiroshima University and Kiichiro Nakatani, Professor Emeritus at Hiroshima University, opened my eyes to the pleasure of philological studies of English when I was an undergraduate student.

I particularly wish to thank Terry Hoad, St. Peter's College, the University of Oxford, U.K., the Governing Body of which offered me Additional Honorary Membership of the Senior Common Room, when I stayed at Oxford as an overseas research professor of the Ministry of Education, Culture, Sports, Science and Technology, Japan from 30 June 2003 until 28 April 2004.

I have to give my grateful thanks to Raymond P. Tripp, Jr., the late professor of Denver University, U.S.A. and Loren C. Gruber, Professor of English, Missouri Valley College. As to the study of certain "value" words in Chaucer, I shall never forget the valuable suggestion given by Raymond P. Tripp, Jr. Loren C. Gruber has given me a great deal of constant encouragement and helpful advice. He taught me about Chaucer's English and Old English during my stay at Simpson College, U.S.A. as an overseas research student of the Ministry of Education, Science and Culture from 1 September 1974 until 31 August 1975.

I have much benefitted from discussions with my academic colleagues, former and present, as well as the members of Japan Society for Medieval English Studies and the English Research Association of Hiroshima.

I wish also to thank Itsushi Kimura, President of Keisuisha Publishing Co., Ltd. for his generous cooperation and hearty assistance in publishing this book. Then I have to acknowledge gratefully the financial help provided by Japan Society for the Promotion of Science, as a Grant-in-Aid (No.175137) for Publication of Scientific Research Results. Last, but not least, I am much indebted to the following young scholars: Osamu Imahayashi, Hiroji Fukumoto, Hideshi Ohno and Mayumi Sawada, who have spared no pains to proofread my rough draft.

All the errors that remain in this book are, of course, my own.

Graduate School of Leters,
Hiroshima University

December 2005

Akiyuki Jimura

CONTENTS

Preface	v
Contents	vii
Introduction	1
Chapter 1 Analysis of Textual Structure	11
1.0. Introduction	11
1.1. *The Book of the Duchess*	11
1.2. *The House of Fame*	24
1.3. *The Canterbury Tales* and *Troilus and Criseyde*	39
1.4. Hypocritical vocabulary	63
Chapter 2 Dialects	79
2.0. Introduction	79
2.1. Northern dialect	79
2.2. Women's speech	94
Chapter 3 Collocations	117
3.0. Introduction	117
3.1. Troilus and Criseyde	118
3.2. Courtly manners and customs	134
3.3. Nature	152
3.4. God and pagan gods	166
Chapter 4 Grammar	189
4.0. Introduction	189
4.1. "Un"-words	189
4.2. Impersonal constructions	196
4.3. Negative expressions	206
Summary	219
Conclusion	227
Select Bibliography	235
Index	247

INTRODUCTION

The language of Chaucer is so subtle, complicated, and interesting that several studies have been applied to the linguistic analysis of Chaucer's works. We have studied the main stream of previous researches on the language of Chaucer since 1950. We would like to evaluate the present study on Chaucer's language as objectively as possible by looking at the previous language studies carried out during the second half of the twentieth century.

Margaret Schlauch (1952), in "Chaucer's Colloquial English: Its Structural Traits," tried to identify the relationship between language structure and the personality of the speaker, discussing the colloquial features of Chaucer's language such as "looseness, repetition, ellipsis, overlapping, anacoluthon, shifted construction." This paper has helped me to approach sociolinguistic study and write my paper about Criseyde's language in *Troilus and Criseyde*.

Michio Masui (1964), in *The Structure of Chaucer's Rime Words: An Exploration into the Poetic Language of Chaucer*, checking the former language studies of Chaucer, found that the rhyme word is the keyword in the structure of Chaucer's language. He traced the structural relationship between the rhyme words in Chaucer's works, studying the syntactic, semantic, and stylistic structure of the rhyme words. This viewpoint has exercised a great influence on the following generation. The stylistic study of Chaucer's works such as the keywords studies has been very important to interpret the literary works of Chaucer from a linguistic point of view.

J. Kerkhof (1966, 1982^2), in *Studies in the Language of Geoffrey Chaucer*, studied the language of Chaucer from a synchronic point of view, following traditional grammatical standards. However, his corpus was based upon F. N. Robinson's first edition of Chaucer's works. He did not compare Robinson's edition with any other editions, to say nothing of the comparison of the manuscripts, as Manly and Rickert did. Then, he gave us the language materials of Chaucer, but he did not present any interpretation of the text. Kerkhof's second edition added several grammatical items to his first edition.

Norman E. Eliason (1972), in *The Language of Chaucer's Poetry: An Appraisal of the Verse, Style, and Structure*, dealt with the subjective interpretation of Chaucer's language, though the former studies were based upon the facts about the language. Eliason did not use any statistical data of the language.

Ralph W. V. Elliott (1974), in *Chaucer's English*, tried to understand the language of Chaucer from an integrated point of view, and let us recognise the meaning of the usage, reading faithfully the context of Chaucer's literary works word by word rather than linguistically, based upon copious examples of Chaucer's language. His analysis of the impersonal construction has had a great influence upon my book. Elliott seems to have put an emphasis upon Chaucer's vocabulary.

Norman Davis (1974), in "Chaucer and Fourteenth-Century English," indicated that Chaucer made the best use of new words adopted from French, native words and phrases, and the popular speech spoken by ordinary people in the contemporary written language.

Vivian Salmon (1975), in "The Representation of Colloquial Speech in *The Canterbury Tales*," following the course of Margaret Schlauch and discussing Chaucer's colloquial speech, stated that the characters' speeches spoken in *The Canterbury Tales* reflected the living speech spoken by contemporary people in the late fourteenth century. Though Salmon only dealt with *The Canterbury Tales*, we could also discuss the characters' speeches in the other works such as *Troilus and Criseyde*.

Gregory. H. Roscow (1981), in *Syntax and Style in Chaucer's Poetry*, was also concerned with the language of Chaucer from only a syntactic point of view. He did not discuss the problems of Chaucer's vocabulary.

David Burnley (1983), in *A Guide to Chaucer's Language*, discussed the meaning of Chaucer's language in order to understand Chaucer's literary works. His study is divided into two parts: (1) the problems of interpretation of the text from the viewpoints of grammar and syntax and (2) Chaucer's language and vocabulary, concentrating on language use, style, and variety. We should follow his approach to the study of Chaucer's language, because it is basically philological.

Arthur O. Sandved (1985), in *Introduction to Chaucerian English*, gave only a descriptive account of Chaucer's language, especially phonology and morphology, based upon F. N. Robinson's second edition. Though this study is an objective description of Chaucer's English, it is in no way an interpretation of Chaucer's literary works.

M. L. Samuels and J. J. Smith (1988), in *The English of Chaucer and His Contemporaries* discussed the textual criticism, paleography, book-production, dialectology, and graphemics of the language of Chaucer, Gower, and Langland. This book told us that the relationship between the language of the author and that of the scribe was difficult to deal with, because the language of the author could not be read and recognised by the manuscript which the professional scribes have written.

Christopher Cannon (1998), in *The Making of Chaucer's English: A Study of Words*, indicated that the language of Chaucer belonged to nothing but the conventional and traditional English, warning against the blind faith of Chaucerian scholars as to Chaucer's linguistic innovation and originality. As a matter of course, we should not overemphasise the literary and linguistic meanings of Chaucer's words and works and we should also be careful not to read them too literally, but there is no clear reason why we should not practice creative reading of Chaucer's texts. It is not too much to say that any author would consider his words carefully and deliberately and integrate his thoughts and ideas into them, when he or she tries to write his or her literary works. Therefore, we could not place high value upon Cannon's approach to the language of Chaucer.

In this way, a brief survey of the previous language studies of Chaucer shows that we have at least two kinds of approach: (1) the literary study of Chaucer's language and (2) the linguistic study of Chaucer's language. However, we will also find an integrated approach between literary and linguistic studies of Chaucer's language. Schlauch, Masui, Davis, Elliott, and Burnley follow this eclectic approach. My study is also based upon this approach, i.e. the literary and linguistic aspect of Chaucer's language, which leads to narrative stylistics, when Chaucer's words are organically studied in his works.

This kind of language study is closely connected with a textlinguistic approach to Chaucer's works. Before we discuss the outline of this book, we would like to investigate a textlinguistic approach in general and then an experiment with Chaucer's texts in particular.

It is generally known that textlinguistics analyses and describes several conditions and rules constituting discourse or text which consists of the sentences occurring in succession.[1] Broadly speaking, there exist two kinds of approach to textlinguistics. (1) One is that linguists regard the text as the extension of the traditional concept of the text (i.e., an analysis of intra-sentential elements), and deal with the linguistic studies of several conditions bringing about inter-sentential elements beyond the sentences. (2) The other is that linguists regard the text as the field where communicative activities are performed, and try to make patterns and models including the intentions and behaviours of addressers and addressees.

The former is divided into two approaches: (a) a microscopic approach, which examines the conditions bringing about the text from the viewpoints of the grammatical and semantic relationships between sentences, and (b) a macroscopic approach, which deals with restrictions on the construction of the whole text. Appraoch (a) is called an analysis of cohesion, where several lexical features are focused on, with special attention to the recurrent words and the repetitions of synonyms or semantically related phrases. Approach (b) deals with the structural analysis of texts such as the narrative structure of a novel. The latter focuses on language behaviour as one of the social activities of human beings, taking the field of language expression into consideration. Socio-linguistic factors would be dealt with in this approach, e.g. how women's language functions in a certain text organically or effectively.

This study is mainly based upon the former approach, although a sociolinguistic study of *Troilus and Criseyde* belongs to the latter. Here we should consider the stylistic approach to the literary works. Stylistics has something in common with textlinguistics because stylistics aims at analysing the style of the language expression as a whole and of the narrative structure such as stories or myths. This study is concerned with the textlinguistic or stylistic approach to fourteenth-century literary works in England.

Leo Spitzer's idea of a philological circle supports our study. Literary works have their own organic unities and they consist of smaller parts, which are closely connected with the whole work.[2] When we investigate those smaller units, it is possible to understand the whole organically. For example, keywords, dialects, collocations, and syntactical units are related to the structure of literary works and create organic unities of the narratives.

Now let us turn to the narrative stylistics of Chaucer's language. We would like to take L. D. Benson's text as the basis for the stylistic investigation of Chaucer's language. Since his edition was published after a comprehensive survey of Chaucerian scholarship, we would like to follow it unless we can establish a more authoritative basis through a textual comparison of Chaucer's edited texts. My study consists of four chapters: Chapter 1 Analysis of Textual Structure, Chapter 2 Dialects, Chapter 3 Collocations, and Chapter 4 Grammar. It is important to understand the meanings of words such as "herte," "soth" and "fals," "hous," and of hypocritical vocabulary in the textual structure, regional dialects and social dialects such as women's language, collocations such as the value words and nouns, and grammatical expressions such as negative expressions, impersonal constructions, when we discuss the narrative stylistics of Chaucer's language. Chaucer would be consciously using the words in the textual structure, the dialects, the collocations, and grammar when he narrated his story before the audience. This study is concerned with Chaucer's intentional use of language in his narratives.

All Chaucer citations, as indicated above, are from L. D. Benson (ed.), *The Riverside Chaucer*, 3rd edition (Boston: Houghton Mifflin, 1987). Italics in the passages are mine. All the data in this study, except for texts specially referred to, are based on Benson's edition. The computer programme used in this study was developed by Masatsugu Matsuo, Hiroshima University.

When we consider how Chaucer's language is skilfully connected with his narrative stylistics, his use of keywords, collocations, dialects, grammatical expressions are important. We will see how they allow Chaucer to narrate before the audience. In Chapter 1, we will deal with the textual structure of *The Book of the Duchess*, *The House of Fame*, *Troilus and Criseyde*, and some tales of *The Canterbury Tales*.

In *The Book of the Duchess*, the apparently inconsistent structure is organised throughout by the word "herte" (=heart). It is used throughout this work; it invites us to think about the details of this poem. This word not only becomes a part of wordplay, but it also results in relating all the episodes of this book to each other. In section 1 of Chapter 1, we would like to investigate the meaning of the keyword "herte" which seems to unify the whole work.

In section 2 of Chapter 1, we will not examine *The House of Fame* from a viewpoint of love, but instead we would like to interpret the structure of this work, though partially, while considering the importance of the antithetical keywords "soth" (=true) and "fals" (=false). These are more often used in this work than in Chaucer's other works, and therefore play an important role in *The House of Fame*.

"The Tale of Melibee" is one of the two tales narrated by Chaucer the pilgrim. The first, "The Tale of Sir Thopas," is apparently a self-mocking, satirical poem of a faded knight riding from the fading days of gallantry. Chaucer the pilgrim is cut short by the Host who says that his "drasty rymyng is nat worth a toord!" (filthy rhyming is not worth a turd!) (I.930). The poet then turns to reciting a translation of the French *Livre de Melibee et de Dame Prudence*. Why the masterful Chaucer would have his poetic persona recite this pair of tales has often troubled scholars. An examination of the symbolism of "The Tale of Melibee" will shed light upon the question, and perhaps provide at least one answer. The concerns of Chaucer and his sensitive contemporaries were not about physical exploits, but exploits of the mind and soul.

In section 3 of Chapter 1, we will discuss Chaucer's expression of "hous," which symbolises the body of the human beings, considering the role the house plays in "The Knight's Tale" and "The Miller's Tale" of *The Canterbury Tales* and *Troilus and Criseyde*.

In discussing "The Reeve's Prologue and Tale" of *The Canterbury*

Tales, it is not enough to deal only with the northern dialect, because we find the other characters such as the Miller, the narrator Reeve's rival, who use other dialects rather than the students' northern dialect. The Miller, who does not use the northern dialect, is represented in the first half of "The Reeve's Tale" as a man of hypocritical nature, which is in striking contrast to the Cambridge students who speak simple and naïve dialects. Hearing the unadorned speech of the students, the Miller decides definitely to equivocate with them. In section 4 of Chapter 1, we will examine the characterisations of the Miller and his family, who regard country speech as "inferior." We will investigate the real figures of the people who pretend to belong to the upper and intellectual class, making little use of the dialects.

In Chapter 2, we will see an overview of the variation in Chaucer's English: the regional and social varieties of English which might have existed in Chaucer's age. In section 1, we would like to discuss the effects of the northern dialect in "The Reeve's Prologue and Tale," by paying special attention to the relationship between the characters and their northern dialect, after briefly surveying some scholars' opinions about them. Although studies of regional dialects in Middle English writings have progressed remarkably, sociolinguistic studies of Middle English have been insufficiently developed. In particular, we still await a study of women's speech in the language of the female characters in Chaucer's works. In section 2 we will deal with the language of Criseyde in Chaucer's *Troilus and Criseyde*, focusing mainly on her vocabulary. Comparing Criseyde's vocabulary with those of Troilus and Pandarus, we will concentrate on the characteristics of women's language in fourteenth-century upper class society, few though they may be.

In Chapter 3, we will discuss collocations between adjectives and nouns, considering that adjectives, which define the nature, appearance, and attributes of people, in conjunction with detailed and concrete description, constitute Chaucer's description of characters. It is not too much to say that Chaucer's adjectives play an important role in *Troilus and Criseyde* and that they may determine and direct the characters.

In Chapter 4, we deal with the grammatical expressions, showing Chaucer's stylistic devices. In section 1, we would like to concentrate on the negative elements of words, especially the "un"-words in "The Clerk's Tale" where the negative expressions seem to be used frequently. We would like to see briefly how effectively the "un"-words, especially "unsad" (=unstable), "untrewe" (=unfaithful), and "undiscreet" (=undiscerning) are used in "The Clerk's Tale." Section 2 aims at recognising how organically the impersonal constructions are used in Chaucer's *Troilus and Criseyde*. Here we will deal with the main matter and problem of some concern: why Chaucer used impersonal constructions in *Troilus and Criseyde*. Section 3, focusing on the speech of the characters, investigates the negatives or negative expressions used in the speeches of the main characters Walter and Griselda and the narrator in "The Clerk's Tale." It should be noted here that the relationship between master and man cultivated and established "gladly" in "The General Prologue" to *The Canterbury Tales* is transferred to the conjugal relationship between Walter and Griselda in "The Clerk's Tale." Griselda, using negative expressions, receives Walter's ascetic teaching gladly and naturally.

Textual structure, collocations between adjectives and nouns, regional and social dialects, grammatical expressions such as "un"-words, impersonal and negative constructions are all connected with one another in Chaucer's works. Textual structure can show the organic relationship between the word and the story or work which Chaucer wrote. Regional dialect is important, because it is only used in Chaucer's works, and social dialect such as women's language must also be considered, because we can understand that it reflects how those people are dealt with, playing an important part in Chaucer's works. Collocations can depict semantically the images of the main characters, to say nothing of the situations, nature, and supernatural beings surrounding them. One of the reasons we call them "grammatical expressions" here is that morphemes such as the prefix "un" are analysed in conjunction with the narrative structure in Chaucer's works, to say nothing of the impersonal and negative constructions. The expressions visualise the characters or the works; in this case, Chaucer's grammatical expressions. Then textual structure, collocations, dialects, and grammar are hypertextually connected with one another and they create Chaucer's narrative stylistics. In this way, the stylistic aspect of Chaucer's language will be studied from the viewpoints of textual structure, dialects, collocations, and grammatical expressions.

Notes
   1   This explanation is based upon *The Kenkyusha Dictionary of English Linguistics and Philology*, edited by T. Otsuka and F. Nakajima (Tokyo: Kenkyusha, 1982).
   2   Leo Spitzer wrote his essay "Linguisitics and Literary History" in 1948, which is included in *Leo Spitzer: Representative Essays*, edited by A. K. Forcione, H. Lindenberger and M. Sutherland (Stanford: Stanford University Press, 1988).

CHAPTER 1

Analysis of Textual Structure

1.0. Introduction

In this chapter we discuss how words function organically in the textual structure of Chaucer's works, which is its own organic unity and consists of smaller parts, closely connected to form a whole. Keywords are related to the structure of the literary works and create the organic unities of the narratives. Words such as "herte" are used as the wordplay in the story and play an important part in *The Book of the Duchess*. Words such as "soth" and "fals" are used as antithetical expressions and show the value judgement or morality concerning what is true or false in *The House of Fame*. "Hous" symbolises both the human body which governs the human mind "herte" and the story of the work which the poet is going to narrate in *Troilus and Criseyde*. Words functioning as "double entendre" (here we use "hypocritical vocabulary" as the title of the section) show the double-faced nature of the characters in "The Reeve's Tale." Those words, i.e. the smaller parts or units of the text, create the understanding of the whole structure integratedly and interlinearly.

1.1. *The Book of the Duchess*

It is sometimes said that the structure of *The Book of the Duchess* is "inorganic."[1] When we read and reread this work, however, the apparently inconsistent structure seems to be organised throughout to its conclusion. The word which supports this impression and informs

11

the work is "herte."

Major scholars agree that the word "herte" seems to make this work organic. As Kökeritz (1954)[2] and Baum (1956)[3] have indicated, the expression "hert-huntyng"[4] used as wordplay is a suitable word to unite this story. This compound word invites us to ask why "herte" is used throughout this work; it invites our thoughts to examine the details of this poem. This word not only becomes a part of wordplay, but it also results in relating all the episodes of this book to each other. In this section, we would like to investigate once again the meaning of the keyword "herte" which seems to unify the whole work.

The Book of the Duchess begins with the description of the poet suffering from insomnia. It should be noted that instead of "herte" we find partial synonyms such as "thoght," "mynde," and "hede,"[5] though his suffering results from his heart. The poet seems not to know where his sorrow is.

The inconsolable heart-sick poet at first reads the story of King Seys and Queen Alcyone, which corresponds to the relationship between the Black Knight and the fair White. As R. Delasanta (1969) states,[6] this story may make the readers or audience expect the following story. Alcyone's "herte" is pitiful because she lost her husband. Here the narrator seems to indicate that her sorrow lies in her "herte" for the first time. It should be noted that "herte" is separated from "body" in a certain sense. We know that "herte" continues to live even though "body" dies. This "herte" is transformed into the "hert" (=hart) and the Black Knight's "herte" (=heart) when the hart is gone.[7] Then, in retrospect, the knight confesses his "herte" in order to make the heavy "herte" easy and light, and he describes his beloved, his sweetheart.

Ultimately, after the "hert-huntyng" is done, the knight discovers his house or palace, where his "herte" rests peacefully. This may be a profound consolation to the poet suffering from insomnia.

In *The Book of the Duchess*, the use of "herte" is divided into the following three parts: (1) the hart, (2) the heart of the body, and (3) the sweetheart or love such as "fair White." The purpose of this chapter is to investigate how the keyword "herte" is related organically to the story of this work. We will study the use of "herte" in the following narrative structure of this work: (1) the poet suffering from insomnia, (2) Seys and Alcyone, (3) the hunting scene of the hart, (4) the Black Knight's sorrowful heart, (5) the Black Knight's declaration of love, and (6) the description of "goode, faire White."

(1) The poet suffering from insomnia
The poet, who could not sleep in his bed, appears to be seized with only mental action or his process of thinking, which is far from the emotions. He cannot recover his presence of mind. Here we do not find the word "herte," but its partial synonyms.[8]

> For sorwful ymagynacioun
> Ys alway hooly in my mynde.
> . . . .
> Suche fantasies ben in myn hede
> So I not what is best to doo.
> . . . .
> And in this bok were written fables
> That clerkes had in olde tyme,
> And other poetes, put in rime
> To rede and for to be in minde,
> While men loved the lawe of kinde. (14-56)

As is clearly shown in the noun "hede" (the *OED*, "2. As the seat of the mind, thought, intellect, memory, or imagination;.... Often contrasted with heart, as the seat of emotions;...," and the *MED*, "3. (a) The seat of the mind; the mind; *hed and herte*, heart and mind; *leien (putten hedes togeder*, to confer; *with a hol hed*; unanimously."), the words about internal pains[9] reveal the state of mind where he tries to solve his inexplicable pains only intellectually and logically.[10] This is in contrast with the emotional state of mind seen in the noun "herte." With this kind of reasoning the poet probably cannot set his mind at ease and calm himself. However, reading the ancient stories in the old books, he recovers himself slowly and steadily and drifts into a peaceful sleep.[11]

(2) Seys and Alcyone

The poet, who has been suffering from insomnia, reads the episode of Seys and Alcyone. Here we find the word "herte" for the first time. The noun "herte" is used to show Alcyone's sorrowful state of mind caused by the loss of her husband Seys.

> Anon her herte began to [erme];
> ....
> That certes it were a pitous thing
> To telle her hertely sorowful lif
> That she had, this noble wif,
> For him, allas, she loved alderbest. (80-87)

The verb "erme," derived from Old English, means "grieve," but this semantically corresponds to the following word "hertely," which A. C. Baugh takes as the adverb meaning "genuinely."[12] Furthermore, E. T. Donaldson takes it as the adjective meaning "heartfelt."[13] According to the MED, in Chaucer's works, the adjective "hertely" collocates with the nouns such as "wyl" or "wordes," while the adverb "hertely" with the verbs "welcome," "lyke," "pray," "thank" and love" or the adverb "wele." We would like to accept Donaldson's interpretation, judging from the etymology that "hertely" is derived from her sorrowful "herte," but the etymology might not be a sure guide here. It would be natural that "hertely" intensifies the meaning of the adjective "sorwoful," according to the syntactical unit of collocation.

Alcyone, complaining of her sorrow in the chest, implores mercy from Juno with all her heart. The word "herte" is used in her speech:

> And hooly youres become I shal
> With good wille, body, herte, and al; (115-16)

It is as if Juno read Alcyone's sorrowful heart; she lets Morpheus revive King Seys. When Morpheus picks up the body of Seys, the god of sleep puts "herte" (which is of course invisible, so the word "herte" does not appear in the text) in Seys's "body."

> He take up Seys body the kyng,
> ....
> Bid hym crepe into the body
> ....
> And do the body speke ryght soo, (142-49)

In this passage, we see that the body is separated from the heart. Even though the body dies, the "herte" continues to live and later it appears. The dominant idea of this work seems to be that the "herte" lives for ever even though the body disappears.

In the end, Alcyone's inconsolable "herte" leads to Seys's "herte." King Seys speaks to Alcyone in a gentle tone of voice, appearing in her dream.

> Took up the dreynte body sone
> And bar hyt forth to Alcione,
> Hys wif the quene, ther as she lay
> ....
> By name, and sayde, "My swete wyf,
> Awake! Let be your sorwful lyf,
> For in your sorwe there lyth no red;
> For, certes, swete, I am but ded.
> Ye shul me never on lyve yse.
> But, goode swete herte, that ye
> Bury my body, for such a tyde
> Ye mowe hyt fynde the see besyde;
> And farewel, swete, my worldes blysse!
> I praye God youre sorwe lysse.
> To lytel while oure blysse lasteth!" (195-211)

What is important in this passage is the identity of the greeting or the term of address: "goode swete herte." This literally indicates Alcyone, but since this speech is her sweetheart Seys's, the king's "herte" approaches his dear wife's "herte," and both hearts are in harmony with each other. The expression "our blysse" may show that they are strongly attached to each other. We know that their true hearts live eternally even though the body becomes a corpse and the happiness in this world is but short-lived.

In this way, this story not only consoles the poet's painful state of mind, without benefit of sleep or rest, but the word "herte" is also transformed into the different shapes in the following sections.[14]

(3) The hunting scene of the hart

The poet, who has not slept enough till the present time, dreams "so ynly swete a sweven," (276). The dream begins with the description of spring, according to the Middle English convention.[15] The gentle twittering of the birds, along with the transparent glassed-in chamber of the dreamer-poet may show the poet's cheerful and clear state of mind. Here the glazed window corresponds to the eyes leading to the "herte." Additionally, the sound of the hunting of the hart echoes to the poet's "herte."[16] He sees the "hert" (=hart).

> And as I lay thus, wonder lowde
> Me thoght I herde an hunte blowe
> T'assay hys horn and for to knowe
> Whether hyt were clere or hors of soun.
> . . . .
> And al men speken of huntyng,
> How they wolde slee the hert with strengthe,
> And how the hert had upon lengthe
> So moche embosed — y not now what. (344-53)

The poet hears the sounds of deer hunting, symbolising courtship, as though in harmony with the comfortable chirpings of the birds and the water-clear sky. The "huntyng" of the "hert" seems to seize the poet's "herte." This "hert" had formerly "embosed," i.e., taken shelter in a wood or thicket. What with the hunter losing sight of the hart, and what with the discovering of the hart, the hart's action of appearing and disappearing is repeated.

> Withynne a while the hert yfounde ys,
> Yhalowed, and rechased faste
> Longe tyme; and so at the laste
> This hert rused, and staal away
> Fro alle the houndes a privy way. (378-82)

Despite the discovery of the hart, as in "yfounde ys," it "rused," i.e., made a detour or other movement in order to escape from the dogs.

Thus, it is during the chase that the "hert" escaped the hunters; it may also be important that the poet sees many harts, many hinds, many fawns and many others, symbolising breeding and reproduction, when he is bathed with the greenery in the wood and the warmth in spring. All of nature's creatures, including the poet, are released from the heaviness of the cold winter.

> And many an hert and many an hynde
> Was both before me and behynde.
> Of founes, sowres, bukkes, does
> Was ful the woode, and many roes, (427-30)

The discoveries of various deer and the findings of many young ones may show the recovery from the loss of the "hert."

(4) The Black Knight's sorrowful heart

When the poet in the dream, who thinks the "hert" has been finally lost, is wandering in the woods (which themselves may symbolise the entangled emotions and untamed thoughts), he, guided by the dog,[17] meets a Black Knight by chance.[18] He meets with the black knight's sorrowful "herte," instead of the "hert." We know that the lost hart is transformed into the knight's heart. The poet understands that the knight's "herte" is about to burst forth, judging from this knight's great lamentation. The loss of his sweetheart leads to the state where he loses his own "herte" in the body. (In fact, his sweetheart owned his "herte.")

> Hys sorwful hert gan faste faynte
> And his spirites wexen dede;
> The blood was fled for pure drede
> Doun to hys herte, to make hym warm —
> For wel hyt feled the herte had harm —
> To wite eke why hyt was adrad
> By kynde, and for to make hyt glad,
> For hit ys membre principal
> Of the body;
> . . . .
> Hym thoughte hys sorwes were so smerte
> And lay so colde upon hys herte. (488-508)

The noun "herte" is treated as a normal inanimate noun and referred to by the pronoun "hyt," but it is not too much to say that this "herte" is the knight himself because the subject "his sorwful herte" collocates with the verbs "faynte," "feled," and "was adrad," which may also reveal compassion and empathy. The "blood" which recognises the cold "herte" of the knight vitalizes him, since it gives the heat to the knight under the influence of Nature, according to medieval beliefs about physiology.

The poet therefore plays the part of the "blood" which warms his "herte." Although G. L. Kittredge does not evaluate this poet's speech, because he believes it not to be suitable for the elegiac tone of this poem,[19] this is not the case. As H. Phillips indicates,[20] the poet acts as a consolation to the sorrowful knight "herte."

> Anoon ryght I gan fynde a tale
> To hym, to loke wher I myght ought
> Have more knowynge of hys thought.
> "Sir," quod I, "this game is doon.
> I holde that this hert be goon;
> These huntes konne hym nowher see." (536-41)

This speech seems to appear suddenly in this stage, but this functions not only as the connection between one episode and another, but it also plays an important part for the Black Knight's "herte." The poet says: "this game is doon" and "this hert be goon," using the demonstrative pronoun "this," in order to communicate the intimate relationship with the knight. In the passage, "this" literally refers to the hart itself; later "this" may be more closely connected with the "herte" whom the knight truly lost.

It does not matter to the knight that the hart disappeared, but it should be noted that the expression "this hert" is the part of the wordplay. The knight has been tormented by the loss of his "herte." Even though he says: "Y do no fors therof" (542), it may be thought that such a negative statement would be spoken all the more consciously to illustrate the relationship between his "herte" and him.

The speech: "this hert is goon" may soften the knight's painful heart a little, because the knight, using the technique of antithesis, begins to confess about his sorrowful heart after the poet says: "And telleth me of your sorwes smerte; / Paraunter hyt may ese youre herte" (555-56). Although the knight's speech does not touch the core of his heart, we understand that his sorrowful heart becomes soothed gradually.

On the other hand, the poet's heart is charmed more and more by the knight's sad story, where his sorrowful fortune is told, mixed with the story of the chess queen.

> And whan I herde hym tel thys tale
> Thus pitously, as I yow telle,
> Unnethe myght y lenger dwelle,
> Hyt dyde myn herte so moche woo. (710-13)

The poet's "herte" is moved to sympathy as he listens to the knight's sorrowful story. The fact that his story made the poet feel compassionate may mean that the knight met with a person of understanding. The "herte" is thus rescued, because the knight can talk about his good and unforgettable memory, even though he had undergone a bitter and sad experience previously. Remembering his sweet memories, the knight states that his "herte" is harmonised with his lady.

> ... She was lady
> Of the body; she had the herte,
> And who hath that may not asterte. (1152-54)

The lady was the master of the knight's "body" and owned his "herte," so the knight's "herte" is also the lady's "herte." Here we do not see the separation of "body" and "herte" which we found in the episode of Seys and Alcyone. The knight was controlled by the lady who incorporated his "body" and "herte" in one. We therefore know that when she passed away his "herte" which is "membre principal / Of the body" (496-97) felt a deep sorrow. However, since the knight begins to talk about his sweet remembrance with his lady, his "herte" has just extricated itself from adverse circumstances.[21]

(5) The Black Knight's declaration of love
It may be a generally acknowledged truth that in the medieval world love enters in the heart through the eye: i.e. the window of the heart. So does the knight's love. As a matter of course, the knight sees the most charming lady of all.

> "Among these ladyes thus echon,
> Soth to seyen, y sawgh oon
> That was lyk noon of the roote;
> . . . .
> For al the world so hadde she
> Surmounted hem alle of beaute, (817-26)

Since she enters in the knight's "herte," both the intellectual and emotional states of mind are governed by the lady.

> That she ful sone in my thought,
> As helpe me God, so was ykaught
> So sodenly that I ne tok
> No maner counseyl but at hir lok
> And at myn herte; for-why hir eyen
> So gladly, I trow, myn herte seyen (837-42)

The knight falls in one-sided love with the lady, thinking that "hir eyen," the window of her "herte," must have shown a friendly feeling for the knight's "herte." This may be little more than his subjective feeling, as in the epistemic clause "I trow."

We notice the recurring expressions of joy and sorrow when we see the knight's one-sided love, just as Troilus's. It may be true that love is a sweet torment so the expressions concerning "herte" are used variously: when he tries to divert the mind from yearning (1171-72), when he cannot decide whether or not to unlock his heart to her (1193), and when he declares his deep love to her for the first time (1211). These uses of the noun "herte" may show his inconsolable state of mind, since the knight does not know whether or not he can earn the lady's love.

We will deal with the passage where the knight swears his deep courtly love to the lady with all his heart. This speech may be the final destination of the wandering "herte."

> Whan that myn hert was come ageyn,
> To telle shortly al my speche,
> With hool herte I gan hir beseche
> That she wolde be my lady swete;
> And swor, and gan hir hertely hete (1222-26)

He tries to serve the lady from the bottom of his heart. It seems that the lady who binds the knight's "herte" in this way is a perfect marvel of beauty.

(6) The description of "goode, faire White"[22]

When we see the "herte" of "faire White," we cannot ignore the description of her "body" over two hundred lines,[23] to say nothing of her eyes showing the window of her "herte." This may be the traditional description of courtly love,[24] but it should also be noted here that the "eyen," which are the windows of the body, may reflect the internal world where the "herte" exists. Based on that conventional idea, we would like to investigate the description of the lady.

As the heart's letter is read in the eyes, her charming eyes may show her pure and noble heart.

> "And whiche eyen my lady hadde!
> Debonaire, goode, glade, and sadde,
> Symple, of good mochel, noght to wyde.
> Therto hir look nas not asyde
> Ne overthwert, but beset so wel
> Hyt drew and took up everydel
> Al that on hir gan beholde.
> Hir eyen semed anoon she wolde
> Have mercy —
> . . . .
> But ever, me thoght, hir eyen seyde,
> 'Be God, my wrathe ys al foryive!'
> . . . .
> But many oon with hire lok she herte,
> And that sat hyr ful lyte at herte,
> For she knew nothyng of her thoght; (859-85)

Ironically enough, however, the verb "herte" (=hurt) is used when the beautiful eyes hurt the man's "herte." As Kökeritz indicates,[25] this pun is another use of wordplay of "herte" in this work. The "herte," the window of the eyes, did "herte," i.e. injure, the man's "herte" and the knight's "herte" itself, damaged by her eyes, feels a great pain.

Declaring his deep love to the lady, he calls her "myn herte swete" (1233), as if he were conveying his feelings in his "herte." This may be the knight's one-sided love, as we have already seen in the knight's declaration of love. Although he is once ignored by his sweet heart's "herte," each "herte" nevertheless becomes united and the knight and the lady are strongly attached to each other.

> Oure hertes wern so evene a payre
> That never nas that oon contrayre
> To that other for no woo.
> For sothe, ylyche they suffred thoo
> Oo blysse and eke oo sorwe bothe;
> Ylyche they were bothe glad and wrothe;
> Al was us oon, withoute were.
> And thus we lyved ful many a yere
> So wel I kan nat telle how." (1289-97)

The "herte" in one-sided love, as in the former section, arrives at the house of the sweetheart's "herte." His "herte" is deeply connected with the lady's "herte." Although the use of the demonstrarive pronoun "they" in the fourth line shows "oure hertes" being viewed objectively, it should be noted that the first person pronoun "we" is used in the second line from the last. This change to a more subjective view may indicate that their hearts become one heart in the end.

After this narration, the poet knows what the knight really lost and the book comes to the last scene.

> "She ys ded!" "Nay!" "Yis, be my trouthe!"
> "Is that youre los? Be God, hyt ys routhe!"
> And with that word ryght anoon
> They gan to strake forth; al was doon,
> For that tyme, the hert-huntyng. (1309-13)

This passage is important, as most critics note,[26] because it may show that the word "herte" is intentionally used as wordplay in this work. Though this passage literally denotes the end of the hart-hunting, the "hert" of the compound performs multiple functions: the "herte" meaning sweetheart whom Alcyone has sought; the Black Knight's sorrowful "herte," the dear "herte" whom the knight has wished for. This expression seems to play a concluding part of this work.

Ultimately, the "herte" is at the point of being lost or it is really lost.

The hart disappears in a certain place. The function of the knight's "herte" is about to stop. The beautiful white lady passes away. When the poet finishes telling about his lost lady, the "hert-huntyng" is done. Since the hart which is pursued by the hunters is also the sweetheart and the heart of the body, and since they are all going to be lost, the bereavement of the "herte" may very well be the theme of *The Book of the Duchess*.[27]

The final rescue occurs, however, when "this kyng" has returned to the white house, symbolising the white lady, which also protects the "herte."[28]

> With that me thoghte that this kyng
> Gan homwarde for to ryde
> Unto a place, was there besyde,
> Which was from us but a lyte —
> A long castel with walles white,
> Be Seynt Johan, on a ryche hil,
> As me mette; but thus hyt fil. (1314-20)

The expression "this kyng," as E. Reiss indicates,[29] literally refers to the king who has been hunting in this work, but the king and the knight pursuing his love also overlap each other in this passage. This last scene may suggest the recovery from the deprivation of love. This house, playing the part of the "body" of the human beings,[30] protects the "herte" while healing the king's sorrowful "herte." The house is the ultimate destination of the "herte." It may also be the suggestion that the poet is released from insomnia.

1.2. The House of Fame

It may be a generally acknowleged truth that Chaucer is a love poet. Though some scholars focus their studies on the theme of fame reflecting the ambivalent or contradictory nature of various things in the work, his second dream poem *The House of Fame* also deals with the theme of love, since "tydynges of love" ultimately come at the last scene of this work.[31]

It is a fact, however, that we do not see the words concerning "love" except where the poet narrates the stories of false love in the first half of this work and where he reveals the "newe tydynge" at the last stage of Book III.[32] This may mean that had Chaucer completed Book III he may have written a love-story; the extant text does not show this aspect of the poet's attitude of love, however. In this section, we will not examine *The House of Fame* from a viewpoint of love, but we would like to interpret the structure of this work, though partially, while considering the importance of the antithetical keywords "soth" and "fals." These are more often used in this work than Chaucer's other works, and therefore play an important role in *The House of Fame*. The following Table 1 shows the frequency of "soth" and "fals" and their variants and derivatives:

Table 1 Frequency of "soth" and "fals" and their variants and derivatives

	soth	sothe	sothly	fals	falsly
CT	60	34	75	109	11
BD	13	3	0	13	0
HF	17	3	1	11	2
ANEL	1	0	0	13	0
PF	3	1	3	2	0
BO	32	17	3	27	5
TC	56	11	4	22	3
LGW	5	2	9	28	4
SHP	3	0	2	5	0
ASTR	3	0	14	0	0
RR	23	14	10	24	4
total	216	85	121	254	29

These words are not so frequently used as the word of the title "fame" and its related words (see Table 7), but they seem to play an important part in this work, because we find these keywords in *The House of Fame* more often than in Chaucer's other works.

When Chaucer was writing *The House of Fame*, he might have

groped in the dark to discover what was true, using and experimenting with various methods of writing, as "a preve by experience" (a proof by experience) (878).[33] We do not know whether or not this is indeed Chaucer's attitude or practice, but we often find "soth" and "fals" and semantically related words and at the same time we see the stories true and false juxtaposed in this work. This fact may indicate that the poet might have felt keenly how he could get the correct answer to the following question: what on earth can he trust? "Soth" belongs to a set of words semantically connected through their expressing favourable judgement of moral or other qualities. "Fals," conversely, belongs to a set of words expressing unfavourable judgement of such qualities. The frequency of words in these sets is shown in the following tables 2 and 3.[34] (We do not distinguish their parts of speech, but we list them mechanically according to the frequency.)

Table 2   Frequency of words in the "soth" set

certeyn (16), kynde (9), goode (8), faire (7), famous (5), kyndely (7), trouthe (6), clere (5), redely (5: including the meaning of "soon"), trewely (5), worthy (5), certeynly (4), deserved (4), certes (3), Nature (3), propre (3), trowe (3), desserve (2), feythfully (2), godnesse (2), goodly (2), kyndes (2), naturel (2), thewes (2), verray (2), whit (2), white (2), better (1), certayn (1), certaynly (1), certein (1), certeinly (1), fayre (1), feir (1), fynest (1), godlyhed (1), godlyhede (1), iwys (1), juste (1), justice (1), kyndelyche (1), parfey (1), purely (1), ryghtfully (1), ryghtis (1), sikerly (1), stedfastly (1), trewe (1), trowen (1), trust (1), truste (1), trusteth (1), verraily (1).

Table 3   Frequency of words in the "fals" set

bad (5), shame (4), blake (3), foul (3), lyes (3), shrewes (3), vice (3), devel (2), envye (2), fantasye (2), fantome (2), hate (2), foule (2), lesinges (2), lewed (2), lye (2), shrewed (2), shrewednesse (2), untrouthe (2), wikkednesse (2), ydel (2), black (1), countrefete (1), countrefeteth (1), deface (1), derke (1), derkly (1), diffame (1), feyned (1), fouler (1), foules (1), lesyng (1), lesynge (1), lewedly (1), shrewe (1), unfamous (1), unkynde (1), unkyndely (1), wikke (1), wikked (1), wikkidly (1), yhated (1), yshamed (1), yvel (1).

It should be noted here that the keywords in this work vary in Books II and III, though we understand that the keyword "fals" is repeatedly used in Book I and again found in Book III.[35] Here we list the summary table of word counts in *The House of Fame* (Table 4) and then the frequency of "soth" and "fals" and their variants and derivatives in each Book of this work (Table 5):

Table 4 Word counts in *The House of Fame*

	token	type	lines
Book I	03085	0966	0508
Book II	03585	1052	0582
Book III	06579	1635	1068
total	13249	2646	2158

Table 5 Frequency of "soth" and "fals" and their variants and derivatives in each Book

	soth, etc.	fals, etc.
Book I	3	9
Book II	6	1
Book III	12	3

Now let us investigate the functions of "soth" and "fals" in *The House of Fame*, and how they establish harmony with the development of this work.

1.2.1. Book I

In Book I, the poet applies the keywords "fals" and "falsly"[36] to, especially, the action of central figures in the legandary narratives he relates. The poet is particularly interested in the love affairs between men and women — especially the stories of women betrayed by men. Above all, he is attached to the story of Dido and false Aeneas; the false figure of man stands out in relief, forming a striking contrast to the faithful woman.[37]

> And when she wiste that he was fals,
> She heng hirself ryght be the hals,
> For he had doon hir such untrouthe.

> ....
> Eke lo how fals and reccheles
> Was to Breseyda Achilles,
> And Paris to Oenone,
> ....
> How fals eke was he Theseus,
> That, as the story telleth us,
> How he betrayed Adriane —
> ....
> And for she had of hym pite,
> She made hym fro the deth escape,
> And he made hir a ful fals jape; (393-414)

Though the poet states facts as they are, he may have presented to himself the following question: "What is the truth in the world?" Both the keyword "fals" and the "fals" story are emphasised. The fact that the poet apparently doubts what he has seen may drive him to continue narrating the following story. He does so to reascertain what is apparently true for him.[38]

The poet goes out of the "fals" world through the "wicket" or "dores." Looking around, he stands in "a large feld" which may be an indefinitely expanding vague world.[39] Looking up to the "hevene" and paying the sublime devotion, he meets with "an egle."[40] This eagle guides him to the external world. Here we see magnificent and glorious images of light. New light may have been thrown on him, as is shown in the expressions: "gold" and "shon so bright." This may suggest that he has already taken a step forward into the "soth" world, escaping from the "fals" one.

1.2.2. Book II

The scene moves from the temple of Venus to the House of Fame. Book II lets the poet see and hear more of the new things. Here we find the keywords: "kynde" and "kyndely."[41] Table 6 shows the frequency of the keyword "kynde," its variants, its derivatives, and its related words in each Book:

Table 6 Frequency of the keyword "kynde," its variants, its derivatives, and its related words in each Book

	Book I	Book II	Book III
kynde	2	5	2
kyndely	0	7	0
kyndeliche	0	1	0
kyndes	1	1	0
nature	1	0	2
naturel	1	0	1
unkynde	1	0	0
unkyndely	1	0	0

Unfortunately, the keyword "fals" conceals itself. We may have to understand the natural law in order to judge what is "soth" or "fals." We do not know the reason exactly why the keyword "soth" appears at the final stage of Book III, but at least we may say that the keyword "soth" is necessary there in order to give the last judgement.

In Book II, the verb "here" has the auditory sense and is often used instead of the verb "see" which has the visual sense. The poet hears new things as though they represented "soth." It is importrant how the poet gets new information from the "egle."[42]

> Thoo gan y wexen in a were,
> And seyde, "Y wot wel y am here,
> But wher in body or in gost
> I not, ywys, but God, thou wost," (979-82)

This kind of objective thought corresponds to the former feeling of doubt in Book I. The poet, however, does not swallow what the eagle said, but he, thinking carefully, feels dubious and inquires of the eagle. Here we do not find the keywords "soth" and "fals," but we will understand the theme of "soth" and "fals" running beneath the surface text.

It is a matter of course that the naïve poet has doubts about the eagle's speech, since the eagle says that every "speech" goes to the

House of Fame. Here the eagle discusses the matter of actual "sound" of "speech."[43] He instructs us what sorts of physical laws are related to the sounds of everyday speech. He vividly and scientifically lectures the poet on such laws, as though he were a professor of university and knew well the epochal laws such as law of gravitation or wave mechanics. It is doubtlessly a fact that the "tydynges," which are transmitted one after another by the eagle, are based on the law of "kynde."[44]

> "Geoffrey, thou wost ryght wel this,
> That every kyndely thyng that is
> Hath a kyndely stede ther he
>   May best in hyt conserved be;
> Unto which place every thyng
> Thorgh his kyndely enclynyng
> Moveth for to come to
> Whan that hyt is awey therfro;
> . . . .
> That every thyng enclyned to ys
> Hath his kyndelyche stede:
> That sheweth hyt, withouten drede,
> That kyndely the mansioun
> Of every speche, of every soun,
> Be hyt eyther foul or fair,
> Hath hys kynde place in ayr.
> And syn that every thing that is
> Out of hys kynde place, ywys,
> Moveth thidder for to goo,
> . . . .
> Than ys this the conclusyoun:
> That every speche of every man,
> As y the telle first began,
> Moveth up on high to pace
> Kyndely to Fames place. (729-852)

Here we see the recurrent adjective and adverb derived from "kynde." All kinds of new "tydynges" governed by the natural order of "kynde" come to the House of Fame. The poet tries to investigate the "tydynges" by "experience": i.e. making the best use of his own eyes and ears.

This "egle" says that the sounds, which are conveyed to the house by the law of "kynde," consist of both "soth" and "fals" things.

> "What?" quod I. "The grete soun,"
> Quod he, "that rumbleth up and doun
> In Fames Hous, full of tydynges,
> Bothe of feir speche and chidynges,
> And of fals and soth compounded. (1025-29)

Both extremely opposite values exist in the House of Fame. Then the poet arrives at the house and the chapter concludes. The eagle leaves the poet there in order to make him "lerne" new things in front of the House of Fame. Finally, the poet has to pass careful and objective judgement on this kind of composite values where "soth" and "fals" things are mixed ambivalently.

1.2.3. Book III

Book III is the concluding chapter. In this chapter the poet must arrive at his own view of things, after ascertaining the facts in Book I and the "egle" enlarges upon knowlege and experience in Book II.

As a matter of course, the things have to depend on the law of "kynde,"[45] but in addition the poet is greatly conscious of his "craft" here.[46] "Craft" belongs to a set of words expressing the poet's great technique of language. The frequency of the words in the "craft" set is as follows:

Table 7 The frequency of the words in the "craft" set

art (5), craft (3), craftely (3), queynte (3), kunnynge (2), poete (2), poetrie (2), curiosite (1), curious (1), curiouse (1), poetical (1), queynt (1), queyntelych (1), skiles (1), skille (1), skilles (1), subtil (1), subtilite (1)

It should be noted that even though he took good care of the "craft," he does not wholly devote himself on poetic technique. He says in the following passage:

> Nat that I wilne, for maistrye,
> Here art poetical be shewed,
> ....
> And that I do no diligence
> To shewe craft, but o sentence. (1094-1100)

This, an invocation of the god Apollo, is a passage which corresponds to common people's prayers for "fame" before the goddess Fame. Here the poet states modestly and courteously that he does not indulge himself only in the artistic and superficial technique of poetry.[47]

It is necessary for the poet to imitate nature faithfully, but if he pursues the objective description of nature only, he may not build his own magnificent structure of the house. So he needs not only "craft" but also the deep meaning of words: "sentence."

Now let us deal with the keywords "craft" and "art," both of which are often synonymous in this medieval age.[48] That the poet, using the creative "craft," tries to make the artistic expressions concerning the House of Fame is an experimental endeavour on his past.[49] The "craft" shows the power to express beauty, the artistic nature of House itself, the skilful art of playing the harp and the ingenious art of blowing the pipe in the House of Fame.

> That al the men that ben on lyve
> Ne han the kunnynge to descrive
> The beaute of that ylke place,
> ....
> So that the grete craft, beaute,
> The cast, the curiosite
> Ne kan I not to yow devyse;
> ....
> Ther herde I pleyen on an harpe,
> That sowned bothe wel and sharpe,
> Orpheus ful craftely,
> ....
> And smale harpers with her glees

> Sate under hem in dyvers sees,
> And gunne on hem upward to gape,
> And countrefete hem as an ape,
> Or as craft countrefeteth kynde. (1167-213)

The poet states modestly that he does not have "kunnynge" or the artistic power of expressing the beautiful place where the House of Fame stands magnificently (1167-69), and that he does not have enough ability to express "the grete craft," "beaute," "that cast" and "curiosite." The House of Fame in this section, however, may be an experimental house built by the poet himself.

The products of "craft" may have varying properties. The house is described by shining images, as is typically shown in "gold,"[50] while the cold and dark side of the house is shown at the same time.[51] (It should be noted that we see the transparent image as well as the bright one, illustrated by the phrase "lyk alum de glass" (1124) which corresponds to the image of "ice": "a roche of yse, not of stel" (1129-30). This complex image of the house may show the composite nature of this place.) The double-faced image of this house represents both "soth" and "fals" beings.

> So unfamous was woxe hir fame.[52]
> . . . .
> For on that other syde I say
> Of this hil, that northward lay,
> How hit was writen ful of names
> Of folkes that hadden grete fames
> Of olde tyme, and yet they were
> As fressh as men had writen hem here
> The selve day ryght, or that houre
> That I upon hem gan to poure. (1146-58)

When things are under the influence of "soth" light, they may be left perpetually; but, in fact, the "hete" makes them melt instantly. On the contrary, when things are in the shade, they may be abandoned eternally, because the "cold" makes them well-preserved for ever. Here we find the scrupulous mixture of contradictory nature in this house.

The unmelted names are "olde," since they got their great fame in ancient times, but now the poet uses the adjective "fresh." This may show the poet's integrated technique of poetry, mixing shining images with cold and dark images.

This kind of expression itself may show a new and experimental use of "craft." Here it seems that the poet begins to accept the "fals" world, although he felt dubious about it in Book I.

When the poet describes the goddess Fame, he uses his own "craft" mixing contradictory values:[53]

> Y saugh, perpetually ystalled,
> A femynyne creature,
> That never formed by Nature
> Nas such another thing yseye.
> For alther-first, soth for to seye,
> Me thoughte that she was so lyte
> That the lengthe of a cubite
> Was lengere than she semed be.
> . . . .
> For as feele eyen hadde she
> As fetheres upon foules be,
> . . . .
> And soth to tellen, also she
> Had also fele upstondyng eres
> And tonges, as on bestes heres;
> And on hir fet woxen saugh Y (1364-91)

It should be noted that the goddess Fame has the character of everlasting nature, while she is described as a variable and capricious character, as is in "Ryght as her suster, dame Fortune," (1547). Although she has the golden hair typical of human females, she has many eyes, ears, tongues, and legs which remind us of thickly-haired animals. She is an androgynous being, as well. The poet, using this complex expression, does not seek after the unified value, but reveals multiple, often contradictory, values simultaneously.

However, we find the keyword "craft" only in the first half of Book III, while the words "fame" and "soth" are often used in the second half of this Book. Table 8 shows the frequency of the word "fame" and its related words. The word "trewe," the synonym of "soth," is not often used in this work.[54]

Table 8 Frequency of the word "fame" and its related words

	Book I	Book II	Book III
fame	2	6	38
fames	0	5	16
name	2	1	18
names	0	1	5
renoun	0	0	6

Here we quote some examples of "soth."

> Now herke how she gan to paye
> That gonne her of her grace praye;
> And yit, lo, al this companye
> Seyden sooth, and noght a lye. (1549-52)

> And than he tolde hym this and that,
> And swor therto that hit was soth — (2050-51)

> And somtyme saugh I thoo at ones
> A lesyng and a sad soth sawe,
> That gonne of aventure drawe
> Out at a wyndowe for to pace; (2088-91)

The meanings of "fals" and "soth" in the noun "fame" are sometimes shown in the form of the adjectival antonyms: "olde" and "newe." The great characters, standing on the various metal pillars supporting this House of Fame, are described by the adjective "olde":

> The halle was al ful, ywys,
> Of hem that writen olde gestes
> As ben on trees rokes nestes; (1514-16)

These "olde" persons are not so important, because they are described by the dark colour and hoarse voice of the rook, while Bennett indicates that the piquant simile such as rookery prefigures "the action, ambience, and atmosphere of the remainder of the poem."[55] It should be also noted here that Havely says: "it seems more likely that the image reflects, ..., 'the lack of any authoritative standard to negotiate among the different songs and stories.'"[56]

On the other hand, various kinds of people come to the House of Fame and the poet hears various sorts of things. He expects something "newe" to hear, but Fame is very capricious and she gives "good fame" or "shrewed fame" or "wikkyd loos" randomly as she likes it. Here we see both aspects of "fame": "soth" and "fals" meaning of "fame."[57]

Furthermore, it should be noted that the colours of Aeolus's trumpet show two kinds of opposite colours: gold and black. Which trumpet would be blown depends upon the capricious judgement of Fame. The same person has the trumpets of the opposite colours: "soth" trumpet and "fals" trumpet. This means that he has the mutually contradictory values, although he does not blow these two antithetical values simultaneously.[58]

The poet cannot yet find the "newe" thing which he has been seeking after. When the poet is asked his identity by Fame, he states his position definitely.

> For what I drye, or what I thynke,
> I wil myselven al hyt drynke,
> Certeyn, for the more part,
> As fer forth as I kan myn art." (1879-82)

This passage may show that he is greatly conscious of the "art" which he tries to create, as in "myn art." Making the best use of "art," he can describe even a little what he wants to express. The contents described by the "art" should not be the fabricated "tydynges" made by a capricious judgement. It seems that the people who have sought for fame till now are not fresh to the poet, because they belong to the "olde" world and they are governed by the whimsical goddess Fame.

Then the poet tries to state his position more definitely in the following passage:

> Somme newe tydynges for to lere,
> Somme newe thinges, y not what,
> Tydynges, other this or that,
> Of love or suche thynges glade. (1886-89)

Judging from the adjective "glade" and the repetitive use of the adjective "newe," the "tydynge" should refresh and entertain the people.[59] But then the "House of Rumour" is full of reports and gossip.[60] At first, this house is not the one which the poet has wanted. It stands as though it pleased only "Aventure"(who is the mother of "tydynges" and as capricious as Fame in the world of contingency).

Then the wise "egle"[61] who is now "myn egle" appears again and plays the part of imparting the last "newe tydynges." The fact that the house seems to stop revolving, as in "me thoughte hit (= this hous) stente" (2031), may show that the poet becomes more composed. The house stops revolving, so the poet stands on the "flor." Here he meets with the people whom he has never seen. There are too many people for the poet to put his leg into the crowd. Those people impart the apparent "soth" and somewhat enlarge it one after another, depending on the natural law of transmission. They transmit the tidings before the news grow "olde." They seem not to care for whether the "tydynge" is "soth" or "fals."

Here the poet is taken to a new dimension and he goes into the unified world of truth and falsehood. As we see in the following passages, truth and falsehood live in the same world and they try to go out of the "wyndow" at the same time.[62]

> And somtyme saugh I thoo at ones
> A lesyng and a sad soth sawe,

> That gonne of aventure drawe
> Out at a wyndowe for to pace; (2088-91)
>
> Thus saugh I fals and soth compouned
> Togeder fle for oo tydynge. (2108-09)

This kind of antithetical presentation of "soth" and "fals" may correspond to the former contrastive techniques of describing the House of Fame itself in the beginning of Book III: the contrast of the melting place by heat and the cold place which remains constant, that of the north and south sides of the house, that of the light and shadow, that of "gold" and "roche of yse," the double-faced aspects of fame itself. This kind of technique reflects skilful art which combines the contradictory values in the same level. Perhaps after the poet experimented with various endings, the technique of employing contradictory values is suitable for the conlusion of this poem.

Finally he hears the "tydynges of love." After he learns the new information about love, he decides to go into the "compouned" world of love where the "soth" and the "fals" are scrupulously mixed with each other,[63] as is shown in the following expression: "We wil medle us ech with other," (2102) and "... this hous in alle tymes / Was ful of shipmen and pilgrimes, / With scrippes bret-ful of lesinges, / Entremedled with tydynges" (2121-24). The poet may recognise what kind of "fame" he has to seek, living in the complex world where the various ambivalent values of love exist. He meets with the famous person who gives him some confidence. Here his "fame" has just connected with the "auctoritee."

"A man of gret auctoritee" appears at the final stage of this work:

> Atte laste y saugh a man,
> Which that y [nevene] nat ne kan;
> But he semed for to be
> A man of gret auctorite.... (2155-58)

He should be the most trustworthy person. As Masui states, "The man of authority who has appeared ghostly in the poet's imagination must be the person who tells the truth to the poet."[64] The poet who has ever sought after the "soth" from the first could find the true person at the concluding line of this work, as a result of his continuous experiments. This expression may be suitable for the conclusion of *The House of Fame*. Even if this work is criticised as "unfinished," this expression suggests the bridge between this work and Chaucer's following great works. Chaucer the poet, influenced by the magnificent power of "auctoritee," has created many famous works which are to transmit his true fame to posterity.[65]

1.3. *The Canterbury Tales* and *Troilus and Criseyde*

"The Tale of Melibee" is one of two tales narrated by Chaucer the pilgrim. The first, "The Tale of Sir Thopas," is likely a self-mocking, satirical poem of a faded knight riding from the fading days of gallantry. Chaucer the pilgrim is cut short by the Host who says that his "drasty rymyng is nat worth a toord!"(I.930). The poet then turns to recite a translation of the French *Livre de Melibee et de Dame Prudence*, which is now generally attributed to Renaud de Louens, according to R. M. Correale and M. Hamel's *Sources and Analogues of the Canterbury Tales*.[66] Why the masterful Chaucer would have his poetic persona recite the pair has often troubled scholars. An examination of the symbolism of "The Tale of Melibee" will shed light upon the question, and perhaps provide at least one answer. We should note, before we proceed, that Loren C. Gruber has suggested that Geoffrey Chaucer was one of the first English poets, if not the first, to recognise and write about a subtle, internal isolation as opposed to the physical isolation experienced by "The Wanderer" of the Old English elegies.[67] It would seem that Chaucer knew he was the poet of epochal change, that the old physical heroic exploits of Sir Thopas were but comic throwbacks, worthy only of derisive laughter. The concerns of Chaucer and his sensitive contemporaries were not about physical exploits, but exploits of the mind and soul. The new man of Chaucer's era was concerned with how to be a Christian, if not Humanistic, hero—one who must conquer himself and his passions before he can conquer or control others. It is this central question, how does a man control himself in order to govern others, around which "The Tale of Melibee" revolves?

1.3.1. *The Canterbury Tales*

Let us turn to the tale and its symbolism. Melibeus goes out to his fields to play, only to find that his wife Prudence and his daughter Sophia have been attacked by three old foes of Melibeus. Melibeus's wife Prudence later explains an allegorical meaning in this tale:

> Thy name is Melibee, this is to seyn, 'a man that drynketh hony'. / Thou hast ydronke so muchel hony of sweete temporeel richesses, and delices and honours of this world / that thou art dronken, and hast forgeten Jhesu Crist thy creatour. /... for certes, the three enemys of mankynde — that is to seyn, the flessh, the feend, and the world — / thou hast suffred hem entre in to thyn herte wilfully by the wyndowes of thy body, / and hast nat defended thyself suffisantly agayns hire assautes and hire temptaciouns, so that they han wounded thy soule in fyve places; / this is to seyn, the deedly synnes that been entred into thyn herte by thy fyve wittes, / And in the same manere oure Lord Crist hath woold and suffred that thy three enemys been entred into thyn house by the wyndowes / and han ywounded thy doghter in the forseyde manere." (Mel, VII.1410-26)

After she explains that the proper noun "Melibee" means "a man that drynketh hony," she says that Melibeus has drunk too much of the worldy wealth and the honey of honour, and the three enemies are "flessh," "feend" and "world." The enemies are "deedly synnes" who went through the "wyndowes" of the "body," violated the "herte" and gave incurable wounds to Melibeus's "doghter."

Before we examine the poetic translation further, it is time to note that, as the Tale says, Melibeus is a name standing for one who drinks honey. Bees and their honey have long been associated with "be-ing," wisdom, and even the basic ingredient for poetic inspiration, the Scandinavian mead which the poet-god Odin sought. In its negative connotation, honey is associated with the honey-tongued Belial of Milton's *Paradise Lost*. Honey, and one who drinks honey, resonate with the symbolism of wisdom and articulate grace necessary for being an individual. Skilled words alone are not enough. They must be balanced with prudence and wisdom: hence the trial of Melibeus, Prudence, and Sophia. It is as though Chaucer the poet — and Chaucer the poet-pilgrim — is saying that playful words must be accompanied by prudence and wisdom. In the tale, however, Prudence and Wisdom were locked away—and the playfulness became heedless. Consequently, the three (Christian) foes of mankind—the world, the flesh, and the devil—attacked Prudence and beat her and struck Sophia with five mortal wounds. The playful Melibeus, like playful words, was caught off-guard. Although he left his wife and daughter securely shut in the house, presumably for safe-keeping, his enemies reached them by entering the house through the windows. Having left his wife and daughter safe, he thought at home, Melibeus could play unfettered and uninterrupted.

The "house" described in this tale is one without a husband to defend it. Even if the door were completely shut, the house might be unguarded. Wisdom and Prudence are unprotected without proper words. The housekeeper might not have been aware of the importance of the "windows." A window is the point at which the house is most vulnerable to intrusion from outside. It is the most suitable way to let the devils pass through. In this way, this house which seems to be defended completely is invaded easily. This fact illustrates how important the function of the windows is in the house. Melibeus's house, metaphorically speaking, symbolises his body. Since the house's "dore" was "faste yshette," he armed himself and his body might have been secure. Though he, ready to fight against the foes, was completely clad in armour, his "wyndowes" of the body, i.e. his eyes were off-guard. He was so careless that it was not surprising that his dear daughter Sophia, i.e. his wisdom, was mortally wounded.

Now let us examine the function of the "wyndowes" which plays the part of "eyen." The "herte" in the "body" can have contact with the outside world through the "wyndowes." In Melibeus's case, his heart or mind is too weak to instinctively recognise a good person, though his eyes should see distinctly what is good. In this way, the function of the windows in the house is as important as that of the eyes of the human beings. We would, therefore, protect automatically our "herte" from the enemy, if we had usual ability enough to discriminate carefully and acknowledge danger instinctively.

Melibeus, isolated by the loss of Sophia, is bombarded by words of wisdom, ancient and modern: Classical Greek and Roman on the one hand; Judeo-Christian on the other. When Classical words do not convince him, those from the Old Testament or those from the New Testamant seem to sway him to Prudence's way of thinking. Generally speaking, it is the more modern arguments that convince him: that is, Melibeus chooses to utterly forgive his arch foes with the Christian charity of the new Testament. We are left to assume, perhaps, that in light of Christian teaching, Sophia will recover from her wounds. As Chaucer has moved from physical isolation of the heroic knight, he has moved to the emotional and spiritual isolation of the modern man who cannot be healed by playful words alone, or, for that matter, by serious words alone, either. He must be healed by a union of wisdom and prudence with his words.

Prudence advises Melibeus to keep his plan secret in order not to be caught in a snare, quoting that "Whil that thou kepest thy conseil in thyn herte, thou kepest it in thy prisoun," (Mel, VII.1144). Here the "herte" in the house leads to the "prisoun." Then we would like to turn from the case of a house which is a dwelling place to one where it is a "prisoun" which plays an important role as a house,[68] namely in "The Knight's Tale" in *The Canterbury Tales*. Masui has already studied the stylistic effect of the expression of "perpetual prisoun" from a rhetorical point of view.[69] Nakatani has dealt with the relationship between the recurrent expressions of "perpetual prison" and the main theme of the story.[70] In this present chapter, we would discuss again how the "prisoun" plays an important part as a house in this work. The characters locked in the "prisoun" are the noble princes of Thebes, Palamon and Arcite, who have fought against Duke Theseus. The "prisoun," which is a keyword in this work, functions organically. Here the "prisoun" symbolises the "body" and the "herte" corresponds to the two imprisoned intimate friends. In this work, neither Palamon nor Arcite may be paid particular attention, but as Muscatine states[71] it may be natural to think that the story develops with both Palamon and Arcite keeping a well-balanced mutual relationship and helping each other. It would then be better to regard these two characters as the only one "herte." Thus we recognise that the "body" is the "prisoun" and the "herte" is shown by the main characters.

This tale takes a fresh and vivid development when the main characters see Emelye, the beautiful daughter of Thesus, through the "wyndow" of the "prisoun."[72]

> This passeth yeer by yeer and day by day,
> Till it fil ones, in a morwe of May,
> That Emelye, that fairer was to sene
> Than is the lylie upon his stalke grene,
> And fressher than the May with floures newe —
> . . . .
> She was arisen and al redy dight;
> For May wole have no slogardie a-nyght.
> The sesoun priketh every gentil herte,
> And maketh it out of his slep to sterte,

> ....
> The grete tour, that was so thikke and stroong,
> Which of the castel was the chief dongeoun,
> ....
> Was evene joynant to the gardyn wal
> Ther as this Emelye hadde hir pleyynge.
> ....
> And so bifel, by aventure or cas,
> That thurgh a wyndow, thikke of many a barre
> Of iren greet and square as any sparre,
> He cast his eye upon Emelya,
> And therwithal he bleynte and cride, "A!"
> As though he stongen were unto the herte. (KnT, I (A), 1033-79)

As a matter of course, the "wyndow" is not only the eye of the "prisoun" but also that of Palamon and Arcite who, having "gentil herte" there, want to get out of the prison. Their present state is wretched but they would like to be in a happier situation. Here Palamon happens to see Emelye through an iron-barred window, and Arcite also is captivated by her, as in the following passage: "And with that sighte hir beautee hurte hym so, / That, if that Palamon was wounded sore, / Arcite is hurt as muche as he, or moore" (KnT, I (A), 1114-16).

In this way, the window of the prison is the best and concrete means of expressing not only the feelings of love but also of developing the story. The pair want to go beyond themselves, and their prison walls.

Palamon and Arcite, the "herte" of this "prisoun," become antagonistic and quarrel with each other. Arcite happens to get out of the prison by the request of Perotheus. Palamon succeeds in escaping from the prison by chance. Each wants to approach Emelye and they fight each other for her hand. Arcite gets the better of Palamon, but he suddenly dies. Then Palamon's fortune is turned in his favour. The tale ends with Theseus's philosophic speech imbued with Boethius's ideas.[73] Had the story not developed without the main characters' accidental meeting with Emelye, we might say that the "wyndow" of the "prisoun" in this work would not become the valuable and indispensable means of symbolic expression.

In "The Miller's Tale," Chaucer uses the window in a skilful and burlesque sense this time. This work, as many critics indicate, may be contrasted with the above-mentioned "The Knight's Tale."[74]

Here the window of the house would also play a dramatic role. Before we discuss the function of the window, we should summarise the story. A young student Nicholas boards at the house of a rich carpenter named John who lives in Oxford. This student excels in astrology, song, and love affairs. Alison, who is the carpenter's wife, is eighteen years old. She is so sexually charming and attractive that it is no wonder that we expect something will happen in this house. Nicholas locks himself in his chamber, thinking up a cunning and sly plan in order to have intercourse with Alison. Portraying himself as one who is captivated by astrology, Nicholas foretells a more terrible flood than that of Noah and indicates the way to escape the calamity. The three, namely Nicholas, Alison, and John, enter separate tubs hanging from the ceiling. Nicholas and Alison quietly come down from their tubs and have a good time in bed. Then Absolon, who has longed for Alison for some time, comes to her house to woo her, since it seems that John the carpenter is absent. He declares his love to Alison near the window of the bed chamber, but in vain. He is refused flatly and positively.

> He rometh to the carpenteres hous,
> And stille he stant under the shot-wyndowe —
> Unto his brest it raughte, it was so lowe — (MillT, I (A), 3694-96)
>
> "Go fro the wyndow, Jakke fool," she sayde; (MillT, I (A), 3708)

We understand that instead of the "dore" of the "hous" the "wyndow" is made the best use of even in this kind of love affair. (It may be possible even for the eyes of human beings to see the objects of the outer world secretly. When the eyes are prudent, they can judge what they should enter.) In this case, since Absolon is not a lover to Alison in the "hous" and because Alison has a secret and enjoyable relationship with the young student, it is no wonder that the "wyndow" is locked cautiously. It is a matter of course that she says to Absolon: "Go fro the wyndow."

Absolon desperately and sorrowfully asks her to give a kiss at least. Here the burlesque scene is disclosed to the audience.

> The wyndow she undoth, and that in haste.
> "Have do," quod she, "com of, and speed the faste,
> Lest that oure neighebores thee espie."
> This Absolon gan wype his mouth ful drie.
> Derk was the nyght as pich, or as the cole,
> And at the wyndow out she putte his hole,
> And Absolon, hym fil no bet ne wers,
> But with his mouth he kiste hir naked ers
> Ful savourly, er he were war of this.
> Abak he stirte, and thoughte it was amys,
> For wel he wiste a womman hath no berd. (MillT, I (A), 3727-37)

Absolon knows that he tasted a passionate and burning kiss to her behind put out of the window and he gets quite mad with anger. His thought of being her true love is in vain. Rather than losing at this point, he seeks to take revenge on her, coming back to the window. The person who first succeeded in using the window, ironically enough, fails to do so later. Absolon, who is boiling inside, goes to the smith, borrows a hot coulter from a blacksmith, comes back to the window of the bed-chamber of the carpenter's house as quick as lightning, and asks her to kiss again as before.

> He cogheth first, and knokketh therwithal
> Upon the wyndowe, right as he dide er.
> ....
> This Nicholas was risen for to pisse,
> And thoughte he wolde amenden al the jape;
> He (=Absolon) sholde kisse his (=Nicholas's) ers er that he scape.

> And up the wyndowe did he hastily
> And out his ers he putteth pryvely
> Over the buttok, to the haunche-bon; (MillT, I (A), 3788-803)

Then Nicholas's fabricated event, Noah's flood, happens humorously as this tale ends with the flood of the irresitible laughter.

In this way, Chaucer makes an extreme and humorous event in "The Miller's Tale," which might never happen in the real world.[75] Fictional though the situation may be, the "wyndow" acts as a link between Alison and Nicholas, the true lovers inside the house, and Absolon, the would-be lover who is shut out from Alison's affections. On the other hand, Chaucer represents the subtle feelings of love through the use of the prison window in "The Knight's Tale." In this tale, Palamon and Arcite look outside from their prison into the garden where they see Emelye. The window therefore depicts the entrance to the heart; it produces not only a romantic love but makes a mean, obscene, and burlesque love plausible and moves the audience to irresistibly uproarious laughter. Chaucer, who is hiding himself behind the tales, seems to be enjoying, and making the consistently best use of the tools of expression.

1.3.2. *Troilus and Criseyde*

Now we would like to discuss how the house and the window work in *Troilus and Criseyde*. This poem is supposed to have been written before most of *The Canterbury Tales* were composed. It may be useful to see how Chaucer describes the house before he created the collection of Tales; that way, we can follow a process of Chaucer's thinking and artistry.[76] We find the description of the house in *Troilus and Criseyde* to parallel that in "The Knight's Tale." Because of the lofty nature of *Troilus and Criseyde* we do not find the burlesque which permeates "The Miller's Tale."

Now let us examine the use of the house in each Book of *Troilus and Criseyde*. Broadly speaking, the meaning and use of the house in

Troilus and Criseyde may be summarised by the following theme of this work: the construction and destruction of the house of love.

In Book I, Troilus, who is a young knight and courtier, languishes for love and Pandarus plays the part of "matchmaker" to ease him of lovesickness. Though Troilus has despised love affairs, ironically enough he becomes involved in the whirlwinds of love. With longing pains in his heart, he locks himself in his own chamber. Troilus imprisoned in the building is a solitary person, just as Palamon and Arcite longing for Emelye suffer from lovesickness. The following passage shows Troilus's hopeless and helpless pains of love.

> And fro this forth tho refte hym love his slep,
> And made his mete his foo, and ek his sorwe
> Gan multiplie, that, whoso tok kep,
> It shewed in his hewe both eve and morwe. (I.484-87)

Troilus has deprived himself of "slep" and "mete"; because of his passionate and disgusting love and he feels "sorwe" more and more. Shutting himself in his own chamber, he is isolated from the outside world.[77]

When Pandarus appears he happens to find a sorrowful Troilus and decides to go into the window of Troilus's mind. Pandarus plays a part of constructing the house of love for Troilus, as is shown in the narrator's description of the image of a carpenter:

> For everi wight that hath an hous to founde
> Ne renneth naught the werk for to bygynne
> With rakel hond, but he wol bide a stounde,
> And sende his hertes line out fro withinne
> Aldirfirst his purpos for to wynne.
> Al this Pandare in his herte thoughte,
> And caste his werk ful wisely or he wroughte. (I.1065-71)

This passage distinctly shows that Pandarus must build a solidly imposing structure, working out a design for it and setting up immovable pillars one after another. This may be connected with Chaucer's art and his way of constructing narrative structures.[78] Let us focus now on Pandarus's way of constructing the house in *Troilus and Criseyde*. Pandarus is obliged to go between Troilus and Criseyde and construct a solid and splendid structure of courtly love. In the above quotation, we find that Pandarus deliberately and sincerely acts as a go-between in the love affair, making the best use of his "hertes line," i.e. his well-balanced eyes. Because Pandarus promises to mediate between Troilus and Criseyde, the young knight, formerly languishing in his one-sided love, is light-hearted and regains his chivalric composure.[79]

It is in Book II that Pandarus shuts himself in the chamber. Pandarus as a carpenter builds a splendid structure, where he makes Troilus and Criseyde live. His method is as follows.

Pandarus goes to Criseyde's house[80] to fulfill an important matter. Here Pandarus's very skilful technique is shown. He introduces the name of Troilus to Criseyde, keeping her in suspense. In this situation, however, Criseyde is imprisoned in her chamber[81] just as Troilus is in Book I. Then Pandarus plays the part of opening her door and window as an ingenious and creative architect.

> But as she sat allone and thoughte thus,
> Ascry aros at scarmuch al withoute,
> And men criden in the strete, "Se, Troilus
> Hath right now put to flighte the Grekes route!"
> With that gan al hire meyne for to shoute,
> "A, go we se! Cast up the yates wyde!
> For thorwgh this strete he moot to paleys ride;
> "For other wey is to the yate noon
> Of Dardanus, there opyn is the cheyne," (II.610-18)

An arch of triumph is now opened to celebrate Troilus's victory. When the Trojans from noble Troilus down are going to parade the street before Criseyde's house, the servants in her house would like to see their valiant figures through the "yates." Then, because the gates are suddenly opened when she is "allone," an unforseen occurrence happens. This "paleys," Troilus's house, is located along "this strete" which runs before Criseyde's house. Both houses are thus connected to each other by this magnificent march. As a matter of course, Criseyde would accidentally met Troilus; it is through artifice, however, that Pandarus made them meet with each other. In other words, it was the matchmaker's way of building a structure of love — deliberately.

Pandarus goes to Criseyde's house with Troilus's love letter. Then he forces her to take it in the garden.[82] Criseyde reads his letter, locking herself again in her chamber. Then Pandarus skilfully leads Criseyde to the window, as is in the following:

> And after noon ful sleighly Pandarus
> Gan drawe hym to the wyndowe next the strete,
> And seyde, "Nece, who hath araied thus
> The yonder hous, that stant aforyeyn us?"
> "Which hous?" quod she, and gan for to byholde,
> And knew it wel, and whoso it was hym tolde;
> And fillen forth in speche of thynges smale,
> And seten in the wyndowe bothe tweye.
> ....
> She shette it (: the lettre), and to Pandare gan goon,
> Ther as he sat and loked into the strete,
> And down she sette hire by hym on a stoon
> Of jaspre, upon a quysshyn gold-ybete,
> ....
> And right as they declamed this matere,
> Lo, Troilus, right at the stretes ende,
> Com rydyng with his tenthe som yfere,
> Al softely, and thiderward gan bende
> Ther as they sete, as was his way to wende
> To paleis-ward; ...
> ....
> With that he gan hire humbly to saluwe,
> With dredful chere, and oft his hewes muwe;
> And up his look debonairly he caste,
> And bekked on Pandare, and forth he paste.
> God woot if he sat on his hors aright,
> Or goodly was biseyn, that ilke day!

Chapter 1   Analysis of Textual Structure

> God woot wher he was lik a manly knyght!
> What sholde I drecche, or telle of his aray?
> Criseyde, which that alle thise thynges say,
> To telle in short, hire liked al in-fere,
> His person, his aray, his look, his cheere,
> His goodly manere, and his gentilesse,
> So wel ... (II.1185-268)

We see in the above passage that the window of Criseyde's house, which Pandarus has made the best use of helps to arouse and cultivate a romantic love between Troilus and Criseyde. It is by looking through the window of her chamber that Criseyde sees a worthy and valiant figure in Troilus, completely clad in armour. Thus, this window lets them effectively connect with each other, after they get out of their respective imprisoned chambers.

As Troilus nears Criseyde, they exchange glances, and the scene is set. Troilus "saluwes" Criseyde with a smile as he passes the window. In Book II, Chaucer describes Criseyde's situation more minutely when she feels the flames of passion, puts off her widow's weeds, and goes out of the prison, her house. Chaucer shows an exquisite touch.

Book III begins with the scene of Deiphebus's house, where Troilus and Criseyde succeed in privately building the house of love. As a matter of course, their success is based upon Pandarus's deliberate "hertes line." In short, Book III shows the glorious completion of the house of love to which Troilus and Criseyde have already escaped from their respective closed chambers. Let us now look into how much they complete their magnificent house of love.

After Troilus and Criseyde pledge themselves to their secret courtly love, it goes well with Pandarus's sincere help. The following passage is the scene which shows their secret meeting at Pandarus's house.

> That it bifel right as I shal yow telle:
> That Pandarus, that evere dide his might
> Right for the fyn that I shal speke of here,

> As for to bryngen to his hows som nyght
> His faire nece and Troilus yfere,
> Wheras at leiser al this heighe matere,
> Touchyng here love, were at the fulle upbounde,
> Hadde out of doute a tyme to it founde. (III.511-18)

With the affair going well, Pandarus plans for them to meet clandestinely at his "hows," and make a good night of it. Pandarus's planning reaches the culmination with the genial and pleasant atmosphere of nature,[83] and all goes well with Pandarus's efficient hopeful execution, as is in "with gret deliberacioun" (III.519). This is Pandarus's way of building the structure deliberately; it is the same as described in the end of Book I. His method is clearly shown in "This tymbur is al redy up to frame;" (III.530). The "tymbur" is quite ready to "frame,"[84] i.e. to construct the house of love.

How could Troilus look for a better chance? Troilus is on the top of the world, looking at Criseyde's (and her servants') arrival at Pandarus's house of love through "a litel wyndow in a stewe."

> But who was glad now, who, as trowe ye,
> But Troilus, that stood and myght it se
> Thoroughout a litel wyndow in a stewe,
> Ther he bishet syn mydnyght was in mewe,
> Unwist of every wight but of Pandare? (III.599-603)

According to the *OED*, "stew," an earliest citation, means "a heated room; a room with a fireplace." The *MED* also quotes this word: "1. (c) a small room, closet; also, a heated room" and three of five quotations are from Chaucer's works. According to the *OED*, "mewe" means "phr. In mew: in hiding or confinement, cooped up. *Obs.*" The *MED* also explains this word as follows: "3. (a) A place of security or confinement; hiding place, shelter; cage, prison...; in ~, in a place of security or shelter; in safety; in confinement or withdrawal from society; in concealment or hiding." Troilus is still "bishet" (which means "2. (a) of persons: confined, locked in; imprisoned;..., according to the *MED*) in the heated secret room, but he will soon be out. We have already seen the expression "in mewe" in Book I, when Troilus, captured by love, tries to proceed his secret love. That phrase recurs in this situation. Could Troilus escape from the "mewe"?

Pandarus's house may be said to be a kind of labyrinth, although not one that leads people astray — at least not yet. Instead, the possessor Pandarus lets his house become a house of love. Pandarus's house may be a Gothic one.[85] The word which shows this Gothic feature may be "trappe."

> And with that word he gan undon a trappe,
> And Troilus he brought in by the lappe. (III.741-42)
>
> "What! which wey be ye comen, benedicite?"
> Quod she "and how, thus unwist of hem alle?"
> "Here at this secre trappe-dore," quod he. (III.757-59)

According to the *OED*, "trappe" and "trappe-dore" are earliest citations and "trappe" means "A movable covering of a pit, or of an opening in a floor, designed to fall when stepped upon." The *MED* also gives the following definition: "A contrivance, usu. disguised, designed to catch and restrain animals and men, a pitfall, snare; ..." Since this word literally means "A contrivance set for catching game or noxious animals; a gin, snare, pitfall," Pandarus's "trappe" is a thing that not only deceives people's eyes but is also set to fulfill the love between Troilus and Criseyde privately. Pandarus, therefore, attaches the adjective "secre" to the "trappe-dore." Pandarus can also make up a maze without letting anybody know about it. Pandarus's power of execution is shown in the following passage:

> Youre wommen slepen alle, I undertake,
> So that, for hem, the hous men myghte myne, (III.766-67)

Pandarus can put his plans into practice so secretly that he lets a person make his way under the house, with the women sleeping silently and soundly.[86]

After Troilus and Criseyde have a night of passion in Pandarus's house, the cruel morning comes to them at last. We will end Book III, quoting the scene in which the "wyndow" of Criseyde's house goes between them.

> And whan that he com ridyng into town,
> Ful ofte his lady from hire wyndow down,
> As fressh as faukoun comen out of muwe,
> Ful redy was hym goodly to saluwe. (III.1782-85)

When Troilus comes back to Troy after his hunting during the truce between the Trojans and the Greeks, Criseyde salutes him with a comforting smile as she stands at the side of the window of her house.

According to the *MED*, "faukoun" means "The peregrin falcon, esp. the female of the species as used in falconry; also, any of various other hawks so used" and tends to be collocated with the adjective "gentil."[87] This passage describes Criseyde's fresh feeling and appearance, including the adjective "fresh" which is suitable for the lovers Troilus and Criseyde. Furthermore, it is noteworthy that Criseyde shows her face at the window of her house, just as the "faukoun" gets out of her "muwe." The word "muwe" was already used to Troilus's imprisoned chamber in Book I.[88] Just as Troilus emerged from his closed world, Criseyde in Book III becomes "out of muwe" to build the world she holds in common with Troilus.

As we can see, the house of love between Troilus and Criseyde is thus built in Book III, through Pandarus's skilful and deliberate plan. Although his design goes well with Heaven's merciful grace in this book, Goddess Fortune unfortunately does not help the pair in Books IV and V. This means that Pandarus cannot control Fortune.

Books IV and V describe the cruel process of destroying the magnificent house of love which was built magnificently by Pandarus. In Book IV, Troilus, certainly knowing that there will be an exchange of hostage involving Criseyde and Antenor, feels similar great pains to those he felt in his solitary chamber in Book I. Criseyde, having also heard the convincing and dreadful rumour of the exchange of hostage, laments for her sorrowful situation. She locks herself in her own room, as does Troilus. Their house of love is at the point of collapsing utterly.

The last lines of Book IV reveal their symbolical departure from the house of love.

> For whan he saugh that she ne myghte dwelle,
> Which that his soule out of his herte rente,
> Withouten more out of the chaumbre he wente. (IV.1699-701)

When they are to part, they go out of the chamber of love without delivering their farewell speech to each other. Troilus knows well Criseyde's definite wish to go to the Greek camp. The blissful light of their chamber is going to be extinguished. Troilus goes out of "the chaumbre," since Criseyde no longer dwells there. She has deprived "his soule" of "his herte." Though Troilus has steeped himself in a merry atmosphere with Criseyde, he is destined to go away. Since their house stands on the ground of their deep love, it will become groundless if one of them leaves. (A groundless love is like the cold and frosty scene of the house which does not keep the owner in Book V.) Symbolically, the collapsed house is shown in Book IV.

Book V reveals the fatal and eternal separation between Troilus and Criseyde. The formidable isolation of each house and the inevitable collapse of Criseyde's are described impressionistically in this book.

At first, let us see the solitary scene after Troilus sent off Criseyde.

> To Troie is come this woful Troilus,
> . . . .
> Tho sodeynly doun from his hors he sterte,
> And thorugh his paleis, with a swollen herte,
> To chaumbre he wente; of nothyng took he hede, (V.197-202)

The first line of this passage corresponds to the sentence: "And Troilus to Troie homward he wente" (V.91), which describes his actions soon after her love's departure. Troilus alone goes back to his "paleis" in Troy and shuts himself in his own chamber.

Troilus, looking forward to Criseyde's return, tells Pandarus with a sorrowful tone of voice that he should go to see Criseyde's house[89] which is left masterless, in order to dissipate the depressing melancholy:

> "For love of God," ful pitously he sayde,
> "As go we sen the palais of Criseyde;
> For syn we yet may have namore feste,
> So lat us sen hire paleys atte leeste." (V.522-25)

Since he cannot meet Criseyde herself, he would like to see at least her house which serves for Criseyde herself. As has been already shown in "The Tale of Melibee" discussed earlier in this chapter, it seems that a symbolic meaning of "hous" is the "body" of human beings.[90] In this sense, Criseyde's house symbolically represents her "body," in this case, her remains. Troilus and Pandarus come to her house.

> And to Criseydes hous they gonnen wende.
> Lord, this sely Troilus was wo!
> Hym thoughte his sorwful herte braste a-two.
> For whan he saugh hire dores spered alle,
> Wel neigh for sorwe adoun he gan to falle.
> Therwith, whan he was war and gan biholde
> How shet was every wyndow of the place,
> As frost, hym thoughte, his herte gan to colde; (V.528-35)

Troilus feels "sorwful" when he understands that "hire dores" are "spered"(= fastened, barred).[91] "Every wyndow of the place" which has served for the development of their lovely house, going between them, is "shet." Communication between them is completely shut out. The expression of the third line in this passage recurs when the narrator describes objectively Criseyde's state of mind: "Hire thoughte hire sorwfull herte brast a-two" (V.180), showing the complete collapse of their common house; neither "sorwfull herte" can live there. This kind of sorrowful state is furthermore described "as frost," a concrete, visual simile.

The house is masterless, but it substitutes for Criseyde, and so Troilus exclaims at the top of his voice:

> Than seide he thus: "O paleys desolat,
> O hous of houses whilom best ihight,
> O paleys empty and disconsolat,
> O thow lanterne of which queynt is the light,
> O paleys, whilom day, that now art nyght,
> Wel oughtestow to falle, and I to dye,
> Syn she is went that wont was us to gye!
> "O paleis, whilom crowne of houses alle,
> Enlumyned with sonne of alle blisse!
> O ryng, fro which the ruby is out falle,
> O cause of wo, that cause hast ben of lisse!
> Yet, syn I may no bet, fayn wolde I kisse
> Thy colde dores, dorste I for this route;
> And farwel shryne, of which the seynt is oute!"
> ....
> "And at that corner, in the yonder hous,
> Herde I myn alderlevest lady deere
> So wommanly, with vois melodious,
> Syngen so wel, so goodly, and so cleere,
> That in my soule yet me thynketh ich here
> The blisful sown; and in that yonder place
> My lady first me took unto hire grace." (V.540-81)[92]

In this description the nouns "paleys" or "hous," restricted by the emotional adjectives, reflect Troilus's delicate state of mind. The scene in Book V where Troilus goes to see Criseyde's "paleys" is most impressive. The description of the "paleys" here suggests Troilus's hopelessness, even though we see his faint expectation. It should be noted that most adjectives show coldness.

The more Troilus expresses the present desolate scene, the more it reminds us of the past splendid and gorgeous moments. The coldness of this palace reflects Troilus's hopeless state of mind. As the adjective "disconsolat"[93] shows, Criseyde's palace seems to be gloomy because of her absence, i.e. its "empty" state. Troilus's heart is in a bleak and frosty condition. Therefore, the "dores" of the palace may show the coldness, as in the adjective "colde," which seems to suggest the coldness of Criseyde's remains.

This kind of coldness makes us feel the splendid state of her palace, as in "best ihight" or "enlumyed with sonne of alle blisse." Troilus continues his speech: "in the yonder hous," remembering his past joy and glory. The recurrent adjective "yonder" in Book V reveals Troilus's sense of alienation and his sorrow at his departure from the world of love — actually and psychologically. Furthermore, the expression "in that yonder place" seems to indicate that Troilus is still thinking about Criseyde's Greek camp. The description of Criseyde's palace as her remains thus reflects Troilus's sorrowful, retrospective state of mind.

Needless to say, the walls between the two armies that separate this palace from Criseyde's Greek camp are also the walls that alienate Troilus from Criseyde. Now let us consider the psychological effect of the walls.

> Upon the walles faste ek wolde he walke,
> And on the Grekis oost he wolde se;
> And to hymself right thus he wolde talke:
> "Lo, yonder is myn owene lady free,
> Or ellis yonder, ther tho tentes be.
> And thennes comth this eyr, that is so soote,
> That in my soule I fele it doth me boote.
> "And hardily, this wynd that more and moore
> Thus stoundemel encresseth in my face
> Is of my ladys depe sikes soore.
> I preve it thus, for in noon othere place
> Of al this town, save onliche in this space.
> Fele I no wynd that sowneth so lik peyne:
> It seyth 'Allas! Whi twynned be we tweyne?' (V.666-79)

Troilus, who is waiting for her return ten days hence, looks at the

CHAPTER 1 ANALYSIS OF TEXTUAL STRUCTURE   59

Greek side, going to the "walles." Troilus feels Criseyde's heavy sighs in the blowing winds from the Greek camp, as if "this eyr" and "this wynd" were Criseyde's "depe sikes sore." In this situation the "walles" play the part of the windows of the house. We see here Troilus's protracted and faint expectation especially in the recurrent word "yonder."

This scene corresponds to the situation where Criseyde draws a deep sigh sorrowfully, looking at Troy.

> Ful rewfully she loked upon Troie,
> Biheld the toures heigh and ek the halles;
> "Allas!" quod she, "the plesance and the joie,
> The which that now al torned into galle is,
> Have ich had ofte withinne yonder walles!
> O Troilus, what dostow now?" she seyde. (V.729-34)

The rhyming pair "Troie" and "joie"[94] is used when Criseyde recollects "Troie" which was full of "joie" for her. We do not know whether or not she would like to recover her joy, but it may be noteworthy that she uses the recurrent adjective "yonder" in Book V, as in "yonder walles," as though Criseyde fully understood Troilus's feelings of love. Criseyde's "joie" was "withinne tho yonder walles," i.e. inside "Troie." If she had been within the walls, they could have protected the house of love adequately and effectively. (This sorrowful speech of Criseyde's becomes impressive, because there exist the alliterative expressions "heigh" and "halles" and the rhyming words "halles" and "walles," besides of the above-mentioned rhyming tag "Troie" and "joie.")

Criseyde decides to get out of the Greek camp the next night and go wherever Troilus wants to go, but she cannot remove the impenetrable barrier which separates them. Criseyde's heart falters within two months.

> For bothe Troilus and Troie town
> Shal knotteles thorughout hire herte slide; (V.768-69)

Despite her resolute determination, this passage again points to her being, as the narrator elsewhere says, "slydynge of corage." (V.825) The nouns "Troilus" and "Troie town" formerly gave her the lovely "joie," and this town of Troy was magnificent enough to satisfy Criseyde's self-respect. Therefore, when she goes to the Greek camp as part of the hostage exchange, she grieves heavily about her misfortunes and remembers her town of Troy. Immediately after that, however, the narrator shows her "slydynge of corage" in a "knotteles" way, the adjective which is the *OED*'s earliest citation and means "without a knot, free from knots, unknotted," while it is the only citation in the *MED* and means "Of a thread: without a knot; — used *fig.*" The love knot is untied; the lovers are no longer bound to each other. (This strikingly contrasts with the former use of the adjective "noble" in "al this noble town" (II.737)). Troy was formerly "noble" to Criseyde, binding her closely and firmly, and now it undoes the knot of her heart. Though her house stood on "Troilus" and "Troie town," it now becomes baseless. So the house of love between Troilus and Criseyde has completely collapsed. Their union is untied, unraveled, as it were. The cords of love are no longer binding their hearts.

The day has come when they made a heartfelt promise. Troilus and Pandarus go to the "walles" and wait for her exultantly.

> And on the walles of the town they pleyde,
> To loke if they kan sen aught of Criseyde. (V.1112-13)

Troilus does not know her "slydynge" nature at all. He keeps on waiting for her. Then he tells Pandarus to go to the gate with him.

> Com forth; I wole unto the yate go
> Thise porters ben unkonnyng evere mo,
> And I wol don hem holden up the yate
> As naught ne were, although she come late." (V.1138-41)

Time passes quickly, because time and tide wait for no man, to say nothing of Troilus. Criseyde does not come back. As is shown in the passage: "He loketh forth by hegge, by tre, by greve, / And fer his hed over the wal he leyde" (V.1144-45), Troilus cannot see her, no matter how eagerly he looks this way and that. The "yate," which may be Troilus's "wyndow" on the world, is open, but regretably Criseyde does not appear in the presence of Troilus.

Looking forward to Criseyde's return, Troilus sees her as if she were there. It is an illusion of his "eyen."

> Have here my trouthe, I se hire! Yond she is!
> Heve up thyn eyen, man! Maistow nat se?"
> Pandare answerde, "Nay, so mote I the!
> Al wrong, by God! What saistow, man? Where arte?
> That I se yond nys but a fare-carte." (V.1158-62)

As Troilus looks at the Greek side through the walls, it seems to him as if Criseyde had just come back there, so he says: "yond she is!" The adjective "yond" which refers to "a visible object at a distance but within view"[95] would be directly connected with the existence of Criseyde by Troilus's subjective "eyen." It may be perfectly true in Troilus's eyes, but it is not so in the light of reality. Pandarus's thinking is based on the fact, as if he were a man of logic. So he states the fact as it is, without understanding Troilus's perception of truth, and says that "I se yond nys but a fare-carte."[96]

We have discussed the function of the house in this work, including the expression of "walles" between the main characters. In Book V, we do not find the "wyndow" which promotes the mutual relationship between them, but there exist the "walles" which let them lock into their imprisoned house. Even though the gate served for the window, it does not help their communication of love. The barrier of war caused by the two armies has completely destroyed their house of love.

Finally the story comes to the last stage. Having known the definite fact that Criseyde had already broken faith with him, Troilus fights a duel with Diomede desperately. However, their fight remains unsettled and Troilus is murdered by "the fierse Achille." Afterwards, Troilus's soul is completely separated from his body, and he laughs as he ascends into Heaven. Troilus finds the suitable house of love instead of the transitory house of love on earth.

> And in hymself he lough right at the wo
> Of hem that wepten for his deth so faste,
> And dampned al oure werk that foloweth so
> The blynde lust, the which that may nat laste,
> And sholden al oure herte on heven caste;
> And forth he wente, shortly for to telle,
> Ther as Mercurye sorted hym to dwelle. (V.1821-27)[97]

Troilus, with his laugh which "sounds unsubstantial, hollow, ephemeral, or ironical (in the symbolical sense of the word),"[98] despises all the worldly things in this book: Troilus's one-sided blind love, his pleasant contact with Criseyde, her sorrowful departure from him, her ultimate "slydynge," Pandarus's help in building the house of love through his deliberate "hertes line," the collapse of the house influenced by Fortune, and so on.[99] Troilus ascends into "heven" and dwells in the new world. He desires us to turn the "herte" in the body on the "heven."

We have discussed Chaucer's expression of "hous," considering the role the house plays in *Troilus and Criseyde*. We will summarise as follows: the house represents the human body and the window symbolises our eyes. We see this symbolism in "The Tale of Melibee." On the other hand, the house and the windows are effectively and adequately used to show the "noble" courtly love in "The Knight's Tale"; they represent the bawdy, physical love in "The Miller's Tales." Both tales certainly represent the extreme aspects of the meaning and use of the house. In such a late work as *The Canterbury Tales*, Chaucer applied the descriptions of the house clearly to separate the spiritual aspect of love from the physical one.

However, he does not view human affairs with an entirely

philosophic eye in *Troilus and Criseyde*. We see the delightful and intoxicating harmony between the spiritual love and the physical love at Pandarus's house in Book III. Troilus and Criseyde fulfill completely the house of love based on Pandarus's prudent "hertes line" and they live there physically and spiritually in an ecstasy of joy. But Troilus, who finally ascends into the house of Heaven, seeks for the world of spiritual love such as God's love, understanding the vanity and dwarfishness of the worldly love which shows the connection between the body and the spirit. We find the separation between the body and the spirit in the final stage of *Troilus and Criseyde*. This may show a slight and important change of Chaucer's mood and thinking which will have a great influence on his later works.

1.4. Hypocritical vocabulary

In Chapter 2,[100] we will discuss the meaning and use of the English northern dialect in the two young students' speech in "The Reeve's Prologue and Tale." It is not enough to deal only with the northern dialect in discussing this prologue and tale, however, because we find the other characters such as the pilgrim Miller, the narrator Reeve's rival, who use other dialects rather than the students' northern dialect. Symkyn the Miller, who does not use the northern dialect, is represented in the first half of "The Reeve's Tale" as the man of hypocritical nature, which is in striking contrast to the Cambridge students who speak their simple and naïve dialect. Hearing the unadorned speech of the students, the Miller decides definitely to equivocate with them. In this section, we will examine the characterisations of the Miller and his family, who regard country speech as "inferior." We will investigate the real figures of the people who pretend to belong to the upper and intellectual class, making little of the dialects.

We should always remember their hypocritical nature whenever we talk of the Miller and his family. Eliason indicates the use of "double entendre" seen in "person" and "wif,"[101] and this also applies in the case of the Miller himself. We will examine the double-faced character of the Miller, keeping in harmony with the story. It should be noted here that the character about whom the Reeve speaks is cast in harsh, ironic terms by the poet.

Furthermore, the Reeve speaks about the Miller bitterly and ironically.

> A millere was ther dwellynge many a day.
> As any pecok he was proud and gay. (RvT, I (A) 3925-26)

The alliterative expression: "pecok" and "proud"[102] may illustrate the vainglorious and pretentious character of the Miller; the *OED* says that "pecok" represents "a type of ostentatious display and vainglory." This kind of hypocritical nature is shown in the following example.

> He was a market-betere atte fulle.
> Ther dorste no wight hand upon hym legge,
> That he ne swoor he sholde anon abegge. (RvT, I (A) 3936-38)

As the *OED* explains, a "market-betere" is "one who idles or lounges about a market." The *MED* also says that he is "one who loiters around a market place, an idler." The Miller likes to go around the market, loitering on the way. He is expert at making a false show of power, and he thinks highly of himself. In addition to his vanity, he easily loses his temper. So, he is too dangerous for people to make friends with.

The Miller, who is hated and disliked by the narrator, is shown as the person who always steals something important.

> A theef he was for sothe of corn and mele,
> And that a sly, and usaunt for to stele. (RvT, I (A) 3939-40)

The narrator discloses the true nature of the Miller, as is shown in "for sothe." Though the key to this tale is the Miller's stealing, he usually hides his true character. Ironically enough, his appearance is covered with a humorous expression.

> Round was his face, and camus was his nose;
> As piled as an ape was his skulle. (RvT, I (A) 3934-35)

The word "camus," the *OED*'s citation, means "Of the nose: low and concave." The *MED* says that it is "Of the nose: turned up, pug, refroussé; ?as surname: the pug-nosed." His face seems not to be handsome and clear-cut, but it is "round." His head is "piled" (the *OED*'s citation, which means "deprived or bereft of hair, feathers, etc., bald, shaven, tonsured" and the *MED* indicates that the word is used in a set-phrase, meaning "bald as an ape (a magpie)"). It is interesting that he is bald and his head is like an ape. In this way, he is a typical example of an ugly man.

As the Miller is bitterly attacked by the narrator in this way, the hypocritical nature of Symkyn's wife is also rebuked as follows:

> A wyf he hadde, ycomen of noble kyn;
> The person of the toun hir fader was.
> With hire he yaf ful many a panne of bras,
> For that Symkyn sholde in his blood allye.
> She was yfostred in a nonnerye;
> For Symkyn wolde no wyf, as he sayde,
> But she were wel ynorisshed and a mayde,
> To saven his estaat of yomanrye. (RvT, I (A) 3942-49)

Though she seems to be of good lineage, Spearing indicates "the contemputuous irony of noble."[103] The adjective "noble" creates a stereotyped picture of a person of high birth, but Chaucer uses this adjective in an ironical way.[104] Spearing also points to the irony in the word "allye" when used to define their marriage; he says that "bras is an alloy, a cheap metal superficially resembling the noble gold, and this might suggest that the marriage was alloy of the same kind."[105] In this situation, their substance is criticised indirectly, and soon the readers and audience know the true character of the Miller's wife directly. In fact, the narrator reveals her real figure, using adjectives and similes.

> And she was proud, and peert as a pye.
> ....
> And she cam after in a gyte of reed;
> ....
> And eek, for she was somdel smoterlich,
> She was as digne as water in a dich,
> And ful of hoker and of bisemare. (RvT, I (A) 3950-65)

She has the same "proud" character as her husband Symkyn. This kind of pride is symbolised by the colour "reed." As for the alliterative phrase: "peert as a pye," the adjective "peert" in the *OED*'s earliest citation, means "forward in speech and behaviour; unbecomingly ready to express an opinion or give a sharp replay; saucy, bordering upon 'cheeky'; malspert:... Said usually of children, young people, or persons inferior position, such as are considered to be too 'uppish' or forward in their address." The *MED* also says that this word means "3. (c) apt, clever; cunning; of words: subtle." Consequently, we understand that Symkyn's wife belongs to "persons in inferior position" and that she is not a person of "noble" birth. We cannot feel that she is courteous and gentle, since the noun "pye" figuratively shows "a chattering or saucy person."[106] The adjective "smoterlich," which has one citation not only in the *OED* but also in the *MED*: "besmirched in reputation," reminds us of her secrecy of her birth, i.e. that she is a natural daughter.[107] Although we cannot define the clear meaning of this adjective, we are sure that her double-faced character is shown clearly and distinctly.

Next, their daughter is described ironically:

> This wenche thikke and wel ygrowen was,
> With kamus nose and eyen greye as glas,
> With buttokes brode and brestes rounde and hye.
> But right fair was hire heer, I wol nat lye.
> ..., for she was feir, (RvT, I (A) 3973-77)

She is a glamorous-looking girl, except for her peasant's nose. She is sexy enough to remind us of Prioresse in "The General Prologue," except for her broad buttocks. Her eyes are as clear as a crystal, as if she were the main character of a romance.[108] The shape of her nose is inherited from her father, who also has a "camus nose."[109] Just as the adjective "proud" connects Symkyn with his wife, the adjective "camus" relates Symkyn to his daughter. Their daughter, with ignoble nose and peasant buttocks, definitely is not of a blue-blooded "noble" family. It may be a slight, but important, change of the narrator's mood toward the Miller's daughter when the adjective such as "fair" or "feir," located at the central position in the medieval field of beauty,[110] is used to describe her. The narrator may feel pity stirring in his heart,[111] though we cannot interpret the adjective "fair" literally. After the daughter was raped by the student, the Miller says: "Who dorste be so boold to disparage / My doghter, that is come of swich lynage?" (4271-72). Though the Miller burns with anger, knowing that the student did "disparage"[112] his daughter of so-called noble blood, the readers nevertheless understand the real meaning of "swich lynage."[113]

We have investigated the appearance and reality of the Miller and his family through the examination of keywords in "The Reeve's Tale." As a final stage of this chapter, we would like to see the humourous scene which shows the reality of the Miller.

> For therbiforn he stal but curteisly,
> But now he was a theef outrageously, (RvT, I (A) 3997-98)

As for the couplet of rhyming adverbs, Masui indicates that "there can be no doubt that the audience would have been impressed with the humorously pointed contrast of the rime, a contradictory notion which Chaucer articulated through rime which was intended to appeal to them" and further explains that Chaucer, or the narrator, has been conscious of "the psychological effect" of the rhyming couplet given to the audience.[114]

Thus, in the first half of "The Reeve's Tale" the anger of Reeve, the narrator, toward the Miller and his family is shown clearly by the ironic description in which they are presented as characters of hypocritical nature. It is interesting that the Miller and his family, who acknowledge themselves "noble," are defeated by the two country boys who use the northern dialect seemingly regarded as "inferior."

Notes

1   R. M. Jordan, "The Compositional Structure of *The Book of the Duchess*," *Chaucer Review*. Vol. 9, No. 2 (1974-75), 99-117, p. 114.

2   H. Kökeritz, "Rhetorical Word-play in Chaucer," *PMLA* LXIX (1954), 937-52, p. 945 and p. 951.

3   P. F. Baum, "Chaucer's Puns," *PMLA* LXXI (1956), 225-46, p. 239.

4   J. Leyerle indicates that the word "hert-huntyng" functions as the keyword in *The Book of the Duchess*. ("The Heart and the Chain," *The Learned and the Lewed: Studies in Chaucer and Medieval Literature* edited by L. D. Benson (Cambridge, Mass.: Harvard University Press, 1974), 113-45, p. 114). Cf. A. Rooney, "*The Book of the Duchess*: Hunting and the 'UBI SUNT' Tradition," *RES* 38 (1987), 299-314, p. 303.

5   As for the use of the rhyme words, see M. Masui, *The Structure of Chaucer's Rime Words: An Exploration into the Poetic Language of Chaucer* (Tokyo: Kenkyusha, 1964). See also M. Masui, *A New Rime-Index to the Canterbury Tales based on Manly and Rickert's Text of the Canterbury Tales* (Tokyo: Shinozaki Shorin, 1988).

6   R. Delasanta, "Christian Affirmation in "*The Book of the Duchess*,"" *PMLA* LXXXIV (1969), 245-51, p. 249.

7   *Ibid.*, p. 251.

8   J. C. Cooper, *Symbolisms: The Universal Language* (Wellingborough: The Aquarian Press, 1982), pp. 115-16.

9   J. M. Hill, based on Burton's theory, regards the narrator's disease as "head melancholy." ("*The Book of the Duchess*, Melancholy, and that Eight-Year Sickness," *Chaucer Review*. Vol. 9, No. 1 (1974), 35-50, p. 39.)

10   C. P. R. Tisdale, "Boethian "Hert-Huntyng": The Elegiac Pattern of *The Book of the Duchess*," *American Benedictine Review* 24 (1973), 365-80, p. 375.

11   G. R. Wilson, "The Anatomy of Compassion: Chaucer's *Book of the Duchess*," *Texas Studies in Literature and Language* XIV 3 (1972), 381-88, p. 388.

12   A. C. Baugh, *Chaucer's Major Poetry* (London: Routledge and Kegan Paul Ltd, 1963), p. 6.

13   E. T. Donaldson, *Chaucer's Poetry: An Anthology for the Modern Reader* (New York: The Ronald Press Company, 1958, 1975²), p. 586.

14   Delasanta, p. 249.

15   As for the relationship between this description and *The Romaunt of the Rose*, see J. I. Wimsatt, *Allegory and Mirror: Tradition and Structure in Middle English Literature* (New York: Pegasus, 1970), pp. 66-67.

16   M. Thiebaux, *The Stag of Love: The Chase in Medieval Literature* (Ithaca and London: Cornell University Press, 1974), p. 119.

17   S. P. Prior, "Routhe and Hert-Huntyng in *The Book of the Duchess*," *JEGP* 85 (1986), 3-19, p. 12.

18   B. F. Huppe and D. W. Robertson, Jr. *Fruyt and Chaf: Studies in Chaucer's Allegories* (Princeton: Princeton University Press, 1963, repr. 1972), p. 52.

19   S. Manning, in a sharp contrast to Kittredge's bitter criticism (G. L. Kittredge, *Chaucer and His Poetry* (Cambridge, Mass.: Harvard University Press, 1915, repr.1972)), regards the dreamer's folly as playing an important role in this work. ("That Dreamer Once More," *PMLA* 71 (1956), 540-41.)

20   H. Phillips (ed.), *Chaucer: The Book of the Duchess*, Durham and St. Andrews Medieval Texts, No. 3, (Durham, 1982), p. 37.

21   M. Masui, "Chaucer's Tenderness and the Theme of Consolation," *Neuphilologische Mitteilungen* 73 (1972), 214-21, p. 218.

22   S. Manning, "Chaucer's Good Fair White: Woman and Symbol," *Comparative Literature* Vol. X, No. 2, 1958, 97-105, p. 100.

23   J. O. Fichte, "*The Book of the Duchess* — A Consolation?" *SN* 45, 1973, 53-67, p. 65.

24   N. Coghill, *Geoffrey Chaucer*, London: Longman, 1956, p. 34. Cf. J. I. Wimsatt, "The Apotheosis of Blanche in *The Book of the Duchess*," *JEGP* 66, 26-44, p. 26.

25   Kökeritz, p. 945.

26   The latest paper is S. P. Prior's "Routhe and Hert-Huntyng in *The Book of the Duchess*," *JEGP* 85 (1986), 3-19.

27   D. Scot-Macnab, "A Reexamination of Octovyen's Hunt in the *Book of the Duchess*," *Medium Ævum* LVI 2, 1987, 183-99, p. 195.

28   Tisdale, p. 378. As for the castle image, see R. A. Shoaf, "Stalking the Sorrowful H(e)art: Penitential Lore and the Hunt Scene in Chaucer's *The Book of the Duchess*," *JEGP* 78 Vol. 3, 1979, 313-24, p. 322.

29   E. Reiss, "Chaucer's Parodies of Love," *Chaucer the Love Poet* edited

by J. Mitchell and W. Provost (Athens: University of Georgia Press, 1973), 27-44, p. 36.

30   The present writer's papers: "Chaucer no Yakata no Hyogen," *Hito no Ie — Kami no Ie*, (Kyoto: Apollon-sha, 1987) and "Chaucer's Use of "hous" and Its Synonyms: With special reference to *Troilus and Criseyde*" *Jinbun Ronso* No. 6, Mie University, 1989, 19-39.

31   W. O. Sypherd, *Studies in Chaucer's Hous of Fame* (London, 1907, reprint, New York: Haskell House, 1965). B. G. Koonce, *Chaucer and Tradition of Fame: Symbolism in the House of Fame* (Princeton: Princeton University Press, 1966), p. 4. P. Boitani, *Chaucer and the Imaginary World of Fame* (London: Brewer, 1984), p. 168. H. Phillips and N. Havely, *Chaucer's Dream Poetry* (London: Longman, 1997), p. 115. A. J. Minnis, *The Shorter Poems* (Oxford Guide to Chaucer) (Oxford: Clarendon Press, 1955), p. 208 ff. The total number of the word "love" and its derivatives is thirty five: "love"(19), "lovers"(9), "loved"(2), "love-daunces"(1), "love-dayes"(1), "love-tydynges" (1), "lovede"(1), and "loven"(1). We find 12 examples in Book I, 11 in Book II, and 12 in Book III, but these words are used in the lines 37-370 in Book I, in the lines 625-683 except the line 1056 in Book II, and in the lines 1489-2144 except the line 1235. So these words are intensively used in the first half and second half in this work.

32   W. Clemen, *Chaucer's Early Poetry* (London: Methuen, 1963), p. 110.

33   "Experience" is the *OED*'s earliest citation and means "experiment" here. The *MED* says that this word means: "1b. Demonstration, proof, or confirmation of a proposition, theory, or expectation on the basis of facts observed or investigated..." In the *MED*, 3 of 7 examples are Chaucer's.

34   As Tables 2 and 3 show, these words are frequently used in this work. The poet tries to represent the world of truth, using the keyword "soth" in this work, while he often uses the keyword "trewe" in *Troilus and Criseyde*. Since the word "trewe" is related to Troilus and his surroundings, the meaning of "trewe" is more specific in *Troilus and Criseyde*. As for the frequency of "trewe" and "trewely" in Chaucer's works, see Table 9 in the note 54.

35   This fact may show that in this work the words become more complicated than in the former work: *The Book of the Duchess* where the keyword "herte" was consistently used.

36   K. G. Stevenson, *The Structure of Chaucer's House of Fame* (Michigan: University Microfilms, 1978), p. 23. Cf. F. Sasaki, "*The House of Fame* to And" *Festshrift for Prof. Sachiho Tanaka* (Tokyo: Kirihara-shoten, 1988), 141-49, pp. 147-88.

37   This corresponds to the "tydynges of love" in the final stage of Book III. Cf. N. Coghill, *The Poet Chaucer* (Oxford: Oxford University Press, 1949), p. 47.

38   The first person singular pronoun "I" and the verbs of perception are repeated in this work, as in "I saugh." Cf. J. Finlayson, "Seeing, Hearing, and Knowing in *The House of Fame*," *Studia Neophilologica* 58 (1986), 47-57.

39   J. M. Steadman, "Chaucer's "Desert of Libye," Venus, and Jove," *Modern Language Notes* 76 (1961), 196-201, p. 199.) J. O. Fichte, *Chaucer's Art Poetical: A Study in Chaucerian Poetics* (Tübingen: Narr, 1980), p. 71. R. R. Edwards, *The Dream of Chaucer* (Durham and London: Duke University Press, 1989), p. 102.

40   In *The Book of the Duchess*, the "dog" played the part of a going-between of the lost "hart" and the Black Knight's sorrowul "heart." Jimura, *op. cit.*

41   J. Leyerle, "Chaucer's Windy Eagle," *UTQ* Vol. 40, No. 3 (1971), 247-65, p. 257.

42   It is also a fact that the words "hous" and "dore" are used to show the enclosed space. As is shown in "Thou goost him to thy hous anoon" (655), this house shows the isolated situation of the person. This leads to "an hermyte" (659). The "hous" also plays the part of freeing from the enclosed situation. This house gives us "som disport and game" (664) in everyday "labour and devocioun" (666). In this way, the "hous" has two kinds of functions.

43   N. Isenor and K. Woolner, "Chaucer's Theory of Sound," *Physics Today* 3 (1980), 114-16.

44   The law of transmission that speech is nothing but the vibration of the air makes us think that the keywords in the work is organically connected with the other words. The poet may have been conscious of the organic function of his words in the works.

45   According to the *MED*, "kynde" means "nature as a source of living things or a regulative force operating in the material world." The *OED* says that "kynde" is "nature in general, or in the abstract, regarded as the established order or regular course of things." As the adjectives "regulative," "established," and "regular" show, "kynde" is used to ascertain an accomplished fact.

46   J. M. Gellrich, *The Idea of the Book in the Middle Ages* (Ithaca and London: Cornell University Press, 1985), p. 186.

47   A. C. Spearing, *Readings in Medieval Poetry* (Cambridge University Press, 1987), p. 86.

48   See "craft" in the *OED*.

49   J. I. Wimsatt, *Allegory and Mirror: Tradition and Structure in Middle English Literature* (New York: Pegasus, 1970), p. 43.

50   The gold images of the house are used in 1306, 1346, and 1348. The magnificence of the house is shown by the expression: "lusty and ryche" (1356).

51   This kind of antithetical description of the house is found in the analogue: *Le Dit de la Panthere d'Amours*. (B. A. Windeatt (ed.) *Chaucer's Dream Poetry: Sources and Analogues* (London: Brewer, 1982), p. 130.) However, the description of the house in the analogue cannot be compared with Chaucer's skilful representation of the house carrying the contradictory values such as "soth" and "fals." J. A. W. Bennett interprets that the image of "glass" resembles that of Fortune. (*Chaucer's Book of Fame: An Exposition of 'The House of Fame'* (Oxford: Oxford University Press, 1968), pp. 104-106.) Cf. A. C. Spearing, *Medieval Dream-Poetry* (Cambridge: Cambridge University Press, 1976), p. 81.

52   Bennett, p. 107.

53   Boitani, p. 16.

54   In this book, we do not distinguish the set phrase "soth to telle" from the other use of "soth," since it seems that in *The House of Fame* "soth" is not so fixed as in Chaucer's later works. In fact, both "soth" and "fals" are used at the same time in this work. In *Troilus and Criseyde* we have 71 examples of "soth," its variants, and its derivatives, among which 28 examples are used as set phrases and 12 examples are connected with the verb "sey." So more than half examples are stereotyped expressions. In addition, the expressions which are not used as fixed expressions are converged on Book IV. The frequency of "trewe" and "trewely" in Chaucer's works is as follows.

Table 9   The frequency of "trewe" and "trewely" in Chaucer's works

	CT	BD	HF	ANEL	PF	BO	TC	LGW	SHP	ASTR	RR
trewe	86	4	1	5	4	6	39	43	13	3	19
trewely	47	10	5	0	0	0	31	8	1	0	4

55   See the *OED* "rook." J. A. W. Bennett, *Chaucer's Book of Fame*, p. 145.

56   N. R. Havely, *Chaucer: The House of Fame* (Durham: Durham Medieval Texts, 1994), p. 178.

57   Sheila Delany, *Chaucer's House of Fame: The Poetics of Skeptical Fideism* (Chicago: The University of Chicago Press, 1972). Cf. F. Sasaki, "*The House of Fame* no Shudai to Buntai" *Katahira* 19 (Okazaki: Chubu Katahirakai, 1983), 32-47. As for Fame herself, see S. S. Hussey, *Chaucer: An Introduction* (London: Methuen, 1971), p. 41. Boitani, "Old Books Brought to Life in Dreams: the *Book of the Duchess*, the *House of Fame*, the *Parliament of Fowls*," *The Cambridge Chaucer Companion* edited by P. Boitani and J. Mann (Cambridge: Cambridge University Press, 1986), 39-57, p. 54.

58   R. W. Hanning, "Chaucer's First Ovid: Metamorphosis and Poetic Tradition in *the Book of the Duchess* and *the House of Fame*," *Chaucer and the Craft of Fiction* edited by L. A. Arrathoon (Michigan: Solaris Press, 1986),

p. 149. However, each petitioner's attitude is a little differnt from each other, so we cannot draw a hasty conclusion that the poet shows the perfectly mixed world of dualistic values here, because the person gets his good fame when he does not overestimate his own abilities. The poet's modest attitude, as in the Invocation of Book III, may be easily connected with his good fame.

59   R. C. Goffin, "Quiting by Tidings in *The House of Fame*," *Medium Ævum* XII (1943), 40-44.

60   W. A. Davenport, *Chaucer: Compaint and Narrative* (London: Brewer, 1988), p. 71.

61   Bennett, p. 177.

62   S. Delany, p. 111. C. P. Chiappelli, *Chaucer's Anti-scholasticism Opposition and Composition in the House of Fame*, (Michigan: University Microfilms, 1977), p. 151. L. J. Fitzpatrick, *Chaucer the Word-master: The House of Fame and The Canterbury Tales* (Michigan: University Microfilms, 1974), p. 180.

63   Bennett states that "In the house of tidings and Aventure he had glimpsed the possiblities of a narrative art that would range far beyond the classical and the courtly; and it had even suggested the ideal vehicle for accommodating *a medley of stories false and true*" (italics mine), p. 187.

64   M. Masui, *Chaucer no Sekai* (*The World of Chaucer*) (Iwanami Shoten, 1976), p. 85.

65   D. Traversi also indicates that this work is deeply connected with *The Canterbury Tales* (*Chaucer: the Earlier Poetry* (Newark: University of Delaware Press, 1977), p. 77.), and last but not least, the present author indicates that there exist Chaucer's other works: *Parliament of Fowls*, *Troilus and Criseyde*, and *The Legend of Good Women* written before *The Canterbury Tales*.

66   R. M. Correale and M. Hamel's *Sources and Analogues of the Canterbury Tales* (Cambridge, D. S. Brewer, 2002), p. 322 ff.

67   See also his article, "The Wanderer and Arcite: Isolation and the Continuity of the English Elegiac Mode" in *Four Papers for Michio Masui*, ed. Raymond P. Tripp, Jr. (Denver: The Society for New Language Study, 1972), pp. 1-10.

68   According to Tatlock and Kennedy's *A Concordance to the Complete Works of Geoffrey Chaucer and to the Romaunt of the Rose* (Gloucester, Mass.: Peter Smith, 1963), there are 78 examples of the word "prisoun" including those of *The Romaunt of the Rose* and among them we find no less than 31 examples in "The Knight's Tale."

69   Michio Masui, *Studies in Chaucer* (in Japanese) (Tokyo: Kenkyusha, 1962), pp. 224-25.

70   Kiichiro Nakatani, "A Perpetual Prison: The Design of Chaucer's Knight's Tale," *Hiroshima Studies in English Language and Literature* IX, i,

ii (The English Literary Association of Hiroshima University, 1963), 75-89.

71　Charles Muscatine, "Form, Texture, and Meaning in Chaucer's *Knight's Tale*," *PMLA* LXV (1950), 911-29. However, if the present writer's reading were justified, we could not help thinking that the narrator seemingly sympathized with Arcite, as stated in the paper: "The Characterisations of Troilus and Criseyde through Adjectives in Chaucer's *Troilus and Criseyde*: "trewe as stiel" and "slydynge of corage," *Phoenix* XV (Department of English, Hiroshima University, 1979), 101-22.

72　The narrator describes this event as the accidental occurrence when Emelye happens to walk around the "gardyn" looking down through the "prisoun" in a tall tower in a morning of May. This kind of description, conventional as it may be, would be Chaucer's effective and skilful means of expressions. See A. Jimura, "Chaucer's Use of Impersonal Constructions in *Troilus and Criseyde*: by aventure yfalle," *Bulletin of Ohtani Women's College*, XVIII, i (1983), 14-27.

73　M. Masui, *Chaucer no Sekai* (Tokyo: Iwanami), pp. 162-63.

74　For example, see Trevor Whittock, *A Reading of the Canterbury Tales* (Cambridge: Cambridge University Press, 1968), pp. 75-95.

75　It is generally said that Chaucer wrote over this story based on the contemporary "fabliau" in Europe. See Tetsuji Shomura, "Chaucer no *The Miller's Tale* to sono Ruiwa: Dento to Sozo,*" Kumamoto Tandai Ronshu* LI (1975) 1-18.

76　As for the word "hous," we should deal with the expression of "hous" in *The Hous of Fame*.

77　Troilus keeps the matter to himself, controlling his feelings, as in "Bywayling in his chambre thus allone" (I.547) and "... he wolde werken pryvely, / First to hiden his desir in muwe / From every wight yborn, al outrely" (I.380-82). It is clear that he is imprisoned in his own house of love.

78　M. Masui, "Chaucer no Geijutsu to Humanism: Buntaiteki Kenchi kara," *Chusei to Renaissance* (Tokyo: Aratake Shuppan, 1977), pp. 73-104. Masui explains Chaucer's well-balanced way of versification, referring to "his hertes line" as one of the characteristics showing 'Gothic' Chaucer. The books dealing with 'Gothic' aspects of Chaucer are as follows: Charles Muscatine, *Chaucer and the French Tradition* (Berkeley: University of California Press, 1957), D. W. Robertson, Jr., *A Preface to Chaucer* (Princeton: Princeton University Press, 1962), Robert M. Jordan, *Chaucer and the Shape of Creation* (New York: Harvard University Press, 1967), D. S. Brewer, "Gothic Chaucer," *Writers and Their Background: Geoffrey Chaucer*, ed. by Derek Brewer (London: G. Bell and Sons, 1974), pp. 1-32. An expository comment is made by Hisashi Shigeo's article: "Chaucer to Gothic Geijutsu" *Eigo Bungaku Sekai* XI, ii (Tokyo: Eichosha, 1976), 30-33.

79　A. Jimura, "Chaucer's Depiction of Characters through Adjectives,"

Ohtani Studies XV, i (1980), pp. 1-20, see p. 9.

80   See note 89.

81   The "closet" plays the part of protecting her internal world, as in "But (Criseyde) streght into hire closet anon, / And set hire doun as stylle as any ston," (II. 599-600).

82   The imagery of "garden" is thoroughly explained and studied in Toshio Kawasaki's following books: *Marvel no Niwa* (Tokyo: Kenkyusha, 1974), *Niwa no England* (Nagoya: Nagoya University Press, 1983), *Rakuen to Niwa* (Tokyo: Chukoshinsho, 1984).

83   The impersonal constructions which show happening and occurrence, as matter of course, closely related to the natural phenomena, impart the crucial turning point and the momentous event in this work. "Chaucer's Use of Impersonal Constructions," *op. cit.*

84   The narrator uses the noun "werk" to show what Pandarus intends to do from now, as in "his werk" (III.697) and "al this werk" (III.702). This "werk" indicates that he does "frame" the structure, using the "tymbur." It may be Pandarus's deliberate use of "hertes line."

85   See note 78.

86   This kind of Pandarus's practical activity, as in "This Troilus,... / Is thorugh a goter, by a pryve wente, / Into my chaumbre come in al this reyn, / Unwist of every manere wight, certeyn." (III.786-88), may be connected with his skilful use of a temporary expedient as an excuse for Criseyde.

87   According to M. P. Tilley's *A Dictionary of the Proverbs in England* (Michigan: The University of Michigan Press, 1950), p. 201, "as gentle as a falcon" may be a set phrase.

88   See Book I, 381 and Book III, 602. While in the former, we read the symbolical meaning in the expression "in muwe," in the latter "in mewe" shows the literal meaning, as is already stated in this article.

89   It should be noted that Criseyde's house is described as such a "palais" as Troilus's "palais." This "palais" means "A dwelling-place of palatial splendour; a stately mansion," according to the *OED* and "A palatial house; a large building," according to the *MED*. But Whitmore states that Criseyde's house may have been the house of common people in the city and that Criseyde's house also may have been so. However, we stand against her opinion, since we would read a literal meaning of "palais," if the "palais" were not merely the "hous," as the *OED* and the *MED* indicate. Sister Mary Ernestine Whitmore, *Medieval English Domestic Life and Amusements in the Works of Chaucer* (New York: Cooper Square Publishers, Inc., 1972), p. 13.

90   Bachelard states that "Elle (= la maison) est corps et ame." (Gaston Bachelard, *La poetique de l'espace* (Paris: Presses Universitaires de France, 1967), p. 26.) Bollnow also says that "... so kann man das Haus doch in einer gewissen Hinsicht als einen erweiterten Leib betrachten,..." O. F. Bollnow,

Mensch und Raum. (Stuttgart: W. Kohlhammer, 1963, p. 292.)

91   This meaning depends on *A Chaucer Glossary*, compiled by Norman Davis, *et al.* (Oxford: Clarendon Press, 1979).

92   The nouns "palais," "house" and "place" are used to describe the house in this passage. We find four times the noun "palais." Since Troilus defines the "palais" as "house of houses" and "crowne of houses alle," we should not be prompt in deciding that the "palais" is merely a private house commonly found in the city.

93   This adjective is the *OED*'s earliest citation and means "Of places or things; causing or manifesting discomfort; dismal, cheerless, gloomy," and the *MED* regards this word as the earliest of four quotations and means: "2. (a) Of a place: cheerless, depressing."

94   This use of Chaucer's rhyme words is shown in the following books. Michio Masui, *The Structure of Chaucer's Rime Words: An Exploration into the Poetic Language of Chaucer* (Tokyo: Kenkyusha, 1964), p. 270 and pp. 278-80. Norman Davis, "Chaucer and Fourteenth-century English," *Writers and Their Background: Geoffrey Chaucer*; ed. by D. S. Brewer, pp. 76-77.

95   See the first definition of the adjective "yon" in the *OED*.

96   Masui states that "... Pandarus's 'That I see yond ... a fare-cart,' cruel though it may be, is a correct answer." *Studies in Chaucer*, p. 120. I have translated Masui's Japanese text into English.

97   Windeatt indicates that both the line 1825 and "oure werk" in the third line of the quotation do not exist in the original text *Teseida*. B. A. Windeatt, *Troilus and Criseyde: A new edition of 'The Book of Troilus,'* (London: Longman, 1984), p. 561.

98   Masui states that "... the laugh sounds unsubstantial, hollow, ephemeral, or ironical (in the symbolical sense of the word) — as if echoing that all is vanity that is on earth, life and love and blind lust and what-not else." "Chaucer's Use of 'Smile' and 'Laugh'" *Anglica*, III, iii (1958), pp. 1-16. Anglica Society (Kansai University), p. 16.

99   This kind of technique is called "palinode," which shows the way of condemning and compensating for a set of conducts. Two of famous examples of "palinode" are: *The Legend of Good Women* and the last "retracciouns" of *The Canterbury Tales*. See J. A. Cuddon (ed.), *A Dictionary of Literary Terms* (London: André Deutch, 1977), pp. 476-77.

100   See also the present writer's article: "Chaucer's Use of Northern Dialects in *The Reeve's Prologue and Tale*," *Festschrift for Professor Kazuso Ogoshi* (Kyoto: Apollon-sha, 1990), pp. 159-83.

101   Norman E. Eliason, "Some Word-Play in Chaucer's Reeve's Tale" *Modern Languages Notes* LXXI (1956), 162-64.

102   Alliterative expressions like this passage are often used in this work: "my fodder is now forage" (3868), "Myn herte is also mowled as myne heris"

(3870), "... for she was somdel smoterlich, / She was as digne as water in a dich" (3963-64), "And forth with 'wehee,' thurgh thikke and thurgh thenne" (4066), and so on.

103 A. C. and J. E. Spearing, *The Reeve's Prologue and Tale with the Cook's Prologue and the Fragment of his Tale* (Cambridge: Cambridge University Press, 1979), p. 97.

104 See the present writer's paper: "Chaucer's Depiction of Characters through Adjectives: Troilus and Criseyde" *Ohtani Studies*, XV, i (1980), 1-20, p. 1.

105 Spearing, p. 97.

106 The *OED*'s definition (2.b.). Spearing states that this alliterative phrase adds "its jaunty effect" (Spearing, p. 98).

107 Spearing, p. 98.

108 The description of Prioresse' eyes in "The General Prologue" is just like the same expression: "... hir eyen greye as glas" (152). In *The Romaunt of the Rose*, the noun "yen" is not connected with "glas," but the adjective "greye" is used, as in the following: "Hir yen grey as is a faucoun" (546) and "hir yen greye and glad also" (862). It is noted that the "grey" eye is not always restricted to a woman. Cf. "Fetys he was and wel beseye, / With metely mouth and yen greye" (821-22).

109 Hart indicates that this nose shows Malin's individual character, which is not found in the original version, stating that "she is individualized, however, and distinguished from all French sisters or prototypes by the 'camuse nose' inherited from Simkin." (W. M. Hart, "The Reeve's Tale: A Comparative Study of Chaucer's Narrative Art," *PMLA* XXIII (1908), 1-44, p. 40.

110 S. Wyler, *Die Adjective des mittelenglischen Schönheitsfeldes unter besonderen Berucksichtigung Chaucers* (Diss. Zurich, Biel: Graphische Anstalt Schuler, 1944).

111 In Trevor Whittock's *A Reading of the Canterbury Tales* (Cambridge: Cambridge University Press, 1968), the author takes up this daughter as an example of "the compassionate portrayal of human beings" (p. 103). He also says that "even this rather ugly-looking girl of such unbecoming parents has fair hair and a tender heart, and is really beautiful" (p. 100). On the other hand, Pearsall sees his daughter differently: "The pride Symkyn takes in his wife is openly abused in her too (3963-65), and the daughter is contemptuously dismissed, in a few lines totally without Chaucerian affection." (Derek Pearsall, *The Canterbury Tales* (London: George Allen & Unwin, 1985), p. 187).

112 The *OED* quotes this as the earliest citation and the meaning is "to bring discredit or reproach upon; to dishonour, discredit; to lower in credit or esteem" and the *MED* explains this word (which is also the earliest example) as follows: "2. (a) To sully or defile (a woman); treat (sth.) with indignity." However, Muscatine states that "to translate 'disparage' simply as 'dishonour'

or 'discredit' is to miss the point. In context the word has clearly a strong flavor of the older meaning, 'to match unequally; to degrade or dishonour by marrying to one of inferior rank'" (C. Muscatine, p. 204).

113   In the following passage, "for hooly chirches good moot been despended / On hooly chirches blood, that is descended. / Therfore he wolde his hooly blood horioure, / Though that he hooly chirche sholde devoure," (RvT, I (A) 3983-86), we will notice the recurrent adjective: "hooly." This kind of repetition lets us ask what is "hooly" and finally we know his real figure who tries to "devoure" his church, under the pretense of the adjective "hooly." This is a good example where the repetition of words produces an intriguing irony.

114   M. Masui, *The Structure of Chaucer's Rime Words* (Tokyo: Kenkyusha, 1964), pp. 276-77. Burnley also states that "in the line of the Reeve's Tale which tells how the rascally miller stole his customers grain curteisly (A. 2997), the act is contrasted with his conduct when he finds himself no longer under supervision, when he steals outrageously. The contrast with this last word points the contextual sense of curteisly, which is here 'with moderation'" and he reads "metonymic restriction" as the meaning of "curteisly." (D. Burnley, "Courtly Speech in Chaucer," *POETICA* 24 (1986), Shubun International Co., Ltd., pp. 16-38. See pp. 21-22). However, it is a matter for regret that Burnley does not deal with the stylistic value of this rhyme word.

CHAPTER 2

Dialects

2.0. Introduction

When we consider the dialects in Chaucer's English, we ought to deal with them from the viewpoints of regional dialects and social dialects. We need to bear in mind that in Chaucer's time, unlike the present day, there was no established standard language, and that London English was just one regional dialect among many. In this chapter, we limit our discussion to the use of northern dialect (2.1) and the language of Criseyde (2.2), which show the marked features of dialects in Chaucer's works.

2.1. Northern dialect

"The Reeve's Prologue and Tale," one of Chaucer's *The Canterbury Tales*, is characterised by the marked features of the northern dialect which were commonly used in Chaucer's lifetime. Why did Chaucer use the northern dialect in "The Reeve's Prologue and Tale" when he never used it in the other works? What was Chaucer's intention? Was the poet satirising and mocking the poetic technique of alliterative verse, e.g. in *Sir Gawain and Green Knight*, stating "... I am a Southren man; / I kan nat geeste, 'rum, ram, ruf,' by lettre," ("The Parson's Prologue," X (I) 42-44)?[1]

In this section, we would like to discuss the effects of the northern dialect in "The Reeve's Prologue and Tale," by paying special attention to the relationship between the characters and northern dialects, after briefly surveying some scholars' opinions about them.

2.1.1. Previous Studies

First, we will examine briefly the scholarship concerning the role of the northern dialect in "The Reeve's Prologue and Tale." Generally speaking, most scholars tend to take the view that the dialect reflects a low social status. Muscatine states that it is "an indication of social inferiority" and gives "a superficial appearance of rustic simplicity," after he says that in old French mimes, a century before Chaucer, dialect means social or intellectual inferiority."[2] Traversi also says it portrays "... two young men whose dialect reflects a mean social status,"[3] but he praises the narrator's careful use of northern dialect, saying it is "the careful reproduction of North country speech."[4] (This point will be considered later.) Copland comments that the northern speech gives a barbarous impression, stating, "in any case their extreme northern origin identifies them completely in southern eyes as mere barbarians ..., and their dialect speech makes it impossible for us to forget this status."[5] Pearcy, as if responding to Copland's calling them "mere barbarians," affirms his position in a severe tone, using the adverb "barbarously," as in "the clerks in *The Reeve's Tale*, with their barbarously provincial northern accents, ..."[6]

On the other hand, it is J. R. R. Tolkien and N. F. Blake who regard the northern dialect as Chaucer's "joke" or "fun." Tolkien, in his pioneer study, "Chaucer as a Philologist: *The Reeve's Tale*," observes that "of all the jokes that Chaucer ever perpetrated the one that most calls for philological annotation is the dialect talk in the *Reeve's Tale*. For the joke of this dialogue is (and was) primarily a linguistic joke, and is, indeed now one at which only a philologist can laugh sincerely."[7] Furthermore, he praises Chaucer's correct use of the northern dialect, after conducting an exhaustive survey of the texts.

Blake, in "The Northernisms in *The Reeve's Tale*," refutes the general view that the dialect shows the "inferior" aspect of the language, on the basis of an actual investigation of the dialects in the Hengwrt MS., and positively asserts that "... the undergraduates are far superior culturally and educationally to the miller, despite his pretension ..."[8] Finally, he takes the view that "the dialect that they speak is probably intended to increase the sense of light-hearted fun."[9]

The northern dialect, which has always been the scholars' and critics' greatest concern, is already used in "The Reeve's Prologue." The Reeve, the narrator in this work, speaks a Northern and East Midland form of English, as is in the following passage.

> "So theek," quod he, "ful wel koude I thee quite
> With bleryng of a proud milleres ye,
> If that me liste speke of ribaudye.
> But ik am oold; me list not pley for age; (RvPro, I (A) 3864-67)

The northern form "ik," the first person singular pronoun, is adequately explained in the *OED*:

> OE. *ic* remained in ME. as *ic*, *ik* in the north; in midl. and south it was early palatalized to *ich* (ɪtʃ) in the 14th c. *ik* and *i* were still used before vowel and consonant respectively in the north, but *I* alone appears in north and midl. after *c*1400.

In short, in the north "ik" was used during the Middle English period, but in the north and the Midlands the sound "k" of "ik" began to drop before the consonant and became the shortened form "i."

The pronoun "ik" (though the compound "theek"[10] in the line 3864 is used before a consonant) belongs to this systematic rule. So the pronoun "i" instead of "ik" is used in the following examples: "But if I fare as dooth an open-ers —" (RvPro, I (A) 3871) and "For sikerly, whan I was bore, ..." (*Ibid.*, I (A) 3891).[11] The pronoun "ik" is used when the sound "h" is not clearly pronounced, as in "And yet ik have alwey a coltes tooth," (*Ibid.*, I (A) 3888).[12]

As R. W. V. Elliott intuitively stated, it may be possible that the use of dialects in "The Reeve's Prologue" was a "signpost" — one that "was all that was needed at this point to prepare the audience for the linguistic hurdles ahead."[13] The Northern and East Midland form of English in "The Reeve's Prologue," prepares the audience for "The Reeve's Tale."

In fact, this kind of conversation in the northern dialect is reflected in two provincial young students' speech in the Tale instead of the old Reeve's in the Prologue. Their speech, however, is not consistent with the dialect. The dialect is arbitrarily used in the Tale, which may be intended by Chaucer the poet. The audience who are aware of the dialect in "The Reeve's Prologue" must have smiled to hear the students speak in their naïve provincial dialects. Further, the fact that they use the northern dialect unaffectedly and straightforwardly seems to be connected with their direct and straight behaviour reflecting their internal physical desires. The audience may have laughed jovially and gleefully over the students' bold and dynamic actions.

The dialects, however, are not used by the Miller and his family. The Miller, of course, is the Reeve's rival, and Chaucer may have scrupulously cared that these characters do not use the dialect speech, at least in "The Reeve's Tale," though the Miller is presumably from Cambridge or thereabouts. The hypocritical nature of the Miller and his family is consistently emphasised in this work. It should also be noted, however, that the persons who do not use the dialect speech do not always show the hypocritical nature.

Now, let us study Aleyn and John, the students of Cambridge University, and their northern speech in detail. At first, we will study the way the speech of the students reflects the northern colouring. Then, we will discuss the unreserved and outspoken behaviour of the students who speak the northern dialect plainly and frankly. It seems that words and actions are closely related to each other, at least in their case. In reality, they have a lively time of it in such a place as bed and triumphantly get the better of the Miller who pretends to belong to the upper and intellectual class of people.

The narrator Reeve in "The Reeve's Tale" comes from Bawdeswell, Norfolk, according to "The General Prologue" to *The Canterbury Tales*. Bawdeswell is some 20 kilometres to the northwest of Norwich, the county borough in eastern England.[14] It is also some 160 kilometres to the northeast of London. The dialect around Norwich is East Midland, according to Brook's classification of Middle English Dialects.[15] In this respect, we see that "ik" is the only Northern and East Midland form of English used by the Reeve in his Prologue. On the other hand, Strother, which might be the birthplace of the two young students in "The Reeve's Tale," is, as Blake says, "probably a fictitious name in Northumbria."[16] Though there does not exist the place name "Strother," it might indicate "Castle Strother," as is in the following: "There is a Castle Strother in Northumberland."[17] Bennett indicates that the place "is now found only north of the Tees, in Durham and Northumberland — further north, that is, than Yorkshire."[18]

The Reeve living between the northern area and London, is in the best position to tell this story, as Spearing declares: "the Reeve was therefore unusually well placed to understand the northern dialect and to represent some of its salient features to an audience of southerners."[19] Chaucer may have taken scrupulous care of even this kind of geographical matter.

Here we will briefly survey the general characteristics of northern dialects in this story, as objectively as possible. The remarkable achievements in this venture are as follows: Tolkien (1934) and Blake (1979).

Tolkien's published paper "Chaucer as a Philologist: The Reeve's Tale," originally presented at the meeting of Philological Society on 16 May, 1931,[20] divides the features of northern dialects into two parts: A. sounds and forms and B. vocabulary. As for the sounds and forms, Tolkien enumerates the seven features: (i) *a* for *o*: *na, nan* ..., (ii) similarly in the combinations *ald*: *tald* ..., (iii) *ang* for *ong*: *wanges* ..., (iv) *e* for *i*: *dreuen* ..., (v) *k* for *ch*: *quilk* ..., (vi) verbal inflections: (a) *es*, *s* for *eth*, *th* in 3 sg. pres. *fares* 103 ..., (vii) various northern forms and contractions (in which he cites the following words: *es, sal, ta, als, boes, gif, ar*).

As for the vocabulary of northern dialects, Tolkien picks up the following twenty-one words: *capel, daf, ferli, folt, fonne, hail, hepen, heping, hougat, il, imell, lape, sel, slik, swain, til, pair, wanges, werkes, wight, yon*, and adds three words: *tulle, gar, greipen*, and then puts four more words in this vocabulary: *auntre, draf-sek, hope, driue*. To sum up, twenty eight words are used as the northern dialects in this work.

On the other hand, Blake, persisting in his view that Hengwrt MS. is the oldest of all and the nearest to Chaucer's own language, studies the northern dialect in the Hengwrt MS.[21] While Tolkien chooses examples of every northern dialectal item found in many manuscripts, Blake states that even a word which shows the northern feature is not purely northern, if it is used in and/or around London. Blake therefore picks up seven words which are not found in the southern texts. Further, he comments that most words which the students use are "of Scandinavian origin" and show "a notable lack of words of literary French origin or of words frequent in courtly romance or sermons."

Blake puts a special emphasis upon the phonological and grammatical features of northern dialects. For example, from a phonological point of view he indicates three patterns: (1) as *a* or *aa* rather than as *o* or *oo*, (2) *lk* instead of *ch*, and (3) *sal* instead of *shal*. From a grammatical point of view, he shows the three patterns as well: (1) the use of *-es*, *-s* for southern *-eth*, *-th* in the third person singular of the present indicative, (2) for the past participle of the so-called strong verbs Chaucer generally omits initial *y-* and includes final *-n* in the undergraduates' language, and (3) *I is, thow is* and (*they*) *ar* instead of *I am*, *thou art* and *they ben*.

In addition to these, Blake states that the northernisms in "The Reeve's Prologue and Tale" are not consistent in the Hengwrt MS., and that the manuscripts supposed to be written after the Hengwrt MS. show more correct and consistent forms of the northern dialect. This fact, Blake says, may reveal that the scribes of those manuscripts could have changed the words into the northern dialect intentionally.

Thus, Blake summarises the features of the northern dialect used in "The Reeve's Prologue and Tale," basing his work upon Tolkien's preceding achievement. It is nevertheless clear that the result of Blake's study is strikingly different from that of Tolkien's, because Blake does not evaluate the northern features from a lexical point of view. He concluded, as we have already quoted in this chapter, that the northern dialect increases "the sense of light-hearted fun." Although we understand that the dialect used in a fabliau produces a comical and light-hearted effect, it does not seem to be enough to explain why Chaucer used the northern dialect only in this work.

Now, we will investigate how much the northern dialect is used in and/or around London before we discuss the relationship between the dialectal examples and the work. Blake, in *Non-standard English in English Literature*, indicates that "as a general principle we may think it unlikely that an author will use a dialect or register which is unfamiliar to the majority of his audience."[22] In Chaucer's lifetime, the northern dialect had already been used in London. We can therefore assume a linguistic environment that would allow Chaucer's audience to recognise the kind of dialect the speaker used when they heard it. They would know where he is from and the part of the country his dialect represents. In order to recognise some linguistic realities and situations in Late Mediaeval English, we consulted *A Linguistic Atlas of Late Mediæval English* edited by A. McIntosh *et al.* and will refer to and then compare the facts set out there with the northern dialects spoken by two students in this Tale.[23] (The volume number and the page number of this atlas are parenthesized at the end of every item.)

(1) The northern form "sal" instead of "shal" is already used in Essex, within the limits of about 20 km. to 40 km. northward from the middle of London. The plural form, however, is "shul," "shull[e]," and "shulle[n]." (Vol. II, p. 98; Vol. IV, p. 37)

(2) The genitive pronoun "their" is used in London. (Vol. II, p. 38; Vol. IV, p. 15)

(3) The northern forms "swilk" and "whilk" instead of "such" and "which" are used in Norfolk where the Reeve, the narrator, comes from. Both forms are co-existent in Norfolk. (Vol. II, p. 44 and p. 50; Vol. IV, pp. 17-18, pp. 20-21)

(4) The northern form "fra" instead of "fro" is used around Essex, about 10km. to the north of London. (Vol. II, p. 128; Vol. IV, p. 49)

(5) The spelling ʒ ("yogh") such as "ʒif" instead of "gif" is used in London. (Vol. II, p. 152; Vol. IV, p. 61)

(6) The northern form "awn" instead of "own" is used in Essex and Middlesex, near to London. (Vol. II, p. 320; Vol. IV, p. 235)

(7) The northern form "say" is not usually found in London where the form "sey" is popular, but we also find the vowel "a" in London. We do not know about the plural form "sayn." (Vol. II, p. 326)

(8) The form "twaie" instead of the northern form "twa" is found in London.[24] (Vol. II, p. 362; Vol. IV, p. 272)

(9) The form "werk" instead of "work" is used in London. (Vol. I, p. 382; Vol. IV, p. 89)

(10) The northern form which belongs to "ba-" type is limited beyond the northern part of East Riding and West Riding, Yorkshire. (Vol. I, p. 396; Vol. IV, p. 134)

(11) The preposition "til" is used at the west end of Norfolk. The word "til" used before the vowel is found in Bedfordshire. (Vol. I, p. 462)

(12) The 3rd per. sing. of present indicative: "-es" or "-s" is used in Buckinghamshire, about 100 km. to the northwest of London. (Vol. I, p. 466; Vol. IV, p. 109)

(13) The northern form "hou" instead of "how" is used in Hertfordshire located in the middle between London and Cambridge. (Vol. I, p. 493)

(14) The northern form "sa-" types of "soul" are mainly used in the northern parts of the British isles, but we find some of them in Norfolk and Warwickshire (Vol. I, p. 506; Vol. IV, p. 257). However, the form "au" of "soul," "know," and "blow" is found in and/or around London. (Vol. I, p. 546)

(15) The form "hethen" is used in Buckinghamshire and Suffolk. We find the word "heythen" in "The Reeve's Tale." (Vol. I, p. 529)

These definite facts, though based upon the spelling rather than the pronunciation, show that the northern dialect, as Blake states, has already deeply penetrated into the London dialect, and has become part of colloquial English. Chaucer, well knowing this kind of linguistic reality, would have the students from Northumberland use their northern dialect which was intelligible to the audience. In doing so, Chaucer could convey the humorous situation of "The Reeve's Tale."

2.1.2. The Effects of Northern Dialect

In order to observe the humorous effect of northern dialect of the students' speech in "The Reeve's Tale," let us consider the kind of thinking reflected by the dialect. In short, the northern dialect, limited though it is to "The Reeve's Tale," reveals the students' straightforward way of thinking and their simple and direct behaviour.

First, the students went to the Miller's house, because they wanted to take revenge for his robbing them: "The millere sholde not stele hem half a pekke / Of corn by sleighte, ne by force hem reve." (RvT, I(A) 4010-11) They are righteous but too simple; the students speak plain words which readily reveal their true intentions to the Miller. John's speech is as follows:

> "By God, right by the hopur wil I stande,"
> Quod John, "and se howgates the corn gas in.
> Yet saugh I nevere, by my fader kyn,
> How that the hopur wagges til and fra." (*Ibid.*, 4036-40)

In this passage, we find northern forms: the third person singular of the present indicative verb: "gas" and "wagges," the interrogative pronoun "howgates" instead of "how," and the set phrase "til" and "fra." John, using this kind of rustic speech including the northern dialects, wants to see the swaying motion of the hopper. The Miller can clearly see through John's intention. His motive is too apparent.

In response to this speech, Aleyn says:

> Aleyn answerde, "John, and wiltow swa?
> Thanne wil I be bynethe, by my croun,
> And se how that the mele falles doun
> Into the trough; that sal be my disport.
> For John, y-faith, I may been of youre sort;
> I is as ille a millere as ar ye." (*Ibid.*, 4040-45)

Here we see such salient features of the northern dialect as the verbal inflections, although we do not find the form "howgates." Instead the form "how" is present. Perhaps Chaucer wished to suggest a northern dialect rather than being completely accurate, just as when he used the pronoun "ik" in "The Reeve's Prologue." Nevertheless, Aleyn's speech and behaviour too obviously reveals that he would like to see the shaking movement of the hopper beneath. It's natural then that the Miller refers to "hir nycetee"; he knows the students' true intention.

Then, when the horse is lost, although it was hitched securely, the dialects show the students' utter confusion skilfully:

> Oure hors is lorn, Alayn, for Goddes banes,
> Step on thy feet! Com of, man, al atanes!
> Allas, our wardeyn has his palfrey lorn."
> . . . .
> "What, whilk way is he geen?" he gan to crie. (*Ibid.*, 4073-78)

CHAPTER 2   DIALECTS

In this passage, we find the following northern dialects: "whilk" instead of "which," the proper noun "Alayn" used when John addresses "Aleyn," the profane expression "for Goddes banes," the adverb "atanes," to say nothing of the verbal inflections mentioned above. All these reflect the rash and uproarious atmosphere and the students' agitation. Heedlessness seems to make Aleyn and John use the most intimate and familiar words of expressions. It should be noted that the following Aleyn's speech does not show his rural characteristics of dialects: "As I have thries in this shorte nyght / Swyved the milleres doghter bolt upright, / Whil thou hast, as a coward, been agast." (*Ibid.*, 4265-67), where he explained his good experience objectively.

Let us turn to the scene in which the students seek their lost horse, after learning from the Miller's wife where it went. The following passage is full of the northern dialect:

> "Allas," quod John, "Aleyn, for Cristes peyne
> Lay doun thy swerd, and I wil myn alswa.
> I is ful wight, God waat, as is a raa;
> By Goddes herte, he sal nat scape us bathe!
> Why ne had thow pit the capul in the lathe?
> Ilhayl! By God, Alayn, thou is a fonne!" (*Ibid.*, 4084-89)

These words, showing the northern features, may be emotional expressions. Here, John became so angry that he made Aleyn an object of his unfounded wrath, all because of an unexpected event. John's true and real internal world is thus revealed. It is interesting that the proper noun "Aleyn" is used in the first line of this passage, and the northern form "Alayn" is in the last line. While this may show an inconsistent use of the northern dialect on Chaucer's or a scribe's case, it could reveal John's unrestrained and confused emotion. The students react directly to their situation. John and Aleyn, as in "thise sely clerkes han ful faste yronne / Toward the fen…," (Both poor students, Allan and John, ran quickly into the marsh.) (*Ibid.*, 4090-

91), act rashly and thoughtlessly.

Even when they chase the horse after this scene, their words are closely related to their action:

> Thise sely clerkes rennen up and doun
> With "Keep! Keep! Stand! Stand! Jossa, warderere,
> Ga whistle thou, and I shal kepe hym heere!" (*Ibid.*, 4100-02)

We see the northern form "ga" as the imperative of the verb of motion; the modal verb is not "sal" but "shal." Although only the imperative form is northern, this passage shows the close connection between the words and their action: the words "keep!" and "stand!" are connected with the students' frantic chase.

Even the students' use of proverbs in their northern dialect reveals the connection between the ideal and their actual behaviour.[25]

> I have herd seyd, 'Man sal taa of twa thynges:
> Slyk as he fyndes, or taa slyk as he brynges.'
> But specially I pray thee, hooste deere,
> Get us som mete and drynke, and make us cheere,
> And we wil payen trewely atte fulle.
> With empty hand men may na haukes tulle;
> Loo, heere oure silver, redy for to spende." (*Ibid.*, 4129-35)

There are many dialectal pronunciations in John's proverbial expression: "one shall take of two things, the thing that one finds or the thing that one brings." Since the students do not have anything but their silver, they are destined to take the thing that they find. John also uses the proverb: "empty hands no hawkes allure," in which his use of "na" may show the northern pronunciation. It is noticeable that these proverbial statements express the students' clear desires and their resulting actions. It is interesting that the latter half of this passage is composed mostly of words in the London dialect, and yet the only dialectal words are in the proverbs. Chaucer may have consciously used the northern dialect as the means to express the close relationship

between the unadorned words and the students' direct action.
This kind of thought process may be also reflected in Aleyn's speech:

> For, John, ther is a lawe that says thus:
> That gif a man in a point be agreved,
> That in another he sal be releved.
> ....
> And syn I sal have neen amendement
> Agayn my los, I will have esement.
> By Goddes sale, it sal neen other bee!" (*Ibid.*, 4180-87)

Aleyn considers his present situation in proverbial legalistic terms,[26] i.e. he considers how to get "esement" because he has "neen amendement" against his loss, except to act.

John also acts similarly. He thinks in practical, proverbial ways:

> And when this jape is tald another day,
> I sal been halde a daf, a cokenay!
> I wil arise and auntre it, by my fayth!
> 'Unhardy is unseely,' thus men sayth." (*Ibid.*, 4207-10)

An alliterative effect of "un"-words (though the prefix 'un-' has the secondary stress) is present,[27] although the proverb is not connected with the northern dialect. When John acts, or plans to, he uses paired alliterated verbs. These words may show the regional features of expression in Chaucer's days.

Lastly, let us turn to the "sely" students' direct action in bed, which reveals their innermost passions. The narrowness of the Miller's "space" or "place" is effectively linked with the word "bed."[28] The students' action in bed reveals the truth of the proverb to take the thing one finds:

> And in his owene chambre hem made a bed,
> With sheetes and with chalons faire yspred
> Noght from his owene bed ten foot or twelve.
> His doghter hadde a bed, al by hirselve,
> Right in the same chambre by and by.

> It myghte be no bet, and cause why?
> Ther was no roumer herberwe in the place. (*Ibid.*, 4139-45)

The affair was caused because the Miller shared "his owene chambre" with the students and his daughter — as well as the students seeking vengeance upon the greedy Miller. This setting is essential to the development of the story.

A brief outline of the events is as follows (*Ibid.*, 4153-206). The Miller goes to "bedde": "To bedde he goth, and with hym goth his wyf." The cradle is put at the foot of the Miller's wife: "The cradel at hir beddes feet is set, / To rokken, and to yeve the child to sowke." The daughter and two students go to "bedde": "To bedde wente the doghter right anon; / To bedde goth Aleyn and also John." Aleyn willingly goes to the daughter's bed: "And up he rist, and by the wenche he crepte." Then John feels mortified all alone in his bed: "And I lye as a draf-sak in my bed." Interestingly, the *OED*'s earliest citation of the northern "draf-sak" means "a sack of draff or refuse; also fig. a big paunch; lazy glutton." John feels worthless, impotent as a man.

John then adds a fresh development to the story, because he changes the position of the cradle to "his beddes feet." Rather than lying impotently, feeling sorry for himself, John acts:

> And up he roos, and softely he wente
> Unto the cradel, and in his hand it hente,
> And baar it softe unto his beddes feet. (*Ibid.*, 4211-13)[29]

For this reason the Miller's wife makes an inevitable mistake after she went to the toilet.

> And cam agayn, and gan hir cradel mysse,
> And groped heer and ther, but she foond noon.
> "Allas!" quod she, "I hadde almoost mysgoon;
> I hadde almoost goon to the clerkes bed.
> Ey, benedicite! Thanne hadde I foule ysped!"
> And forth she gooth til she the cradel fond.
> She gropeth alwey forther with hir hond,

> And foond the bed,and thoghte noght but good, (*Ibid.*, 4216-23)

Not realising that her own "bed" is really "the clerkes bed," she gropes here and there until she finds the "cradel" where, she supposes, her true bed lies. She crawls with a sense of security into the place where the physical love-making takes place. This is the first mistake.

Another happens when Aleyn creeps into what he believes to be John's bed after he made a happy night of it with the Miller's daughter. The cradle also makes him misjudge the place.

> Aleyn up rist, and thoughte, "Er that it dawe,
> I wol go crepen in by my felawe,"
> And fond the cradel with his hand anon.
> . . . .
> I woot wel by the cradel I have mysgo;
> Heere lith the millere and his wyf also."
> And forth he goth, a twenty devel way,
> Unto the bed ther as the millere lay. (*Ibid.*, 4249-58)

Aleyn makes a great mistake. This lets the Miller know the truth.

In this way, the students' action in the "bed" is not only connected with the theme of this work, but also serves as a vehicle to show the students' straightforward and frank thought processes.

A good example of where the dialect produces a humorous effect is the scene where Aleyn, using his own dialect, bids the Miller's daughter a hearty and affectionate farewell:

> Aleyn wax wery in the daweynge,
> For he had swonken al the longe nyght,
> And seyde, "Fare weel, Malyne, sweete wight!
> The day is come, I may no lenger byde;
> But everemo, wher so I go or ryde,
> I is thyn awen clerk, swa have I seel! (*Ibid.*, 4234-39)

Just like a hero in romance,[30] Aleyn should have extended a knightly farewell to his sweet lady, but in fact he uses the bucolic level of speech. The gap between the courtly and the rustic produces a subtle atmosphere of parody. Further, this seems to indicate that the students who use the northern dialect get the better of the miller. This is a humorous passage, indeed.

We have thus discussed the characters who speak the northern form of English, paying special attention to the description of characters. To sum up, the persons who use the dialect in this work tend to take direct and straightforward action which makes the audience laugh lightheartedly. On the other hand, the persons who do not use the dialect in this work are two-faced; they try to deceive other people; i.e. they do not reveal their real intentions. We will discuss the hypocritical vocabulary of the Miller and his family in a further study.

In this way, "The Reeve's Tale" consists of two kinds of contrastive characters. One type of characters uses the London dialect or the city speech, which might normally suggest membership of a middle class superior to the students, while the other type of characters uses the northern dialect or the country speech, which might normally be associated with a less cultivated class. However, it is interesting that the Miller, whose language is that of the superior class, is defeated by the country boys. From this contrastive point of view, unless the dialects were used in this work, "The Reeve's Prologue and Tale" would have become a tasteless and humourless story lacking depth.

2.2. Women's speech

Recently, studies of regional dialects in Middle English writings have progressed remarkably. One of the representative achievements is A. McIntosh *et al.* (eds.), *A Linguistic Atlas of Late Mediæval English* (1986). Another is M. L. Samuels and J. J. Smith's *The Language of Chaucer and His Contemporaries* (1988), in which they discuss regional dialects in "a linguistic community" created by the fourteenth century writers and contemporary scribes.

Much attention has thus been paid to regional dialects, but sociolinguistic studies of Middle English have been insufficiently

CHAPTER 2 DIALECTS

developed. Though there have been a few outstanding researchers, such as M. Schlauch (1952), V. Salmon (1975), N. F. Blake (1981), and D. Burnley (1983), the sociolinguistic approach has not applied to Middle English comprehensively. In particular, we still await a study of women's speech in the language of the female characters in Chaucer's works.

In this section we will deal with the language of Criseyde in Chaucer's *Troilus and Criseyde*, focusing mainly on her vocabulary. Comparing Criseyde's vocabluary with those of Troilus and Pandarus, we will concentrate on the characteristics of women's language in fourteenth century upper class society, few though they may be. In this study, we have used a data-based text of *Troilus and Criseyde* and statistical data analysis to investigate Criseyde's language, making use of a personal computer. Table 1 shows the number of lines and words in each Book and the number of words used by the characters in each.

Table 1 Summary Table of Word Counts

	Book I	Book II	Book III	Book IV	Book V	total
Troilus	1583	338	2441	3601	3392	11355
Criseyde	6	2227	2036	3290	1426	8985
T&C	0	0	12	0	0	12
Pandarus	2808	5426	2924	1783	1282	14223
Narrator	4146	5255	7108	4104	7126	27762
Others	87	973	0	604	1521	3185
total	8630	14219	14521	13382	14747	65522

T&C: Troilus and Criseyde

First of all, let us examine some general characteristics of women's speech in *Troilus and Criseyde*. When we read the scene of the Criseyde-Antenor hostage exchange arranged between Troy and Greece in Book IV, we encounter Criseyde's upper class women friends. Their language might be considered to reflect contemporary

Middle English women's speech.

> Quod first that oon, "I am glad, trewely,
> Bycause of yow, that shal youre fader see."
> Another seyde, "Ywis, so nam nat I,
> For al to litel hath she with us be."
> Quod tho the thridde, "I hope, ywis, that she
> Shal bryngen us the pees on every syde,
> That, whan she goth, almyghty God hire gide!"
> Tho wordes and tho wommanysshe thynges,
> She herde hem right as though she thennes were; (IV.687-95)

The narrator comments on the women's speeches in this passage as being "wommanysshe" (the *OED*'s earliest citation: "2. Characteristic of or proper to a woman or women; womanly, feminine."). The women commonly use the intensive adverbs such as "trewely" and "ywis," and they ask for boons from God, such as "almyghty God hire gide" (expressions from which the language developed many of its oaths); they also use short or abridged sentences in succession.

We also see an aspect of women's colloquial language in Antigone's words of love after she sings her love sonnet.

> "madame, ywys, the goodlieste mayde
> Of gret estat in al the town of Troy,
> And let hire lif in moste honour and joye." (II.880-82)

The characteristics of women's language are shown in the intensive adverb "ywys," Criseyde's use of evaluative terms such as "gret estat" and "moste honour" repeatedly in reference to herself, the adjective "al," and the superlative adjectives such as "goodlieste" and "moste."

These characteristics of women's speech are also reflected in the language of Criseyde. In this section, we would like to investigate Criseyde's speech, using Jennifer Coates' classification (1986), and that of Robin Lakoff (1975). The aspects of language considered here are as follows: (1) Pronunciation, (2) Grammar, (3) Vocabulary, (4) Swearing and taboo language, (5) Literacy, and (6) Verbosity.

2.2.1. Pronunciation

In "The General Prologue" to *The Canterbury Tales*, Chaucer gives an ironic touch to the Prioresse's manner of speech, but we do not find such a subtle description to Criseyde's. (Further, in "The Reeve's Prologue and Tale" of *The Canterbury Tales*, Chaucer, changing his London spellings, gives northern dialects to the students and visualises some rural features of the contemporary pronunciation, but we do not find such a visualised rural dialect in Criseyde's speech.) Chaucer rather favours her speech.

In this section we quote only the passages referring to Criseyde's speech to see how the others evaluate her "speche," "word," and "voice."

> ... ne of speche / A frendlyer,... (I.884-85)
>
> And goodly of hire speche in general, (V.822)
>
> And with hire goodly wordes hym disporte
> She gan,... (III.1133-34)
>
> With pitous vois, (I.111)
>
> With broken vois, al hoors forshright, (IV.1147)
>
> Herde I myn alderlevest lady deere
> So wommanly, with vois melodious,
> Syngen so wel, so goodly, and so clere (V.576-78)

It seems that Criseyde speaks in a compassionate tone of voice, never in a harsh voice, for, as Burnley states, "a woman was expected to have a gentle and sweet tone" (1986: 27). Her speech is refered to by the favourable adjectives such as "frendly" or "goodly." The adjective "melodious" is also used when Troilus remembers Criseyde's beautiful voice in Book V.[31]

2.2.2. Grammar

Now we would like to consider the grammatical differences between men and women. In the first half of this section, we will deal with some grammatical items; in the second half, some problems of grammatical constructions will be considered.

2.2.2.1. Ellipsis, repetition, interrogative sentences, etc.

It seems that men used more formal language than women, because formerly men were more likely to have received an education than women (Coates 1985: 24). Criseyde, however, seems to have received a fair education, judging from her courtly speech, although as Taylor points out there are some loose constructions in her speech (1969: 147). In this section are presented examples of ellipsis, repetition, and interrogative sentences from Criseyde's speech. Criseyde tends to use them more often than Troilus and Pandarus do.

(a) ellipsis

Criseyde sometimes cuts short and leaves out sentences. Some of the instances are as follows:

> What! Bet than swyche fyve? I! Nay, ywys! (II.128)
>
> "And whi so, uncle myn? Whi so? (II.136)
>
> "Which hous?" (II.1189)
>
> "I? no," (II.1470)
>
> "Horaste! Allas, and falsen Troilus? (III.806)
>
> O, mercy, God! Lo, which a dede! (IV.1231)

(b) repetition

Sometimes Criseyde repeats words and phrases. Some of the instances are as follows:

> "And whi so, uncle myn? Whi so? (II.136)
>
> But harm ydoon is doon, whoso it rewe: (II.789)
>
> Do wey, do wey, (II.893)

Welcome, my knyght, my pees, my suffisaunce!" (III.1309)

(c) interrogative sentences

Criseyde often uses interrogative sentences. This may mean that she always consults with others for their judgement, and is obedient to them. Though it is a quite feminine style of expression, in Book IV, we find that she persuades Troilus of her honesty, pledging herself to come back to Troilus without fail. When she makes up her mind to do something, however, she is not obedient to others at all. Some of her interrogative sentences are as follows:

> Sey ye me nevere er now? What sey ye, no? (II.277)
>
> "Now em," quod she, "what wolde ye devise?
> What is youre reed I sholde don of this?" (II.388-89)
>
> Ye seyn, ye nothyng elles me requere?" (II.473)
>
> "Why, no, parde; what nedeth moore speche? (II.497)
>
> "Kan he wel speke of love?" (II.503)
>
> "Who yaf me drynke?" (II.651)
>
> "It reyneth; lo, how sholde I gon?" (III.562)
>
> "What, which wey be ye comen, benedicite?" (III.757)
>
> Why doth my deere herte thus, allas?" (III.843)
>
> And ye therwith shal stynte al his disese? (III.884)

2.2.2.2. Parataxis or hypotaxis

Traditionally speaking, the grammatical distinction between parataxis and hypotaxis is used as criteria to differentiate men and women's speech. Both written language and men's speech are likely to use hypotaxis, while both spoken language and women's speech tend to use parataxis (Coates 1985: 26). We would, therefore, expect to find more sentences involving coordinate clauses than sentences involving subordinate clauses in Criseyde's speech.

We will regard "and," "but,"[32] and "or"[33] as representative of coordinate sentences and "if" and "which"[34] as representative of subordinate sentences. Since all of these words except "if" play an important role in the narrative parts of this work, the narrator uses these conjunctions most frequently. However, when we compare Criseyde's use of "if" and "which" with that of the other characters, we do not detect any striking difference. We do, however, find the conjunctions "and" and "or" in Criseyde's speech used in Books II, III, and IV more than in the other characters'. There does seem to be some relationship between the choice of parataxis and hypotaxis and the language differences between the sexes. In particular we find a striking difference between Troilus and Criseyde in their longest speeches. Troilus uses the conjunction "and" 19 times in his speech: Book IV 958-1078 (121 lines), while Criseyde uses "and" 45 times in her speech: Book IV 1254-1414 (161 lines). In order to build up extended speech, Criseyde seems to need the conjunction "and."

2.2.3. Vocabulary

In this section, (1) intensive adverbs, (2) adjectives, and (3) nouns which show the salient features of Criseyde's language are dealt with.

2.2.3.1. Criseyde's Use of Intensive Adverbs

As Lakoff (1975: 54-55) indicates, intensive adverbs seem to show an aspect of women's language. They tend to be used among the women more than the men in the Middle English period. Taylor (1969: 148-49) also points out that they have a high frequency of use in Criseyde's language. Her choice of adverbs, however, depends on the kinds of adverbs. Here, we would like to investigate the differences between the sexes in the use of adverbs such as "trewely," "certes," and "iwis."

The adverbs "trewely" and "trewelich(e)" are used 12 times in

Criseyde's speech, compared with only 8 in Troilus's speech and 6 in Pandarus's. The adverb "trewely" and its variants are used mainly by Criseyde. One of the instances is as follows:

> "Myn honour sauf, I wol wel trewely,
> And in swich forme as he gan now devyse.
> Receyven hym fully to my servyse, (III.159-61)

In this speech, Criseyde faithfully accepts Troilus's declaration of love. Criseyde makes balanced use of the adverb "trewely" from Book II to Book V. Ironically, she uses this adverb most often in Book V, when she truly submits herself to Diomede's will.

The adverb "certes" and its related words are used mainly by Troilus: 14 in Troilus's speech, 5 in Criseyde's, and 6 in Pandarus's. One of Criseyde's uses of "certes" is given below. It is significant that she skilfully uses the negative expressions rather than the adverb "certes."

> "But certes, I am naught so nyce a wight
> That I ne kan ymaginen a wey
> To come ayeyn that day that I have hight. (IV.1625-27)

In addition, the adverbs "sikerly" and "sikirly," which are of Old English origin and at present mainly used in Scotland and other northern dialects, are never spoken by Criseyde.

The adverbs "iwis," "iwys," "ywis," and "ywys," which are obsolete in Present-day English, are of Old English origin. It should be noted that, though Troilus uses these adverbs as many as 24 times, and Criseyde 26 times, in some parts of the poem Criseyde uses them significantly more often than Troilus. This is especially the case in Book III, where Troilus uses these adverbs 2 times, Criseyde so 10 times. As can be seen in the examples below, Criseyde uses an adverb when she states her feelings definitely. These adverbs, however, do not show clear differences between Troilus and Criseyde, as Taylor has pointed out (1969: 148-49). Troilus uses them when he persuades himself in his monologue: "For in hym, nede of sittynge is, ywys, / And in the, nede of soth; and thus, forsothe (For in him there is certainly the necessity of sitting, and in you the necessity of truth.) (IV.1034-35) and "That right as whan I wot ther is a thyng, / Iwys, that thyng moot nedefully be so;" (IV.1073-74). Criseyde, on the other hand, speaks to her friend quite at ease:

> "Iwis, so wolde, and I wiste how,
> Ful fayn," quod she. "Allas, that I was born!"
> ....
> "Iwys, my deere herte, I am nought wroth,
> Have here my trouthe!" (III.1102-11)

This is an example of colloquial speech and may be taken as characteristic of not only Criseyde's speech but also that of her upper class women contemporaries.

2.2.3.2. Criseyde's Use of Adjectives

Jespersen regards adjectives such as "pretty" and "nice" as typical of women's language, and Lakoff sees empty adjectives such as "divine," "charming," and "cute" as characteristic of women's language (Coates 1985: 18-19). Here, we would like to check the intensive adjectives which show the differences between Troilus and Criseyde. The following items are discussed: (a) the adjective "verray," (b) the superlative of the adjectives, and (c) the collocation of "al" and "my(n)."

(a) "ver(r)ay," "verrey"

The adjective "ver(r)ay" or "verrey" are usually collocated with the nouns "God" and "lord," and are used by Troilus, Criseyde, and Pandarus. However, the collocation of "verray" and nouns meaning pleasure such as "joie" is used only in Criseyde's speech. We see the noun "slouthe" attached to the adjective "verray" in Pandarus's speech. Criseyde also uses the noun "tene" with the adjective "verray." We find 5 examples of "verray" in Criseyde's speech, 3 in Troilus's, and 6 in Pandarus's.

(b) The superlatives of adjectives
Some superlatives of adjectives are mainly used by Criseyde. They are "gentileste," "thriftieste," and "worthieste," the last of which is used by Criseyde three times and only once by Pandarus where Pandarus, facing Criseyde, refers to Troilus (III.781). The superlative "goodlieste" is used twice by both Criseyde and Antigone respectively. This adjective may symbolise women's pride.

On the other hand, the superlative "wofulleste" is used only by Troilus. Pandarus and the narrator use "beste" more than the other characters. The following are some examples. Comments are in parentheses:

> "I thenke ek how he able is for to have
> Of al this noble town the thriftieste
> To ben his love, so she hire honour save.
> For out and out he is the worthieste,
> Save only Ector, which that is the beste; (II.736-40)
>
> And though that I myn herte sette at reste
> Upon this knyght, that is the worthieste, (II.760-61)

(N.B. Here "the thriftieste" means the woman who is most "worthy, worshipful, estimable, respectable, well-living," but indirectly suggests Criseyde herself. "The worthieste" is Troilus in this passage.)

> I am oon the faireste, out of drede,
> And goodlieste, who that taketh hede, (II.746-47)

(N.B. Criseyde regards herself as "the faireste, ... goodlieste.")

> For I have falsed oon the gentileste
> That evere was, and oon the worthieste!
> . . . .
> Yet prey I God, so yeve yow right good day,
> As for the gentileste, trewely,
> That evere I say, to serven feythfully,

And best kan ay his lady honour kepe." (V.1056-77)

(N.B. Both "the worthieste" and "the gentileste" refer to Troilus's qualities. The word "best" in line 1077 of Book V is an adverb which describes the manner of Troilus, who had saved Criseyde's "honour" prudently and substantially.)

(c) "al + my(n)"

The idiomatic expression "*al + my(n)*" is used 16 times by Troilus, 15 by Criseyde and 8 by Pandarus. The frequency of Criseyde's use of the expression is not so different from that of Troilus's, but the nouns collocated with this expression differ between the characters. As Taylor indicates, "*al* is a general intensifier which acts both as an adverb with the adjective, *my*, 'entirely my knight,' and an adjective with the noun, *knyght*, 'my complete knight'" (1969: 144). Criseyde uses this expression only in Books III (9 times) and IV (6 times), while Troilus uses it mainly in Books III (5 times) and V (6 times). The examples in Book V show Troilus's sorrowful state of mind as he remembers happy times he spent with his sweetheart Criseyde. Criseyde, however, never uses this kind of sorrowful expression. Criseyde uses the following nouns in collocations: "knyght," "trist," and "estat," none of which are used by Troilus or Pandarus. The nouns "trist" and "estat" may reflect Criseyde's self-consciousness, since she always tries to look about herself. The instances are as follows:

> al my knyght (III.176, III.996), al my myght (III.178, IV.940), al my trist (III.941, III.1023), al my peyne (IV.903, IV.942), al my kyn (IV.1331), al myn herte (III.1001, III.1304, IV.1313)

2.2.3.3. Criseyde's Use of "estat," "honour," etc.

The nouns "honour," "estat," and "name" may characterise Criseyde. Taylor regards "estat" as one of Criseyde's favourite words, stating that this word shows "her concern for social status and wealth" (1969: 163-65), while Shirley regards "honour," "estat," and "name" as the keywords of Criseyde (1978: 50-55).

(a) "estat"

The noun "estat" often collocates with the pronoun of the first person genitive singular "myn" in Criseyde's speech. The other examples also tend to suggest Criseyde's present state as well as her rank. She uses it 8 times: 5 in Book II and 3 in Book IV. This fact may indicate that she needs this noun "estat" when she faces dangerous situations. It should be noted that the narrator uses "estat" when Criseyde begins to feel Diomede's "gret estat" in Book V, as in "Retornyng in hire soule ay up and down / The wordes of this sodeyn Diomede, / His grete estat, and perel of the town" (V.1023-25).

> And thus she seyde, "Al were it nat to doone
> To graunte hym love, yet for his worthynesse
> It were honour with pley and with gladnesse
> In honeste with swich a lord to deele,
> For myn estat, and also for his heele. (II.703-07)

(b) "honour"

The frequency of the noun "honour" (including "honure") is very high in Criseyde's speech (16 times), while it is equally distributed between Troilus and Pandarus (8 times respectively). The noun "honour" always means the magnificent high moral virtue, when collocated with the adjective "sauf," as well as the verbs "kepe" and "have." Moreover, "honour" reveals the reverence of human beings for each other. It suggests the virginity of women, in this case, Criseyde's. The frequency of this important value word diminishes with the development of the story. Interestingly, or perhaps ironically, the diminishing use of "honour" may be connected with Criseyde's "slydynge" behaviour.

Ever since her father Calkas had to escape from Troy in the first stage of Book I, leaving her in a dangerous situation which threatened her "honour," Criseyde needs to continually guard her honour. Her hardship is shown in the following speech of Hector's:

> "And al th'onour that men may don yow have,
> As ferforth as youre fader dwelled here,
> Ye shul have, and youre body shal men save,
> As fer as I may ought enquere or here." (I.120-23)

Since she sincerely and honestly asked the nobles around her for help, she was in fact saved by the "honour" of those who tried to take care of her. This situation leads to the last stage of the work. When talking of Criseyde, the narrator, Pandarus, and Troilus all make much of her "honour." Thus, her "honour" is preserved well not only by Criseyde herself but also by the nobles around her.

As we have stated above, Criseyde's use of "honour" diminishes with the development of the story. We find only one example of "honour" in Book V, where she states that she was well loved and cared for by Troilus when she was in Troy.

> Yet prey I God, so yeve yow right good day,
> As for the gentileste, trewely,
> That evere I say, to serven feythfully,
> And best kan ay his lady honour kepe." (V.1074-77)

Does not she carry her "honour" in this situation? We do not know whether or not this kind of attribute of "honour" is applied to Chaucer's women contemporaries (in fact, a certain woman in this work uses the noun "honour"), but it should be noted that this speech is very suitable for Criseyde herself.

(c) "name"

The noun "name" is used in the same context as the "honour." It is used differently from "honour." The noun "name" is used as a rhyme word, and though "name" is rhymed with the noun "fame" in *The House of Fame*, it is interesting that it is also rhymed with the noun "shame," which has a meaning contrary to that of "fame" in this work. The frequency of this noun is as follows: 6 times by the narrator, 3 by Troilus, 5 by Criseyde, and 7 by Pandarus. One of Criseyde's examples is:

> And though that I myn herte sette at reste
> Upon this knyght, that is the worthieste,
> And kepe alwey myn honour and my name,
> By alle right, it may do me no shame." (II.760-63)

2.2.4. Swearing and Taboo Languages

In the Middle English period, women generally tended to avoid ignoble or bawdy words. Coates has commented that in fabliaux women liked dirty deeds but disliked indecent and vulgar words (1985: 20).

Since *Troilus and Criseyde* does not belong to the genre of fabliaux, we cannot apply Coates' excellent idea of women in the Middle Ages to Criseyde. She does not use dirty words; rather, she controls her emotions as much as possible. In this section, we will deal with swearing which might determine the sex differentiation between men's speech and women's, as well as interjections such as "o" or "allas." Criseyde uses more moderate and less varied swear words than men (Kawai 1983: 196).

2.2.4.1. Criseyde's Use of Interjections

(a) "o"

The interjection "o" is "a natural (or what now seems a natural) exclamation, expressive of feeling," according to the *OED*. As a matter of fact, Criseyde uses this interjection in this work, but in her speech we do not find any more such interjections than in Troilus's speech. In Book V, Troilus anaphorically repeats the interjection "o" when he sees Criseyde's empty house. One of the reasons why Criseyde does not use the interjection "o" as often as Troilus may be because she is always modest, leaving almost everything to the judgement of others. The following is one example which shows Troilus's anaphoric use of the interjection "o."

> Than seide he thus: "O paleys desolat,

> O hous of houses whilom best ihight,
> O paleys empty and disconsolat,
> O how lanterne of which queynt is the light,
> O paleys, whilom day, that now art nyght,
> ....
> "O paleis, whilom crowne of houes alle,
> ....
> O ryng, fro which the ruby out falle,
> O cause of wo, that cause hast ben of lisse! (V.540-50)

(b) "allas"

Criseyde uses the interjection "allas" almost as many times as Troilus: 40 times as compared with Troilus.[35] While Criseyde uses this interjection 9 times in Book II, 12 in Book III, 10 in Book IV, and 9 in Book V, Troilus mainly uses it in the latter half of the story, 12 times in Book IV and 15 in Book V. This fact may show that Criseyde can say the interjection "allas" more easily than Troilus, even though she is not in a sorrowful state of mind. Criseyde speaks little in Book V but uses "allas" 9 times, and this high frequency which may show that Criseyde finds her situation difficult in Greece:

> She seyde, "Allas, for now is clene ago
> My name of trouthe in love, for everemo!
> ....
> "Allas, of me, unto the worldes ende,
> Shal neyther ben ywriten nor ysonge
> No good word, for thise bokes wol me shende.
> O, rolled shal I ben many a tonge!
> Thoroughout the world my belle shal be ronge!
> And wommen moost wol haten me of alle.
> Allas, that swich a cas me sholde falle! (V.1054-64)

2.2.4.2. Criseyde's Use of Oaths

(a) "by God" and other oaths

We find the expression "by God" 22 times in this work: used 3 times by Troilus, 10 by Criseyde, and 3 by Pandarus. This swear word is mostly used with the phrase "by my trouthe" (always/frequently in rhyme) which may be considered as a key-expression in this work. Criseyde uses this swear word most often. One example is as follows:

> "I, what?" quod she, "by God and by my trouthe,
> I not nat what ye wilne that I seye." (III.120-21)

As for the pagan gods, Criseyde prefers to use "Jove" as an address form rather than "Venus" (which she only uses in Book IV, and which Troilus uses often). Unlike Troilus and Pandarus, Criseyde never invokes "Mars," "Neptunus," "Fortune," "Furies," "Mercurie," "Imeneus," "Latona," or "Minerve" (although she uses the proper noun "Pallas" 3 times). This may show that Criseyde speaks a polite, non-violent language and does not make use of the variety of oaths used by the male characters.

Using the oath "on or for + noun," as well as "by + noun," Criseyde invokes various pagan gods.

> Saturnes doughter, Juno, thorugh hire myght,
> As wood as Athamante do me dwelle
> Eternalich in Stix, the put of helle!
> "And this on every god celestial
> I swere it yow, and ek on ech goddesse,
> On every nymphe and deite infernal,
> On satiry and fawny more and lesse,
> That halve goddes ben of wildernesse;
> And Attropos my thred of lif tobreste
> If I be fals! (IV.1538-57)

Invocating the goddess "Juno" (this proper noun may not be an oath but rather an appeal to the goddess "Juno"), the pagan gods and the nymphs, satyrs, and fauns who live in the woods, she pledges her truth. Though she is usually cool and stable, here her heart is a little too subtly exalting.

When she pledges never to have had improper connection, she uses oaths one after another:

> But, for my devoir and youre hertes reste,

> Wherso yow list, by ordal or by oth,
> By sort, or in what wise so yow leste,
> For love of God, lat preve it for the beste; (III.1045-48)

The noun "devoir" means "perform one's duty, due service" and the noun "ordal" means "an ancient mode of trial regarded as the immediate judgement of the Deity." Both of them are used only once by Criseyde in this work. In this passage, we find the following impersonal constructions: "yow list" and "you leste." This kind of impersonal speech is very suitable for Criseyde, because she leaves almost everything to the judgement of others.

2.2.5. Literacy

Educated women in the Middle English period would have likely acquired French, Latin, and Greek, as representatives of the upper class. While it is as a matter of course that upper class men knew these languages, they may have been restricted to a few upper class ladies such as Criseyde who were able to learn and use them. As Taylor indicates, Criseyde sometimes uses academic and fashionable words such as the derived words from Latin (Taylor 1969: 156), i.e., the "goodly" words when we cite Chaucer's language. This fact may show Criseyde's wide learning and her careful usage concerning the contemporary fashion.

Now we would like to enumerate the words which Criseyde uses only once in this work. We will exclude words with variant spellings or those which have derivatives. Verbal nouns and the adjectival use of past participles are regarded as independent words. An asterisk (*) shows that the word is cited in the *OED*.

> abstinence, *amphibologies**, angwissous*, *bakward**, bille, bisshop, bridlede, brotel, *busshel**, byword*, byquethe, carie, causyng, cave, chartres, chekmat*, chep, cherisynge, childissh*, conceyved, constellecioun*, *continuance**, cors, court, covenable, coveyteth, *coye**, crowned, debat, *depeynted**, *deprive**, devoir, *disseveraunce**, *dissmulyng**, doubleth, dowves, dronkenesse,

drynkeles*, *enchaunten*, *entrecomunen*, *excusable*, *fawny*, *ferventliche*,* floureth, forlong, fox, *future*,* gentily, gnat, greyn, grucche, habundaunce, handle, harmyng, heleles, *hemysperie*,* herteles, hove, hyve, *infortuned*, *injure*, *janglerie*,* jugement, *juparten*,* kynrede*, leful, lesyng, letuarie*, likkere, *lustinesse*,* maisterfull*, maistresse*, *marcial*,* me-ward, mencioun, misericode, *mocioun*,* morter*, muable, *mysbyleved*,* nobleye, *noriture*,* novelrie*, nymphe, office, ordal*, papir*, plukke, *poeplissh*,* pompe, *rave*,* rebounde, *refut*,* regioun, religious, remenant, *remuable*,* repentaunce*, *repressed*, *repressioun*, *resistence*,* reyneth, *rooteles*,* salve, satiry, saufly, scrit*, *shove*,* skilfully, *slyvere*, *sourmounteth*, *sours*, *sovereignete*,* spie, sporneth, spotted, stoppen, stormy*, *suffrant*,* thewes, threteth, *torney*, *transitorie*,* tribulacioun*, twynnyng*, *underserved*,* ungiltif*, unhappy,*unshethe*,* unstable, *unteyd*,* unthonk, *unthrifty*,* untriste*, venym, *voluptuous*,* wanteth, weddynge*, wether, wildernesse, wolf, *worthily*,* wyvere*, ypleynted.

Looking up the vocabulary of the above list, we will summarise as follows:

(1) There are many words quoted as the earliest citation in the *OED*. Those are itlicised in the list.

(2) There are many words derived from Old French, Anglo-French, and Latin: e.g. in the above list most words are derived from Romance languages, except for some words which originated in Old English such as "bakward," "lustinesse," "mysbyleved," "rooteles," "unshette," "unteyd," and "worthily," and some words originated in Old Norse such as "unthrifty" or "untriste" whose prefix "un-" comes from Old English.

(3) We find some scholarly and scientific terms such as astronomy, astrology, and rhetoric: "constellecioun," "hemysperie," and "amphibology."

(4) The stem with the Old English prefix "un-" originated in Old French, Old English and Old Norse.

(5) Other features:

(a) The meaning of some words is explained as "figurative" in the

OED: "enchaunten," "sours," "stormy," and "wyvere."

(b) The meaning of some words is explained as "loosely" in the *OED*: "busshel."

(c) Some words have a pejorative meaning: "depeynted."

(d) Some words are quoted in the only one citation in the *OED*: "mysbyleved," "poeplissh," and "suffrant."

(e) We find a literally translated word from Latin to English: "byword," which is modeled on Latin proverbium.

2.2.6. Verbosity

The Wife of Bath is a very talkative woman, as Chaucer says: "In felaweshipe wel koude she laughe and carpe" (Well could she laugh and prate in company.) (I (A) 474). Criseyde seems not only talkative at times like the Wife of Bath, but also silent at other times like Griselda in "The Clerk's Tale."

In order to investigate whether or not Criseyde is verbose, we have compared the length and the total words of Criseyde's speech with those of the other characters. Please see Table 1, which shows the total words of each character. The lineage of the longest speech of each character is as follows: Troilus 121 lines (IV.958-1078), Criseyde 161 lines (IV.1254-1414), and Pandarus 105 lines (III.239-343). The frequency of each character's speech is as follows: Troilus 153 times (the total words of Troilus's speech: 11,355 words), Criseyde 172 times (8,985 words), and Pandarus 227 times (14,223 words). Thus we have two kinds of facts concerning Criseyde's verbosity. First, we find that she has the most speech of the three characters. Second, she tends to be less wordy, though she speaks more often than the other characters. We, however, must not jump to the conclusion that these facts show her talkativeness, but it is also a matter of fact that this kind of statistical analysis helps us to see at least one aspect of Criseyde's speech.

We have investigated Criseyde's language from various points of view. Her language, closely related to her critical situation in this work, tends to be influenced by her surroundings: her uncle Pandarus, playing the part of go-between; the natural phenomena encompassing the lovers, Troilus and Criseyde, especially their deep love covered with the rain fallen by chance; the political dealing such as the hostage exchange; and her obedience forced on her by her father Calkas. All these happenings may indicate that Criseyde is unable to make up her mind, and leaves almost everything to the judgement of others. She may find it convenient that her "honour" is guarded by others, especially Troilus and Pandarus, since this allows her to live life to the full.

From this study we are unable to say exactly what kind of relationship exists between the language of Chaucer's women and that of Criseyde and what kind of language the main character Troilus uses. These points will be the subjects of a further study.

From this study we are able to state the following. As Masui states "Chaucer's language becomes dramatic in fact, since he dynamically connects the speech with the character and that such a dynamic language is reflected in Criseyde's speech and Pandarus's from a courtly point of view" (1962, 1973: 203), Criseyde's language shows at least one aspect of women's language in the fourteenth century courtly society of England where Criseyde, created and characterised by the poet Chaucer, lives with flesh and blood as well as her contemporary women.

Notes

1   R. W. V. Elliott states that "For Chaucer the dialect of the north of England was truly a literary dialect. We may assume that he never spoke it himself although he will have heard it often enough to recognise, and in due time repeat, it with a fair degree of accuracy," reading his paper, "Literary

Dialect in Chaucer, Hardy, and Alan Garner" at Kumamoto University on 27 May, 1988.

2   C. Muscatine, *Chaucer and French Tradition* (Berkeley: University of California Press, 1957), pp. 201-02.

3   Derek Traversi, *The Canterbury Tales: A Reading* (London: The Bodleyhead, 1983), p. 87.

4   *Ibid*, p. 87.

5   M. Copland, "'The Reeve's Tale': Harlotrie or Sermonyng?" *Geoffrey Chaucer* herausgegeben von Willi Erzgraber (Darmstadt: Wissenshaftliche Buchgesellschaft, 1983), 357-80, p. 369.

6   Roy J. Pearcy, "The Genre of Chaucer's Fabliau-Tales," *Chaucer and the Craft of Fiction* edited by Leigh A. Arrathoon, (Michigan: Solaris Press, Inc., 1986) 329-84, p. 354.

7   J. R. R. Tolkien, "Chaucer as a Philologist: *The Reeve's Tale*," *Transactions of the Philological Society* (1934), 1-70, p. 2.

8   N. F. Blake, "The Northernisms in The Reeve's Tale" *Lore and Language* 3, 1. The Centre for English Cultural Tradition and Language, University of Sheffield (1979), 1-8, p. 7.

9   *Ibid*, p. 7.

10   According to the explanatory notes of Benson's edition, "So theek: The suffixed ik, "I" (cf. I.3867), is a Northern and East Midland form, appropriate to a Norfolk man." (p. 848)

11   It should be noted here that as for Blake's edition we see the northern form "ik" rather than "i" in these two examples. This fact may show that Blake's edition is based upon the manuscript written earlier than the others. (*The Canterbury Tales* (London: Edward Arnold, 1980))

12   This fact that the sound "h" is not pronounced clearly is seen in the use of "my" and "myn" or "thy" and "thyn." The pronoun "myn" or "thyn" rather than "my" or "thy" is chosen before the initial "h" of the following word.

13   It may be possible to connect the Reeve's Prologue with his Tale, according to Elliott's idea. However, we do not know why the pronoun "I" is used in the Tale, though we see "ik" in the Prologue. If *OED*'s explanation (see p. 67) were true, we would conjecture that in the Tale the scribe may have secured unity in the pronoun "I" which he uses in everyday life. We see also the pronominal form "thair" (not usual in Chaucer) in the Tale, which might be prevalent in London area. These may show that the Tale was written later than the Prologue.

14   Elliott says that "... Baldeswelle, modern Bawdswell, in the northern part of Norfolk, a region which combined a predominantly midland dialect with some northern features." ("Literary Dialect in Chaucer, Hardy, and Alan Garner," *op. cit.*)

15   G. L. Brook, *English Dialects* (London: André Deutsch, 1963), p. 62.
16   Blake, *The Canterbury Tales*, p. 162.
17   *The Riverside Chaucer*, p. 850.
18   J. A. W. Bennett, *Chaucer at Oxford and at Cambridge* (Oxford: Clarendon Press, 1974), p. 101.
19   A. C. and J. E. Spearing, *The Reeve's Prologue and Tale with the Cook's Prologue and the Fragment of his Tale* (Cambridge: Cambridge University Press, 1979), p. 27.
20   Tolkien, p. 2.
21   Blake, "The Northernisms in *The Reeve's Tale*," pp. 1-7.
22   Blake, *Non-standard Language in English Literature* (London: André Deutsch, 1981), p. 32.
23   A. McIntosh et al. eds., *A Linguistic Atlas of Late Mediæval English* (Aberdeen University Press, 1986).
24   This form "twaie" may be the descendant of the masculine of the OE. numeral. (See the word "twain" in the *OED*.)
25   Whiting's book does not include the proverbial expressions in Aleyn's speech, though he states that "*The Reeve's Tale* contains seven proverbs, five of which are spoken by John and one by the miller."(B. J. Whiting, *Chaucer's Use of Proverbs* (Cambridge: Harvard University Press, 1934), pp. 86-88.
26   See Spearing's "Notes," p. 106.
27   Many alliterative expressions are used in this work: (I (A) 3868, 3870, 3875, 3963-64, 3974-75, 4066).
28   The expressions concerning the space are mainly used in the latter half of the Tale, but we would notice that the image concerning the house is found from the first (W. M. Hart, "*The Reeve's Tale*: A Comparative Study of Chaucer's Narrative Art," *PMLA* XXIII (1908), 1-44, pp. 12-13.). Then we see the expression of the tub in the Prologue: "Til that almoost al empty is the tonne" (3894). N. E. Eliason states that the description of "places" is not so effective, as in "Chaucer's description of places is usually less complete and detailed than his description of persons" (*The Language of Chaucer's Poetry: An Appraisal of the Verse, Style, and Structure* (Copenhagen: Rosenkilde and bagger, 1972, p. 96). However, as Robertson indicates: "... all we know about the dwelling is that it was small and contained the beds, cradle, and staff necessary for the action" (D. W. Robertson, Jr., *A Preface to Chaucer* (Princeton: Princeton University Press, 1962), p. 259), it seems that these spatial expressions are made the best use of in this Tale, even though they were not "complete" and "detailed." These expressions are the supplementary means of describing the students.
29   Hart states that Chaucer's work produces "the effect of suspense" more than the original version: "in the fabliau it occurs to the clerk to misplace

the cradle only after seeing the miller's wife leave the room... Chaucer's change increases the effect of suspense, since the reader does not know why the cradle is moved" (p. 16). We understand that Chaucer gave a subtly scrupulous care to the use of the spaces. The expressions of "hous" are also used organically in *Troilus and Criseyde*. As for the use and meaning in *Troilus and Criseyde*, see A. Jimura,"Chaucer no Yakata no Hyogen," *Hito no Ie Kami no Ie* (Kyoto: Apollon-sha, 1987), pp. 5-44.

30   In T. Whittock's *A Reading of the Canterbury Tales* (Cambridge: Cambridge University, 1968), he regards this daughter as the person showing "the compassionate portrayal of human beings" and he states that "even this rather ugly-looking girl of such unbecoming parents has fair hair and a tender heart, and is really beautiful" (p. 100). Jun Sudo explains in "Two Approaches to Chaucer's Style and Expression," read at Kyoto Conference of Chaucer's English held in Doshisha University on 3 and 4 October, 1987 that it is Chaucer's own skilful technique that Chaucer makes the best use of the style, as if it were deviating from the theme, quoting this passage. He states that "Chaucer deliberately employs different styles according to the levels of characters in a certain subject matter."

31   We find the expression "wikked speche" (V.1610) in Criseyde's letter. This is used when Criseyde says that one of the reasons why she cannot return from Greece to Troy is because she is extremely conscious of the evil speech around her. This shows Criseyde's self-consciousness which makes her aware of the un-courtly speech around her and consequently leads her to using the courtly speech.

32   Here we include the word "but" meaning "unless," because we have collected the examples mechanically, using a personal computer.

33   Here we include not only the paratactic constructions of sentences but also those of words and phrases.

34   We notice that Troilus uses "which(e)" (61 times) more often than Criseyde does (35 times).

35   The frequency of Troilus's use of the interjection "allas" becomes proportionally higher as the total frequency of "allas" increases in this work.

CHAPTER 3

Collocations

3.0. Introduction

It is well-known that William Blake expressed great admiration for Chaucer's character paintings in *The Canterbury Tales*, stating: "of Chaucer's Characters as described in his *Canterbury Tales*, some of the Names are altered by Time, but the Characters themselves for ever remain unaltered." We can find such excellence as moved Blake in the character portraits which are presented even in "The General Prologue" to *The Canterbury Tales*. The admirable and delicate precision which defines each character is Chaucer's skilful use of adjectives and similes. For example, we remember the following adjectives: "worthy," "wise," "gentil," and "goode" in the description of the Knight, "yong," "as fressh as is the month of May," and "curteis" in the description of the Squire, and "of hir smylyng was ful symple and coy," "estatlich," "plesaunt," "amyable," and "charitable" in the description of the Prioress. These adjectives, which define the nature, appearance, and attributes of people, in conjunction with detailed and concrete description, constitute Chaucer's description of characters.

The adjectives and similes also play a significant part in depicting characters in *Troilus and Criseyde*. The most impressive example may be the passage which shows each persona of Troilus, Diomede, and Criseyde in the middle of Book V. It is not quite certain why the poet felt that he had to summarise each character in the closing stage of this narration, but we cannot deny that the poet tried to sum up each character, in the order of Diomede, Criseyde, and Troilus, and that it gave the readers the concise effect of contrast.[1] It is adjectives and similes which are the framework of this passage. The description is not superficial and conceptual, since if it is based upon the deep understanding of human beings, we recognise a certain concreteness in it; perhaps ultimately the living image of human beings in the passage. It is not too much to say that Chaucer's adjectives play an important role in *Troilus and Criseyde* so that they may determine and direct the characters.

3.1. Troilus and Criseyde

In this section, we wish to examine the adjectival descriptions of Chaucer's characters, Troilus and Criseyde. J. R. Firth took the initiative by collocating adjectives and nouns, and we will use his approach as a model for this study. In "Modes of Meaning," he considers, for example, the kinds of adjectives which are connected with the noun *ass*:

> There are only limited possibilities of collocation with preceding adjectives, among which the commonest are *silly, obstinate, stupid, awful*, occasionally *egregious. Young* is much more frequently found than *old*. The plural form is not very common.[2]

Those adjectives grouped or associated with the noun *ass* show unfavourable meanings. Although Firth states only that the noun *ass* collocates with the above adjectives, we can assume that the noun is restricted by these adjectives. To put it another way, they attach unfavourable meanings to *ass*, and its territory of meaning is thus determined. In *Troilus and Criseyde*, on the other hand, certain collocations have elevated meanings which Chaucer consciously chose to colour his work: Troilus and Criseyde, as we shall see, are depicted in pleasant terms commensurate with their noble and beautiful character. Even if collocation does not solve every complicated literary problem, it might nevertheless provide some clues leading us to the resolution of problems dealing with the meaning of Chaucer's poem.

3.1.1. The Image of Troilus

The character of Troilus is described by various adjective-noun collocations, and they reveal a variety of facets of his nature. When his aspect of a warrior is represented, the noun "knyght" is used; when Troilus is a man, the noun "man" or "wight" is used. The proper noun "Troilus" is most often used, however. It is an interesting fact that the noun "lovere," illustrating his amorous nature, is used only once in this work. We will not deal with some nouns, such as "herte," "lord," "frend," and "brother," when they occur in the vocative.

(1) "Troilus"
Generally speaking, the proper noun "Troilus" is restricted by (a) the adjectives which define the qualities of a warrior, a knight, and a courtier; e.g., "fresh," "noble," and "worthy," as well as (b) the adjectives which show a man who languishes for love; e.g. "sorwful" and "woful."

Some of the former examples, evoking Trolius's courtly qualities, are:

"Now, nece myn, the kynges deere sone,
The goode, wise, worthi, fresshe, and free,
....
The noble Troilus, so loveth the, (II.316-19)

And Troilus wel woxen was in highte,
....
So wel that kynde it nought amenden myghte;
Yong, fressh, strong, and hardy as lyoun;
Trewe as stiel in ech condicioun; (V.827-33)

In the lines II.316-9, when Pandarus tells Criseyde that Troilus loves her, Pandarus uses many adjectives "goode, wise, worthi, fresshe, and fre, ... noble" to describe the chivalric Troilus. These adjectives are those attached to the Knight and the Squire in "The General Prologue" to *The Canterbury Tales*: Chaucer used the adjectives "wise" and "worthi" and the noun of "fre" or "fredom" to describe the Knyght. Similarly he attached the adjective "noble" to the knight's army and "goode" to his horse. The most important quality, "trewe," appears as the noun "trouthe." Troilus thus possesses the virtues comparable to those of the Knight in "The General Prologue."

Chaucer, on the other hand, used the adjective "fressh" to symbolise Troilus's youth as well as that of the Squire who is "as fressh as is the month of May." The adjective "yong" and the noun "strengthe," similarly, collocate with each other to describe "Squier." Troilus, then, is not only a virtuous knight, but also a young and strong warrior. The narrator's skilful description of Troilus in the middle of Book V, comparing him with Diomede and Criseyde, provides an example of his prowess. While the adjective "hardy" describes Diomede, the narrator needs a simile, "hardy as lyoun," when he compares Troilus's bravery with that of Diomede. Moreover, the word "lyoun" is emphatically placed in rhyming position. "Trewe as stiel," on the other hand, provides a striking contrast to Criseyde's "slydynge of corage," as Masui states.[3] The value word "trewe," recurrent throughout the poem, therefore, describes Troilus's ideal knightly character, and the similes, conventional as they are, make Troilus's strength and faithfulness appealing to us.

Some of the latter examples, describing Troilus's love-lorn characteristics, are:

> thow woful Troilus (I.519) / this sorwful Troylus (I.597) / sely Troilus (I.871) / sely Troilus (II.683) / this woful Troilus (IV.360) / this woful Troilus (IV.372)* / this woful Troilus (V.197)* / this sely Troilus (V.529) (N. B. The asterisk shows that the noun is put in the rhyming position for emphasis.)

Troilus's pain is stressed by the recurrent word "woful." The expression "woful Troilus," in particular, is used often in Books IV and V, where two examples are positioned as rhyme words, but it is used only once in Books II and III. We can say, therefore, that the distribution of these adjectives shows the development of a love theme.[4] There appear three uses of "woful Troilus" in Book I, when he experiences one-sided love, and there are four occurrences in Books IV and V, when he begins to experience his tragedy.

In this way, the proper noun "Troilus" is restricted by (1) the adjectives which define the qualities of a warrior, a knight, and a courtier, as well as (2) the adjectives which show a man who languishes for love.

(2) "Knyght" and "the" + the superlative of the adjective
Next, let us discuss the collocation of adjectives and the noun "knyght" or a noun or pronoun synonymous contextually with one of Troilus's characteristics. We have the following two types: (a) the noun "knyght" and attached adjectives as well as (b) "the" + the superlative of the adjective. In both instances, these adjectives illustrate knightly virtues. The noun "knyght," however, is sometimes omitted after the superlative in the latter type because the superlatives of the adjective modify a variety of nouns and occasionally a pronoun referring to Troilus.

(a) The noun "knyght" and attached adjectives
The narrator, Pandarus, and Criseyde use the adjectives to depict Troilus's knightly virtue. They are "worthy," "noble," "trewe," and so on. We find:

> this fierse and proude knyght (I.225)* / A worthi knyght (I.986) / that noble gentil knyght (II.331)*/ a manly knyght (II.1263)* / the worthieste knyght (III.781)* / trewe knyght (III.1648)* / this ilke noble knyght (V.1752)* The gentilest, and ek the moost fre, The thriftiest and oon the beste knyght (I.1080-81)

These collocations of adjectives and "knyght" (except the second) are used as rhyme words. The noun "wight" instead of "knyght" can be chosen as a rhyme word, but in the above instances Chaucer used the noun "knyght" of necessity. It is a self-evident fact that the noun "knyght" shows a man of courage, and the last example is most impressive. Because Pandarus promises to mediate between Troilus and Criseyde, the young knight, formerly languishing in his one-sided love, is lighthearted and regains his chivalric composure. This kind of expression is grammatically equivalent to that which describes the great king Beowulf in the last two lines in *Beowulf*: "cwædon þæt he wære wyruldcyning(a) / manna mildust ond mon(ðw)ærust, / leodum liðost ond lofgeornost." (3180-82)[5]

(b) "the" + the superlative of the adjective

The adjectives of this type also refer to Troilus's knightly virtues. The adjectives such as "beste," "worthiest," and "gentileste" are often found in this work. The examples are:

> Founde oon the beste, and lengest tyme abiden (I.474)
>
> For out and out he is the worthieste
> Save only Ector, which that is the beste (II.739-40)
>
> Upon this knyght, that is the worthieste, (II.761)
>
> He was, and ay, the first in armes dight,
> And certeynly, but if that bokes erre,
> Save Ector most ydred of any wight (III.1773-75)
>
> That Troilus was nevere unto no wight,
> As in his tyme, in no degree secounde
> In durryng don that longeth to a knyght.
> Al myghte a geant passen hym of myght
> His herte ay with the first and with the beste
> Stood paregal, to durre don that hym leste (V.835-40)
>
> For I have falsed oon the gentileste
> That evere was, and oon the worthieste! (V.1056-57)

> As for the gentieste, trewely, (V.1075)

Troilus's virtuous and noble figure as a knight is represented by these adjectives, most of which are placed in the position of rhyme words.

Now we would like to comment on the deliberate use of these adjectives, especially the word "beste." The narrator's use of this word is a little different from Pandarus's or Criseyde's. The narrator always describes Troilus as "the beste," "the first," and "in no degree secounde." Criseyde, on the other hand, in the line II.740 uses "the beste" to praise Hector; similarly Pandarus says: "And ek his fresshe brother Troilus, / The wise, worthi Ector the secounde" (II.157-58). Here Pandarus does not consider Troilus to be the first among knights, but, rather, "the secounde." When Criseyde and Pandarus use "beste" to describe Troilus, they give him its attribute only in a partial sense, not an inclusive one. Davis Taylor indicates that "Pandarus and Criseyde normally use this superlative only when it qualifies a particular attribute of a person. Pandarus says that Troilus is the best in keeping fellowship (II.206); Criseyde, that he is the best in honor (V.1077). Criseyde uses best in all inclusive sense only once, and then to praise Hector, not Troilus."[6] What we insist upon here is that the narrator, unlike Pandarus and Criseyde, attaches the adjectives "beste" and "first" to Troilus in an inclusive sense. The narrator thus describes Troilus twice in this way (III.1775; V.1804), but he does not use "the beste" for Hector. The narrator therefore seems to sympathize with Troilus.[7]

In this way, the noun "knyght" is not collocated with the adjectives which show Troilus's emotional suffering, but those which show his noble and courageous virtue as a knight.

(3) "man" and "wight"

In this section, Troilus is regarded as "man" and "wight." The noun "man," is restricted by adjectives such as "trewe," "gentil," and "hardy," illustrating Troilus's character as a warrior, a knight, a courtier, as well as adjectives such as "sorwful," revealing Troilus's fluctuating state of mind. "Wight" collocates mainly with the adjectives such as "woful."

(a) "man"

The noun "man," as shown above, collocates with two types of adjectives: (1) the adjectives which show the attributes of a warrior, a knight, and a courtier, and (2) the adjectives which show those of a man who languishes for love. The former examples are:

> the frendlieste man (II.204)* / That trewe man (II.331) / this gentil man (III.963)* / hardy man (IV.601) / this ilke worthi man (V.1765)*

In this way, even when Troilus is a "man," his noble, chivalric nature is revealed. Pandarus uses the first three adjectives when he explains Troilus's honourable and worthy character to Criseyde. The last example is the narrator's description.

Let us then turn to the adjectives which show the attributes of a man who languishes for love.

> this sorwful man (IV.233)* / This sorwful man (IV.1160) / this sorwful man (IV.1697)*

The grief-stricken Troilus, who loses heart, is described primarily with the collocation of "sorwful" and "man," which is often placed at the end of the line. The noun "man" is never collocated with the adjective "woful" though it is often attached to the proper noun "Troilus."

(b) "wight"

The noun "wight," often collocating with the adjective "woful," shows Troilus's painful state of mind. This may be a fixed expression, since it is used alliteratively, and it is not placed in the rhyming position (I.13; III.103; IV.365; V.1320). When Troilus is the most sorrowful, the superlative "wofulleste" is used: "Of me, that am the wofulleste wyght" (IV.516) is under the restriction of rhyme. The synonymous "woful wrecche" is used as a rhyme word twice in this work (IV.1444; V.321).

Each occurrence of "wight" reveals sorrow, except for one: "For he bicom the frendlieste wight (=knyght)" (I.1079), which shows that Troilus is ecstatic with joy. Chaucer apparently chose the noun "wight" this one time to rhyme with the noun "knyght" when describing the lover's happiness.

We may conclude then, that the noun "man" showing both the noble and the love-lorn Troilus, has a wider territory of meaning than the noun "wight." The image of Troilus, in addition, is idealistic as Muscatine says: "Troilus represents the courtly, idealistic view of experience.... Troilus is described in conventional, hyperbolical terms."[8] But his particular characteristics are subtly represented according to the context of *Troilus and Criseyde*. The nature of Troilus is variously restricted by the nouns "Troilus," "knyght," "man" and "wight," and their respective collocated adjectives.

3.1.2. The Image of Criseyde

Criseyde is also described by various nouns. When she is a gentlewoman, the noun "lady" is used; when she is a sweetheart, the noun "herte" is used; when she is a woman, the noun "creature" or "wight" is used. Pandarus uses the noun "nece" of course to describe their relationship. The proper noun "Criseyde" is most often used in this work. It should be noted here that the noun "fo" is employed in a special context. We do not deal with some nouns, such as "herte," "lady," and "nece," when they occur in the vocative.

(1) "Criseyde"

The proper noun "Criseyde," collocated with the adjectives "brighte" and "untrewe," is used only three times in Book V. When the adjectives are used as substantives, they are those which show Criseyde's beauty, such as "goodly" and "fair."

> They spaken of Criseyde the brighte; (V.516)

To gete ayeyn Criseyde, brighte of hewe; (V.1573)

Both examples are used when Troilus nostalgically remembers Criseyde. The adjective "brighte" is often attached to "woman," just as the *OED* indicates: "3. Of persons: 'Resplendent with charms' (J.); beautiful, fair. *arch.*"

> "Ne I nevere saugh a more bountevous
> Of hire estat, n'a gladder, ne of speche
> A frendlyer, n'a more gracious
> For to do wel,... (I.883-86)
>
> I am oon the faireste, out of drede,
> And goodlieste, who that taketh hede, (II.746-47)

In the first example, Pandarus describes Criseyde to Troilus after he has at last confessed his love for her. Pandarus, using a series of adjectives, describes Criseyde's excellent character. Pandarus's use of the comparative adjectives emphasises her good quality. In the second example, after Criseyde listens to Pandarus's speech, she has an immoderate opinion of her own beauty and character. Criseyde's use of the superlative reveals her pride. Thus the proper noun "Criseyde" is restricted by the adjectives which show her beauty.

(2) "lady"

This word shows that Criseyde is Troilus's "lady." According to the *OED*, it means "A woman of superior position in society, or to whom such a position is conventionally or by courtesy attributed." It strikingly contrasts with the noun "lord" used by Pandarus. Just as Pandarus renders service to Troilus, Troilus performs service for Criseyde. The attached adjectives are "deere," "righte," "brighte," and so on, in which "righte" is, as the *OED* notes, "17. Justly entitled to the name; having the true character of; true, real, veritable. a. Of persons, their character or position." Some of examples are as follows:

> First he gan hire his righte lady calle, (II.1065)

"As to my lady right and chief resort,
With al my wit and al my diligence; (III.134-35)

For al this world, in swych present gladnesse
Was Troilus, and hath his lady swete. (III.1244-45)

"And at that corner, in the yonder hous,
Herde I myn alderlevest lady deere (V.575-76)

And by this bor, faste in his armes folde,
Lay, kyssyng ay, his lady bryght, Criseyde. (V.1240-41)

But natheles, though he gan hym dispaire,
And dradde ay that his lady was untrewe, (V.1569-70)

In the first two examples, Troilus calls Criseyde "righte." They occur in the beginning of his first letter to Criseyde and in Troilus's first speech, pledging loyalty, to Criseyde. The adjective "righte" shows his fidelity and deep emotion. In the third example, Troilus calls Criseyde "swete" when both of them are happiest. "Myn alderlevest lady deere," the fourth example, is Criseyde remembered when Troilus went to see her empty palace. Troilus may have seen Criseyde's phantom before him because the adjective "alderlevest" emphasises his strong desire to see her goodness and beauty, rather than her actual figure. Troilus, however, dreams a terrible dream that the "bor" raped his beloved Criseyde for whom he had been waiting for a long time. Criseyde, in the dream, however, is not pale but still "bryght." Troilus's love continues to grow despite their separation and his fears. In the last example, Troilus knows that Criseyde betrayed him, as the adjective "untrewe" shows. What is important here is the expression "brighte of hewe" rhymes not only with the above-mentioned adjective "untrewe," but with "newe": "he soughte ay newe / To gete ayeyn Criseyde, brighte of hewe" (V.1572-73). Even though she betrayed Troilus, he still loved her, and he tried to regain her affection. Troilus continues to serve faithfully his "lady" Criseyde, although she left him for another.

(3) "herte"

The word "herte" reveals that Criseyde is Troilus's sweetheart, and that he is, for a time, hers. The noun "herte," in short, shows their mutual love for one another. As the *OED* states, "14. Used as a term of endearment, often qualified by dear, sweet (see Sweetheart), etc.; chiefly in addressing a person," the adjectives "deere" and "swete" are attached to this noun.

> Whan shal I next my deere herte see? (II.982)

> And Troilus in lust and in quiete
> Is with Criseyde, his owen herte swete (III.1819-20)

> "And yonder have I herd ful lustyly
> My dere herte laugh; ... (V.568-69)

In the first example, Troilus uses the expression "my deere herte" to describe Criseyde to whom he has not spoken. Truly, Criseyde is Troilus's sweetheart at the end of Book III. This relationship is described in the second example. In the third example, Troilus remembers her beautiful figure. Thus, since the noun "herte" means sweetheart, it collocates with the adjectives such as "deere" and "swete" which show tenderness and gentleness.

(4) "nece"

The word "nece" shows Criseyde's relationship to Pandarus. The attached adjectives, such as "deere," "faire," and "bright," primarily show her beauty. These adjectives may also indicate their intimate relationship.

> But wo is me, that I, that cause at this,
> May thynken that she is my nece deere,
> And I hire em, and traitour ek yfeere! (III.271-73)

> As for to bryngen to his hows som nyght
> His faire nece and Troilus yfere, (III.514-15)

How trewe is now thi nece, bright Criseyde! (V.1712)

In the first example, Pandarus explains his relationship with Criseyde to Troilus, using the adjective "deere" to emphasise his avuncular affection for her. In the second example, the narrator uses the expression "His faire nece." These adjectives show his affection as a family relationship. It is important to note that in the third example, the collocated expression "bright Criseyde" is an appositive to "thi nece." Criseyde, in this situation, is neither "lady" nor "herte" to Troilus; she is nothing but "thi nece." Troilus, aware of Criseyde's treachery, and avoiding her, spoke to Pandarus in a rather ironic tone. This speech may ultimately satirize Pandarus's role, too, because Troilus emphasises "thi nece." This sentence is likely ironic because there are semantic gaps between the nouns "nece," "Criseyde" and the adjective "bright" this situation, these nouns "nece" and "Criseyde" refer to one who is "untrewe." Then, if they are collocated with the adjectives "bright" and "trewe," there is a disparate meaning between the courtly, loving terms and the nouns.

(5) "creature" and "wight"

Here we will deal with the nouns "creature" or "wight" and their attached adjectives. The noun "creature" collocates with (a) the adjectives such as "hevenyssh perfit" or "fair" which demonstrate Criseyde's beauty and (b) the adjectives such as "sorwful" or "woful" which indicate Criseyde's sorrowful state of mind. When Criseyde is described as an attractive woman, the former adjectives are used in this work. The noun "wight," on the other hand, collocates with the adjectives such as "ferfulleste" or "sorwful" which show Criseyde's emotional state.

(a) "creature"

First let us examine the adjectives which show Criseyde's beauty. They are used especially in the beginning of Book I, when Troilus is attracted by Criseyde's charms.

> That lik a thing inmortal semed she,
> As doth an hevenyssh perfit creature, (I.103-04)
>
> And that she was so fair a creature; (I.115)
>
> ... that creature
> Was nevere lasse mannyssh in semynge. (I.283-84)

Criseyde is unparalleled in beauty, as the narrator describes her, using the adjective "hevenyssh," which, according to the *OED*'s first citation, means "*obs*. Of or pertaining to heaven; celestial, heavenly," as well as the adjective "perfit." She is so beautiful it is as if she were of heaven. As a matter of course, she also possesses a woman's femininity. She is not "mannyssh," which, also the *OED*'s first citation, means "2. Of a woman, her attributes, etc.; Resembling a man, manlike, masculine. Chiefly contemptuous." It is interesting that the narrator, making careful use of the contemptuous adjective "mannyssh," stresses that Criseyde is not so. There were probably many women in Chaucer's audience and society, and we can imagine that some of them must have been "mannyssh." Chaucer took care to contrast Criseyde with those "loathly hags," such as that in "The Wife of Bath's Tale," who lived in his times. Criseyde's beautiful figure is also described in Book V, when the narrator gives us her Gestalt (V.808).

Let us next discuss the adjectives which show Criseyde's sorrowful state or mind.

> ... for which disaventure
> She held hireself a forlost creature. (IV.755-56)
>
> How shal she don ek, sorwful creature? (V.241)
>
> And thus despeired, out of alle cure,
> She ladde hire lif, this woful creature. (V.713-14)

In Book IV, she laments for the miserable decision of the parliament.

In Book V, she sighs away her days in the Greek camp, after Troilus sent away her. Criseyde is as "woful" as Troilus has imagined. The adjectives "sorwful," "woful" and "forlost" are used in order to describe her sorrow.

It is noticeable that the noun "creature" is always a rhyme word. So Chaucer may have chosen this word rather consciously. When Criseyde is a "creature," she is described as heavenly, just like an angel; but, when her mortal existence is a burden, she grieves at sorrowful events, just like an ordinary person.

(b) "wight"

When Criseyde is called a "wight," the noun tends to be collocated with the adjectives such as "woful" or "sorwful." Most of these examples occur in Book IV, but in Troilus's case these adjectives are used throughout this work. The phrase "the wofulleste wight" (IV.516) reveals Troilus's emotional intensity, but it is the collocation "the ferfulleste wight" (II.450) that illustrates Criseyde's timorous mind. And it suggests her fragile character, liable to variation. It also seems that this characterisation leads us to her figure as "tendre-herted, slydynge of corage." Some of examples are as follows:

> Criseyde, which that wel neigh starf for feere,
> So as she was the ferfulleste wight (II.449-50)
>
> "Allas," quod she, "out of this regioun
> I, woful wrecche and infortuned wight, (IV.743-44)

As we have already explained, the adjective "ferfulleste," the *OED*'s first citation and which means "II. *subjectively* 3. Frightened, timorous, timid, apprehensive. a. *simply* Now somewhat *rare*.," shows her delicate character. The adjective "infortuned" in the second example, also the *OED*'s first citation, means "*v. Obs. trans*. To cause misfortune to, to afflict; in Astrol. to 'afflict' (a planet or house) with an unfortunate 'aspect'. *ppl. a.*, unfortunate." The *MED* also quotes this adjective and explains: "(b) unhappy, miserable, plagued by misfortune." Using an astrological term unconsciously, she thinks of her misery which is of cosmic proportion, as would be typical of a mediaeval person. This kind of thinking is in character: her father is a priest proficient in astrology. Moreover, although Criseyde deeply laments her ill-fated chance, adding the prefix "in" showing negation to the verb "fortune," she is a woman submissive to fate, or as it were Dame Fortune. Criseyde does little to alleviate her suffering at the hands of fate.

The noun "wight," in short, collocates with the adjectives which show Criseyde's sorrowful situation. An exception, however, is "so swete a wight" (: right) (III.1284).

(6) "fo"

Finally, we will deal with the special use of the noun "fo" and its attached adjective. We can find two examples of "fo" which are collocated with the adjective "swete" to show the feeling of intimacy.[9] It is also related to Troilus's tender feeling of love.

> And seyde, "Allas, of al my wo the welle,
> Thanne is my swete fo called Criseyde!" (I.873-74)

> O herte myn, Criseyde, O swete fo!
> O lady myn, that I love and na mo, (V.228-29)

As Troilus says: "For wel fynde I that Fortune is my fo" (I.837), he regards "Fortune" as his foe or love's existence farthest from him. Judging from this expression, we may consider that Criseyde, who is also a foe who thwarts his amorous advances, is also distant from him. However, as he is charmed by Criseyde, she is the existence nearest to him; that is, she is "swete." Therefore, she is the love farthest from — and nearest to — him; that is, "my swete fo."[10] We cannot find this expression from Book II to Book IV, because Troilus has an intimate relationship with Criseyde. In Book V, however, this expression recurs when Criseyde is definitely apart from him. Here we cannot see a flash of hope, as in the former example.

It is interesting that Criseyde is thus regarded as the changeable existence just like "Fortune." Is it for this reason that "bothe Troilus and Troie town / Shal knotteles thorughout hire herte slide" (V.768-69)? It is, as a matter of course, connected with her "slydynge of corage," as Muscatine states, since "she represents earthly instability. She is as the world is and goes as the world goes."[11] But it must be noted here that her slydynge is caused by her tender heart, because she must ultimately choose between her lovers. She must decide between them, even though she wants to serve both Troilus and Diomede tenderly and sincerely.

3.1.3. The essential natures of both Troilus and Criseyde

We have discussed the characterisations of Troilus and Criseyde by investigating the meanings of adjectives attached to each noun illustrating their natures. Troilus, who languishes for love, is represented as a strong, faithful, idealistic knight and courtier; Criseyde is a beautiful and charming lady, who shows her subtle and delicate feeling, suggesting something fragile to touch."[12] The essential natures of both Troilus and Criseyde, in conclusion, are summarised in the middle of Book V. We will end this section, borrowing Chaucer's words:

>   She sobre was, ek symple, and wys withal,
>   The best ynorisshed ek that myghte be,
>   And goodly of hire speche in general,
>   Charitable, estatlich, lusty, and fre;
>   Ne nevere mo ne lakked hire pite;
>   Tendre-herted, slydynge of corage;
>   . . . .
>   And Troilus wel woxen was in highte,
>   . . . .
>   Yong, fressh, strong, and hardy as lyoun,
>   Trewe as stiel in ech condicioun;
>   Oon of the beste entecched creature
>   That is, or shal, whil that the world may dure. (V.820-33)

3.2. Courtly manners and customs

In section 3.1. Chaucer's character paintings in *Troilus and Criseyde* have already been examined, from the viewpoint of the use of the adjectives attached to the nouns referring to each person. Certainly we understand how important the characters and their relationship are in *Troilus and Criseyde*. However, if it is a fact that the poet Chaucer, playing the part of the narrator, relates this story to the audience[13] — the tale which, differently from a work describing only human relations, is based upon courtly elements —, it is necessary that we should look closely at Chaucer's depiction of courtly manners and customs surrounding Chaucer's character paintings in this work.

It is difficult to encompass such a large and complex grouping as courtly manners and customs. When we study what kinds of adjectives have to be connected with the nouns referring to courtly elements, we may understand, little though it may be, how the narrator considers the manners and customs, or how the characters in this work consider these things. It is also important to consider how structurally these expressions are developed in this work. In this sense, we have classified the courtly manners and customs into the following four types: (1) Town and Buildings, (2) Clothes, Arms and Accessories, (3) Culture and Amusement and (4) Customs and Society.

Roughly speaking, the narrator or the characters feel themselves identified with objects in courtly manners and customs. In other words, they experience the process of what is called Einfühlung or empathy.[14] This may mean that the description of courtly manners and customs is not only gorgeous, as in the description of "lystes" in "The Knight's Tale" (e.g., "swich a noble theatre" (I(A) 1885), "a gate of marbul whit" (I(A) 1893), and "Of alabaste whit and reed coral" (I(A) 1910) or in the description of "Heorot" in *Beowulf* (e.g., "healærna mæst (78) and "heah and horngeap" (82)), but also shows the psychological aspect of this work or the internal mental processes of especially the persons Troilus and Criseyde.

In the first category "Town and Buildings," the description of "town" reflects Criseyde's state of mind: "slydynge of corage," and the personification of "paleys" shows Troilus's present sorrow and his past joy. The terms, that is, symbolise some key aspects of the characters of Criseyde and Troilus respectively. In the second category "Clothes, Arms, and Accessories," Criseyde's "blak" clothes make a striking contrast with her "fair" figure and Troilus's arms symbolise his strength. In the third category "Culture and Amusement," we deal with the cultural background in the court. It is not only the background of this work *Troilus and Criseyde* but also that of the narrator himself who speaks to the audience. Therefore, the narrator regards himself as "the sorwful instrument," he often uses the following expression "as olde bokes tellen us," and at last he modestly states that his book *Troilus and Criseyde* is "litel bok." In addition to them, the expressions such as "Letter, a blisful destine" and "th'amorouse daunce" are connected with the main characters Troilus and Criseyde. In the last category "Customs and Society," it is notable that both Troilus and Criseyde satirize the customs and present world subjectively and emotionally. Troilus attacks "lewed observaunces" or "blynde world" and Criseyde makes little of "this false world." Both of them fall into the condition which they have criticised so caustically, and they end in tragedy. Therefore, the narrator curses the present life such as "rites" or "world." In this way, the objects in courtly manners and customs reflect the situation of the narrator or the delicate emotion of the characters. Let us closely examine the description of the courtly elements.

3.2.1. Town and Buildings

In this section, we have the following three categories of nouns: (1) "town," (2) "paleys" or "hous," and (3) "chaumbre." The nouns ought to have collocated with adjectives which show only gorgeous images,[15] but in fact it is noted that most attached adjectives reflect the delicate emotions of Troilus and Criseyde.

(1) "town"

Since the main setting of the story is laid in Troy, it is natural that we find the description of the city Troy. At first the noun "town" which Criseyde describes is connected with the adjective "noble," which lends dignity to her town.

> "I thenke ek how he able is for to have
> Of al this noble town the thriftieste,
> To ben his love, so she hire honour save. (II.736-38)

The adjective "noble" may mean "distinguished by splendour, magnificence, or stateliness of appearance; of imposing or impressive proportions or dimensions," according to the *OED*. This town of Troy is magnificent enough to satisfy Criseyde's self-respect. Therefore, when she goes to the Greek camp in the hostage exchange, she grieves about her misfortunes, remembering her town of Troy: "the toures heigh and ek the halles" (V.730) and "yonder walles" (V.733). Immediately after that, however, the narrator shows her "slydynge of corage." The nouns "Troilus" and "Troie town" are connected with the quasi-adverb "knotteles":

> For bothe Troilus and Troie town
> Shal knotteles thorughout hire herte slide; (V.768-69)

The word "knotteles" strikingly contrasts with the former use of the adjective "noble." Troy was formerly "noble" to Criseyde, but now it is nothing but "knotteles"[16] (which is the *OED*'s earliest citation and means "without a knot, free from knots; unknotted"). Criseyde's heart is moving in a sliding manner.

(2) "paleys" or "hous"

The nouns "paleys" or "hous," restricted by the emotinal adjectives, as we have already explained, reflect Troilus's delicate state of mind. Especially in Book V, the scene where Troilus goes to see Criseyde's "paleys" is most impressive. The description of "paleys" here suggests Troilus's hopelessness, even if we can see his faint expectation. Most adjectives show coldness:

> Than seide he thus: "O paleys desolat,
> O hous of houses whilom best ihight,
> O paleys empty and disconsolat,
> ....
> "O paleis, whilom crowne of houses alle,
> Enlumyned with sonne of alle blisse!
> ....
> Yet, syn I may no bet, fayn wolde I kisse
> Thy colde dores, dorste I for this route;
> ....
> And at that corner, in the yonder hous,
> Herde I myn alderlevest lady deere
> So wommanly, with vois melodious,
> Syngen so wel, ... (V.540-78)

This description is in striking contrast to the past splendour.[17] The more Troilus expresses the present desolate scene, the more it reminds us of past splendid and gorgeous moments. The coldness of this palace reflects Troilus's hopeless state of mind. As the adjective "disconsolat" shows (the word which is the *OED*'s earliest citation and means "Of places or things: causing or manifesting discomfort; dismal, cheerless, gloomy"), Criseyde's palace seems to be gloomy because of her absence. Troilus's heart is in a bleak and frosty condition. Therefore, the "dores" of the palace may show the coldness, as in the adjective "colde." This kind of coldness makes us feel the splendid state of her palace, as in "best ihight" or "enlumyned with sonne of alle blisse." Troilus continues his speech: "in the yonder hous" which often recurs in Book V, remembering his past joy and glory.[18] This leads to the following comment: "…and in that yonder place / My lady first me took unto hire grace" (V.580-81). In this way, the description of Criseyde's palace reflects Troilus's sorrowful mind.

When Troilus is in his happiest state and returns home, the narrator describes Troilus's palace, as in "his real paleys" (III.1534). The place where Troilus stays, in the description of his dream, is explained: "In place horrible makyng ay his mone" (V.250). The tent of Criseyde's father at the Greek camp is described as follows: "Whan that Criseyde unto hire bedde wente / Inwith hire fadres faire brighte tente" (V.1021-22), where the expression "faire brighte" contrasts with the forlorn scene of Criseyde's palace.[19]

The noun "trappe-dore" (which is the *OED*'s earliest citation and means "A door, either sliding or moving on hinges, and flush with the surface, in a floor, roof, or ceiling, or in the stage of a threatre"), in addition to the noun "dore," is used to show the door of the buildings. When Pandarus goes to Criseyde's room secretly, the adjective "secre" is attached to the noun, as in "'Here at this secre trappe-dore,' quod he" (III.759).

(3) "chaumbre"

The nouns such as "chaumbre" (which is the interior structure of the buildings) collocate with the concrete and physical adjectives. The expressions are "the grete chaumbre" (II.1712) and "this myddel chaumbre" (III.666).

> And Pandare, that ful tendreliche wepte,
> Into the derke chambre, as stille as ston, (IV.353-54)

Pandarus is much surprised to hear the news of the hostage exchange decided at the parliament, and then he in deep grief goes to "the derke chambre." The adjective "derke" shows not only the physical sense or the darkness of the surrounding but also suggests Pandarus's grief indirectly.

Criseyde's room is described as follows: "a paved parlour" (II.82) (the adjective "paved" is the *OED*'s earliest citation and means "Laid with a pavement; having a pavement; set or laid together as a pavement (*obs*.)") and "a quysshyn goldybete" (II.1229), the adjective which probably means "embroidered," according to Benson's explanatory notes.[20]

We also find some examples of the light in the chamber: "Light is nought good for sike folkes yen!" (III.1137) where Pandarus makes a joke about Troilus and Criseyde. Remembering his past happiness, Troilus compares Criseyde's palace to a "lantern": "O thow lanterne of which queynt is the light" (V.543). Her palace which had emotionally sent out rays of light is now "queynt" ("pp. quenched, extinguished").[21]

3.2.2. Clothes, Arms, and Accessories

Under this heading we may classify the following three kinds of nouns: (1) clothes, (2) arms, and (3) accessories. The description of clothes and accessories shows Criseyde's beautiful figure, but her black dress is much more emphasised. The description of arms symbolises Troilus's strength.

(1) Clothes

Criseyde's clothes, suitable for a woman at court, are elegant and gorgeous, as the expression "In widewes habit large of samyt broun"(I. 109) shows. The noun "samyt," according to the *OED*, means "a rich silk fabric worn in the Middle Ages, sometimes interwoven with gold" and "also, a garment or cushion of this material." However, the adjective "broun" shows her clothes a little tinged with experience, and perhaps sadness. She has already carried the heavy burden of widowhood on her shoulders. Therefore, the adjective "blak" is attached to her dress (I.170, 309). The following description is indicative of such an aspect:

> Nor under cloude blak so bright a sterre
> As was Criseyde, as folk seyde everichone

> That hir behelden in hir blake wede. (I.175-77)

As Brewer indicates that "'Brightness' is the usual attribute of the medieval heroine, who always had bright golden hair, etc." and that "Criseyde's black dress was an effective contrast,"[22] the recurrent adjective "blak" forms a remarkable contrast with her "aungelik" and "fair" figure, and the colour "blak" makes her beauty more prominent. Furthermore, the fact that she wears "hir blake wede" suggests that she does not have a husband; that is, "makeles."[23] In some way or another, this expression makes us expect that she wants to make friends with a certain companion. Then it is not until in Book IV that we can find this kind of expression again. She does not need the "blake wede" in Books II and III, because she has a close relation with Troilus.

> "And Troilus, my clothes everychon
> Shul blake ben in tokenyng, herte swete,
> That I am as out of this world agon,
> That wont was yow to setten in quiete; (IV.778-81)

When she has to part from Troilus in Book IV, she pledges her loyalty to him sincerely and honestly. She is going to put on the "blake" dress for ever. To our regret, however, it is noted that we do not find any instances of this expression in Book V. There Diomede has succeeded in gaining her heart. It seems that her black dress makes Criseyde's beauty prominent and attracts Diomede's heart. In this way, her black dress symbolically shows her beauty, connected with the subsequent event.

Troilus's clothes will be dealt with in the following section arms." The next examples are not concerned with his arms: "this furred cloke" (III.738) ("furred" means "1. (b) trimmed or lined with fur."[24] and "his bare sherte" (III.1099). Pandarus uses the expression of the battered hat: "myn olde hat" (III.320).

(2) Arms

Most examples are those which show Troilus's bravery and courageousness. The nouns are: "swerd," "helm," "sheeld," and "stede":

> That, as that day, ther dorste non withstonde,
> Whil that he held his blody swerd in honde. (II.202-03)

> His helm tohewen was in twenty places,
> That by a tyssew heng his bak byhynde;
> His sheeld todasshed was with swerdes and maces, (II.638-40)

When Pandarus explains Troilus's strength to Criseyde, he attracts her heart, using the expression "his blody swerd." Then Criseyde is charmed with Troilus's valiant figure, when the narrator emphasises his gallant deed at the battle field, using the intensifying prefix "to-." And Pandarus advises Troilus to show her the inspiring sight, as in "Ye, hardily, right in thi beste gere – / And ryd forth by the place, as nought ne were" (II.1012-13). Therefore, Criseyde finds her affections drawn irresistibly toward him, as in "God woot wher he was lik a manly knyght!" (II.1263).

The narrator further describes the battle between Troy and Greece and the fierce and bloody situation is shown by the enumeration of the arms and the adjectives put in the position of rhyme words: "The longe day, with speres sharpe igrounde, / With arwes, dartes, swerdes, maces felle, / They fighte..." (IV.43-45). The bitter battle between Troilus and Diomede is described as follows: "Assayinge how hire speres weren whette" (V.1760).

Lastly, let us discuss the "stede" which Troilus rides on. The adjective "bay" (which is, according to the *OED*, "A reddish brown colour; a. generally used of horses, and taken to include various shades") is often used. Troilus who appears before Criseyde is described as follows: "This Troilus sat on his baye steede, / Al armed, save his hed, ful richely" (II.624-25). But in Book V Criseyde gives this "baye stede" to Diomede, as in "And after this the storie telleth us / That she hym yaf the faire baye stede" (V.1037-38), where it is of great moment that the noun "stede" is restricted by the expression "faire baye." Here we notice not only Criseyde's changeability, but we see also that "baye" colour seems a symbol of pride, for Troilus's proud attitude is compared to "proude Bayard" (I.218) in Book I. The noun "bayard" is the *OED*'s earliest citation and means "Proper name of the bright-bay-coloured magic steed given by Charlemagne to Renaud (or Rinalds), one of the four sons of Amon, famous in mediaeval romance; *whence* a. formerly used as a kind of mock-heroic allusive name for any horse."

(3) Accessories

The nouns "gemme," "ryng," and "broche" are used to show Criseyde's beauty or token of their affection. When Pandarus advises Criseyde to accept Troilus's deep love, Criseyde's beauty is compared to the "gemme," as in "Wo worth the faire gemme vertulees!" (II.344), where the adjective "vertulees," the *OED*'s earliest citation meaning "Destitute of efficacy or excellence; ineffective, worthless," which the *MED* cites with Gower's passage (*CA*, VII.1315), is a stinging word. The "broche" which Criseyde gave Troilus as a token of her love is attached to the paired words "gold and asure" (III.1370). The noun "ryng" collocates with "blewe," as in "this blewe ryng" (III.885).

3.2.3. Culture and Amusement

Culture and amusement obviously reveal the main characteristics in the courtly life, as D. S. Brewer says, "The courtesy books with their emphasis on good manners influenced the way the court actually worked, and the way the court worked affected the nature of the ceremonies and amusements which took place."[25] In this section, we will deal with the following objects: (1) music and verse, (2) books, (3) correspondence, and (4) courtly games such as "daunce." In the first type, we find the blissful music of the harp and the narrator's modest attitude towards versification. In the second type, we find the recurrent expression "olde bokes," which shows the fact that this work is based upon the classics. The third type shows the love letter between Troilus and Criseyde. And lastly the fourth type shows the courtly entertainment of games.

(1) Music and verse.

We find most examples of musical terms and references in Book V. When Troilus, waiting for Criseyde, enjoys himself with Pandarus at Sarpedoun's house, the happy state is emphasised: "Nor in this world ther is non instrument / Delicious, thorugh wynd or touche of corde, / As fer as any wight hath evere ywent" (V.442-44), where the adjective "delicious" may mean "Highly pleasing or delightful; affording great pleasure or enjoyment," according to the *OED*. Then when he goes to see her palace, he remembers that she was merrily singing in that place: "That in my soule yet me thynketh ich here / The blisful sown; ..." (V.579-80). When they had a pleasant time, there existed "the blisful sown." The adjective "blisful" is often attached to the noun "Venus." Here Troilus seems to imagine Criseyde to be just like Venus. Lastly when he died a heroic death, surprisingly he heard the heavenly music, ascending into heaven.

> And ther he saugh with ful avysement,
> The erratik sterres, herkenyng armonye,
> With sownes ful of heuenyssh melodie. (V.1811-13)

This may be conventional, since Tillyard states that "... there was the further notion that the created universe was itself in a state of music, that it was one perpetual dance."[26] (Cf. the following passage in *The Parlament of Fowls*: "And after shewede he hym the nyne speres; / And after that the melodye herde he / That cometh of thilke speres thre, / That welle is of musik and melodye / In this world here, and cause of armonye," (59-63) where the harmonious music is heard in heaven.) The narrator must have expressed great admiration for the sincere and faithful figure of Troilus. Besides these examples, when Pandarus teaches Troilus how to write a love letter, he compares the person refined in wording to "the best harpour," and says, "For though the best harpour upon lyve / Wolde on the beste sowned joly harpe / That evere was, with alle his fyngres fyve" (II.1030-32).

In the beginning of Book I and the Proem of Book II, the narrator explains the "vers" or the "tale" which he is going to relate. The narrator may have keenly felt the need of such explanations because he is the user of the following refined diction:

> Thesiphone, thow help me for t'endite
> Thise woful vers, that wepen as I write.
> . . . .
> Thow cruwel Furie, sorwynge evere yn peyne,
> Help me, that am the sorwful instrument,
> . . . .
> For wel sit it, the soth for to seyne,
> A woful wight to han a drery feere,
> And to a sorwful tale, a sory chere. (I.4-14)

In this passage, the narrator regards the tale he is going to narrate as "thise woful vers"[27] and "a sorwful tale," in which the narrator is nothing but "the sorwful instrument." We see the narrator's modesty here. Although he is a poet, he never claims that he is. The narrator who thus comments on the whole verse also explains the words in the Proem of Book II. He knows well the limits and changes of the words.

> Disblameth me, if any word be lame,
> For as myn auctour seyde, so sey I.
> . . . .
> Ye knowe ek that in forme of speche is chaunge
> Withinne a thousand yeer, and wordes tho
> That hadden pris, now wonder nyce and straunge
> Us thinketh hem, (II.17-25)

Here the adjective "lame" is the *OED*'s earliest citation and means "*fig*. Maimed, halting; imperfect or defective, unsatisfactory as wanting a part or parts. Said esp. of an argument, excuse, account, narrative, or the like." The *MED* also quotes this word, as in "(e) of language, verse, meter: halting, defective," where the passage (a 1420) Lydgate is quoted before Chaucer's passage, but Chaucer's may be the first. The second example "wordes ... nyce and straunge" shows that the narrator understands the changes of meaning in the words. Then we recognise how much he, relating his story to the audience, is conscious of language. In this way, the narrator, explaining the tale and the words in this work, makes a refined description of Troilus and Criseyde.

(2) Book

Since this work is based upon the classics, the narrator often repeats the following expression: "as olde bokes tellen us" (V.1563). The example "olde bokes" is a kind of set phrase.

> I wol yow telle, as techen bokes olde. (III.91)
>
> As writen clerkes in hire bokes olde, (III.1199)
>
> As for to looke upon an old romaunce. (III.980)
>
> As men may in thise olde bokes rede, (V.1753)
>
> Lo here, the forme of olde clerkis speche (V.1854)

Cassandre also uses this kind of expression:

> Thow most a fewe of olde stories heere, (V.1459)
>
> "Of which, as olde bokes tellen us, (V.1478)
>
> By ligne, or ellis olde bookes lye. (V.1481)
>
> And so descendeth down from gestes olde
> To Diomede,... (V.1511-12)

Criseyde explains the letters which she has just finished reading: "And here we stynten at thise lettres rede" (II.103), where "lettres rede," according to Benson, are "the rubrics that regularly set off titles and sections of works in medieval manuscripts."[28]

Lastly, the narrator thinks of his work as "litel bok":

> Go, litel bok, go, litel myn tragedye,
> Ther God thi makere yet, er that he dye,
> So sende myght to make in som comedye!
> But litel book, no makyng thow n'envie,
> But subgit be to alle poesye; (V.1786-90)

Masui states that "although it is a modest speech, it is possible to listen to the triumphant tone of voice in the internal world of the poet."[29] No matter how great this work may be, the narrator is modest in telling about his own book. This tone of voice seems to correspond to the expression "the sorwful instrument" in the beginning of Book I.

(3) Correspondence

Expressions referring to letters show the love affair between Troilus and Criseyde. So we find the examples only in Books II and V, where Pandarus advises Troilus to write to Criseyde. Let us look into the expressions about letters, keeping up with the development of the story.

Troilus begins to write a love letter to Criseyde under Pandarus's advice. Pandarus teaches him how to write properly: "And if thow write a goodly word al softe, / Though it be good, reherce it nought to ofte" (II.1028-29). He advises Troilus to use "a goodly word" but not to repeat it too often. In Book V, the narrator explains Criseyde's answer: "This Troilus this letter thoughte al straunge, / When he it saugh, and sorwfullich he sighte" (V.1632-33). It may be natural for Troilus to consider her letter "straunge," for Criseyde shows even a general and objective consideration concerning a letter: "Yet preye ich yow, on yvel ye ne take / That it is short which that I to yow write; ... Ek gret effect man write in place lite" (V.1625-29). She shows an easy attitude towards Troilus. In this way, the expressions about the letter are described, conforming entirely to the development of this story.

(4) Courtly games such as "daunce"
We will find the following expressions referring to "daunce": "the newe daunce" (II.553) and "the olde daunce" (III.695). And the noun "daunce" also collocates with the adjective "amorouse."

> For which the grete furie of his penaunce
> Was queynt with hope, and therwith hem bitwene
> Bigan for joie th'amorouse daunce; (IV.1429-31)

After Troilus agrees to Criseyde's temporizing solution, they are strongly attached to each other.

Another noun referring to games is "pley" and the examples are as follows. Criseyde regards Calcas's trickery as "his queynte pley" (IV.1629) which may mean his "cunning devices," according to A. C. Baugh's text.[30] When Troilus is determined to die, he asks Pandarus to prepare for the feasts and games at the wake: "And of the feste and pleyes palestral / At my vigile, ... (V.304-05), where the adjective "palestral" is the *OED*'s earliest citation and means "Of or pertaining to the palaestra, or to wrestling or athletics; athletic." When the people kept a watch over the dead such as a noble person Troilus in that age, the "athletic games" must have been played. According to Benson, "Chaucer may also have had in mind the pyre and funeral games of Archemorus in Theb.6."[31] Another sport "torney" is described as follows: "in werre or torney marcial" (IV.1669), where the noun "torney" is the *OED*'s earliest citation and means "Originally, A martial sport or exercise of the middle ages, in which a number of combatants, mounted and in armour, and divided into two parties, fought with blunted weapons and under certain restrictions, for the prize of valeur; later, A meeting at an appointed time and place for knightly sports and exercises."

3.2.4. Customs and Society

As a matter of course, we find the description of customs and society in Troy and Greece in which the setting of this story is laid. They are sometimes objectively described by the narrator, but most of them are often subjectively satirized by both Troilus and Criseyde. Troilus despises the blind world of love and Criseyde does silly and mischievous rumours or the "false" world. However, ironically enough both of them fall into the world which they have despised and end in the tragedy. Therefore, in the Epilogue of this work, the narrator satirizes the customs and society of the present world, though he is in part referring specifically to the lives of the pagans of the past. The following is a good example:

> Lo here, of payens corsed olde rites!
> Lo here, what alle hire goddes may availle!
> Lo here, thise wrecched worldes appetites! (V.1849-51)

In this way, the narrator curses the "rite" (which means "a formal procedure or act in a religious or other solemn observance"[32] and the "world" (i.e., "this present life"[33]) in which the characters worship and behave themselves. Here let us discuss more exhaustively the customs and society which the narrator satirizes in a bitter and pungent manner.

(1) Customs

When the customs of Troy are described, the nouns "usage" or "observaunce" are chosen in this work. Collocating with the adjective "olde," they show the traditional and fixed ceremony.

> But though that Grekes hem of Troie shetten,
> And hir cite biseged al aboute,
> Hire olde usage nolde they nat letten,
> As for to honoure hir goddes ful devoute;
> . . . .
> In sondry wises shewed, as I rede,

> The folk of Troie hire observaunces olde,
> Palladiones feste for to holde. (I.148-61)

This passage represents Trojans who are absorbed in the religious customs. Troilus also goes to such a ceremony with his soldiers.[34] The noun "usage" means "habitual use, established customs or practice, customary mode of action, on the part of a number of persons; long-continued use or procedure; custom, habit."[35] The noun "observaunce" means "an act performed in accordance with prescribed usage, esp. one of religious or ceremonial character; a practice which is customarily observed, customary rite or ceremony, customs: something which has to be observed; an ordinance, rule, or obligatory practice (*obs.*)."[36] Both show synonymous meanings and seem to be somewhat stereotyped, judging from the attached adjective "olde." (The adjective "olde" is also connected with the noun "ensaumple" (which means "an illustrative instance"[37]), and Troilus satirizes bitterly Pandarus's "olde ensaumples," as in "Lat be thyne olde ensaumples, I the preye (I.760).)

When Troilus makes little of the foolish love of the young in the present world, he says, "I have herd told, pardieux, of youre lyvynge, / Ye loveres, and youre lewed observaunces" (I.197-98), where the adjective "lewed" means ignorant. Ironically Troilus goes into "lewed observaunces" himself. Then the narrator tries to describe the story of how Troilus wins Criseyde's affection, telling that he is going to write about Troilus's love as an example of various "usages," as in "Ek for to wynnen love in sondry ages, / In sondry londes, sondry ben usages" (II.27-28).

In this way, it seems that the narrator and Troilus think of the customs as something "olde" or fixed. Consequently it may correspond to the fall of Troy. Is it a coincidental conjunction that the fall of Troy is keeping with the tragedy of Troilus? Just as both Troilus and Troy became "knotteles" in Criseyde's heart (V.768-69), the downfall of both of them may have been predestined. Therefore, the narrator instead of Troilus curses old "rites" at the end of this work.[38]

(2) Society

Society in this work is mainly represented by the noun "world," which, a little wider in application than the customs, means "the earthly state of human existence; this present life," according to the *OED*. The meaning of the noun "world" may be difficult to recognise, but we can understand the field of meaning if we look at the attached adjectives. Since the adjectives such as "blynde," "false," and "wretched" tend to be collocated with the noun "world," the society around the human beings may be regarded as an unfavourable one. Therefore, the characters are too much conscious of society.

> O blynde world, O blynde entencioun!
> How often falleth al the effect contraire
> Of surquidrie and foul presumpcioun; (I.211-13)

Troilus is somewhat detached from society and sees the lovers more as a bystander at first. This kind of attitude to society may be also "blynde." He later becomes a blind person in love. As well as this example, when their love affair is going on, the narrator states that the people in the society do not know this affair, as in "Now al is wel, for al the world is blynd / In this matere, bothe fremed and tame" (III.528-29).

On the other hand, we have often discussed that Criseyde is over-conscious of society. When Criseyde is asked to accept Troilus's deep love by Pandarus, Criseyde points out the falsehood of society: "This false world – allas! – who may it leve ?" (II.420). After Pandarus tells her that Troilus has heard that she is in love with Horaste, she laments for the rumour and satirizes it (but it is Pandarus's plausible lie):

> so worldly selynesse (III.813)
>
> fals felicitee (III.814)

> Condicioun of veyn prosperitee (III.817)
>
> O brotel wele of mannes joie unstable! (III.820)
>
> ... thow, joie, art muable (III.822)
>
> ... joie is transitorie,
> As every joie of worldly thyng mot flee (III.827-28)
>
> Ther is no verray weele in this world here (III.836).

In this way, she indicates the false world, but taking the whole situation into consideration, she seems to be in such a false society from the very beginning. At first, her father Calcas escapes from Troy and abandons her. Widow though she is, she falls in love with Troilus. Lastly she gives her heart to Diomede. This series of events shows the false world itself.

In Book IV the narrator satirizes this present world. Although the people demand the return of Antenor, he brings about the ruin of Troy. So he says, "O nyce world, lo, thy discrecioun!" (IV.206). The rumour of the hostage exchange spreads fast, just as "The swifte Fame ... / Was thorughout Troie yfled with preste wynges / Fro man to man ..." (IV.659-62).[39]

Ultimately, this work ends in tragedy and Troilus meets his fate like a brave man. Ascending into heaven, he despises society or the present world. In *Troilus and Criseyde*, to sum up, Troilus makes his appearance, looking down on the present world; he falls into the blind world; and finally he despises the wretched world again, going to the glorious world of heaven:

> ... and fully gan despise
> This wrecched world, and held al vanite
> To respect of the pleyn felicite (V.1816-18)

> ... and thynketh al nys but a faire,
> This world, that passeth soone as floures faire. (V.1840-41)

It seems that "floures faire" are not "wrecched" but transitory. Thus Troilus knew the transitory life in this world through the luckless and unrequited love affair.

In this way, we have discussed Chaucer's depiction of courtly manners and customs through adjectives in *Troilus and Criseyde*. These descriptions surrounding Chaucer's characters are important, because they may make the characters in *Troilus and Criseyde* stand out clearly and distinctly.

3.3. Nature

The word "nature," according to the *OED*, means "the creative and physical power which is conceived of as operating in the material world and as the immediate cause of all its phenomena." In this section, I will deal with the creative and regulative physical power in Chaucer's description of natural phenomena which surround "Human Beings" and "Court and Society" in *Troilus and Criseyde*.

Chaucer's description of nature has been traditionally accepted, as W. H. Hudson says: "A specially charming feature of his poetry is its fresh out-of-doors atmosphere. His descriptions of the country are often indeed in the conventional manner of his time, and his garden landscape and May flowers are to some extent things of tradition only. But he has a real love of nature and particularly of the spring, and when he writes of these, as in the *Prologue* and the *Knightes Tale*, the personal accents unmistakable."[40] It is a well-known fact that the best example of his description of nature, as Hudson points out, is found in "The General Prologue" to *The Canterbury Tales* (I(A) 1-11), where appear the following adjectives: "swoote," "sweete," "tendre," and "yonge." These adjectives create a pleasing atmosphere of spring which provides the setting of the scenes in *The Canterbury Tales*.

Chaucer's description of natural phenomena in *Troilus and*

Criseyde also achieves a pleasant springlike effect. The narrator, by describing the beauty of natural objects, plants, and animals, produces a gentle atmosphere around the human beings. He also provides the setting of nature in *Troilus and Criseyde*, such as April in Book I, May in Book II, "reyn" in Book III. Those natural objects will keep up with the development of the story: i.e., they reflect the characters' state of mind, harmonizing the contents of the story.

Moreover, it is not too much to say that the descriptions of nature in this work reflect the delicate emotion of the characters. Their subtle states of mind are seen especially when they curse the natural order at the end of Book III, or when they see the animals in their dreams.

Nature controls both the development of the story and the characters' states of mind in this work. If they act in harmony with nature, everything will follow the natural course of events. However, once they try to break down this harmony or natural order, as at the end of Book III and in Book IV, they tend to be destroyed by nature's uncontrollable power. In Book V, the narrator emphasises the transcendental aspect of nature. Even though the characters end up tragically, nature stands aloof from them, just as Taylor states: "In this book, the narrator no longer confined nature to art. He does not limit it to the garden of love; he does not reduce it by personification of love; he does not allude to it to transform death. He writes of it now on the grandest of scales, as the intermediary between man and God, the veil partially hiding the final vision."[41] Therefore, majesty of nature remains stable, even though Troilus and Criseyde end tragically. After he dies a heroic death, however, Troilus ascends to heaven in harmony with nature. This may be the last rescue to the hero Troilus.

> And ther he saugh, with ful avysement
> The erratik sterres, herkenyng armonye
> With sownes ful of hevenyssh melodie. (V.1811-13)

Let us closely examine the description of nature, which, thus looking at the characters with a detached air, reflects the development of the story and the characters' subtle states of mind. This section will proceed in the following order: (1) Natural Objects, (2) Plants, and (3) Animals.[42]

3.3.1. Natural Objects

Natural objects are represented by nouns such as "moon, rein, see, sonne, sterre, wynd, etc."[43] Here I will discuss the kinds of adjectives that collocate with these nouns. The following types are dealt with in this section: (1) natural objects in the air and (2) day and night.

(1) Natural objects in the air

We find the following nouns: the objects which exist in the air such as "cloude," "sterre," "Bole," "moone," and "sonne;" those which are created by the physical power of the former objects, such as "bemes" and "reyn." (The nouns "day" and "nyght" are dealt with in the following section.) These nouns generally collocate with the adjective "brighte" which shows the beauty of nature, but sometimes with the adjective "blak" which provides an effective contrast with the former adjective.

In the following instance, Criseyde's beautiful figure contrasts powerfully with her black dress through natural description. The colour of her black dress is, strangely enough, coincident with that of "cloude blak" and her fair figure corresponds to "so bright a sterre," as previously quoted in the section 3.2.2. (1).

> Nas nevere yet seyn thyng to ben preysed derre,
> Nor under cloude blak so bright a sterre
> As was Criseyde, as folk seyde everichone
> That hir behelden in hir blake wede. (I.174-77)

Criseyde's appearance harmonises with the natural objects. We can imagine how "bright" Criseyde's beauty is against the dark sky. Here the expression "so bright a sterre" contrasts strongly with "cloude blak."

Let us now discuss the natural objects which show brightness in this work. The adjective "bright" is attached to the nouns "Phebus," "sonne," and "moone." Further the proper noun "Phebus" collocates with the compound adjectives "gold-ytressed" and "laurer-crowned" which refer to the superior and dignified aspect of nature.

> Whan Phebus doth his bryghte bemes sprede
> Right in the white Bole, it so bitidde,
> As I shal synge, on Mayes day the thrydde, (II.54-56)

> But right as floures, thorugh the cold of nyght
> Iclosed, stoupen on hire stalke lowe,
> Redressen hem ayein the sonne bright,
> And spreden on hire kynde cours by rowe, (II.967-70)

> The gold-tressed Phebus heighe on-lofte
> Thries hadde alle with his bemes cleene
> The snowes molte, and Zepherus as ofte
> Ibrought ayeyn the tendre leves grene, (V.8-11)

> The brighte Venus folwede and ay taughte
> The wey ther brode Phebus down alighte; (V.1016-17)

> The laurer-crowned Phebus with his heete
> Gan, in his cours ay upward as he wente,
> To warmen of the est as the wawes weete, (V.1107-09)

The first quotation describes "bryghte" Phebus, who seems to cooperate with Pandarus in furthering the object Pandarus has in view. The epithet "white," in harmony with the brightness of the sun, "has been traced to Ovid's description of the snow-white bull in the form of which Jupiter visited Europa (Met., ii, 852)."[44] In the second instance, the favourable progress of their love affair, in harmony with "the sonne bright," makes Troilus's heart feel happy. In the Proem of Book III, as a matter of course, we again find expressions of brightness, but they are not related to the sun but to the blissful state of the goddess Venus. In Book IV, there are few expressions of brightness, but we find one instance which shows harmonious nature, when Troilus and

Criseyde have been temporizing. Dancing "th'amrouse daunce," they go into the harmony of nature, as in "And as the briddes, whanne the sonne is shene, / Deliten in hire song in leves grene," (IV.1432-33). This may be an attempt by the narrator to rescue them from their harsh and dark situation. In this way, the tragedy draws near. It must be noticed, however, that majestic nature makes her appearance, in the last three instances. The adjective in the expression "the gold-tressed Phebus" shows the eternal nature of the sun. This nature does not change, even as time passes. This eternity is applicable to the planet "Venus," which, according to the *OED*, means "5. *Astr*. The second planet in order of distance from the sun, revolving in an orbit between those of Mercury and the earth; the morning or evening star." It is associated with the goddess Venus. The figure of Phebus is also shown in the adjective "laurer-crowned."

As for the natural objects which show darkness in this work, we may consider nouns such as 'reyn' and 'wynd'. It is noticeable that the rain, which contrasts with the above-mentioned sun, functions to promote the couple's love affair in Book III.

> Now is ther litel more for to doone,
> But Pandare up and shortly for to seyne,
> Right sone upon the chaungynge of the moone,
> Whan lightles is the world a nyght or tweyne,
> And that the wolken shop hym for to reyne, (III.547-51)

> The bente moone with hire hornes pale,
> Saturne, and Jove, in Cancro joyned were,
> That swych a reyn from heven gan avale,
> That every maner womman that was there
> Hadde of that smoky reyn a verray feere; (III.624-28)

> And seyde, "Lord, this is an huge rayn! (III.656)

> The sterne wynd so loude gan to route
> That no wight oother noise myghte heere; (III.743-44)

These natural phenomena play a significant role in preventing Criseyde from escaping from Pandarus's house. The rain may be unfortunate for Criseyde, but it is fortunate for both Troilus and Pandarus. (The adjective "bente" is the *OED*'s first citation and means "1. Constrained into a curve, as a strung bow; curbed, crooked, deflected from the straight line." The *MED* also cites this word. The adjective "smoky" is also the *OED*'s first citation and means "2. Of vapour, mist, etc.: Having the character or appearance of smoke; resembling smoke; smoke-like." The *MED* also cites this word.) In this way, Pandarus's plan harmonises with the natural phenomena in Book III.

Lastly, at the end of Book V when Troilus ascends into heaven, he is bathed in the harmonious light of nature. Although in Book IV we lose the sense of Troilus being in harmony with nature, he gains a bird's-eye view of several planets around him.

> And ther he saugh, with ful avysement,
> The erratik sterres, herkenyng armonye
> With sownes ful of hevenyssh melodie.
> And down from thennes faste he gan avyse
> This litel spot of erthe,... (V.1811-15)

In this passage, "the erratik sterres" are "the (seven) planets"[45] and the adjective "erratik" is a first citation in the *OED* and means "A. Wandering; prone to wonder. 1. First used in certain special applications: a planet. *obs*." Passing these 'sterres', he looks down at "this litel spot of erthe." The whole description of nature forms a fine panorama of great nature and it shows the hierarchical order of human beings, nature, and God.

We find the following astrological expressions:

> And caste and knew in good plit was the moone
> To doon viage, and took his way ful soone (II.74-75)

> I, woful wrecche and infortuned wight,
> And born in corsed constellacioun, (IV.744-45)

The verb "caste" (which is the first citation in the *OED* and means "39. To calculate astrologically, as to cast a figure, horoscope, nativity, etc.; also *absol.*, though the *MED* does not quote this word.") shows that Pandarus uses an astrological calculation to discover that the moon is in a favourable position. The other astrological expression is the noun "constellacioun," which, according to the *OED*, means "†1. *Astrol*. The configuration or position of 'stars' (i.e. planets) in regard to one another, as supposed to have 'influence' on terrestrial things; esp. their position at the time of a man's birth; my constellation = 'my stars.'"

(2) Day and night

The contrast between day and night continues the development of the theme in this work. When things are in the right order, "the derke nyght" corresponds to "sorwe" and "the glade morwe" to "joie," as can be seen when Pandarus is preaching to Troilus: "And next the derke nyght the glade morwe; / And also joie is next the fyn of sorwe" (I.951-52). We can also understand this contrast, when we consider that it is not in the morning but at night that Grendel made an attack on Heorot in *Beowulf*. The advent of night is connected with the colour "blake," as in "And white thynges wexen dymme and donne / For lak of lyght, and sterres for t'apere, / That she and alle hire folk in went yfeere" (II.908-10), where the adjective "donne" is the *OED*'s second citation and means "2. More vaguely: Dark, dusky (from absence of light); murky, gloomy."

However, a clear-cut distinction between black and white is not always applicable to a work of psychological depth such as *Troilus and Criseyde*. As is clear in Book III, when Troilus and Criseyde further their love affair at night, the value of day and night turns upside down. Nature seems to offer a hand of help to Troilus and Criseyde, but in fact it does not help them, and both Troilus and Criseyde complain of the day and night which Nature has created. This situation will be found in Books III and IV. At first, the narrator describes Troilus and Criseyde's happy night, using the adjective "blisful," as in "O blisful nyght, of hem so longe isought, / How blithe unto hem bothe two thow weere!" (III.1317-18). Although they enjoy themselves at night, however, they complain of both the night and day. The following is Criseyde's complaint.

> "O blake nyght, as folk in bokes rede,
> That shapen art by God this world to hide
> At certeyn tymes wyth thi derke wede, (III.1429-31)
>
> Thow rakle nyght! Ther God, maker of kynde,
> The, for thyn haste and thyn unkynde vice, (III.1437-38)

Criseyde compains of the swiftly passing night, using the adjectives "blake" and "rakle." (This may be natural, because the night is of course "blake.") On the other hand, Troilus complains of the coming day, according to the lover's convention or aubade.

> "O cruel day, accusour of the joie
> That nyght and love han stole and faste iwryen,
> Acorsed be thi comyng into Troye,
> For every bore hath oon of thi bryghte yen!
> Envious day, what list the so to spien? (III.1450-54)
>
> "Allas! what have thise loveris the agylt,
> Dispitous day? Thyn be the peeyne of helle! (III.1457-58)

This kind of "day" is against the natural laws. It is just the opposite of Pandarus's proverbial expression. Troilus wishes to stay with his love Criseyde, and curses the day, which is regarded as the "cruel," "envious," and "dispitous" being (the adjective "dispitous" is the *OED*'s first citation and means "2. Cruel; exhibiting ill-will, or bitter enmity, malevolent"). These expressions lead to the following instances: "cruel day" (III.1695) and "Callyng it traitour, envyous, and worse," (III.1700). (It is interesting to note that Pandarus's saying, "How stant it now / This mury morwe?" (III.1562-63), when the morning comes, may show his optimistic and joyous state of mind.) Troilus's emotional reaction to the day is described in the serious words in Book IV. When Criseyde is destined to be sent away to the Greek camp, Troilus complains of the day, losing his heart in grief: "O deth, allas! why nyltow do me deye? / Acorsed be that day which that Nature / Shop me to ben a lyves creature!" (IV.250-52).

In Book V, Troilus appears to regain the tranquil state of mind, but, in fact, he is in a fever of impatience. Being anxious, he feels he has waited for Criseyde much longer than he really has waited.

> The dayes moore, and lenger every nyght
> Than they ben wont to be, hym thoughte tho, (V.659-60)

In this way, the expressions about the day and night reflect the characters' state of mind, especially Troilus's sensitive emotions.

3.3.2. Plants

In this section, I will deal mainly with the description of spring, such as found in "The General Prologue" to *The Canterbury Tales*. This natural phenomenon is often present in other Middle English verses; for example, in *Sir Orfeo* the scene is set in the gentle atmosphere of spring, and this atmosphere provides a surrounding in which an event occurs: "Bifel so in þe comessing of May, / When miri and hot is þe day, ... And blosme breme on eueri bouȝ / Oueral wexeþ miri anouȝ" (57-62),[46] where the emotional expression "miri" is used to show the joyous state of the characters and the narrator.

In *Troilus and Criseyde*, however, unlike *Sir Orfeo*, the narrator connects the description of nature to the development of the story and to the characters' states of mind. In this poem, the narrator uses not only the description of spring, but also the 'turning of the seasons.' The description of the seasons is subtly differentiated in each one of the Books. It should be noted here that the changes of the seasons in this work correspond to the characters. Raymond P. Tripp, Jr. points out this fact in "The General Prologue": "The emotion is gentler in Chaucer and the sense of time even more subtly internalized. The motion is toward spring and life, rather than toward winter and death; but the vital welling of time is still there: life is movement and pilgrimage — man's "season."[47] We should note how deeply the "turning of the seasons" is connected with that of the characters' minds and with their circumstances. I will quote one passage from each Book and compare their descriptions of nature.

> And so bifel, whan comen was the tyme
> Of Aperil, whan clothed is the mede
> With newe grene, of lusty Veer the pryme,
> And swote smellen floures white and rede, (I.155-58)

> In May, that moder is of monthes glade,
> That fresshe floures, blew and white and rede,
> Ben quike agayn, that wynter dede made,
> And ful of bawme is fletyng every mede, (II.50-53)

> But right as thise holtes and thise hayis,
> That han in wynter dede ben and dreye,
> Revesten hem in grene when that May is,
> Whan every lusty liketh best to preye;
> Right in that selve wise, soth to seye,
> Wax sodeynliche his herte ful of joie,
> That gladder was ther nevere man in Troie. (III.351-57)

> And as in wynter leves ben biraft,
> Ech after other, til the tree be bare,
> So that ther nys but bark and braunche ilaft,
> Lith Troilus, byraft of ech welfare,
> Ibounden in the blake bark of care, (IV.225-29)

> The gold-tressed Phebus heighe on-lofte
> Thries hadde alle with his bemes cleene
> The snowes molte, and Zepherus as ofte
> Ibrought ayeyn the tendre leves grene, (V.8-11)

In Book I, the narrator describes April rather objectively. Taylor says that the description is "purely conventional,"[48] but we know that the description of spring foreshadows a subsequent event in this work. Spring has come, just as "Veer" (which is the *OED*'s first citation and means "the season of spring; spring-time") is "lusty" (="pleasant, delightful"). The flowers are "white and rede," as in "The General Prologue." The whole field is full of life. We expect that something will happen.

In Book II, April turns into May. The description of nature is more cheerful than in Book I. The recurring sounds /m/ and /f/ are alliteration as having effect of heightening the beautiful movements of nature. The proper noun 'May' is personified.[49] The flowers are described by the adjectives "fresshe" (just like "as fressh as is the month of May" in the description of "Squier") and "blew," in addition to "white" and "rede" in Book I. The pleasing spring strikingly contrasts with the "dede" winter. In this way, the narrator creates an atmosphere of cheerfulness and Troilus and Criseyde's love affair proceeds successfully.

In Book III, the harmony of nature is described by the narrator. Especially in the Proem of this Book, we find eternal nature in harmony with the goddess Venus, as in "As man, brid, best, fissh, herbe, and grene tree / Thee fele in tymes with vapour eterne" (III.10-11). The passage (III.351-57) shows that the description of nature also plays a role in depicting Troilus's state of mind; when he does not know if Criseyde can accept his love, his mind is in "wynter", and later, when he realises what her feelings are and wins her affection, he enjoys the cheerful spring. The narrator also explains this in the following way: "For I have seyn of a ful misty morwe / Folowen ful ofte a myrie someris day; / And after wynter foloweth grene May;" (III.1060-62).

It is winter that the narrator describes in Book IV. The passage (IV.225-29) reminds us of a cold and severe winter, because of the expressions "til the tree be bare" and "the blake bark of care."

In Book V, however, surprisingly the beauty of nature is described again. To use Taylor's words, "the imagery here is epic, presenting time's relentless course, and although the passage of time portends sorrow, nature maintains its beauty" and the passage creates "the impression of an eternal order, benevolent and beautiful although distant from man."[50] The eternal beauty of nature is represented here. Since nature is stable and constant, she keeps her dignified air, regardless of the fate of the characters.

In this way, the setting of the scene is the spring, as in Book I. The love affair goes well with the help of nature. But as soon as the harmony of nature is disturbed in Book IV, her cheerful and lovely aspect turns into a cold and severe winter. In Book V, however, nature displays her magnificent beauty. The more dignity nature has in Book V, the more the situation reminds us of the miserable state of Troilus. This is also true of Criseyde, miserable as she is, whose beauty also makes Diomede love her, though. Although nature seems to be detached from the characters, she is, in fact, deeply connected with them.

3.3.3. Animals

The animals which make their appearance in this work are the "swalowe," the "nightingale," the "egle," and the "bor." The description of the animals also reflects the development of the story and the characters' state of mind.

First, let us discuss the animals 'swalowe' and 'nightingale.' As Brewer states,[51] they are based upon Ovid's *Metamorphoses*. However, the narrator does not simply quote it, but he seems to make use of it in order to represent the characters' delicacy of feeling.

> The swalowe Proigne, with a sorowful lay,
> Whan morwen com, gan make hire waymentynge,
> Whi she forshapen was; and ever lay
> Pandare abedde, half in a slomberynge,
> Til she so neigh hym made hire cheterynge
> How Tereus gan forth hire suster take,
> That with the noyse of hire he gan awake, (II.64-70)

When Pandarus is going to let Criseyde know of Troilus's passionate love, this "swalowe" begins to chirp outside the house. The bird's "sorwful" twitterings may suggest the beginning of the love affair. It seems that in some way or another the "suster" Philomela of this "swalowe" reminds us of Criseyde, because Pandarus soon visits Criseyde and goes between Troilus and Criseyde in Book II. Criseyde may be obliged to accept Troilus's love through Pandarus's earnest commendation of Troilus to her. Criseyde may be "forshapen" by Pandarus. Afterwards, she is compared to the "nyghtingale:" "And as the newe abaysed nyghtyngale, / That stynteth first whan she bygynneth to synge, / Whan that she hereth any herde tale / Or in the hegges any wyght stirynge, / And after siker doth hire vois out rynge" (III.1233-37).[52] Just as the nightingale trembling with fear begins to sing again when she is released from fear, Criseyde has a joyful time with Troilus.

Next, let us discuss the animals which make their appearance in the characters' dreams. Their dreams are affected by expectations and fears. Criseyde dreams of a figure in the shape of an "egle" and Troilus dreams of a "bor."

The "egle" appears in Criseyde's dream. The word "egle," according to the *OED*, means that "the strength, keen vision, graceful and powerful flight of the eagle are proverbial, and have given to him the title of the king of birds."

> And as she slep, anonright tho hire mette
> How that an egle, fethered whit as bon,
> Under hire brest his longe clawes sette, (II.925-27)

Criseyde, fascinated with Troilus's bravery, anticipates a successful relationship with Troilus. That may show her psychological reality. It seems that this courageous white "egle" is the knightly figure of Troilus, who is on the point of captivating Criseyde's mind.

In comparison with Criseyde's dream, in Book V Troilus dreams a terrible dream in which Criseyde is raped by the "boor."

> And up and doun as he the forest soughte,
> He mette he saugh a bor with tuskes grete,
> That slepte ayeyn the bryghte sonnes hete. (V.1237-39)

This dream reflects Troilus's apprehension. The "bor with tuskes grete" instead of Troilus makes his appearance before Criseyde. Cassandre foretells that the boar will turn out to be Diomede and this prediction comes true. The adjective "stronge" and "gret" are attached to the animal "bor:" "And hire bisoughte assoilen hym the doute / Of the stronge boor with tuskes stoute;" (V.1453-54) and "For with a boor as gret as ox in stalle / She made up frete hire corn and vynes alle" (V.1469-70).

3.3.4. Summary

We have discussed the description of nature which controls both courtly elements and human beings in Chaucer's *Troilus and Criseyde*. First, as for the description of natural objects, the relationship between the cloud and the star reflects Criseyde's black dress and her bright figure. Furthermore, the description of natural objects shows the delicate feelings of the characters; in particular, "the sonne bright" represents a joyous state of mind. The fatal "reyn" heightens the drama as the story develops. The rain, governing the human beings and the palace, facilitates the love affair between Troilus and Criseyde. However, when Troilus and Criseyde go against nature, she does not support them, as is shown in the fact that they complain of the day and night at the end of Books III and IV. Second, the plants also reflect the delicate emotions of the characters. The descriptions of plants suggest the harmonious development of the love affair in Books I, II, and III, as the adjectives "newe grene," "fresshe," "blew and white and rede," and "lusty" show, while they may show that in Book IV the natural order is about to break down, as in the expressions: "til the tree be bare" and "the blak bark of care," the adjectives reminding us of the severe winter and the coldness of the human beings. However, the description of Phebus as "gold-tressed" signals a return to the harmony of nature in Book V. In spite of the characters' tragic end, nature remains undisturbed. Finally, the animals are also deeply connected with the characters in this work: "the newe abaysed nyghtyngale" is compared to Criseyde, "an egle, fethered whit as bon" in Criseyde's dream suggests the manly figure of Troilus, and the "bor" in Troilus's dream is associated with Diomede. In this way, the descriptions of nature in *Troilus and Criseyde* mirror faithfully the actions and states of minds of the characters.

3.4. God and pagan gods

The Middle Ages are, in a sense, the age of religion. As D. S. Brewer states, "all levels of society took shape from religion, and God seemed very near in the fourteenth century, sometimes."[53] We usually recognise the existence of one God who rules over human beings, society, and nature.[54] In Chaucer's works, however, the Christian God coexists with pagan gods and it is often difficult to distinguish between them. Obviously, pagan gods play a more important role in *Troilus and Criseyde*, as well as in "The Knight's Tale," than in any other of Chaucer's works. Particularly noteworthy, however, is Troilus's ascension to the heavenly world of the Christian God in the Epilogue of *Troilus and Criseyde*. While W. W. Skeat always uses the lower case for the noun "god," F. N. Robinson and L. D. Benson seem to discriminate carefully between the Christian God and the pagan gods, using upper/lower case to distinguish between them. However important the aforesaid issues may be, here we do not attempt at the explication of them in this book, say, in terms of the interrelationships and hierarchy of the gods. we have studied what kinds of adjectives have to collocate with the noun "god," written in both upper and lower cases in *Troilus and Criseyde*. It must be noted that we have classified the pagan gods in accordance with Masui's classification.[55] The following table shows the adjectives attached to each "god" or personified forces.

Table 1   A List of the Nouns and Their Attached Adjectives

Nouns	Adjectives
God	almyghty, myghty, blisful, holy, heighe, verray, etc.
Christ	sothfast
Venus	blisful, brighte, deere, debonaire, goodly, lief, etc.
Cupid	benigne, blisful, blynde, cruel, dredful, heighe, mighty, verray, etc.
Jove	almyghty, blisful, heighe, natal, etc.
Marte	cruel, dispitouse, heighe, fierse, etc.
Fortune	adverse, brighte, comune, cruel, etc.
destyne	blisful, fatal, etc.

It must be incidentally noted here that the adjective "almyghty"[56] which was imported with the introduction of Christianity to England is not only attached to the Christian God but also to the pagan god "Jove."[57] Furthermore, the God of Love "Cupid," by whom Troilus's heart is bound tightly, abundantly displays the god's manipulating ability. It may be for this reason that the adjectives "myghty," "benigne," and "holy" are attached to Cupid.

3.4.1. God

This section deals with the adjectives attached to the Christian God, who is, according to the *OED*, "In the specific Christian and monotheistic sense. The One object of supreme adoration; the Creator and Ruler of the Universe." The attached adjectives are as follows: "almyghty," "myghty," "blisful," "holy," and "verray." In addition, the nouns "purveyaunce" and "prescience" are discussed. It is worth while noticing Troilus's peculiar disposition to the necessity of events which is particularly seen in Book IV.

To begin with, let us analyse the adjectives "almyghty" and "myghty" used by every character in this work. The narrator speaks to the audience, as if he were a mouthpiece of Troilus, before Troilus converses with Criseyde in the end of Book II: "And was the firste tyme he shulde hire preye / Of love; O myghty God, what shal he seye?" (II.1756-57). The adjective "myghty," to say nothing of the word "almyghty," is straightforwardly descended from Old English. We can notice the following example in *Beowulf*.

> Wundor is tō secganne,
> hū mihtig God manna cynne
> þurgh sīdne sefan snyttru bryttað,
> eard ond eorlscipe; hē āh ealra geweald. (1724b-27)

Here the expression "mihtig God," though "mihtig" alliterates "manna," is used as a set phrase, one which has been used traditionally by Christians since early Middle Ages. Consequently, "myghty God" in Chaucer's work seems likewise to be a fixed expression. A further example is: "Ther myghty God yet graunte us see that houre!" (II. 588).[58] The adjective "almyghty" is also used in the following speech of Pandarus: "And fro this world, almyghty God I preye / Delivere hire soon! I kan namore seye" (V.1742-43). Pandarus, praying seriously to God, expresses his hatred for Criseyde. This is the last speech of Pandarus's in this work.

However, the adjective which Troilus uses is a little different from that which Criseyde and Pandarus use. The adjective "blisful" is used twice by Troilus. He prays to "blisful God," as if God were Venus: "And blisful God prey ich with good entente, / The viage, and the lettre I shal endite," (II.1060-61) and "As wolde blisful God now, for his joie, / I myghte hire sen ayeyn come into Troie!" (V.608-09). This expression "blisful God" seems not to be descended from Old English, although the adjective "blisful" is a native complex word. Rather, it is because the Christian God is also a god of love.

On the other hand, Criseyde uses the adjectives such as "holy" and "heighe": "Ye, holy God," quod she, "Why thyng is that?" (II.127), (since we can find the following examples in *Beowulf*: "halig God"

(1553) and "halig Dryhten" (686), the expression "holy God" may be a fixed expression.) and "But that woot heighe God that sit above," (III.1027). Further, Pandarus and Criseyde use the adjective "verray" (which is, according to the *OED*, "1. Really or truly entitled to the name or designation; possessing the true character of the person or thing named; properly so called or designated."): "He seide, "O verray God, so have I ronne!" (II.1464) and "As wisly verray God my soule save" (III.1501). This word is derived from Old French.

In this way, the adjectives attached to the noun "God," conventional as they may be, are used somewhat differenly by the various characters. At last, the narrator in his conclusive remarks of this story uses the adjective "sothfast" for the noun "Crist" (=Son of God). He prays to "Crist" for mercy, cursing every one of the pagan gods:

> And to that sothfast Crist, that starf on rode,
> With al myn herte of mercy evere I preye,
> And to the Lord right thus I speke and seye: (V.1860-62)

It would seem that the noun "Crist" unexpectedly appears before the audience. As pagans, the characters could not speak of Christ. But in fact, "Crist" is deeply connected with the noun "God" to whom the characters and the narrator have often committed themselves. They, always keeping "God" in mind, speak and act in their daily life. As Christians, they also commit themselves to Christ. This may be a typical medieval world, reigned over by "almyghty God," whose son Jesus Christ is His viceroy over the earth.

In addition to the noun "God," the nouns "purveiaunce" and "prescience" are dealt with. The noun "purveiaunce" is, according to the *OED*, "3. In full, providence of God (etc.), divine providence: The foreknowing and beneficent care and government of God (or of nature, etc.); divine direction, control, or guidance." And the noun 'prescience' is, according to the *OED*, "Knowledge of events before they happen; foreknowlege. a. esp. as a divine attribute." Both are religious terms, which are used twice in *Troilus and Criseyde*.

The first occurrence shows that, when Pandarus explains Troilus's sorrowful speech to Criseyde, Pandarus becomes a spokesman of Troilus: "'O god, that at thi disposicioun / Ledest the fyn, by juste purveiaunce" (II.526-27), in which Pandarus uses the lower case "god" perhaps referring to Cupid instead of the Christian God, even though "juste purveiaunce" in fact refers to the Providence of God. In Book I Troilus prays to God (not "god") for mercy, but Pandarus, changing the expression, uses the noun "god" instead of "God."

Second, the instances are found in Troilus's speech when he, meditating on the necessity of events, laments his misfortune. The noun "purveyaunce" collocates with the adjectives "divine" and "sovereyne" and the noun "prescience" with the adjective "eternal." He recognises that everything is governed by the divine providence of God (IV.960-1078).

> So myghte I wene that thynges alle and some
> That whilom ben byfalle and overcome
> Ben cause of thilke sovereyne purveyaunce
> That forwoot al withouten ignoraunce. (IV.1068-71)

Troilus, thus realizing the necessary outcome of events, speaks: "Almyghty Jove in trone" (IV.1079), in which Troilus prays to "Jove," as if "Jove" were the Christian God. In contrast, Pandarus invokes "God" in the subsequent speech: "O myghty God ... in trone" (IV.1086). How contrastive they are! Troilus seems to contradict himself when he prays to a controlling god who may direct him to the tragic end, although Troilus may be thinking of Christianity when he prays to the pagan god "Jove" for mercy.[59]

In this way, the noun "God" is used throughout this work. In the last stage of this work, the narrator prays to the Christian God, despising the pagan gods. Almighty God rules over nature, court, and human beings in *Troilus and Criseyde*. Even if Troilus's end is tragic, we will see a certain harmonious world when we put his tragedy in perspective. It is certain that the harmonious world is brought about by the almighty power of God.

3.4.2. Pagan Gods

In this section, we will discuss pagan gods who are based upon the classic mythology. Though many pagan gods appear in this work, here I will focus on the following gods: (1) Venus, (2) Cupid, (3) Jove, (4) Marte, (5) Palladium, and (6) Diana, and I would like to give a comprehensive survey of what kinds of adjectives have to be collocated with these pagan gods. Though Troilus and Criseyde appreciate especially Venus and Cupid in their loving each other, they enter into tragedy, abiding the unfortunate destiny. Therefore, the narrator finishes this work, cursing the pagan gods (V.1849-53). However, pagan gods play an important role in *Troilus and Criseyde*, because the characters often pray to pagan gods for love and mercy, just as Palamon, Arcite, and Emelye pray to Venus, Marte, and Diana respectively in "The Knight's Tale."

(1) Venus

"Venus" is, according to the *OED*, "1. *Mythol*. The ancient Roman goddess of beauty and love (esp. sensual love), or the corresponding Greek goddess Aphrodite." and the adjective "blisful" is often chosen for "Venus."[60] "Venus" thus collocated keeps in step with the development of the love affair, because it is often used in Books I, II, and III.

> And also blisful Venus, wel arrayed,
> Sat in hire seventhe hous of hevene tho,
> Disposed wel, and with aspectes payed,
> To helpe sely Troilus of his woo. (II.680-83)

The goddess "Venus" in the seventh heaven helps Troilus. In fact, Troilus supplicates to her for his love,[61] as in "Now blisful Venus helpe, er that I sterve" (I.1014) and "O Venus deere, / Thi myght, thi grace, yheried be it here!" (II.972-73). The blissful state of Venus is collectively described in the Proem of Book III.

> O blisful light of which the bemes clere
> Adorneth al the thridde heven faire!
> O sonnes lief, O Joves doughter deere,
> Plesance of love, O goodly debonaire,
> In gentil hertes ay redy to repaire!
> O veray cause of heele and of gladnesse,
> Iheryed be thy myght and thi goodnesse! (III.1-7)

This may be equivalent to the beautiful description of nature in Books I and II. In this passage, the special emphasis is put upon the comfortable and lovely atmosphere, as in the expression "blisful light." The fact that the noun "light" is used instead of "Venus" may show that the poet emphasises the bright and pleasant atmosphere around Troilus and Criseyde. This kind of expression continues successively in Book III: "blisful Venus" (III.705, 712), "O Venus ful of myrthe" (III.715), and "Venus mene I, the wel-willy planete!" (III.1257).[62] They may symbolise Troilus's spiritual exaltation. In this way, most examples of "Venus" are used by Troilus and the narrator. On the other hand, Pandarus uses it in his swearing: "by the blisful Venus that I serve" (II.234).

Though the scene becomes dark in Books IV and V, the striking examples of "Venus" make their appearance. When Criseyde pledges her loyalty to Troilus, she uses the expression "blisful Venus":

> "And blisful Venus lat me nevere sterve
> Er I may stonde of plesaunce in degree
> To quyte hym wel that so wel kan deserve;" (IV.1661-63).

It seems that this scene somewhat corresponds to the description of the goddess "Venus" in Book V:

> "The brighte Venus folwede and ay taughte

Chapter 3 Collocations

> The wey ther brode Phebus down alighte;
> ....
> Whan that Criseyde unto hire bedde wente
> Inwith hire fadres faire brighte tente," (V.1016-22).

While in the former speech Criseyde tells Troilus that Venus lets them meet again each other, this passage shows Criseyde's appearance before her father Calcas. Though it is natural that "the brighte Venus" should show herself with the coming of night, this expression, connected with the following "faire brighte tente," may suggest the beautiful figure of Criseyde who takes on the attributes of the goddess when she is subsequently wooed and won by Diomede.

The expression of "Venus" in *Troilus and Criseyde*, often used in Books I, II, and III by the narrator and Troilus, shows the supreme bliss of love. On the other hand, it seems that Venus symbolises Criseyde's beautiful figure and her gliding movement in Books IV and V.

(2) Cupid

"Cupid," who is called "the God of Love" by Chaucer, is "1. In Roman Mythology, the god of love, son of Mercury and Venus, identified with the Greek Eros.," according to the *OED*. The attached adjectives are "blisful," "benigne," "heighe," and so on. Troilus is from the first under the influence of Cupid when he is shot and bound by the god. Then Troilus prays to Cupid:

> "Ye stonden in hir eighen myghtily,
> As in a place unto youre vertu digne;
> Wherfore, lord, if my service or I
> May liken yow, so beth to me benigne; (I.428-31)

As is shown in the expressions: "Benigne Love, thow holy bond of thynges" (III.1261) and "Loves heigh servise" (III.1794), Troilus seems to gain Criseyde's heart.[63] Similarly, the narrator addresses Cupid and Venus, as in "Thow lady bryght, the doughter to Dyone, / Thy blynde and wynged sone ek, daun Cupide," (III.1807-08). On the other hand, Pandarus uses "Immortal god" (III.185) and Criseyde "blisful god" (II.834) to describe Troilus's blissful state brought by Cupid.

However, the scene becomes dark in Books IV and V: "O verrey lord, O Love! O god, allas! / That knowest best myn herte and al my thought," (IV.288-89). In Book IV, Troilus invokes Cupid: "verray lord," but Troilus's bright hope is fading in this expression. Then he prays to Cupid, while waiting for Criseyde in Book V.

> Thanne thoughte he thus: "O blisful lord Cupide,
> . . . .
> Wel hastow, lord, ywroke on me thyn ire,
> Thow myghty god, and dredefull for to greve!
> Now mercy, lord! Thow woost wel I desire
> Thi grace moost of alle lustes leeve,
> . . . .
> Now blisful lord, so cruel thow ne be
> Unto the blood of Troie, I preye the, (V.582-600)

Even if he prays to Cupid sincerely, regarding him as "blisful lord" or "myghty god," Cupid ultimately turns out to be "dredefull" and "cruel," because he is not helpful to Troilus.

Thus Cupid controls Troilus almost from the beginning to the end. Troilus enters into the blind world of love, after he is shot and bound by Cupid and he remains blind in love to the end.

(3) Jove

"Jove" is "1. A poetical equivalent of Jupiter, name of the highest deity of the ancient Romans," according to the *OED*. He holds the highest rank among the gods in mythology. The attached adjectives are suitable for his rank: "almyghty," "heighe," "blisful," "cruel," and so on: "As wolde blisful Jove, for his joie, / That I the hadde, wher I wolde, in Troie!" (IV.335-36) and "Thanne seyde he thus: "Almyghty Jove in trone, / That woost of al thys thyng the sothfastnesse," (IV.1079-80).

Jove seems to be paralled to the Christian God, since the adjective "almyghty," usually collocated with Christian God, is attached to the god "Jove." It is only in Book IV that Troilus prays to the god "Jove." When Fortune stands aloof from Troilus in Book IV, he earnestly wishes to enlist the help of "Jove."[64] "Jove," however, does not help Troilus, because Fortune is ruled over by "Jove," as is in the following:

> Fortune, which that permutacioun
> Of thynges hath, as it is hire comitted
> Thorugh purveyaunce and disposicioun
> Of heighe Jove, as regnes shal be flitted
> Fro folk in folk, ... (V.1541-45)

Pandarus uses the noun "Jove" in his swearing, when he tries to persuade Criseyde: "Now, nece myn, by natal Joves feste, / Were I a god, ye sholden sterve as yerne," (III.150-51), in which the adjective "natal" is the only one citation in the *OED* and means "presiding over birthdays or nativities." Perhaps this is an echo of Jesus's nativity, Christmas, when Christians celebrate the birth of the Son of God who brought love to the world.

(4) Marte

"Marte" is "1. The Roman god of war; identified from an early period with the Greek Ares. Often, after Roman practice, used for: Warface, warlike prowess, fortune in war.," according to the *OED*. Since "Marte" holds the high rank as the god of war, the adjectives such as "heigh," "cruel," and "fierse" are attached to him. The narrator uses the following expressions in the Proems of Books III and IV: "fierse Mars" (III.22) and "Thow cruel Mars" (IV.25). It is noted that in Book IV the narrator invokes "Mars" instead of "Venus."

> ... with all his fulle myght,
> By day, he was in Martes heigh servyse —
> This is to seyn, in armes as a knyght; (III.436-38)

The narrator thus describes Troilus's valiant deed and strength in the battle field.[65]

When Pandarus forcibly persuades Criseyde, he says, "O cruel god, O dispitouse Marte, / O Furies thre of helle, on yow I crye!" (II.435-36). Pandarus often invokes many gods, as well as "Marte," but almost all the time only for persuading his companion.

In this way, "Marte" symbolises warlike prowess.

(5) Palladium

"Palladium" is "1. *Gk.* and *Lat. Myth.* The image of the goddess Pallas Athena, in the citadel of Troy, on which the safety of the city was supposed to depend, refuted to have been thence brought to Rome.," according to the *OED*. Troy is said to be in safety as far as the image of the goddess Pallas Athena exists there. Trojans make a point of worshipping at the temple of "Palladium," as is in "The folk of Troie hire observaunces olde, / Palladiones feste for to holde" (I.160-61).

Criseyde, who is forced to go to the Greek camp, worries about her misfortune. Even though she wants to return to Troy, she cannot convince her father of it. Then she is obliged to accept Diomede's love. In this situation, Criseyde prays to Pallas Athena for mercy:

> And er ye gon, thus muche I sey yow here:
> As help me Pallas with hire heres clere,
> If that I sholde of any Grek han routhe,
> It sholde be youreselven, by my trouthe! (V.998-1011)

This passage shows that Criseyde gives her heart to Diomede. Criseyde, who sincerely loved Troilus, is destined to bend to Diomede's will as she shows her good faith to Diomede. It is noted that she prays to Pallas Athena, a guardian goddess of Troy, for help, even though she is on the side of the Greeks. If her prayer is answered, Pallas Athena may reprove the Trojans. How ironic her sincerity is!

Pallas Athena is also shown by "Minerva" who is, according to the

OED, "1. The Roman goddess of wisdom, anciently identified with the Greek Pallas Athene, 'the goddess of wisdom, warlike prowess, and skill in the arts of life.'" Before Troilus writes to Criseyde, he prays to "Minerva."

(6) Diana

"Diana" is "1. An ancient Italian female divinity, the moon-goddess, patroness of virginity and of hunting; subsequently regarded as identical with the Greek Artemis, and so with Oriental deities, which were identified with the latter, e.g. the Artemis or diana of the Ephesians.," according to the *OED*. This goddess symbolises virginity and hunting.[66] The relationship between "Diana" and the Greeks is shown in Cassandre's speech:

> "Diane, which that wroth was and in ire
> For Grekis nolde don hire sacrifice,
> Ne encens upon hire auter sette afire, (V.1464-66)

"Diana" seems to be ignored by Greeks in this poem.

The proper nouns "Cinthia" and "Lucina" are used in *Troilus and Criseyde*. According to the *OED*, "Cinthia" is "the Cynthian goddess, i.e. Artemis or Diana, said to have been born on Mond Cynthus; hence the Moon. A poetic name for the Moon personified as a goddess." Criseyde pledges her loyalty to Troilus, praying to the "Cinthia":

> Now for the love of Cinthia the sheene,
> Mistrust me nought thus causeles, for routhe,
> Syn to be trewe I have yow plight my trouthe. (IV.1608-10)

She takes an oath to Troilus with sincerity. In the same scene, Criseyde prays to the goddess "Lucina": "And trusteth this: that certes, herte swete, / Er Phebus suster, Lucina the sheene, / The Leoun passe out of this Ariete, / I wol ben here, withouten any wene" (IV.1590-93), in which "Lucina" is also connected with "Diana," as the *OED* explains that it is "In Roman mythology, the goddess who presided over childbirth, sometimes identified with Juno or with Diana; hence, a midwife."

Thus Criseyde promises to return to Troy, swearing by the goddess related to "Diana." Goddess such as "Diana" seems to be ignored by the Greeks in Book V. Therefore, we probably cannot find any examples of "Diana" except those in Cassandre's speech.

3.4.3. Supernatural Beings

The word "supernatural" means, according to the *OED*, "That is above nature; belonging to a higher realm or system than that of nature; transcending the powers or the ordinary course of nature." I will closely discuss what part the supernatural beings such as "Fortune" or "destyne" are playing in the development of theme. It should be noted, first of all, that "Fortune" plays a capital role in determining the fate of Troilus and Criseyde in this poem. In this connection, several synonymous words like "aventure," "cas," and "chaunce" will be dealt with.

"Fortune" is "1. Chance, hap, or luck, regarded as a cause of events and changes in men's affaris. Often (after Latin) personified as a goddess, 'the power supposed to distribute the lots of life according to her own humour' (J.); her emblem is a wheel, betokening vicissitude.," according to the *OED*. In other words, Fortune can make a puppet of Troilus and Criseyde. But Troilus's attitude toward "Fortune" is quite different from Criseyde's and Pandarus's. Troilus is hostile to "Fortune" from the beginning of the work, since he believes that "Fortune is my fo"(I.837). Therefore, he may use the adjective "cruel" in Books I and IV. Although he seems to be able to do everything owing to his unparalleled power, he cannot have "Fortune" under his control. On the contrary, he is buffeted by her. Troilus's end is tragic, as a result of his hostility toward "Fortune"; so is Criseyde's, because she leaves herself to "Fortune." How contrastive they are!

Fortune seems to represent a rigid, unyielding predestination. Cupid, on the other hand, appears to represent a freedom of will in Troilus's eyes.

In Book I, Troilus regards "Fortune" as his foe: "Ne al the men that riden konne or go / May of hire cruel whiel the harm withstonde;" (I.838-39). On the other hand, Pandarus regards "Fortune" as "comune": "Woost thow nat wel that Fortune is comune / To everi manere wight in som degree?" (I.843-44). Even though Troilus strives against "Fortune," she remains helpful to him till Book III, as in the following: "But O Fortune, executrice of wierdes, / O influences of thise hevenes hye!" (III.617-18), where Troilus and Criseyde are able to achieve their love affair, under the divine aid of fortune.

But the scene becomes dark in Book IV. In the Proem, the narrator describes "Fortune" who is leaving Troilus: "That [=Fortune] semeth trewest whan she wol bygyle / And kan to fooles so hire song entune / That she hem hent and blent, traitour comune!" (IV.3-5) and "From Troilus she gan hire brighte face / Awey to writhe, and tok of hym non heede," (IV.8-9). The wheel of Fortune goes round and she, standing aloof from him, tries to place him in the lowest position. The narrator, as a matter of course, sympathizes with Troilus, as in "traitour comune." Then Troilus utters curses against "Fortune": "thi foule envye" (IV.275) and "thi gerful violence" (IV.286), while Pandarus pacifies Troilus, using the same adjective "comune" as before: "hire yiftes ben comune" (IV.392). Troilus keeps cursing: "cruel Fortune" (IV.1189) and "Fortune adverse" (IV.1192). Ultimately "the fatal destyne" comes in Book V:

> Aprochen gan the fatal destyne
> That Joves hath in disposicioun,
> And to yow, angry Parcas, sustren thre,
> Committeth, to don execucioun; (V.1-4)

D. S. Brewer comments on this passage: "fatal destyne: 'the inexorable course of events' ... Boethius makes it clear that the course of events in the world, however mysterious or little to one's liking, is ultimately guided by God, here mythologically called Jove."[67] No matter how much Troilus is hostile to Fortune, as the adjectives "cruel" and "adverse" show, Fortune is nevertheless ruled over by the almighty power of God.

In this way, Troilus's life ends tragically, but Criseyde, unlike Troilus, never goes against the will of Fortune. She pledges herself to come back to Troy without fail: "And this may lengthe of yeres naught fordo, / Ne remuable Fortune deface." (IV.1681-82). The adjective "remuable" (which is the *OED*'s first citation and means "a. *Obs. rare.* 1. that may remove (=depart) or be removed; changeable, unstable.") shows the changeable quality of Fortune. Although Criseyde insists that the mutability of Fortune cannot prevent her from returning to Troy, she eventually abandons herself to Fortune, as if Criseyde were "remuable fortune." This figure of Criseyde is just the opposite of that of Troilus who says, "Fortune is my fo" (I.837) and "thanne is my swete fo called Criseyde!"(I.874).

Finally, I will consider what kinds of adjectives are attached to the nouns "aventure," "cas," and "chaunce." The word "aventure" is "That which comes to us, or happens without design; chance, hap, fortune, luck. *Obs.*," according to the *OED*. The attached adjectives are as follows: "good," "goodly," "fair," and "unsely," of which the adjective "good" is most noticeable. In the beginning of Book I, the narrator summarises Troilus's love affair: "In Troilus unsely aventure" (I.35). However, when Troilus falls in love with Criseyde, the narrator uses the adjective "good" instead of "unsely": "It was to hym a right good aventure / To love swich oon,..." (I.368-69). In his conversation with Criseyde, Pandarus suggests Troilus's love for her, by the following synonymous expressions: "fair an aventure" (II.224), "som goodly aventure" (II.281), and "Good aventure" (II.288). Then, when Troilus is in adversity, he sees the happy lovers with envious eyes and says: "O ye loveris, that heigh upon the whiel / Ben set of Fortune, in good aventure," (IV.323-24).

While the noun "aventure" is most often associated with Troilus's love affair, the nouns "cas" and "chaunce" are related to Criseyde's reaction to the love affair. When she first heard Troilus's love to herself from Pandarus, her reaction was so negative as is shown in the adjectives "dredful" and "sory."

> Is this youre reed? Is this my blisful cas?
> ....
> O lady myn, Pallas!
> Thow in this dredful cas for me purveye, (II.422-26)
>
> "A, Lord! what me is tid a sory chaunce! (II.464)

However, the more she recollects Pandarus's speech alone in her chamber, the more she feels inclined to open her heart to Troilus. Therefore, the adjective "newe" is attached to the noun "cas": "And wex somdel astoned in hire thought / Right for the newe cas," (II.603-04). Then we cannot find any examples of "cas" in Book III, but in Book IV, Criseyde laments for "cas" again, using the adjective "sorwful": "But how shul ye don in this sorwful cas?" (IV.794). However, "this sorwful cas" is taken the place of by the expression "newe chaunce" in Book V.

> He goth hym hom, and gan ful soone sende
> For Pandarus, and al this newe chaunce,
> And of this broche, he tolde hym word and ende, (V.1667-69)

This passage shows Criseyde's betrayal.

The fact that the expressions such as "good aventure," "newe chaunce," and "blisful cas" are used in this poem may show how much the characters and the narrator are interested in contingency (which is as a matter of course governed by Fortune). Troilus and Criseyde happen to fall in love with each other, even though their love affair is predestinated. This naturally reminds us of the characters in *The Canterbury Tales* who happen to meet one another "at the Tabard," as "At nyght was come into that hostelrye / Wel nyne and twenty in a compaignye / Of sondry folk, by aventure yfalle / In felaweshipe,..." (I(A)23-26).

3.4.4. Summary

We have discussed the nouns referring to God and pagan gods and their attached adjectives. In regard to the pagan gods, the noun "Venus," often collocated with the adjective "blisful," is deeply connected with the perfection of love. The god "Cupid" manipulates and binds Troilus's heart, even though "blisful" Cupid is metamorphosed into "cruel" Cupid. The noun "Jove," collocated with the adjective "almyghty" which is often attached to the noun "God," is used in Troilus's speech. The noun "Marte," collocated with the adjective "cruel," shows the strength at war. On the other hand, the nouns "Palladium" and "Diana" are closely related to Criseyde. Although she sincerely prays to them, as in "Pallas with hire heres clere" or "Cinthia the sheene," ultimately they disappear, leaving Criseyde alone. In this way, the pagan gods may determine the mental processes and emotional relationships of the protagonists Troilus and Criseyde, especially.

However, the narrator reveals his attitude to the pagan gods in the Epilogue, as in "Lo here, of payens corsed olde rites!" (V.1849). He unveils the merits of the Christian God. The noun "God" in this work seems to be more widely used than that in *Beowulf*, the fact which may be proved by a variety of the adjectives attached to "God," such as "myghty" and "holy" derived from Old English, "blisful" often collocated with the noun "Venus," and "verray" derived from Old French. Furthermore, the fact that the characters often use the noun

"God," collocated with the above adjectives, shows that Chaucer places them in close contact with the Christian God who is more omnipresent than pagan gods. Then Troilus's profound meditation on "purveyanunce" indicates one of the aspects of medieval Christianity.

Lastly, the problems of the supernatural beings have been discussed. It is important for "Fortune" to be ruled over by God. While Troilus, using the adjective "cruel," is hostile to Fortune, Pandarus, who takes a relative position tries to soothe Troilus by saying: "Fortune is comune." Troilus's wilful attitude to Fortune may have caused his tragedy. Fortune is nothing but a "fo" to him. As for Criseyde, she leaves herself to fate, as if she had the same temperament as "Fortune." Her attitude is in a marked contrast to Troilus's. For this reason, it may safely be said that "Fortune" is regarded as "a cause of events and changes in men's affairs"[68] under the almighty power of God. Although Troilus dies a tragic death, however, the narrator does not leave him alone, but lets him ascend into a heavenly world. Herein lies Chaucer's sympathy towards Troilus.

Thus the world of Troilus changes from that of pagan gods to that of the Christian God. "Providence" means that God will provide for us no matter what path we take; perhaps "Providence" allows Troilus to ascend to the heavenly world. The following passage may be enough to show this fact:

> And to that sothfast Crist, that starf on rode,
> With al myn herte of mercy evere I preye,
> And to the Lord right thus I speke and seye:
> Thow oon, and two, and thre, eterne on lyve,
> That regnest ay in thre, and two, and oon,
> Uncircumscript, and al maist circumscrive,
> Us from visible and invisible foon
> Defende, and to thy mercy, everichon,
> So make us, Jesus, for thi mercy, digne,
> For love of mayde and moder thyn benigne.
> Amen. (V.1860-70)

Notes

1   Michio Masui, *Studies in Chaucer* (in Japanese) (Tokyo, 1973), p. 115.

2   J. R. Firth, "Modes of Meaning," in *Papers in Linguistics 1934-1951* (London, 1969), p. 195.

3   Michio Masui, *Studies in Chaucer*, p. 114.

4   Michio Masui, "A Mode of Word-Meaning in Chaucer's Language of Love," *Studies in English Literature*, English Number 1967, pp. 113-26 (The English Literary Society of Japan, 1967), p. 123.

5   All *Beowulf* citations are from Fr. Klaeber, ed., *Beowulf and the Fight at Finnsburg* (Boston: D. C. Heath and Company, 1922, 1950^3).

6   Davis Taylor, *Style and Character in Chaucer's Troilus* (Michigan, 1969), p. 24.

7   Kittredge, in his *Chaucer and His Poetry*, states that "he (Troilus) is a gallant warrior, second only to the unmatchable Hector in prowess" (p. 122). Edwin J. Howard also says that "Chaucer by no means makes Troilus out as lacking in masculinity; he specifically tells us that Troilus is so highly esteemed as a warrior that he is considered to be Hector the second" (*Geoffrey Chaucer*, p. 112). But they consider the image of Troilus just as Pandarus and Criseyde do.

8   Charles Muscatine, *Chaucer and the French Tradition* (California, 1957), p. 133.

9   This kind of expression is called 'contentio.' See Michio Masui's *Studies in Chaucer*, p. 223.

10   In "The Knight's Tale," when Arcite speaks his noble dying words, he says to Emelye, "Fare wel, my sweets foo, myn Emelye!" (A 2780). Conventional as it may be, it shows Arcite's emotion clearly. Emelye was the existence nearest to him, because he could gain her heart, but she was the existence farthest from him, because he was destined to die.

11   Muscatine, p. 154.

12   The characters of Troilus and Criseyde, from the angle of Troilus's 'trouthe' and Criseyde's 'slydynge', are stated by I. L. Gordon:"Where Troilus exemplifies 'trouthe' in love, albeit in a 'false good', Criseyde, for all that she 'menes wel', exemplifies, both as agent and victim, the 'slydynge corage' inevitable in one whose values are the values of this 'slydynge' world." in her *The Double Sorrow of Troilus* (Oxford, 1970), p. 143.

13   D. S. Brewer, *Chaucer in His Time* (London, 1963), p. 198.

14   The Supplement of *the Oxford English Dictionary* says "The power of entering into the experience of or understanding objects or emotions outside ourselves" and the quotation of 1909 Academy 17 Aug. 209/2 says that "... One had to 'feel oneself in it' (: the object of contemplation)... This mental process he called by the name of *Einfülung*, or, as it has been translated,

Empathy."

15   In *Sir Orfeo*, for example, the buildings of court are represented by the following beautiful and gorgeous expressions: "Amidde þe lend a castel he siȝe, / Riche and real, and wonder heiȝe. / Al be vtmast wal / Was clere and schine as cristal; / An hundred tours þer were about, / Degiselich, and bataild stout; / ... No man may telle, no þenche in þouȝt / Þe riche werk þat þer was wrouȝt; / Bi al þing him þink þat it is / Þe proude court of Paradis" (357-76). This quotation is from *Fourteenth Century Verse and Prose* edited by K. Sisam (Oxford at the Clarendon Press, 1921).

16   An example of "knotte" is found in Book III: "The goodlihede or beaute which that kynde / In any other lady hadde yset / Kan nought the montance of a knotte unbynde, / Aboute his herte, of al Criseydes net." (III.1730-33), where Troilus is bound by Criseyde's net.

17   In Old English elegiac poetry such as "The Wanderer" and "The Seafarer," we see the remarkable contrast between the past grandeur and the present wretchedness. Akiyuki Jimura, "The Anglo-Saxon Poem "The Seafarer" and Ezra Pound's "The Seafarer" – Similarities and differences," *ERA* New Series, The English Research Association of Hiroshima, Department of English, Hiroshima University, Vol. 1, No. 2, pp. 1-18. Winter 1981, pp. 10-12.

18   This kind of retrospection is similar to Wordsworth's imagination. Wordsworth, in "Lines," describes "These beauteous forms" (23), when he remembers in his library the magnificent scenery of nature around "Tintern Abbey."(William Wordsworth, *Poerical Works* edited by Thomas Hutchinson (London, 1904).) While Wordsworth pictures the great nature alone in his library, Troilus remembers his past joy, in front of the very object that is empty and lonely. And it is a definite fact that Wordsworth translated ll. 519-686 of Book V in Chaucer's *Troilus and Criseyde*.

19   Another noun "temple" collocates with the physical adjective "large," as in "In thilke large temple on every side" (I.185).

20   Benson, *The Riverside Chaucer*, p. 829.

21   W. W. Skeat, *The Complete Works of Geoffrey Chaucer* 7 vols., (Oxford at the Clarendon Press, 1894, 1899, 1926, 1972). See the sixth volume.

22   D. S. Brewer and L. E. Brewer (eds.), *Troilus and Criseyde* (abridged) (London, 1969), p. 104.

23   We find a good example: "In beaute first so stood she, makeles" (I.172), where the adjective "makeles," the *OED*'s third citation, means "Without an equal; matchless, peerless." However, it is possible that this adjective may be interpreted into "mateless, husbandless" which is the *OED*'s second definition.

24   The *MED*.

25   Brewer, *Chaucer in His Time*, p. 150.

26   E. M. W. Tillyard, *The Elizabethan World Picture* (London, 1943), p.

94.
27   Davis Taylor critically comments on this expression: "The last line of the stanza in its context may also strike one as rather simple, even simple-minded since the personification of verses is both effusively sentimental and impossibly literal." (*Style and Character in Chaucer's Troilus* (Michigan, 1969), p. 190.)
28   Benson, *The Riverside Chaucer*, p. 1031.
29   Michio Masui, *Chaucer no Sekai* (Tokyo, 1976), p. 134. I have translated Masui's Japanese text into English.
30   Albert C. Baugh (ed.), *Chaucer's Major Poetry* (London, 1963), p. 180.
31   Benson, *The Riverside Chaucer*, p. 1051.
32   See the *OED*.
33   See the *OED*.
34   See 11. 183-7 in Book I. Further, we see a following example: three characters Arcite, Palamon and Emelye in "The Knight's Tale" perform such a ceremony respectively.
35   See the *OED*.
36   See the *OED*.
37   See the *OED*.
38   Another example is as follows: Diomede asks Criseyde twice whether or not "the Grekis gise" is "straunge" (V.120, V.860). This might be his technique to gain her heart.
39   In *The House of Fame*, the noun "fame" collocates with the following adjectives: "wikke," "unfamous," "good," "worse," and "grete."
40   W. H. Hudson, *An Outline History of English Literature* (London, 1966), 26.
41   Taylor, p. 254.
42   Masui, "A Mode of Word-Meaning in Chaucer's Language of Love," p. 115.
43   *Ibid.*
44   Benson (1989: 1031). Cf. Robinson (1957: 818).
45   D. S. Brewer and L. E. Brewer, p. 128.
46   The text of *Sir Orfeo* is from K. Sisam, ed., *Fourteenth Century Verse and Prose* (Oxford, 1921). This description is, as a matter of course, conventional. But it is interesting that the physical adjective "hot" and the emotional adjective "miri" are used at the same time. The word "miri" usually shows the joyous state of the human beings. According to the *OED*, it may mean "of weather, climate, atmospheric conditions, etc: 'pleasant', 'fine'. Of a wind: 'Favourable'."Since the mind of human beings will judge whether or not it is "pleasant" and "favourable," it is the emotional expression.
47   R. P. Tripp, Jr., "On the Continuity of English Poetry between *Beowulf*

and Chaucer" (1-21) in *POETICA* Vol. 6 (Tokyo, 1976), 9. See also the following two articles: C. L. Wrenn, "On the Continuity of English Poetry," *A Study of Old English Literature* (New York, 1967), 17-34, and L. C. Gruber, "The Wanderer and Arcite: Isolation and the Continuity of the English Elegiac Mode," *Four Papers for Michio Masui* (Denver, 1972), 1-10.

48   Taylor, p. 244.
49   The noun 'May' is the *OED*'s first citation.
50   Taylor, pp. 252-54.
51   D. S. Brewer and L. E. Brewer, p. 108.
52   When Criseyde is charmed by Troilus's knightly figure more and more, she falls asleep, listening to the nightingale's chirpings. This male nightingale comes near to Criseyde's room and whispers sweet nothings to her, as if this nightingale were Troilus: "A nyghtyngale, upon a cedir grene / Under the chambre wal ther as she lay, / Ful loude song ayein the moone shene," (II.918-20). This passage corresponds to the one which shows that Arcite in "The Knight's Tale" is dying for Emelye, singing the song of spring: "And loude he song ayeyn the sonne shene" (I(A)1509), where the noun 'sonne' is used instead of the noun 'moone'.
53   D. S. Brewer, *Chaucer in His Time*, p. 204.
54   My earlier papers are as follows: "The Characterisations of Troilus and Criseyde through Adjectives in Chaucer's *Troilus and Criseyde* — "trewe as stiel" and "slydynge of corage"—," *PHOENIX* 15 (1979), Department of English, Hiroshima University, 101-22, "Chaucer's Depiction of Courtly Manners and Customs through Adjectives in *Troilus and Criseyde*," *Philologia* 19 (1987) Association of English Studies, Mie University, 1-26, and "Chaucer's Description of Nature through Adjectives in *Troilus and Criseyde*," *English and English Teaching* 2 (1997), Department of English, Faculty of School Education, Hiroshima University, 57-69.
55   M. Masui, "A Mode of Word-Meaning in Chaucer's Language of Love," p. 115.
56   This word, literally translated from Latin "omnipotens," is "orig. and in the strict sense used as an attribute of the Deity, and joined to God or other title," according to the *OED*.
57   This also may be a convention, judging from Brewer's statement: "... for centuries before Chaucer, as for centuries after, Christian poets also referred to God himself as Jove or Jupiter. It was a well-known convention" (*Introduction to Troilus and Criseyde*, xxxix.).
58   See also III.60, IV.1086, and V.707.
59   Chaucer himself is confusing "God" with "god" for poetic effect. Troilus would have been unable to pray to the Christian God — Christianity did not exist in ancient B.C. E. Greece. It is Chaucer who is likely contrasting the pagan Pandarus who thinks love is simple and largely physical. Troilus

lives for love that permeates his physical and emotional being. Christian love is supposed to be forgiving of all faults — as is the Christian God and His Son. However, Troilus is caught by his pagan culture temporarily. His society is ruled by Jove, and Criseyde has surrendered to Fortune, and he cannot escape that fact. Interestingly, Fortune is the handmaiden to the Christian god. She was medieval Christian's attempt to explain inescapable events and stands for "predestination" while Jesus seems to represent "free will."

60 The examples are found in the following: I.1014, II.234, II.680, III.1, III.705, III.712, IV.1661, and V.1250.

61 In "The Knight's Tale," Palamon also prays to Venus for his love. But it should be noted that Troilus prays to Cupid and Jove as well as Venus.

62 The adjective "wel-willy" is the *OED*'s first citation and means "a. *obs. exc. dial.* Full of good will, benevolent, well-disposed, generous."

63 It is noted that in the end of Book III the narrator attaches such an adjective "benigne" to Troilus as is usual with Cupid: "Benigne he was to ech in general" (III.1802), where the adjective "benigne" is the *OED*'s earliest citation and means "2. Exhibiting or manifesting kindly feeling in look, gesture, or action; bland, gently, mild."

64 In "The Knight's Tale," Arcite invokes "Juppiter" when he dies: "And Juppiter so wys my soule gye" (I(A) 2786) and "So Juppiter have of my soule part" (I(A) 2792).

65 It is "Marte" to whom Arcite prays for his victory in both fight and love. "Marte" gives him the victory only in fight.

66 The typical example is shown in "The Knight's Tale." Emelye prays to Diana for mercy and follows her.

67 D. S. Brewer and L. E. Brewer, p. 124.

68 The *OED*.

CHAPTER 4

Grammar

4.0. Introduction

Words with the negative prefix *un-* (which I will call "un"-words hereafter), impersonal constructions, and negative expressions play an important part in Chaucer's texts, to say nothing of other Middle English writings. The scholars only deal with the syntactic or grammatical use of them, but no one has yet adequately explained the meanings of those expressions in the literary works. This chapter investigates those grammatical expressions used in both the speeches of the main characters and the narrative structures in Chaucer's works.

4.1. "Un"-words

When we read Chaucer's texts, we often encounter negative expressions, not only as sentences, clauses, phrases, and words, but also as morphemes. In this section, we would like to concentrate on the negative elements of words, especially the "un"-words in "The Clerk's Tale," where the negative expressions seem to be used frequently.

As we see in the Tables,[1] the work which shows the second highest frequency of negatives in *The Canterbury Tales* is "The Clerk's Tale." In this work, the "un"-words are used fifteen times: "unnethe" three times, "unnethes" twice, "unworthy" twice, and the following words once: "uncerteyn," "unlyk," "undigne," "untressed," "unreste," "unsad," "untrewe," and "undiscreet." While Griselda describes herself as "undigne" and "unworthy" in her humble speeches to Walter, the narrator describes her as "untressed" and "unreste" (the word "unreste" is not an adjective and it should be noted that it is used of a hypothetical situation rather than of Griselda's own case). Some important "un"-words seem to be thus connected with the characterisation of Griselda. We would like to see briefly how effectively the "un"-words, especially "unsad," "untrewe," and "undiscreet," are used in "The Clerk's Tale."

In "The Clerk's Tale" there seems to be a conflict or tension between the steadfast and the changeable types of people. The "sad" people comment critically regarding the "unsad" and "stormy" people, using the "un"-words continually.

> "O stormy peple! Unsad and evere untrewe!
> Ay undiscreet and chaungynge as a fane! (995-96)

As we shall see, this passage may show that the would-be wise and serious persons make an ironical remark at the changeable nature of the "rude" people who are liable to change easily. It should be noted that we have three "un"-words in this quotation: "unsad," "untrewe," and "undiscreet." Now we do not forget that there exist the stems or bases of the "un"-words, i.e. "sad," "trewe," and "discreet." These adjectives, the bases of the "un"-words seem to play an important part in this work, to say nothing of the "un"-words themselves. In this chapter, we would like to investigate the meaning of these value words, in order to understand the real meanings of the "un"-words: "unsad," "untrewe," and "undiscreet."

4.1.1. "sad"

To begin with, we quote the *OED*'s definition. We find the citations of Chaucer's texts in the following four items.

First, as for the meaning of the adjective "sad" the *OED* says "†1. Having had one's fill; satisfied; sated, weary or tired (of something). Const. *of* (in OE. *gen.*) or *inf.*" and it quotes Chaucer's "Canon's Yeoman's Prologue and Tale" 324 as the ninth instance. Second, the

OED says "†2. Settled, firmly established in purpose or condition; steadfast, firm, constant. *Obs.*" and it quotes Chaucer's *Boece* iii. pr. x. 70 as the fifth instance. Third, the *OED* says "†4. Orderly and regular in life; of trustworthy character and judgement; grave, serious. Often coupled with *wise* or *discreet*. *Obs.*" and quotes Chaucer's "Man of Law's Tale" 37 as the second instance. Fourth, the *OED* says "5. a. Of persons, their feelings or dispositions: Sorrowful, mournful" and quotes Chaucer's *The Romaunt of the Rose* 211 as the earliest instance. However, this quotation seems uncertain, because I find the word *fade* instead of *sad* in the same line of Benson's edition. Instead, the *MED* quotes the line 552 of "The Clerk's Tale" which shows the meaning of "expressive of sorrow," as is shown in the following paragraph.

The second and third meanings of "sad" in the *OED* seem to be the most suitable in "The Clerk's Tale," because the main character Griselda is characterised by the steadfastness and the wisdom and "sad" is often collocated with "stidefast" and "constant." We also remember the "un"-words quoted already: "Unsad and evere untrewe! Ay undiscreet ..."

Although the *OED* does not quote Chaucer's "The Clerk's Tale," the *MED* cites several instances. First, in the item of "2(c) of a person: firm, steadfast; constant; faithful, righteous;..." we find "The Clerk's Tale" 1047 as the fourth instance. Second, in the item of "4a. Of a person, group of nuns: (a) grave, sober, serious; dignified, solemn; discreet, wise; stern; ..." we find "The Clerk's Tale" 754 as the second instance. Third, in the item of "4b. (a) Of one's disposition, demeanor, countenance, etc.: sober, serious, grave; stern; ..." we find "The Clerk's Tale" 693 as the third instance. Fourth, in the item of "4b. (d) of discretion, learning, teaching, etc.: prudent, sober; ... in — wise, in a sober manner;..." we find "The Clerk's Tale" 237 as the earliest instance. Last, in the item of "5. (b) expressive of sorrow;" we find

"The Clerk's Tale" 552 as the second instance. In these instances of the *MED*, most meanings are related to "constant" and "sober," except the last one.

Now we would like to see the usage of the adjective "sad" and its derivatives in "The Clerk's Tale." In order to describe Griselda's stable mind, the adjective "sad" is used: "But thogh this mayde tendre were of age, / Yet in the brest of hire virginitee / Ther was enclosed rype and sad corage;" (218-20). Her stability is also shown in her countenance when she listens to Walter's speech: "And doun upon hir knes she gan to falle, / And with sad contenance kneleth stille, / Til she had herd what was the lordes wille" (292-94). Griselda's general demeanour is connected with her humility.

Walter tries to tempt her "sad" and patient character, because she is too constant to be a typical woman: "This markys in his herte longeth so / To tempte his wyf, hir sadnesse for to knowe," (451-52) where the noun form of "sad" is used. Thus Griselda does not change her face, even when she is going to depart from her beloved daughter. Instead, Griselda embraces her daughter with the serious and stable countenance, as "and hir barm this litel child she leyde / With ful sad face, and gan the child to blisse, / And lulled it, and after gan it kisse" (551-53). While the adjective "sad" is interpreted as "expressive of sorrow" by the *MED*, Donaldson adds a gloss to this "sad": "unmoved."[2] Donaldson's interpretation seems the better one when we consider Griselda's constant and unchangeable nature. The narrator then explains the patient and enduring nature of Griselda's character, as in "Wel myghte a mooder thanne han cryd "allas!" / But nathelees so sad stidefast was she / That she endured al adversitee," (563-65) where the word "sad" is interpreted as an adjective meaning "constant" by Donaldson[3] and as an adverb meaning "firmly" by Benson[4] and Davis.[5]

Though Walter tries to know whether Griselda's appearance and words have changed, he cannot find her emotional and changeable nature at all: "... he nevere hire koude fynde / But evere in oon ylike sad and kynde" (601-02), where the adjective "sad," which means "stable," is paired with the adjective "kynde," which means "having natural (good) qualities." Thus her stable nature is connected with her natural goodness. Walter wonders about her tranquil and serene attitude, because Griselda is so stable and constant even when he tries to detach her son as well as her daughter from her:

> This markys wondred, evere lenger the moore,
> Upon hir pacience, and if that he
> Ne hadde soothly knowen therbifoore
> That parfitly hir children loved she,
> He wolde have wend that of som subtiltee,
> And of malice, or for crueel corage,
> That she hadde suffred this with sad visage. (687-93)

The last line of the passage may indicate that Walter regards her as a suffering figure, but Griselda seems to have the same "sad" contenance as before.

Even though Walter proposes to get a divorce from Griselda, she does not change her mood at all. Instead, she obeys her cruel Fate, as in "she, ylike sad for everemo," (754). Then she asks Walter not to make his new wife endure hardships as she did. Griselda's statement then makes Walter think she has endured his cruelty up until this time, only to fail. So Walter tries to test Griselda's true nature again, but he finds she is always "sad and constant as a wal" (1047). Finally, she holds her children "sadly" (which means "firmly" here) after she knows the truth:

> And in hire swough so sadly holdeth she
> Hire children two, whan she gan hem t'embrace,
> That with greet sleighte and greet difficultee
> The children from hire arm they gonne arace. (1100-03)

Then she loses her senses.

In this way, the meaning of "sad" in the noun "sadnesse," the adjective "sad," and the adverb "sadly" always shows Griselda's constant and stable mind, even though in Present-day English it may mean the emotional state of mind.

4.1.2. "trewe"

The *OED* defines the meaning of the adjective "trewe": "2. In more general sense: Honest, honourable, upright, virtuous, trustworthy (*arch.*); free from deceit, sincere, truthful (cf. 3d); of actions, feelings, etc., sincere, unfeigned ...." and quotes an instance of Chaucer's texts (*L.G.W.* 464 (*Balade*)) as the sixth instance. This lexical meaning is reflected in "The Clerk's Tale," but when we see the details of the context, we find a subtly different meaning from the adjective "sad."

First, we are told that Griselda is not only "sad" but also "trewe" to Walter:

> She was ay oon in herte and visage,
> And ay the forther that she was in age
> The moore trewe, if that it were possible,
> She was to hym in love, and moore penyble. (711-14)

We understand that the virtue "truth" becomes greater with the age, unlike the virtue "sadnesse" which always shows her unchangeable nature. The virtue "sadnesse" does not become greater, but it is always the same with Griselda.

Unlike the adjective "sad," the value word "trewe" is used in Griselda's speech which is spoken when Walter reveals his marriage with a new wife. She says: "... I yaf to yow my maydenhede, / And am your trewe wyf, ..." (837-38). Then the narrator states that men do not have "trewe" character half as much as women.

> Ther kan no man in humblesse hym acquite
> As womman kan, ne kan been half so trewe
> As wommen been, but it be falle of newe. (936-38)

So here "trewe" is used to describe the general characteristics of women, though in *Troilus and Criseyde* Troilus is depicted as "trewe as stiel," which is, as a matter of course, a traditional expression used to emphasise Troilus's faithful character. Again in "The Clerk's Tale," the adjective "trewe" is used to show Griselda's true nature; she vows to Walter: "To love you best with al my trewe entente" (973). Even when he asks her to help his marriage with the new wife, she is glad to help him with all her heart. She is always "trewe" to Walter.

Last, we will deal with the noun "trouthe," which is used only, once in Walter's speech: "As for youre trouthe and for youre obeisance, / Noght for youre lynage, ne for youre richesse;" (794-95) where Griselda's virtues "trouthe," "obeisance," and "goodnesse" are emphasised, with the negation of the superficial values of "lynage" and "richesse." "Trouthe" does not always need lineage and riches, especially in the case of Griselda's "trouthe."

In this way, unlike "sad," which sometimes describes the general characteristics of women, the adjective "trewe," is often used in the speeches, especially in Griselda's, and also emphasises mainly her true and faithful attitude to Walter.

4.1.3. "discreet"

The adjective "discreet" means "showing discernment or judgement in the guidance of one's own speech and action; judicious, prudent, circumspect, cautious; often *esp.* that can be silent when speech would be inconvenient," according to the *OED*. This definition refers to the "discreet" nature of persons and speech, action, and the like. The *MED* supports the *OED*'s definition, adding the third item (c)? civil, polite, courteous. Griselda's wise and deliberate way of speech is described by the adjective "discreet": "... so discreet and fair of eloquence / So digne of reverence" (410-11). The narrator then explains that Griselda behaves much the same way as before, even when she lives secretly in her parental home:

> No wonder is, for in hire grete estaat
> Hire goost was evere in pleyn humylitee;
> No tendre mouth, noon herte delicaat,
> No pompe, no semblant of roialtee,
> But ful of pacient benygnytee,
> Discreet and pridelees, ay honurable,
> And to hire housbonde evere meke and stable. (925-31)

She is as modest and humble as she had been when she was Walter's wife. Winny supports Griselda's constant modesty, when he explains that "discreet and pridelees" are synonymous "self-effacing and modest."[6]

To sum up, these adjectives "sad," "trew," and "discreet" show Griselda's magnificent nature which does not change at all. The virtues of human beings, especially Griselda's, are especially emphasised in this work. So when the negative prefix "un" is attached to these stems, it makes the meaning of the stems heighten the effect contrastively. The meaning of the "un"-words symbolises and represents the "stormy," "unsad," and noisy people in this work. Ultimately, Griselda's stable nature is emphasised. She endures as usual, even though she is under unfavourable conditions.

4.2. Impersonal constructions

The number of impersonal constructions has decreased and fallen greatly during the historical period from Old English through Middle English to Modern English, as is shown in van der Gaaf's pioneer study.[7] Especially, the use of impersonal constructions in Middle English has been studied by modern grammarians, such as Traugott, who make the best use of new linguistic theories.[8] Willy Elmer has made a further study of impersonal constructions, using the technical term "subjectless constructions."[9] This section aims at recognizing how organically the impersonal constructions are used in Chaucer's *Troilus and Criseyde*, after we consider the general characteristics of the impersonal constructions. There are some primary requisites to discuss the syntactic features. One of them is that we need to compare Chaucer's use of impersonal constructions with his contemporaries' use and/or the authors' (or the poets') use before and after Chaucer's lifetime, when we discuss Chaucer's syntactically special use of impersonal constructions. Another is that we need to study and analyse syntactically the impersonal constructions in all of Chaucer's works, and furthermore, since Chaucer did not write his works at the same time, we need to investigate his use of impersonal constructions diachronically according to the chronological order of his works. In the present stage of this study, this kind of syntactic aspect will be a further research project. Here we will deal with the main matter and problem of some concern, namely why Chaucer used the impersonal constructions in *Troilus and Criseyde*.

4.2.1. The general characteristics of the impersonal constructions
When we look at the semantic features of impersonal constructions, i.e. the synonymous sets of impersonal verbs, we should make good use of Nakao's classification.[10] The classified items are as follows:

(1) Verbs which refer to 'happening, seeming, possibility'
(2) Verbs which refer to 'lack, sufficiency, need'
(3) Verbs which refer to 'psychological and physiological phenomena'
(4) Verbs which refer to '(dis)pleasure, preference'
(5) Verbs which refer to 'availing, fitness, relation.'

There are at least two problems with this classification. One of them is that Nakao includes the verbs of judgement such as "seme" or "thynke" in item (1) which shows 'happening or occurrence.'[11] We can put these verbs of judgement into item (5) which shows 'appropriateness or relation'. The other is that we should group items (3) and (4) under one item indicating 'psychological or mental process.'[12]

Thus we will revise Nakao's classification as follows:

(1) Verbs which refer to 'happening or occurrence'
(2) Verbs which refer to 'necessity, need, deficiency'

(3) Verbs which refer to 'appropriateness or relation'
(4) Verbs which refer to 'psychological or mental process'
   (a) 'pleasure or displeasure'
   (b) 'sorrow, pain, complaint, repentance'
   (c) 'dream'

In item (1), there exists the factor governed by contingency, i.e. the supernatural phenomenon in the uppermost part and it influences every phenomenon of nature. Here we can deal with the natural phenomena which tend to be avoided by previous studies.[13] Item (2) includes the impersonal verbs which mean not only physical necessities, needs, and deficiencies but also emotional ones, and ultimately it corresponds to item (4) which denotes psychological or mental processes. So there is something in common between (2) and (4), but item (2) simply means necessities, needs and deficiencies in a literal sense. Item (3) indicates the standards of judgement. Here we will discuss what is appropriate in a certain situation. In item (4), we deal with purely psychological aspects of internal mental processes, which would be divided into the following three subclasses: (a) 'pleasure and displeasure,' (b) 'sorrow, pain, complaint, and repentance,' and (c) 'dream.'

We will add to the aforesaid classification some syntactic features of impersonal constructions. The verbs which show happening and occurrence do not possess an objective case, since they are limited to the contingent instances of natural phenomena. But the verb 'fal' is sometimes used in the structure 'V + O' or 'it + V + O.' In item (2), the verbs may possess an objective case or not. However, in item (3), the verbs carry an objective case more often than (2), and when the verbs completely show the internal mental thinking of human beings, most of the verbs anticipate an objective case. The more internalized the impersonal verbs are, the more they need to have an objective case as Experiencer.[14] Then the objective case, with the change of the times, seems to be subjectivalized[15] as the subject of the sentence.[16]

The constructions which are not subjectivalized are those which belong to category (1), the verbs which follow the impersonal 'it' in Modern English. The typical example of this usage is the impersonal 'it' which shows 'weather' etc.

We can find more examples of impersonal constructions showing emotion than any other. They indicate the psychological mental processes of characters. In a certain internal or emotional process, we do not need the nominative case of personal (pro)noun before or behind the main verb, but we must consider how the thing is felt and perceived by the person represented by the objective case of personal (pro)noun. When we do not need the objective case at all, i.e. in the case of the item (1), we do not admit the necessity of the objective case from the first and then the external phenomena govern the whole sentence. Generally speaking, when the impersonal construction is preferred, we would think the thing by outside help rather than by our own ability, i.e. we would consider that heteronomy should be better than autonomy. The use of impersonal constructions, then, becomes a politer expression, because it holds others in high esteem. We prefer an objective way of thinking to a subjective way of thinking. Namely, the expression that represents objectivity or universality is preferred in the use of impersonal constructions. Thus, the impersonal constructions showing mainly the internal structures of human beings are not likely to be presented as the subjective expression where the human beings are the subject, but as the objective expression, implying the estimation of others.

It is not so easy to distinguish the personal construction from the impersonal construction, though we have seen the characteristics of the impersonal constructions in the above paragraphs. Chaucer's use of these constructions is sometimes at random, according to the editions of Chaucer's works. For example, a certain edition says: "he thoughte," while another says: "hym thoughte."[17] We cannot easily decide which is in fact used by Chaucer himself. However, since Shigehiko Toyama admits a difference between these constructions[18] we would like to forward the discussion on the assumption that there exists even in some measure a difference between these constructions.[19]

Ralph W. V. Elliott, comparing Chancer's impersonal constructions with the personal constructions, indicates that Chaucer's use of impersonal constructions enriches Chaucer's "expressiveness." He illustrates the verb 'long' as an example. Compare, for example, the impersonal construction:

> 'So soore longeth me
> To eten of the smale peres grene,' (Merch T. 2332-33)

with the personal construction:

> Thanne longen folk to goon on pilgrimages. (Gen. Prol. 12)

The latter denotes a straightforward desire, but the former, by making the desire to eat green pears the implied subject of the sentence and making the 'real' subject (*me*) the object, connotes an element of helplessness, a passive surrender to physical or psychological urges, which fit with appropriate irony into the strategy of 'this fresshe May' attempting to deceive her blind, doting husband.[20]

In this way, if Chaucer used the impersonal constructions consciously, as Elliott says, it would not be useless to investigate the effects of these constructions, in accordance with the context and contents of *Troilus and Criseyde*.

Now we will discuss Chaucer's use of impersonal constructions which show happening and occurrence, and then we may see an aspect of Chaucer's expressive arts of language.

4.2.2. Happening and occurrence in *Troilus and Criseyde*

We find the following impersonal verbs: "befal," "hap," "betide," "fal," etc. in this construction. These verbs are usually used when the narrator presents an important event to the readers or the audience. Especially it should be noted that the natural description keeps in perfect harmony with the happening and occurrence in this work. This way of Chaucer's description, as is seen in the beginning of "The General Prologue" to *The Canterbury Tales*, seems to be one of the characteristics of Chaucer's art.

In Book I, when the air is full of spring in April, various ceremonies are held under the influence of the Palladium, which protects Troy and Troians. This happening, shown by the impersonal construction, is harmonised with the warm and fine weather of April (I.155-57). Keeping in step with this occurrence, Troilus, who has always been despising lovers around him, is suddenly enslaved by Criseyde's beauty, as the narrator shows us a general idea, using the impersonal construction, and he states that the God of Love unites everything (I.236-38).

> And upon cas bifel that thorugh a route
> His eye percede, and so depe it wente,
> Til on Criseyde it smot, and ther it stente. (I.271-73)

Troilus falls in love with Criseyde at first sight. Here Troilus does not look at Criseyde consciously, but he turns his eyes upon her by chance. This contingency symbolises the general truth that love will break out in spite of a man.

In Book II, the impersonal construction is used of Pandarus, who goes between Troilus and Criseyde.

> Whan Phebus doth his bryghte bemes sprede
> Right in the white Bole, it so bitidde,
> ....
> That Pandarus, for al his wise speche,
> Felt ek his part of loves shotes keene,
> That, koude he nevere so wel of lovyng preche,
> It made his hewe a-day ful ofte greene.
> So shop it that hym fil that day a teene
> In love,... (II.54-62)

Though the impersonal construction is harmonised with the magnificent description of nature in May, Pandarus's pains of heart become acute, because nobody knows how the relationship between Troilus and Criseyde changes in the world. The date is 3 May, the day which suggests that a certain ominous occurrence may happen, as many critics state.[21] Though May is the season of love, as in "fresshe May," and we, as a matter of course, expect something good and buoyant, the impersonal construction here suggests that the love between Troilus and Criseyde is not so easily performed in the future, because Pandarus feels more and more "a teene in love" in the unlucky day, 3 May. In this way, the use of the impersonal constructions in Book II shows Pandarus's objective position that he takes pains to go between them and unite them by love.

In Book III, Troilus successfully meets Criseyde by Pandarus's continuous efforts and they are beginning to have an enjoyable time. When the affair is going well, Pandarus plans to make them have a clandestine meeting with each other, i.e. Pandarus intends to let them come to his house and make a good night of it.

>That it bifel right as I shal yow telle:
>That Pandarus,...
>.....................
>Hadde out of doute a tyme to it founde, (III.511-18)

In this passage, the impersonal verb "bifel" represents that a most appropriate moment has just come to Pandarus's hands by chance. The evidence that Pandarus's planning is governed by contingency is witnessed by the following atmosphere of nature: the threatening look of the sky. Despite her uncle's invitation, Criseyde says: 'It reyneth; lo, how sholde I gon?" (III.562). The rain is, of course, governed by an impersonal expression, which may suggest that something will happen in some way, though Criseyde does not know what will occur to her. Masui states that "it is the scrupulous care of Chancer who intends to consider the organic function of the natural phenomena in this poem that Chaucer brings natural phenomena into the world of human beings."[22] In other words, we may say that the natural phenomena created by the impersonal expression have a great and subtle influence on the characters in this work. Availing herself of this opportunity, Criseyde understands that she will stay at her uncle's house.

> And syn it ron, and al was on a flod,
> She thoughte, "...
> ....
> For hom to gon, it may nought wel bitide." (III.640-44)

Then, after they went to bed by twos and threes, it rained heavily and ceaselessly: "And evere mo so sterneliche it ron, I And blew therwith so wondirliche loude, / That wel neigh no man heren other koude" (III.677-79). The heavy wind and weather, concealing the existence of the main characters, seem to echo and reflect the exalted feelings of Troilus and Criseyde before their secret meeting. We can see that the natural phenomena of rain expressed by the impersonal constructions produce a great and favourable effect upon the human beings in this work.

In this way, in Books I, II and III, the impersonal constructions which show the happening and occurrence, keeping in perfect harmony with the development of the story, lead to the natural phenomena such as the heavy rain in Book III, as if they symbolised the great exaltation of Troilus and Criseyde's love. In Books IV and V, when the deep love between Troilus and Criseyde is facing ruin, they are to be detached from the graces of natural phenomena. Even in the description of Hector's behaviour in the beginning of Book IV, we see that Nature is keeping aloof from the characters, although Nature should give them warmth intrinsically.

> Byfel that, whan that Phebus shynyng is
> Upon the brest of Hercules lyoun,

That Ector, with ful many a bold baroun,
Caste on a day with Grekis for to fighte,
As he was wont, to greve hem what he myghte. (IV.31-35)

This passage shows that Hector accidentally attempts to fight against the Greeks and give a great damage on them, when Phebus, the god of the sun, is shining in the sky. Hector, loaded with honours of Troy, is the best and first warrior in Troy. His activity, as a matter of course, should have rescued the unfortunate state of the Trojans, but the following narration, as a matter of fact, goes against the Trojans. It is the most important turning point in this work. The story says that Antenor, a brave warrior in Troy, was captured by the Greeks. This happening, it seems, leads to the critical situation that Criseyde must needs go to the Greeks in exchange for Antenor.

Troilus, having known the definite fact of the exchange of hostages, feels great pains. Troilus's sorrow, at the present time, results from the fact that Criseyde must go far from him, though in Book I his sorrow is from his feeling that he cannot get near to Criseyde, whatever he may do. This kind of emotional despair is shown in his following speech: "For which, for what that evere may byfalle, / Withouten wordes mo, I wol be ded." (IV.499-500), where the impersonal verb "byfalle" is used. This speech is much contrasted to that of Diomede who becomes a new sweetheart of Criseyde in Book V: "Happe how happe may, / Al sholde I dye, I wol hire herte seche!" (V.796-97), although he uses the impersonal verb "hap." It should be noted here that, while Troilus leaves himself to supernatural fate, Diomede tries to strive against cruel fate; in short, Troilus is passive and Diomede is active.

In Book V, the impersonal constructions are used to show Criseyde's subtle emotional feeling of heart. Criseyde, having already been taken to the Greeks, cannot do anything despite her attempt to go to Troy. Her following speech, including the impersonal construction, shows objectively that she cannot escape from the Greeks: "And if that I me putte in jupartie, / To stele awey by nyght, and it bifalle / That

I be kaught, I shal be holde a spie;" (V.701-03), which represents her strong self-consciousness. And how ironic it is that on the same tenth day Diomede happens to visit Criseyde, though she, in Book IV, pledged herself with streaming eyes to return to Troy on the tenth day after their sorrowful separation. Diomede's visit to Criseyde's camp is also shown by the impersonal construction: "It fel that after, on the tenthe day / Syn that Criseyde out of the citee yede, / This Diomede, as fressh as braunche in May, / Com to the tente ther as Calkas lay," (V.842-45). Then Criseyde gladly accepts his coming. Though Criseyde, refusing temptation, says that it will never happen that the Greeks will get their revenge on the Troians, using the impersonal construction (V.962-63), her speech appears to suggest that times change and Criseyde with them. So Criseyde, negating her above speech, states as follows:

> Hereafter, whan ye wonnen han the town,
> Peraventure so it happen may
> That whan I se that nevere yit I say
> Than wol I werke that I nevere wroughte! (V.990-93)

Judging from her impersonal speech that she seemingly will do the thing which she has never done before, in spite of her complex feeling, this speech may imply not only her resigned feeling but her own character "slydynge of corage," the problem which has been constantly discussed by a number of critics till the present time.[23]

On the other hand, Troilus, not knowing such a change of Criseyde's mind, keeps on waiting for her. Troilus's great apprehension for Criseyde in fact appears in his dream. In other words, Troilus's dream excites no little fear about Criseyde. Troilus dreams that Criseyde gives herself over to a breach of faith. It happens that this dream does not go by contraries. He chances to discover Diomede's "cote-armure" to which is attached the "broche" that was delivered to Criseyde with all Troilus's heart when they parted from each other.

> And so bifel that thorughout Troye town,
> As was the gise, iborn was up and down
> A manere cote-armure, as seith the storie,
> Byforn Deiphebe, in signe of his victorie;
> The whiche cote, as telleth Lollius,
> Deiphebe it hadde rent fro Diomede
> The same day. (V.1649-55)

By accident, a certain coat of mail is brought to this town as spoils and it allows Troilus to know definitely that the inevitable event has happened in the end, i.e. that Criseyde has already broken faith with Troilus.

In this way, the impersonal constructions which show happening and occurrence, as a matter of course, closely related to the natural phenomena, impart the crucial turning point and the momentous event in this work, and especially produce the transition of the love affair between Troilus and Criseyde. The uppermost part of these impersonal constructions is the supernatural power that governs the natural phenomena, as in the description of rain in Book III. This means the phenomena that occur under the power of inevitability and go beyond the power of human beings. It seems that Chaucer has made the best use of so many impersonal constructions to describe the important contents in *Troilus and Criseyde*, since the poet is much fascinated by the supernatural mighty force of Fortune.

4.3. Negative expressions

When we read Chaucer's texts, we often meet with negative expressions. We find these expressions not only in the poet's sentences, clauses, phrases, and words, but also in the internal structures of the words, i.e. morphemes. Negatives are said to be often used not only in Chaucer's texts but also in other Middle English writings, as Elliott, Mossé, Roscow, Sandved, and others indicate in their essays. These scholars have addressed Middle English negatives from a syntactic point of view.[24] Burnley also discusses Chaucer's use of negatives syntactically, noting the differences of negatives between those in the Ellesmere MS. and the Hengwrt MS.[25]

These scholars only deal with the syntactic or grammatical use of negatives, but no one has yet explained the meanings of negative expressions. We should read closely Chaucer's texts word by word to better understand the meaning of each negative expression within its context. For example, we remember the scene where the narrator describes Criseyde as "nevere lasse mannyssh" (I.284). The adjective "mannyssh" is defined by the *OED*: "Of a woman, her attributes, etc.: Resembling a man, man-like, masculine. Chiefly contemptuous." Since this contemptuous word is negated by the negatives, we understand that Criseyde's feminine virtue is much emphasised. Then we quote a famous passage in "The General Prologue" to *The Canterbury Tales*: "He nevere yet no vileynye ne sayde / In al his lyf unto no maner wight" (I(A) 70-71). The noun "vileynye," meaning "wicked, low, obscene, or opprobrious speech," throws the virtuous speech and the action of the noble knight into relief through the accumulation of negatives.

On the other hand, in *Troilus and Criseyde* we remember the adjective "unkynde," which consists of the negative prefix "un" and the stem "kynde." The adjective "kynde" may mean "having a gentle and sympathetic, or benevolent nature." Criseyde says to Troilus, "Don't be 'unkynde' to me," when she parts from him, as in "And douteles, if that ich often wende, / I ner but ded, and er ye cause fynde, / For Goddes love, so beth me naught unkynde!" (IV.1650-52) Even though Criseyde tries to be "kynde" to Troilus — even believing herself to be so, she nevertheless becomes "unkynde" to Troilus in Book V.

The negatives thus used effectively in Chaucer's works are most often found in "The Clerk's Tale." It may be too hasty to conclude that the high frequency of negatives suggests an important role in the work, but it seems that the use of negatives is directly and closely related to both the contents of "The Clerk's Tale," and the characterisation found therein.[26] Such use may be skilful and intentional by the poet Chaucer. In this section, focusing on the speech of the characters, we would like to investigate the negatives or negative expressions used in the speeches of the main characters Walter and Griselda and the narrator in "The Clerk's Tale."[27]

4.3.1. Negative Expressions Used by Walter

In order to test Griselda's patience, Walter uses various lies which are often connected with the negative expressions. An outstanding feature of Walter's orders to others, including Griselda, not to do anything, is represented by his use of negative expressions. As a marquess, Walter governs not only his subjects but also his wife Griselda, so it is a matter of course that he uses words related not only to his reign and government, but also impressionistic negative expressions.

First, Walter uses negative expressions when he orders his subjects not to make a complaint about his choice of a new wife.

> ... that ye
> Agayn my choys shul neither grucche ne stryve;(169-70)
>
> And but ye wole assente in swich manere,
> I prey yow, speketh namoore of this matere." (174-75)

Second, Walter uses negative expressions again when he requires Griselda's passive obedience to him and deprives her of the free will absolutely:

> "I seye this, be redy with good herte.
> To al my lust, and that I frely may,
> As me best thynketh, do yow laughe or smerte,
> And nevere ye to grucche it, nyght ne day?
> And eek whan I sey 'ye,' ne sey nat 'nay,'
> Neither by word ne frownyng countenance? (351-56)

Third, Walter uses negative expressions, when he tells the truth, negating every lie he told intentionally to test his wife Griselda. In the following instance, negatives are used with the swearing before God. Even his confession has a peremptory tone of vice:

> "This is ynogh, Grisilde myn," quod he;
> "Be now namoore agast ne yvele apayed.
> ....
> "Grisilde," quod he, "by God, that for us deyde.
> Thou art my wyf, ne noon oother I have,
> Ne nevere hadde, as God my soule save!
> ....
> Taak hem agayn, for now maystow nat seye
> That thou hast lorn noon of thy children tweye.
> "And folk that oother weys han seyd of me,
> I warne hem wel that I have doon this deede
> For no malice, ne for no crueltee,
> But for t'assaye in thee thy wommanheede,
> And nat to sleen my children – God forbeede! –
> But for to kepe hem pryvely and stille,
> Til I thy purpos knewe and al thy wille." (1051-78)

Thus, most negative expressions in Walter's speech are used when he governs and orders the others, especially his wife Griselda.

4.3.2. Negative Expressions Used by Griselda

Griselda is a patient wife who gladly endures the trials given by Walter. Her patience is directly revealed in her speech and action, to say nothing of her facial expressions. Using negative expressions, Griselda brings herself under Walter's rule and shows her steadfast faith. Her unchangeable attitude is not unnatural indeed, but it seems to be connected with her naïve joyfulness. Her heart and her speech are united harmoniously; she seems glad to endure steadfastly. So we unexpectedly find many expressions showing joy in this work.

Then we remember a famous passage concerning the Clerk in "The General Prologue" to *The Canterbury Tales*: "And gladly wolde he lerne and gladly teche" (I(A) 308). In "The Clerk's Tale," Griselda gladly receives Walter's compulsive and forcible teaching. Her negative expressions are not always connected with a joyous situation, but it seems that what would normally make everybody else feel pain is a natural joy to Griselda.

Griselda thus obediently submits to Walter's orders gladly and naturally. She enters into the negative world spontaneously, as is shown in the adverb "willyngly":

> She seyde, "Lord, undigne and unworthy
> Am I to thilke honour that ye me beede,
> But as ye wole youreself, right so wol I.
> And heere I swere that nevere willyngly,
> In werk ne thoght, I nyl yow disobeye,
> For to be deed, though me were looth to deye." (359-64)

She does not assent herself, since she is "undigne and unworthy," the adjectives which impart her humble attitude to her lord Walter. She never says that she obeys her lord in her action and thought, but she does not disobey her lord, nor does she break her promise to obey him even if she dies. Such a negative expression emphasises Griselda's unchangeable humble attitude more effectively than the affirmative expression.

While Walter uses the negative imperative, Griselda corresponds to Walter's negative speech, using recurrent negatives. Does this speech somewhat reflect her complaining tone of voice, as Winny states?[28]

> "I have," quod she, "seyd thus, and evere shal:
> I wol no thyng, ne nyl no thyng, certayn,
> But as yow list. Naught greveth me at al,
> Though that my doughter and my sone be slayn, —
> . . . .
> I have noght had no part of children tweyne
> But first siknesse, and after, wo and peyne.
> . . . .
> But now I woot youre lust, and what ye wolde,
> Al youre plesance ferme and stable I holde;
> For wiste I that my deeth wolde do yow ese,
> Right gladly wolde I dyen, yow to plese.
> Deth may noght make no comparisoun

Unto youre love ..." (645-67)

We are impressed that Griselda speaks to Walter gladly: "wiste I that my deeth wolde do yow ese, / right gladly wolde I dyen yow to plese" (664-65). Even though this speech implies Griselda's complaint, we understand that she accepts and practices "gladly" whatever she is ordered to do by Walter.

Then the scene moves to Walter's new wedding ceremony. Walter calls back "sely povre Griselda," on the pretext that he needs many helping hands at the nuptials. As the narrator states: "And she with humble herte and glad visage, / Nat with no swollen thoght in hire corage" (949-50), she is never proud at all and she is modest and glad. Her gladness is naturally revealed in her speech where the negatives are recurrent.

> "Nat oonly, lord, that I am glad," quod she,
> "To doon youre lust, but I desire also
> Yow for to serve and plese in my degree
> Withouten feyntyng, and shal everemo;
> Ne nevere, for no wele ne no wo,
> Ne shal the goost withinne myn herte stente
> To love yow best with al my trewe entente." (967-73)

Griselda says: "I am glad to doon youre lust," and then she, using negative expressions, states that she will not lose her love. She is willing to serve Walter. Her reverent and humble service to Walter is done by her "glad" heart. She tries to devote herself unselfishly to her lord, even though she throws away her life, as is shown in the following negative expressions:

> "Now rekke I nevere to been deed right heere;
> Sith I stonde in youre love and in youre grace
> No fors of deeth, ne whan my spirit pace!" (1090-92)

4.3.3. Negative Expressions Used Mainly by the Narrator

The narrative in "The Clerk's Tale" is narrated by the "Clerk of Oxenford," and also contains negatives. We will examine those negative expressions, and we will include the negatives in the speech of "sadde folk" who might well be regarded in the same light with the narrator's speech. Most negative expressions in the narrator's speech are used to make moralistic comments, which are general considerations and objective descriptions of Griselda's patience and virtue. It may be an excellent expression of negatives, above all, that the "unsadde" people are judged and criticised by the continuous use of "un"-words, which negate the virtues of Griselda. The "sad" people comment critically regarding the "unsad" and "stormy" people. The commentators use "un"-words continually. The "sad" people speak for the narrator, because in the former situation the narrator criticises unfavourably "the rude peple" (750), referring to the people who believe that the divorce between Walter and Griselda is right.

> "O stormy peple! Unsad and evere untrewe!
> Ay undiscreet and chaungynge as a fane! (995-96)

The negative expressions which the narrator uses in his general observations are most often found when the narrator is conscious of those women in the audience who hear his speech. For example, the narrator uses negative expressions when he states that men do not have as half a "trewe" nature as women.

> Though clerkes preise wommen but a lite,
> Ther kan no man in humblesse hym acquite
> As womman kan, ne kan been half so trewe
> As wommen been, but it be falle of newe. (935-38)

The narrator thus uses the negative expressions humorously.

> Thus Walter lowely – nay, but roially –
> Wedded with fortunat honestetee. (421-22)

The negative "nay" is an interjection, but we include it as a negative expression because it ironically connects Griselda's lowly social position with her internal nobleness. In appearance Walter married with a woman of humble condition but in reality he married a woman with a royally noble heart. This kind of contrastive statement is represented humorously by the negative "nay."

It may be a masterpiece that in "Lenvoy de Chaucer" the narrator, humorously making use of negative expressions, states that the audience does not have to be patient like Griselda, considering the ladies attending before the narrator.

> O noble wyves, ful of heigh prudence,
> Lat noon humylitee youre tonge naille,
> Ne lat no clerk have cause or diligence
> To write of yow a storie of swich mervaille
> As of Grisildis pacient and kynde,
> ....
> Ye archewyves, stondeth at defense,
> Syn ye be strong as is a greet camaille;
> Ne suffreth nat that men yow doon offense.
> ....
> Ne dreed hem nat; doth hem no reverence,
> For though thyn housbonde armed be in maille, (1183-1202)

In short, the narrator is so everchangingly protean that he can state opposite meanings, in order to attract the attention of the audience. He has described the patient Griselda in his Tale, but at last he says, "do not be patient" and "do not endure," before the lively and mannissh "wyf of Bath." His negative expressions are a good means of irony.

The relationship between master and man is cultivated and established "gladly" in "The General Prologue" to *The Canterbury Tales* and it is transferred to the conjugal relationship between Walter and Griselda in "The Clerk's Tale." Using negative expressions, Griselda receives Walter's ascetic teaching gladly and naturally.

At last, Griselda's perseverance gets the better of Walter's tyranny. She is blessed by being reunited with her children. However, stating that such a patient woman does not exist in the present world, the narrator denies his story with the use of negative expressions. This kind of the narrator's humorous use of negative expressions shows not only Chaucerian humour but also Chaucer's uniquely well-balanced sense of style.

Notes

1   The frequency of "un"-words in Chaucer's works is shown in the following table 1. The abbreviations of Chaucer's works follow L. Y. Baird-Lange and H. Schnuttgen, *A Bibliography of Chaucer1974-1985* (D. S. Brewer, 1988). SHP shows "The Short Poems" such as "Fortune."

Table 1   The frequency of "un"-words in Chaucer's works

CT	BD	HF	Anel	PF	Bo	TC	LGW	SHP	Astr	Rom
158	4	18	6	12	152	113	24	20	2	50

Word token: CT: 182,037, BD: 8,668, HF: 13,255, Anel: 2,771, PF: 5,522, Bo: 51,479, TC: 65,590, LGW: 25,680, SHP: 10,701, Astr: 14,755, Rom: 48,370.

The frequency of "un"-words in *The Canterbury Tales* is shown in the following table 2. The abbreviations of the tables follow the above-mentioned *Bibliography*. It is noted, however, that each abbreviation includes the prologue or the link attached to the tale.

Table 2   The frequency of "un"-words in *The Canterbury Tales*

GP	KnT	MilT	RvT	CkT	MLT	WBT	FrT	SumT	ClT	MerT	SqT	FranT
2	11	5	4	0	8	4	2	2	15	11	5	8

PhyT	PardT	ShT	PrT	Th	Mel	MkT	NPT	SNT	CYT	ManT	ParsT
2	4	1	4	0	6	6	2	5	9	3	39

Word token: KnT: 17,147, MLT: 9,044, WBT: 9,987, ClT: 9,447, Mel: 16,906, ParsT: 30,964.

The above data are all from M. Matsuo, Y. Nakao, S. Suzuki, and T. Kuya, *Machine Readable Text of Chaucer Project* (Hiroshima University, 1985).

2   E. T. Donaldson (ed.), *Chaucer's Poetry* (New York: The Ronald Press Company, 1958), p. 213.

3   *Ibid*. It seems that the adjectival use of "sad" is better in this context, because Griselda's "sad" nature is much emphasised here. It is also noted that an adverb "sadly" (an adjective "sad" + a suffix "-ly") is used in the line 1100

in this work.
4   Benson, *The Riverside Chaucer* (Boston: Houghton Mifflin, 1987), p. 144.
5   N. Davis, *et al.*, *A Chaucer Glossary* (Oxford: Oxford University Press, 1979), p. 124.
6   J. Winny, *The Clerk's Prologue and Tale* (Cambridge: Cambridge University Press, 1966), p. 83. Cf. It is noted that the adjective "discreet" is attached to the male character Walter: "A fair persone, and strong, and yong of age, / And ful of honour and of curteisye; / Discreet ynogh his contree for to gye," (73-75).
7   van der Gaaf, *The Transition from the Impersonal to the Personal Construction in Middle English* (Heidelberg, 1904).
8   Elizabeth Closs Traugott, *A History of English Syntax* (New York, 1972). Eiko Ito also deals with the impersonal constructions in Middle English, in her paper "A Study of Impersonal Verbs in Middle English," *The Bulletin of Kobe Jogakuin University*, 21-2, 1974, where she depends on Traugott's theory.
9   Willy Elmer, *Diachronic Grammar: The history of Old and Middle English subjectless constructions* (Tübingen, 1981).
10   Toshio Nakao, *Eigoshi II* (Tokyo, 1972), pp. 297-98.
11   We suppose that his idea is that in e.g. 'It seems to me the ice is melting' (or 'The ice seems to be melting', or 'I think the ice is melting'), we are talking about something happening. And if we said 'It seems to me the ice will melt' we are talking about a possibility. This idea does not fit under 'appropriateness or relation', but it seems that the main clauses such as 'it seems to me' or 'I think' is deeply connected with the value judgement of the first person 'me' or 'I'.
12   We can include the impersonal constructions formed by the structure 'be + adjective' in this section. The impersonal construction of preference, e.g. "me were levest," has been fully investigated from a structural point of view by Masui in his paper "Some Observations on the Constructions of Preference in Chaucer," *Gengo Kenkyu*: Journal of the Linguistic Society of Japan, 17 and 18, 1951, pp. 125-33.
13   Even Gaaf and Elmer keep away from the problems of natural phenomena, because natural phenomena do not show the transition from the impersonal constructions to the personal constructions.
14   Traugott's technical terms
15   Traugott's technical terms.
16   Jespersen states one of the causes of the transition from the impersonal construction to the personal construction: "the greater interest taken in persons than in things, which caused the name of the person to be placed before the verb" (*MEG* III, p. 208). Ryoichi Uemura also indicates that this kind of intellectual desire, followed by the development of internal minds,

caused the impersonal verbs to change semantically. The semantic change is as follows: the change from the passive way of perception to the active way of self-realization and the change from the heteronomous to the autonomous behaviour. ("Characteristics of the Impersonal Constructions," *Hiroshima Studies in English Language and Literature*, Vol. 3, No. 1, pp. 82-92. (The English Literary Association of Hiroshima University, 1956), p. 90).

17   While Tatlock and Kennedy's concordance, based on the "Globe" edition of Chaucer's works, quotes: "he thoughte he mighte his herte reste" (TC. II.1326), Skeat and Robinson's texts say: "hym (or him) thoughte...." Since one of Chaucer's reliable manuscripts says: "hym thoughte..." (*Troilus and Criseyde: A Facsimile of Corpus Christi College Cambridge MS 61*), Chaucer may have used the impersonal construction in this part.

18   Shigehiko Toyama, "'Watashi' no Mondai" *Eigo Seinen* (*The Rising Generation*) Vol. CXXVIII, No. 5, Tokyo, August 1, 1982, p. 335.

19   Ralph W. V. Elliott, *Chaucer's English* (London: André Deutsch, 1974), pp. 52-53.

20   Elliott, p. 52.

21   For example, D. S. Brewer states that "this day was one of the traditional unlucky days. Chaucer also uses it in *The Knight's Tale*, I, 1462-3, and *The Nun's Priest's Tale*, VII, 3190." (*Troilus and Criseyde* (abridged), London, p. 108.)

22   Masui, *Studies in Chaucer* (Tokyo: Kenkyusha, 1973), p. 96. Here I have translated Masui's Japanese text into English.

23   Akiyuki Jimura, "The Characterisations of Troilus and Criseyde through Adjectives in Chaucer's *Troilus and Criseyde*: "trewe as stiel" and "slydynge of corage,"" *Phoenix* 15, pp. 101-22. (Hiroshima University, 1979), p. 120.

24   R. W. V. Elliott, *Chaucer's English*. F. Mosse, *A Handbook of Middle English* (Baltimore: The Johns Hopkins University Press, 1952). G. H. Roscow, *Syntax and Style in Chaucer's Poetry* (Cambridge: D. S. Brewer, 1981). A. O. Sandved, *Introduction to Chaucerian English* (Cambridge: D. S. Brewer, 1985).

25   D. Burnley, *A Guide to Chaucer's Language* (London: Macmillan, 1983).

26   The fact that many nagatives are used in "The Clerk's Tale" is shown in the Tables 3 and 4. We deal with the following negatives in this paper: "ne," "nat," "no," "naught (or no(u)ght)," "nothing (or nothyng)," "never(e)," "nay," "neither," "nam(o)ore (or namo)," and "nor." The complex word, which consists of the negative affix "un" and the stem, is also dealt with here. The other contracted forms such as "nolde," "noon," "ny," etc. are omitted in the list. The data is based on *Machine Readable Texts of Chaucer Project*, in which F. N. Robinson's text: *The Works of Geoffrey Chaucer* (Houghton Mifflin, 1957) is the source textbook. Table 3 shows the frequency of negatives in Chaucer's works. Table 4 shows the frequency of negatves in *The Canterbury Tales*.

CHAPTER 4 GRAMMAR

Table 3 Frequency of Negatives in Chaucer's Works

	CT	BD	HF	Anel	PF	Bo	TC	LGW	SHP	Astr	Rom
na	10	0	0	0	1	0	5	0	0	0	0
namo	9	0	0	0	0	0	0	0	0	0	0
namoore	97	0	0	0	0	0	1	0	0	0	0
namore	0	0	0	0	0	1	28	2	0	0	1
nat	1059	17	3	0	20	579	197	142	27	3	38
naught	11	0	1	0	0	12	104	2	0	0	4
noght	190	22	21	2	1	45	0	3	7	0	3
nought	2	3	3	0	1	2	178	7	4	0	100
nay	83	11	7	3	3	15	33	5	5	0	9
ne	901	66	70	16	23	777	234	106	65	19	327
neither	42	0	1	0	0	10	9	1	3	1	18
never	48	37	27	5	0	0	1	6	31	1	100
nevere	223	0	0	1	9	40	150	20	6	4	23
no	825	44	39	12	15	213	219	83	95	13	270
nor	12	6	1	0	0	6	21	3	2	1	32
nothing	1	3	6	2	1	17	12	6	7	0	16
nothyng	40	14	2	0	2	21	19	6	2	0	41
un-	158	4	18	6	12	152	113	24	20	2	50
total	3711	227	198	47	88	1889	1324	416	274	44	1032

Word token: CT: 182,037, BD: 8,668, HF: 13,255, Anel: 2,771, PF: 5,522, Bo: 51,479, TC: 65,590, LGW: 25,680, SHP: 10,701, Astr: 14,755, Rom: 48,370.

Table 4 Frequency of Negatives in *The Canterbury Tales*

	GP	KnT	MilT	RvT	CkT	MLT	WBT	FrT	SumT	ClT	MerT	SqT	FrT
na	0	0	1	6	0	2	0	0	0	0	0	0	0
namo	2	1	0	0	0	1	2	0	0	0	0	1	0
namoore	1	14	1	2	0	4	4	2	3	7	9	5	6
nat	26	63	39	19	5	26	59	31	35	50	57	27	28
naught	1	3	0	0	0	0	1	0	0	1	0	0	0
noght	9	25	4	5	0	15	18	1	5	19	8	4	6
nought	1	0	0	0	0	0	0	0	0	0	0	0	1
nay	0	5	3	1	0	3	8	8	4	5	4	1	4
ne	23	99	18	8	1	26	29	15	16	58	38	28	37
neither	0	6	2	0	0	1	0	0	1	6	6	0	1
never	1	3	0	0	0	3	5	1	1	0	1	4	2
nevere	4	17	2	1	0	7	15	5	3	17	12	8	22
no	25	58	23	14	3	37	67	15	24	66	55	16	36
nor	3	3	1	0	0	0	0	0	0	1	2	1	0
nothing	0	0	0	0	0	0	0	0	0	1	0	0	0
nothyng	0	0	0	0	0	2	1	2	2	3	0	0	2
un-	2	11	5	4	0	8	4	2	2	15	11	5	8
total	98	308	99	60	9	135	213	82	96	249	203	100	153

	PhyT	PardT	ShT	PrT	Th	Mel	MkT	NPT	SNT	CYT	ManT	ParsT
na	0	0	1	0	0	0	0	0	0	0	0	0
namo	0	0	0	0	0	0	0	1	1	0	0	0
namoore	0	4	6	1	1	2	4	5	1	5	2	9
nat	8	30	22	6	5	158	35	29	20	49	17	216
naught	0	0	0	1	0	1	0	0	1	1	1	0
noght	1	5	3	3	1	14	8	2	6	8	5	15
nought	0	0	0	0	0	0	0	0	0	0	0	0
nay	0	7	3	1	1	3	0	3	1	11	1	6
ne	7	16	13	2	3	139	37	25	17	25	12	210
neither	0	1	2	0	1	4	1	1	0	0	0	9
never	0	0	1	0	0	2	2	5	0	7	5	5
nevere	3	6	2	1	0	19	13	7	8	13	5	33
no	22	24	20	3	5	75	34	23	15	33	16	116
nor	0	0	1	0	0	0	0	0	0	0	0	0
nothing	0	0	0	0	0	0	0	0	0	0	0	0
nothyng	0	2	0	0	1	5	1	3	0	4	2	10
un-	2	4	1	4	0	6	6	2	5	9	3	39
total	43	99	75	22	19	428	141	106	75	165	69	668

Word token: KnT: 17,147, MLT: 9,044, WBT: 9,987, ClT: 9,447, Mel: 16,906, ParsT: 30,964.

27   Table 5 shows the frequency of negatives in the female characters' speech. Table 6 shows the frequency of negatives in the male characters' speech.

Table 5   Frequency of Negatives in the Female Characters' Speeches

	Griselda	Criseyde
na, etc.	59	229
word-token	1,292	8,986

Table 6   Frequency of Negatives in the Male Characters' Speeches

	Walter	Troilus	Pandarus
na, etc.	40	229	283
word-token	1,424	11,368	14,212

28   J. Winny (ed.), *The Clerk's Prologue and Tale: from the Canterbury Tales by Geoffrey Chaucer*, p. 78.

SUMMARY

The narrative stylistics of Chaucer's language has been dealt with in this book. Whenever Chaucer the man, the poet, the narrator, the pilgrim, the courtier wanted to tell his story before the audience, he did his best to make his narration understood clearly and distinctly, making use of textual structure, collocations, dialects, and grammatical expressions.

In Chapter 1, the word "herte" in *The Book of the Duchess* organises the apparently inconsistent structure throughout to its conclusion. That word supports this impression and informs the work. Major scholars agree that the word "herte" makes this work organic. As Kökeritz (1954) and Baum (1956) have indicated, the expression "hert-huntyng" used as wordplay is a suitable word to unite this story. This compound word invites us to ask why "herte" is used throughout this work; it invites our thoughts to examine the details of this poem. This word not only becomes a part of wordplay, but it also results in relating every episode of this book to each other. After the "hert-huntyng" is done, the knight discovers his house or palace, where his "herte" rests peacefully. This would be a profound consolation to the poet suffering from insomnia.

Then the "herte" turns into the value words "soth" and "fals" in *The House of Fame*. We do not see the words concerning "love" except where the poet narrates the stories of false love in the first half of this work and where he reveals the "newe tydynge" at the last stage of Book III. This may mean that had Chaucer completed Book III he may have written a love-story; the extant text does not show this kind of the poet's attitude of love, however. We have not examined *The House of Fame* from a viewpoint of love, but we would like to interpret the structure of this work, though partially, while considering the importance of the antithetical keywords "soth" and "fals." These are more often used in this work than the other Chaucer's works, and therefore play an important role in *The House of Fame*. Ultimately, the poet who has ever sought after the "soth" from the first could find the true person "a man of auctoritee" at the concluding line of this work, as a result of his continuous experiments. This expression may be suitable for the conclusion of *The House of Fame*. Even if this work were criticised as "unfinished," this expression suggests the bridge between this work and Chaucer's following great works. Chaucer the poet, influenced by the magnificient power of "auctoritee," has created many famous works which are to transmit his true fame to posterity.

The word "hous" plays the important part of the structure of Chaucer's works. An examination of the symbolism "hous" of "The Tale of Melibee," *The Canterbury Tales*, will shed light upon the problem that Geoffrey Chaucer was one of the first English poets, if not the first, to recognise and write about a subtle, internal isolation. The concerns of Chaucer and his sensitive contemporaries were not about physical exploits, but exploits of the mind and soul. We have discussed Chaucer's expression of "hous," considering the role the house plays in *Troilus and Criseyde*. We will summarise as follows: the house represents the human body and the window symbolises our eyes. We see this symbolism in "The Tale of Melibee." On the other hand, the house and the windows are effectively and adequately used to show "noble" courtly love in "The Knight's Tale"; they represent bawdy, physical love in "The Miller's Tales." Both tales certainly represent the extreme aspects of the meaning and use of the house. In such a late work as *The Canterbury Tales*, Chaucer applied the descriptions of the house clearly to separate the spiritual aspect of love from the physical one. However, he does not view human affairs with an entirely philosophic eye in *Troilus and Criseyde*. We see the delightful and intoxicating harmony between the spiritual love and the physical love at Pandarus's house in Book III. Troilus and Criseyde fulfill completely the house of love based on Pandarus's prudent "hertes line" and they live there physically and spiritually in an ecstasy of joy. But Troilus, who finally ascends into the house of Heaven, seeks for the world of spiritual love such as God's love, understanding the vanity and dwarfishness of the worldly love which shows the connection between the body and the spirit. We find the separation between the body and the spirit in the final stage of *Troilus and Criseyde*. This may show a slight and important change of Chaucer's mood and thinking which will have a great influence on his later works.

We have discussed the meaning and use of the English northern dialect in the two young students' speech in "The Reeve's Prologue and Tale," *The Canterbury Tales*. It is not enough to deal only with the northern dialects in discussing this prologue and tale, however, because we find the other characters such as the Miller, the narrator Reeve's rival, who use other dialects rather than the students' northern dialect. The Miller, who does not use the northern dialect, is represented in the first half of "The Reeve's Tale" as a man of hypocritical nature, which is in striking contrast to the Cambridge students who speak simple and naïve dialects. Hearing the unadorned speech of the students, the Miller decides definitely to equivocate with them. Here we have examined the characterisations of the Miller and his family, who regard country speech as "inferior." We have investigated the real figures of the people who pretend to belong to the upper and intellectual class, making little of the dialects. In the first half of "The Reeve's Tale" the anger of the Reeve, the narrator, toward the Miller and his family is shown clearly by the ironic description in which they are presented as characters of a hypocritical nature. It is interesting that the Miller and his family, who acknowledge themselves "noble," are defeated by the two country boys who use the northern dialects seemingly regarded as "inferior."

In Chapter 2, first we have discussed the effects of the northern dialect in "The Reeve's Prologue and Tale," by paying special attention to the relationship between the characters and northern dialects, after briefly surveying some scholars' opinions about them. To sum up, the persons who use the dialect in this work tend to take direct and straightforward action which makes the audience laugh light-heartedly. On the other hand, the persons who do not use the dialect in this work are two-faced; they try to deceive other people; i.e. they do not reveal their real intentions. We will discuss the hypocritical vocabulary of the miller and his family in a further study. In this way, "The Reeve's Tale" consists of two kinds of contrastive characters. One type of characters, using the London dialect or the city speech, appears to belong to an intellectual class, while the other type of characters, using the northern dialect or the country speech, appears to belong to a less intelligent class. However, it is interesting that a Miller representing the upper class, is defeated by the country boys. From this contrastive point of view, unless the dialects were used in this work, "The Reeve's Prologue and Tale" would have become a tasteless and humourless story lacking depth.

Second, we have dealt with the social dialect of Chaucer's English: this time the language of Criseyde in Chaucer's *Troilus and Criseyde*, focusing mainly on her vocabulary. Comparing Criseyde's vocabulary with that of Troilus and Pandarus, we have concentrated on the characteristics of women's language in fourteenth century upper class society, few though they may be. Criseyde's language shows at least one aspect of women's language in fourteenth century courtly society of England where Criseyde, created and characterised by the poet Chaucer, lives with flesh and blood as well as her contemporary women.

Chapter 3 has dealt with the collocations of Chaucer's English. First, we have discussed the characterisations of Troilus and Criseyde by investigating the meanings of adjectives attached to each noun illustrating their natures. Troilus, who languishes for love, is represented as a strong, faithful, idealistic knight and courtier; Criseyde is a beautiful and charming lady, who shows her subtle and delicate feeling, suggesting something fragile to touch.

Second, we have discussed Chaucer's depiction of courtly manners and customs through adjectives in *Troilus and Criseyde*. These descriptions surrounding Chaucer's characters are important, because they may make the characters in *Troilus and Criseyde* stand out clearly and distinctly.

Third, we have discussed the description of nature which controls both courtly elements and human beings in Chaucer's *Troilus and Criseyde*. As for the description of natural objects, the relationship between the cloud and the star reflects Criseyde's black dress and her bright figure. Furthermore, the description of natural objects shows the delicate feelings of the characters; in particular, "the sonne bright" represents a joyous state of mind. The fatal 'reyn' heightens the drama as the story develops. The rain, governing the human beings and the palace, facilitates the love affair between Troilus and Criseyde. However, when Troilus and Criseyde go against nature, she does not support them, as is shown in the fact that they complain of the day and night at the end of Books III and IV. The plants also reflect the delicate emotions of the characters. The descriptions of plants suggest the harmonious development of the love affair in Books I, II, and III, as the adjectives "newe grene," "fresshe," "blew and white and rede," and "lusty" show, while they may show that in Book IV the natural order is about to break down, as in the expressions: "til the tree be bare" and "the blak bark of care," the adjectives reminding us of the severe winter and the coldness of the human beings. However, the description of Phebus as "gold-tressed" signals a return to the harmony of nature in Book V. In spite of the characters' tragic end, nature remains undisturbed. Finally, the animals are also deeply connected with the characters in this work: "the newe abaysed nyghtyngale" is compared to Criseyde, "an egle, fethered whit as bon" in Criseyde's dream suggests the manly figure of Troilus, and the "bor" in Troilus's dream is associated with Diomede. In this way, the descriptions of nature in *Troilus and Criseyde* mirror faithfully the actions and states of minds of the characters.

Fourth, we have discussed the nouns "God" and pagan gods and their attached adjectives. In regard to the pagan gods, the noun "Venus," often collocated with the adjective "blisful," is deeply connected with the perfection of love. "Cupid" manipulates and binds Troilus's heart, even though "blisful" Cupid is metamorphosed into "cruel" Cupid. The noun "Jove," collocated with the adjective "almyghty" which is often attached to the noun "God," is used in Troilus's speech. The noun "Marte," collocated with the adjective "cruel," shows the strength at war. On the other hand, the nouns "Palladium" and "Diana" are closely related to Criseyde. Although she sincerely prays to them, as in "Pallas with hire heres clere" or "Cinthia the sheene," ultimately they disappear, leaving Criseyde alone. In this way, the pagan gods may determine the mental processes and emotional relationships of the protagonists Troilus and Criseyde, especially. However, the narrator reveals his attitude to the pagan gods in the Epilogue, as in "Lo here, of payens corsed olde rites!" (V.1849). He unveils the merits of the Christian God. The noun "God" in this work seems to be more widely used than in *Beowulf*, a fact which may be proved by a variety of the adjectives attached to "God," such as "myghty" and "holy" derived from Old English, "blisful" (also often collocated with the noun "Venus,") and "verray" derived from Old French. Furthermore, the fact that the characters often use the noun "God," collocated with the above adjectives, shows that Chaucer places them in close contact with the Christian God who is more omnipresent than pagan gods. Then Troilus's profound meditation on "purveyanunce" indicates one of the aspects of medieval Christianity. Lastly, the problems of the supernatural forces have been discussed. It is important for "Fortune" to be ruled over by God. While Troilus, using the adjective "cruel," is hostile to Fortune, Pandarus who takes a relative position tries to soothe Troilus by saying: "Fortune is comune." Troilus's wilful attitude to Fortune may have caused his tragedy. Fortune is nothing but a "fo" to him. As for Criseyde, she leaves herself to fate like "Fortune." Her attitude is in a marked contrast to Troilus's. For this reason, it may safely be said that "Fortune" is regarded as "a cause of events and changes in men's affairs" under the almighty power of God. Although Troilus dies a tragic death, however, the narrator does not leave him alone, but lets him ascend into a heavenly world. Herein lies Chaucer's sympathy towards Troilus. Thus the world of Troilus changes from that of pagan gods to that of the Christian God. "Providence" means that God will provide for us no matter what path we take; perhaps "Providence" allows Troilus to ascend to the heavenly world.

Chapter 4 has investigated the grammatical expressions of Chaucer's English. First, the negative expressions were dealt with. We have concentrated on the negative elements of words, especially the "un"-words in "The Clerk's Tale" where the negative expressions seem to be used frequently. We have seen briefly how effectively the "un"-words, especially "unsad," "untrewe," and "undiscreet," are used in "The Clerk's Tale." To sum up, these adjectives "sad," "trew," and "discreet" show Griselda's magnificent nature which does not change at all. The virtues of human beings, especially Griselda's, are especially emphasised in this work. So when the negative prefix "un" is attached to these stems, it makes the meaning of the stems heighten the effect contrastively. The meaning of the "un"-words symbolises and represents the "stormy," "unsad," and noisy people in this work. Ultimately, Griselda's stable nature is emphasised. She endures as usual, even though under unfavourable conditions.

Second, we have discussed the impersonal constructions in Chaucer's works. This section has aimed at recognizing how organically the impersonal constructions are used in Chaucer's *Troilus and Criseyde*. Here we have dealt with the main matter and problem of some concern why Chaucer used the impersonal constructions in *Troilus and Criseyde*. The impersonal constructions which show happening and occurrence, as a matter of course, closely related to the natural phenomena, signal the crucial turning points and the momentous events in this work, and especially produce the transition of the love affair between Troilus and Criseyde. The uppermost part of these impersonal constructions is the supernatural power that governs the natural phenomena, as in the description of rain in Book III. This means the phenomena that occur under the power of inevitability and go beyond the power of human beings. It seems that Chaucer has made the best use of so many impersonal constructions to describe the important contents in *Troilus and Criseyde*, since the poet is much fascinated by the supernatural mighty force of Fortune.

Third, the negatives have been studied again in the last section. Scholars have only dealt with the syntactic or grammatical use of negatives, but no one has yet explained the meanings of negative expressions. The last section, focusing on the speech of the characters, has investigated the negatives or negative expressions used in the speeches of the main characters Walter and Griselda and the narrator in "The Clerk's Tale." The narrator is so everchangingly protean that he can state opposite meanings, in order to attract the attention of the audience. He has described the patient Griselda in his Tale, but at last he says, "do not be patient" and "do not endure," before the lively and mannish "wyf of Bath." His negative expressions are a good means of irony. The relationship between master and man cultivated and established "gladly" in "The General Prologue" to *The Canterbury Tales* is transferred to the conjugal relationship between Walter and Griselda in "The Clerk's Tale." Using negative expressions, Griselda receives Walter's ascetic teaching gladly and naturally. At last, Griselda's perseverance gets the better of Walter's tyranny. She is blessed by being reunited with her children. However, stating that such a patient woman does not exist in the present world, the narrator denies his story with the use of negative expressions. This kind of the narrator's humorous use of negative expressions shows not only Chaucerian humour but also Chaucer's uniquely well-balanced sense of style.

CONCLUSION

Told just before "The Parson's Prologue and Tale," "The Manciple's Prologue and Tale" sums up Chaucer's narrative techniques. We wish to conclude this book with a consideration of why and how this story has the Manciple render his prologue and tale as he does.

It would seem that the final "The Parson's Prologue and Tale" was written carefully so as to be a summation of Chaucer's poetic techniques, although the collection of *The Canterbury Tales* is incomplete and we do not know what Chaucer intended. Nevertheless, "The Manciple's Prologue and Tale" seems to be the most carefully written tale in the collections. The tale before the last one should show the way to the last stage of *The Canterbury Tales*. Chaucer chooses his words intentionally and carefully when he narrates "The Manciple's Prologue and Tale." Chaucer seems to be focusing on the problems between language and narration in order to consider how "the word moot cosyn be to the werkyng" as he develops his tales. It would seem that "The Manciple's Prologue and Tale" reflects Chaucer's narrative stylistics as he employs language, a matter we would like to discuss.

1. Polysemic Words and Phrases in "The Manciple's Prologue and Tale"

First, there are many pregnant words used in this work. Most of them do not impart one meaning, but may be interpreted in many ways. Chaucer knows that it is true that one word has many meanings and he experiments with his use of words according to the context. While forming not simply the element of wordplay, the multi-layered meanings correspond to the kinds or degrees of the audience. Here we would like to concentrate on the meanings of the following words and phrases: "queen," "lust," "lemman," "semelieste," "countrefete," and "Bobbe-up-and-doun."

(1) quene

We have the word "queen" in "The Manciple's Prologue":

> Or hastow with som quene al nyght yswonk, (18)

The word "quene" means "quean" here, but it has another sense "queen." Although this word implies a degenerated woman in this context, what kind of impression does this give of the ladies belonging to the upper classes like the queen?

(2) lust and lusty

The words "lust" and "lusty" are used as follows:

> Fy, stynkyng swyn! Fy, foule moote thee falle!
> A, taketh heede, sires, of this lusty man. (40-41)
>
> He (=Phebus) was the mooste lusty bachiler. (107)
>
> Whan Phebus wyf had sent for hir lemman,
> Anon they wroghten al hire lust volage. (238-39)

The first instance is the speech where the Manciple has conversed with the Cook in "The Manciple's Prologue." Here "lusty" is the first citation of the *OED* and means "†4. Full of lust or sexual desire; lustful. *Obs.*" This word may foreshadow the use of "lust" in "The Manciple's Tale." Even though the word is used in the serious context, it makes us or the audience associate the former meaning and has the effect of making us laugh ironically. Then the character of the Cook becomes similar to the god Phebus.

(3) lemman

The word "lemman" is quoted in the two passages:

> And so bifel, whan Phebus was absent,

> His wyf anon hath for hir lemman sent. (203-04)
>
> And for that oother is a povre womman,
> She shal be cleped his wenche or his lemman. (219-20)

The former "lemman" means a lover or a gigolo and the latter a love or a prostitute, but, etymologically speaking, both of them mean a darling as "lemman" is a "lief man" and the original meaning has degenerated and a darling becomes a dirty man or woman interestingly. The man is similar to the woman, if the former acts as dirtily as the latter does.

(4) semelieste

> Therto he was the semelieste man
> That is or was sith that the world bigan. (119-20)

The superlative adjective "semelieste" may have a double meaning. Phebus is the man who is the most suitable for the lord. He is the most appropriate lord in appearance, but we do not know what kind of man he is in reality.

(5) countrefete

> Whit was this crowe as is a snow-whit swan,
> And countrefete the speche of every man
> He koude, whan he sholde telle a tale. (133-35)

The crow was able to imitate the speech of the man just like a parrot. So he practiced his way of life, obeying a certain philosophy: "silence is golden"and he did not tell anything more than he needed to. However, he had his great ability to make Phebus become angry with his wife and put her to death. In short, he created a false image that looked real enough to deceive people: in this case, Phebus. He wanted to act like a flatterer who contrived to get to the weak side of Phebus, trying to have his favour. Then he became too wordy and fluent a speaker. The verb "countrefete"suggests various kinds of imitations by human beings.

(6) Bobbe-up-and-doun

We have an important proper noun in "The Manciple's Prologue": "Bobbe-up-and-doun" the place which is near to and on the way to Canterbury, the destination of the Pilgrims.

> Woot ye nat where ther stant a litel toun
> Which that ycleped is Bobbe-up-and-doun,
> Under the Blee, in Caunterbury Weye?
> Ther gan oure Hooste for to jape and pleye,
> And seyde, "Sires, what! Dun is in the myre! (1-5)

Here the conversion from the verb phrase to the noun phrase is intentionally used. This is a grammatical problem since the verb + adverb combination "bobbe up and doun" is turned into the noun, finally becoming the proper noun, but here we should notice a lexical problem, because this word is related to the up and down movement of the Cook when he is riding on the horse, meaning "to move up and down like a buoyant body in water, or an elastic body on land;...," according to the *OED*.

2. Conversions of Narrative Topics in "The Manciple's Prologue and Tale"

Though the Manciple is "lewed," he gets the better of a great many "lerned" people, as in the description of the Manciple himself in "The General Prologue" to *The Canterbury Tales*. The fact that "lewed mannes wit" surpasses "the wisdom of an heep of lerned men" indicates that both lower and higher people are equal without descrimination. Moreover, the narrator seems to say that the "lewed" people are greater than the "lerned."

The story turns "from ernest to game." We do not know whether or not the story is true, because the Cook is drinking heavily. The narrator seems to tell that even if the narrator tells the story seriously or humourously, the result would be the same or the main theme would not change at all. Now the "ernest" becomes equivalent to the "game" in the story-telling.

In fact, it is the Manciple, not the Cook who tells the story. In "The Manciple's Prologue" the Manciple attributes the content of his story to the Cook's bad behaviour, as in "Bobbe-up-and-doun" (2), "Dun is in the mire" (5), "(he) doun the hors hym cast" (48). In "The Manciple's Tale" the Manciple makes the sun God Phebus in the mythology descend on the earth and become one of the human beings who is easily influenced by sentiment. The fact that God becomes man indicates the upside-down element in the story. Thus the Cook in the prologue is similar to Phebus in the tale.

Now we would like to analyse the meaning of the proverbial expression: "The word moot cosyn be to the werking." Chaucer, making the use of Manciple the calculator, presents the important idea of the proverb that each character does not have any meaning of the existence unless his or her action has to coincide with his or her words, which are always connected with his or her thoughts. Chaucer of course satirizes discordance between one's words and actions. Then we would discuss the following topics: first, as the example showing consistency of speech and action, (1) The Cook's tale and action, (2) Phebus's speech and action, (3) the impulsive actions of the animals, and (4) the action of Phebus's wife; second, as the example showing inconsistency of speech and action, (5) the actions of the crow; lastly (6) the deliberate and scrupulous speech and action of the Manciple.

(1) The Cook's tale and action

The Manciple, who is good at calculating money, appears in "The General Prologue" to *The Canterbury Tales*. He does not get along with the Cook. The apprentice in "The Cook's Tale" leaves the house and the Cook seems to hint that the apprentice is the Manciple. And the Cook cuts his story on the way. The incomplete story suggests that the Cook's intoxication caused him to lose his train of thought. In fact, in "The Manciple's Prologue," the Manciple narrates the slovenly behaviour of the Cook, a son of Bachus, as in the description of the hard-drinking Cook coming off a horse. He also shows clearly to the audience the disposition that the Cook is short-tempered and emotional. The Cook's sluggish action is closely related to the Cook's unfinished story.

(2) Phebus's speech and action
The Manciple tries to cheer up the Cook by giving him even more to drink after carefully considering his boozy nature. The Cook is moody and "rakel" enough to be influenced by such a superficial good-will of the Manciple. This Cook's nature is reflected in the character of Phebus in "The Manciple's Tale," who is easy to be carried away by his feelings, although he is not presented as a hard-drinking man. Phebus, believing easily what is told by the crow, acts without thinking at all. He is so "rakel" that he kills his wife. Though he is regarded as a wise ruler, he is transformed into the tirant suddenly. Phebus carefully keeps guard over his wife and suddenly and spasmodically kills her after hearing the crow's words. Both actions of Phebus's are not irrelevant, because they show the one-sided way of his thinking.

(3) The impulsive actions of the animals
The crow is an imitator of a parrot, so the crow's words are not connected with the crow's true actions. Most animals act on their impulse: the bird wants to get out of the cage, the cat wants to eat the mouse, she-wolf tries to get her lover. They act on their impulse and instinct, without thinking any more.

(4) The action of Phebus's wife
The action of Phebus's wife is like that of those animals. She wants to have sexual intercourse with her lover instinctively.

(5) The actions of the crow

The actions of the crow are inconsistent with the words. Though the crow does not say any words, as in "the white crowe ... / Biheld hire werk, and seyde never a word," (240-41) he sings a merry song with the sounds "Cokkow! Cokkow! Cokkow!" (at least Phebus seems to hear like that), which is not only the cry "cuckoo" of the bird, but also means that Phebus is "cuckold." So the word "Cokkow" has the double meaning. Further, this word makes us associate another meaning in the narrative structure. Judging from the fact that this tale is told by the Manciple who is quarrelling with the Cook, the word "cokkow" has a punning effect on the similar sound of the word "cook." The crow is kidding the Cook here. Then this word has the triple meaning. This crow explains the real meaning of "Cukkow," "by wordes bolde" (258) and using the rhetorical device of anaphora: Phebus was cuckolded by his wife's lover. The crow, the mere imitator of the man, becomes the fluent speaker or rhetorician now. We cannot imagine the true character of the crow, because the crow is so complicated, but the crow shows the inconsistent nature between the words and the actions.

(6) The deliberate and scrupulous speech and action of the Manciple

The Manciple is deliberate and careful in his speech. First, he excuses and explains that it is for the faithless and lustful man that he indicated the examples of "bryd," "cat," and "she-wolf" which are obedient to their own instinct. This is also the shrewd speech where the narrator is conscious of the audience, this time, the courtly ladies before the narrator. There were probably many women in Chaucer's audience and society, and we can imagine that some of them must have been submitting themselves to their instinct like "bryd," "cat," and "she-wolf" (187-95). Second, Phebus's wife called her "lemman" when her husband was absent from his house. The narrator excuses his vulgar speech, saying that he used "a knavyssh speech," i.e. "low, vulgar, and obscene" speech. He may have been conscious of the ladies before him. Therefore, the narrator defenses the word with the pejorative meaning such as "lemman," quoting the proverb: "the word moot cosyn to the werking." If the persons act in the similar way, they do not show any differences, no matter how they have the high or low estates. We do not have to care whether they are ladies or not. Here the meaning of "lady" is equivalent to that of "lemman" (205).

This logic applies to two kinds of leaders: "a titlelees tiraunt" and "an outlawe or a theef erraunt." They are different from each other, because they have their different actions and names. However, they are essentially the same, because they rule over the other persons by force. This speech may have been made to the lords or gentlemen before the narrator. If the lords act as tyrannically as the outlaws and the robber, they are not better than they. All of them belong to nothing but the same group.

In this way, the upside-down nature of words and narrations reflects Chaucer's skilful technique of narrative stylistics in using the language, to say nothing of "The Manciple's Prologue and Tale." In this tale, saying nothing is equivalent to talking carelessly and glibly. Consequently, Chaucer has illuminated the wisdom of life, i.e. we should be moderate and our words should be consistent with our actions, when he has arrived at the final stage of his pilgrimage. Chaucer has informed his own son of his valuable philosophy.

SELECT BIBLIOGRAPHY

Awaka, K. (1967) "St. Juliana no Gojun," *The Bulletin of Faculty of Education* 37, Mie University, 100-18.
Bachelard, G. (l967) *La poetique de l'espace*. Paris: Presses Universitaires de France.
Baird-Lang, L. Y. and H. Schnuttgen. (1988) *A Bibliography of Chaucer 1974-1985*. Cambridge: D. S. Brewer.
Baker, Donald C. (1958) "Imagery and Structure in Chaucer's *Book of the Duchess*," *Studia Neophilologica* 30, 17-26.
Barney, S. A. (1993) *Studies in Troilus: Chaucer's Text, Meter, and Diction*. East Lansing: Colleagues Press.
Baugh, A. C. ed. (1963) *Chaucer's Major Poetry*. New York: Appleton-Century-Crofts.
Baum, Paul F. (1956) "Chaucer's Puns," *PMLA* LXX, 225-46.
Bennett, J. A. W. (1968) *Chaucer's Book of Fame: An Exposition of 'The House of Fame.'* Oxford: Oxford University Press.
Bennett, J. A. W. (1974) *Chaucer at Oxford and at Cambridge*. Oxford: Clarendon Press.
Benson, L. D., ed. (1987) *The Riverside Chaucer*, 3rd ed. Boston: Houghton Mifflin.
Benson, L. D. (1992) "Chaucer's Spelling Reconsidered," *English Manuscript Studies 1100-1700*. Vol. 3, 1-28.
Benson, L. D., ed. (1993) *A Glossarial Concordance to the Riverside Chaucer*. Garland.
Blake, N. F. (1979) "The Northernisms in The Reeve's Tale," *Lore and Langauge*, The Centre for English Cultural Tradition and Langauge, University of Sheffield, 3:1, 1-8.
Blake, N. F., ed. (1980) *The Canterbury Tales: Edited from the Hengwrt Manuscript*. London: Edward Arnold.
Blake, N. F. (1981) *Non-standard Language in English Literature*. London: André Deutsch.
Blake, N. F. (1985) *The Textual Tradition of the Canterbury Tales*. London: Edward Arnold.
Blake, N. F., D. Burnley, M. Matsuo, and Y. Nakao, eds. (1994) *A New Concordance to The Canterbury Tales: Based on Blake's Text Edited from the Hengwrt Manuscript*. Okayama: University Education Press.

Blake, N. F. (1998) "Editing *The Canterbury Tales*," *Anglia*. Vol. 116, No. 2, 198-214.
Boitani, P. (1984) *Chaucer and the Imaginary World of Fame*. London: D. S. Brewer.
Boitani, P. and J. Mann eds. (1986) *The Cambridge Chaucer Companion*. Cambridge: Cambridge University Press.
Bollnow, O. F. (1963) *Mensch und Raum*. Stuttgart: W. Kohlhammer.
Brewer, D. S. (1963) *Chaucer in His Time*. London: Thomas Nelson and Sons, Ltd.
Brewer, D. S. and L. E. Brewer. eds. (1969) *Troilus and Crisedye* (abridged). London: Routledge and Kegan Paul.
Brook, G. L. (1963) *English Dialects*. London: André Deutsch.
Burnley, D. (1983) *A Guide to Chaucer's Language*. London: Macmillan.
Burnley, D. (1986) "Courtly Speech in Chaucer," *POETICA* 24, 16-38.
Burnley, D. (1990) *The Sheffield Chaucer Textbase*. Sheffield: University of Sheffield.
Cannon, C. (1998) *The Making of Chaucer's English*. Cambridge: Cambridge University Press.
Carson, M. Angela, O. S. U. (1967) "Easing of the 'Hert' in the *Book of the Duchess*," *Chaucer Review* 1, 157-60.
Chiappelli, C. P. (1977) *Chaucer's Anti-scholasticism Opposition and Composition in the House of Fame*. Michigan: University Microfilms.
Clark, John Frank. (1982) *The Hunt as Metaphor: A Study of the Theme of Death in Four Middle English Poems*. Michigan: Unpublished PhD Dissertation.
Clemen, Wolfgang. (1963,1980) *Chaucer's Early Poetry*. London: Methuen.
Coates, Jennifer. (1986, 1993[2]) *Women, Men and Language*. London: Longman.
Coghill, N. (1949) *The Poet Chaucer*. Oxford: Oxford University Press.
Coghill, N. (1956) *Geoffrey Chaucer*. London: Longmans.
Cooper, H. (1989, 1996[2]) *The Canterbury Tales* (Oxford Guide to Chaucer). Oxford: Oxford University Press.
Cooper, J. C. (1982) *Symbolism: The Universal Language*. Wellingborough.
Copland, M. (1983) "'The Reeve's Tale': Harlotrie or Sermonyng?" *Geoffrey Chaucer*, Herausgegeben von Willi Erzgraber. Darmstadt: Wissenshaftliche Buchgesellschaft, 357-80.
Correale, R. M. and M. Hamel (2002) *Sources and Analogues of the Canterbury Tales*. Cambridge: D. S. Brewer.
Cuddon, J. A. ed. (1977) *A Dictionary of Literary Terms*. London: André Deutch.
Davenport, W. A. (1988) *Chaucer: Compaint and Narrative*. London: Brewer.
David, Luisi. (1971) "The Hunt Motif in *The Book of the Duchess*," *English Studies* 52, 309-11.
Davis, N. (1974) "Chaucer and Fourteenth-Century English," *Writers and Their*

Background: Geoffrey Chaucer, edited by D. Brewer. London: G. Bells and Sons.
Davis, N., D. Gray, P. Ingham, and A. Wallace-Hadrill, eds. (1979) *A Chaucer Glossary*. Oxford: Clarendon Press.
Delany, S. (1972) *Chaucer's House of Fame: The Poetics of Skeptical Fideism*. Chicago: The University of Chicago Press.
Delasanta, Rodney. (1969) "Christian Affirmation in *The Book of the Duchess*," *PMLA* LXXXIV, 245-51.
Demoto, F. (1973) "Shoki Chueishi *The Owl and the Nightingale* no Gojun ni tsuite (I)." *Shinonome Eigo Kenkyu* 7, 10-13.
Demoto, F. (1973) "Shoki Chueishi *The Owl and the Nightingale* no Gojun ni tsuite (II)." *The Bulletin of Hijiyama Women's Junior College* 9, 1-10.
Denison, D. (1993) *English Historical Syntax*. London and New York: Longman.
Donaldson, E. T. ed. (1958) *Chaucer's Poetry: An Anthology for the Modern Reader*. New York: The Ronald Press.
Ebi, H. (1977) "*The Book of the Duchess* ni okeru Hikari to Yami — Gothic Geijutsu no 'Hikari no Bigaku'," *Kwansai Ika Daigaku Kyoyobu Kiyo* 8, 15-126.
Edwards, R. R. (1989) *The Dream of Chaucer*. Durham and London: Duke University Press.
Eldredge, Laurence. (1969) "The Structure of *The Book of the Duchess*," *Revue de l'Universite d'Ottawa* 39, 132-51.
Eliason, N. F. (1956) "Some Word-Play in Chaucer's Reeve's Tale," *Modern Languages Notes* LXXI, 162-64.
Eliason, N. F. (1972) *The Language of Chaucer's Poetry: An Appraisal of the Verse, Style, and Structure*. (Anglistica, XVII.) Copenhagen: Rosenkilde and Bagger.
Elliott, R. W. V. (1974) *Chaucer's English*. London: André Deutsch.
Elmer, W. (1981) *Diachronic Grammar: The history of Old and Middle English subjectless constructions*. Tübingen: Niemeyer.
Fichte, J. O. (1973) "*The Book of the Duchess* — A Consolation?," *Studia Neophilologica* 45, 53-67.
Fichte, J. O. (1980) *Chaucer's Art Poetical: A Study in Chaucerian Poetics*. Tübingen: Narr.
Finlayson, J. (1986) "Seeing, Hearing, and Knowing in *The House of Fame*," *Studia Neophilologica* 58, 47-57.
Firth, J. R. (1969) "Modes of Meaning," in *Papers in Linguistics 1934-1951*. Oxford: Oxford University Press.
Fisher, J. H. (1977) *The Complete Poetry and Prose of Geoffrey Chaucer*. New York: Holt, Rinehart and Winston.
Fitzpatrick, L. J. (1974) *Chaucer the Word-master: The House of Fame and The*

Canterbury Tales. Michigan: University Microfilms.
Fries, C. C. (1940) "On the Development of the Structural Use of Word-order in Modern English," *Language* 16, 199-208.
Fyler, John M. (1977) "Irony and the Age of Gold in *The Book of the Duchess*," *Speculum.* Vol. LII, No. 2, 314-28.
Gaaf, van der. (1904) *The Transition from the Impersonal to the Personal Construction in Middle English.* Heidelberg: Carl Winter.
Gellrich, J. M. (1985) *The Idea of the Book in the Middle Ages.* Ithaca and London: Cornell University Press.
Goffin, R. C. (1943) "Quiting by Tidings in *The House of Fame*," *Medium Ævum*, XII.
Grennen, Joseph E. (1964) "Hert-huntyng in *The Book of the Duchess*," *Modern Language Quarterly* 15, 131-39.
Gruber, L. C. (1972) *Isolation in Old English Elegies and the Canterbury Tales: A Contribution to the Study of the Continuity of English Poetry.* Michigan: Unpublished PhD Dissertation.
Gruber, L. C. (1972) "The Wanderer and Arcite: Isolation and the Continuity of the English Elegiac Mode" in *Four Papers for Michio Masui*, ed. Raymond P. Tripp, Jr. (Denver: The Society for New Language Study, 1972),1-10.
Hanning, R. W. (1986) "Chaucer's First Ovid: Metamorphosis and Poetic Tradition in *the Book of the Duchess* and *the House of Fame*," *Chaucer and the Craft of Fiction,* edited by L. A. Arrathoon. Michigan: Solaris Press.
Harada, H. (1977) "A Japanese Translation of *The Book of The Duchess*," *Hiroshima Shudai Ronshu.* Vol. 18, No. 1, 331-89.
Hart, W. M. (1908) "The Reeve's Tale: A Comparative Study of Chaucer's Narrative Art," *PMLA* XXIII, 1-44.
Havely, N. R. (1994) *Chaucer: The House of Fame.* Durham: Durham Medieval Texts.
Higuchi M. (1996) *Studies in Chaucer's English.* Tokyo: Eichosha.
Hill, John M. (1974) "*The Book of the Duchess*, Melancholy, and That Eight-year Sickness," *Chaucer Review.* Vol. 9, No. 1, 35-50.
Hoad, T. (1992) "Chaucer's Language: On What Is Possible in Stylistic Analysis," *POETICA* 36, 15-37.
Horobin, S. C. P. (1998) "A New Approach to Chaucer's Spelling," *English Studies.* Vol. 79, No. 5, 415-24.
Huppe, Bernard F. and D. W. Robertson, Jr. (1963) *A Fruyt and Chaf: Studies in Chaucer's Allegories.* Princeton: Princeton University Press.
Hussey, S. S. (1971) *Chaucer: An Introduction.* London: Methuen.
Isenor, N. and K. Woolner. (1980) "Chaucer's Theory of Sound," *Physics Today* 3, 114-16.

Ito, E. (1974) "A Study of Impersonal Verbs in Middle English," *The Bulletin of Kobe Jogakuin University*, 1-23.
Iwashita, S. (1980) "'The Tale of Melibee' no Gojun no Kousatu," *Nebyurasu* 8, 113-28.
Jespersen, O. (1917) "Negation in English and Other Langauges," *Selected Writings of Otto Jespersen*. Rptd. Tokyo: Senjo, 1960, 3-151.
Jespersen. Otto. (1947 rpt. of 1922) *Language and Its Nature, Development and Origin*. London: George Allen and Unwin.
Jespersen. O. (1961, rpt. of 1927) *A Modern English Grammar*. Part III. London: George Allen and Unwin.
Jimura, A. (1979) "The Characterisations of Troilus and Criseyde through Adjectives in Chaucer's *Troilus and Criseyde* — "trewe as stiel" and "slydynge of corage"—," *PHOENIX* 15, Department of English, Hiroshima University, 101-22.
Jimura, A. (1980) "Chaucer's Depiction of Characters through Adjectives," *Ohtani Studies* XVI, 1-20
Jimura, A. (1981) "The Anglo-Saxon Poem "The Seafarer" and Ezra Pound's "The Seafarer": Similarities and differences" *ERA* New Series, The English Research Association of Hiroshima, Department of English, Hiroshima University, Vol. 1, No. 2, 1-18.
Jimura, A. (1983) "Chaucer's Use of Impersonal Constructions in *Troilus and Criseyde*: by aventure yfalle," *Bulletin of Ohtani Women's College*, XVIII. i. l4-27.
Jimura, A. (1987) "Chaucer's Depiction of Courtly Manners and Customs through Adjectives in *Troilus and Criseyde*," *Philologia* 19. Association of English Studies, Mie University, 1-26,
Jimura, A. (1987) "Chaucer no Yakata no Hyogen," *Hito no Ie Kami no Ie*. Kyoto: Apollon-sha.
Jimura, A. (1990) "Chaucer's Use of Northern Dialects in *The Reeve's Prologue and Tale*," *Festschrift for Kazuso Ogoshi, Ohtani Women's College*. Kyoto: Apollon-sha. 159-83.
Jimura, A. (1993) "Word-formation of Chaucer's English (I)," *Bulletin of the Faculty of School Education*, Hiroshima University, Part II, Vol. 15, pp. 1-16.
Jimura, A., Y. Nakao, and M. Matsuo, eds. (1995) *A Comprehensive List of Textual Comparison between Blake's and Robinson's Editions of The Canterbury Tales*. Okayama: University Education Press.
Jimura, A. (1997) "Chaucer's Description of Nature through Adjectives in *Troilus and Criseyde*," *English and English Teaching* 2, Department of English, Faculty of School Education, Hiroshima University, 57-69.
Jimura, A. (1998) "Metathesis in Chaucer's English," *A Love of Words: English Philological Studies in Honour of Akira Wada*, edited by M. Kanno,

G. K. Jember, and Y. Nakao, 103-114. Tokyo: Eihosha.
Jimura, A. (1998) "Metathesis in Chaucer's English," *A Love of Words: English Philological Studies in Honour of Akira Wada*, edited by M. Kanno, G. K. Jember, and Y. Nakao. Tokyo: Eihosha, 103-114. .
Jimura, A., Y. Nakao, and M. Matsuo, eds. (1999) *A Comprehensive Textual Comparison of Troilus and Criseyde*. Okayama: University Education Press.
Jimura, A., Y. Nakao, and M. Matsuo, eds. (2002) *A Comprehensive Textual Comparison of Chaucer's Dream Poetry*. Okayama: University Education Press.
Jordan, Robert M. (1974-75) "The Compositional Structure of *The Book of the Duchess*," *Chaucer Review*. Vol. 9, No. 2, 99-117.
Kanayama, A. (1966) "Chaucer no Sanbun ni okeru Gojun — Bun no Shuyoso ni Kanren shite," *Osaka Gaidai Eibei Kenkyu* 5, 1-32.
Kawai, Michio. (1983) "Modes of Swearing in Eighteenth-century Drama," *Festschrift for Michio Masui, Hiroshima University*. Tokyo: Kenkyusha. 191-97.
Kawasaki, K. (1974) *Marvel no Niwa*. Tokyo: Kenkyusha.
Kawasaki, K. (1983) *Niwa no England*. Nagoya: Nagoya University Press.
Kawasaki, K. (1984) *Rakuen to Niwa*. Tokyo: Chukoshinsho.
Kerkhof, J. (1966, 1982²) *Studies in the Language of Geoffrey Chaucer*. Leiden: Leiden University Press.
Kittredge, G. L. (1915) *Chaucer and His Poetry*. Cambridge, Mass: Harvard University Press.
Klaeber, Fr. (1922) *Beowulf and the Fight at Finnsburg*. Lexington, Massachusetts: D. C. Heath and Company.
Kökeritz, Helge. (1954) "Rhetorical Word-play in Chaucer," *PMLA* LXIX, 937-52.
Koonce, B. G. (1966) *Chaucer and Tradition of Fame: Symbolism in the House of Fame* Princeton: Princeton University Press.
Lakoff, Robin. (1975) *Language and Woman's Place*. New York: Harper and Row Publishers.
Leyerle, J. (1971) "Chaucer's Windy Eagle," *UTQ* Vol.40, No.3, 247-65.
Leyerle, John. (1974) "The Heart and the Chain," *The Learned and the Lewed: Studies in Chaucer and Medieval Literature*, edited by Larry D. Benson. Cambridge, Mass: Harvard University Press.
Longsworth, R. (1974) "Chaucer's Clerk as Teacher," *The Learned and the Lewed: Studies in Chaucer and Medieval Literature*, edited by Larry D. Benson. Cambridge: Harvard University Press, 61-66.
Manly J. M. and E. Rickert, eds. (1940) *The Text of the Canterbury Tales*, 8 vols. Chicago: University of Michigan Press.
Manning, Stephen. (1956) "That Dreamer Once More," *PMLA*. LXXI, 540-41.

Manning, Stephen. (1958) "Chaucer's Good Fair White: Woman and Symbol," *Comparative Literature*. Vol. X, No. 2, 97-105.
Masui, M. (1958) "Chaucer's Use of 'Smile' and 'Laugh,'" *Anglica*, III, iii, 1-16.
Masui, M. (1962, 1973) *Studies in Chaucer* (in Japanese). Tokyo: Kenkyusha.
Masui, M. (1964) *The Structure of Chaucer's Rime Words: An Exploration into the Poetic Language of Chaucer*. Tokyo: Kenkyusha.
Masui, M. (1967) "A Mode of Word-Meaning in Chaucer's Language of Love," *Studies in English Literature*. English Number 1967. Tokyo. 113-26.
Masui, M. (1972) "Chaucer's Tenderness and the Theme of Consolation," *Neuphilologische Mitteilungen* 73, 214-21.
Masui, M. (1976) Chaucer no Sekai. Tokyo: Iwanami.
Masui, M. (1977) "Chaucer no Geijutsu to Humanism: Buntaiteki Kenchi kara," *Chusei to Renaissance*. Tokyo: Aratake shuppan.
Masui, M. (1988) *Studies in Chaucer's Language of Feeling*. Tokyo:Kinseido.
Masui, M. (1988) *A New Rime-Index to the Canterbury Tales based on Manly and Rickert's Edition of the Canterbury Tales*. Tokyo: Shinozaki-shorin.
Matsuo, M., Y. Nakao, S. Suzuki, and T. Kuya, comp. (1986) *A PC-KWIC Concordance to the Works of Geoffrey Chaucer Based on Robinson (1957)*. Yamaguchi and Hiroshima: Yamaguchi University and Hiroshima University.
McCall, J. P. (1979) *Chaucer among the Gods*. University Park and London: The Pennsylvania State University Press.
McIntosh, Angus et al. eds. (1986) *A Linguistic Atlas of Late Mediaeval English*. Aberdeen: Aberdeen University Press.
Minnis, A. J. (1982) *Chaucer and Pagan Antiquity*. Cambridge: D. S. Brewer.
Minnis, A. J. (1995) *The Shorter Poems* (Oxford Guide to Chaucer). Oxford: Clarendon Press.
Miura, T. (1967) "Chaucer ni okeru Shugo to Jutsugodoushi no Gojun," *Kobe Miscellany* 5, 85-104.
Mossé, F. (1952) *A Handbook of Middle English*. Baltimore: The Johns Hopkins University Press.
Muscatine, C. (1950) "Form, Texture, and Meaning in Chaucer's *Knight's Tale*," *PMLA*, LXV, 911-29.
Muscatine, C. (1957) *Chaucer and the French Tradition: A Study in Style and Meaning*. Los Angeles and London: University of California Press.
Mustanoja, T. F. (1960) *A Middle English Syntax*. Helsinki: Société Néophilologique.
Nakao, T. (1972) *Eigoshi II*. Tokyo: Taishukan.
Nakao, Y., S. Suzuki, T. Kuya, and M. Matsuo. (1985) "Personal Computer niyoru Chaucer Sakuhin no Yourei Kensaku Shisutemu," *Yamaguchi University Eigo to Eibungaku*, Vol. 20, 61-72.
Nakao, Y. (1994) "Chaucer no *Troilus and Criseyde* ni okeru Text Ido to Juyo

no Mondai," *Eigo to Eibeibungaku* 29, 51-94.
Nakao, Y. (1994) "Chaucer no *Troilus and Criseyde* ni okeru Text Ido to Juyo no Mondai," *Eigo to Eibeibungaku* 29, 51-94.
Nakatani, K. (l963) "A Perpetual Prison: The Design of Chaucer's Knight's Tale," *Hiroshima Studies in English Language and Literature* IX, i, ii.The English Literary Association of Hiroshima University.
Nishimura, H. (1985) "Chueigo ni okeru Gojun to Johokozo," *Eigo to Eibenbungaku* 20, 11-33.
Oiji, T. (1968) *Chaucer to sono Shuhen*. Tokyo: Bunrishoin.
Oizumi, Akio, ed. (1991) *A Complete Concordance to the Works of Geoffrey Chaucer*, programmed by K. Miki, 10 vols. Hildesheim: Olms-Weidmann.
Otsuka, T. and F. Nakajima, eds. (1982) *The Kenkyusha Dictionary of English Linguistics and Philology*. Tokyo: Kenkyusha.
Pearcy, R. J. (1986) "The Genre of Chaucer's Fabliau-Tales," *Chaucer and the Craft of Fiction* edited by Leigh A. Arrathoon. Michigan: Solaris Press, Inc., 329-84
Pearsall, D. (1985) *The Canterbury Tales*. London: George Allen & Unwin.
Phillips, Helen. ed. (1982) *Chaucer: The Book of the Duchess*. Durham: University of Durham.
Phillips, H. and N. Havely. (1997) *Chaucer's Dream Poetry*. London: Longman.
Prior, Sandra Pierson. (1986) "Routhe and Hert-Huntyng in *The Book of the Duchess*," *Journal of English and Germanic Philology* 85, 3-19.
Reiss, Edmund. (1973) "Chaucer's Parodies of Love," *Chaucer the Love Poet*, edited by J. Mitchell and W. Provost. Athens: University of Georgia Press, 27-44.
Robertson, Jr., D. W. (1962) *A Preface to Chaucer*. Princeton: Princeton University Press.
Robinson, F. N., ed. (1957) *The Works of Geoffrey Chaucer*, 2nd ed. Boston: Houghton Mifflin.
Rooney, Anne. (1987) "*The Book of the Duchess*: Hunting and the 'UBI SUNT' Tradition," *Review of English Studies* 38, 299-314.
Root, R. K., ed. (1926) *The Book of Troilus and Criseyde by Geoffrey Chaucer*. Princeton: Princeton University Press.
Roscow, G. H. (1981). *Syntax and Style in Chaucer's Pooetry*. Cambridge: D. S. Brewer.
Ruggiers, Paul G., ed. (1979) *The Canterbury Tales: A Facsimile and Transcription of the Hengwrt Manuscript, with Variants from the Ellesmere Manuscript*. Norman, OK: University of Oklahoma Press.
Saito, T. (1974) "Word-order in Late Middle English," *Murakami Shikou Kyoju Taikan Kinen Ronbunshu*, 433-44.
Salmon, Vivian. (1975) "The Representation of Colloquial Speech in *The Canterbury Tales*," *Style and Text: Studies Presented to N. E. Enkvist*.

Stockholm: Sprakforlaget Skirptor AB and Abo Akademi. 263-77.
Samuels, M. L. and J. J. Smith (1988) *The English of Chaucer and His Contemporaries*. Aberdeen: Aberdeen University Press.
Sandved, A. O. (1985) *Introduction to Chaucerian English*. Cambridge: D. S. Brewer.
Sasagawa, H. (1968a) "Chaucer no Sanbun ni okeru Gojun," *Launch* 1, 44-56.
Sasagawa, H. (1968b) "Chaucer no Sanbun ni okeru Gojun," *The Bulletin of Liberal Arts* 1, Niigata University, 23-34.
Sasaki, F. (1983) "*The House of Fame* no Shudai to Buntai" *Katahira* 19. Okazaki: Chubu Katahirakai.
Sasaki, F. (1988) "*The House of Fame* to And," *Festshrift for Prof. Sachiho Tanaka*. Tokyo: Kirihara-shoten.
Schaar, Claes. (1954) *Some Types of Narrative in Chaucer's Poetry*. Lund: C. W. K. Gleerup.
Schlauch, Margaret. (1952) "Chaucer's Colloquial English: Its Structural Traits," *PMLA*.LXVII, 1103-16.
Scott-Macnab, David. (1987) "A Reexamination of Octovyen's Hunt in *The Book of the Duchess*," *Medium Ævum*. Vol. LVI, No. 2, 183-99.
Shigeo, H. (1958) "'Koushaku Fujin no Sho' Shoron," *Meiji Gakuin Daigaku Ronshu*. Vol. 50, No. 1, 73-84.
Shimogasa, T. (1975) "Chaucer no Sakuhin ni Arawareru 'UN'-words no Kenkyu," *Yamaguchi Women's University Kenkyu Kiyo*. Vol. 1, 59-71.
Shinoda, Y. (1976) "A Research on Major and Minor Sentence Patterns in *Cursor Mundi*," *The Bulletin of Faculty of Letters* 35, Hiroshima University, 171-89.
Shirley, Charles G. (1978) Jr. *Verbal Texture and Character in Chaucer's Troilus and Criseyde*. Michigan: Unpublished PhD Dissertation.
Shoaf, R. A. (1979) "Stalking the Sorrowful H(e)art: Penitential Lore and the Hunt Scene in Chaucer's *The Book of the Duchess*," *Journal of English and Germanic Philology*. Vol. 78, No. 3, 313-24.
Shomura, T. (l975) "Chaucer no *The Miller's Tale* to sono Ruiwa: Dento to Sozo" *Kumamoto Tandai Ronshu* LI, l-l8.
Sisam, K. ed. (1921) *Fourteenth Century Verse and Prose*. Oxford: Clarendon Press.
Skeat, W. W. ed. (1894-1897) *The Complete Works of Geoffrey Chaucer*, 7 vols. Oxford: Clarendon Press.
Smith, J. J.,ed. (1988) *The English of Chaucer and His Contemporaries: Essays by M. L. Samuels and J. J. Smith*. Aberdeen: Aberdeen University Press.
Spearing, A. C. (1976) *Medieval Dream-Poetry*. Cambridge: Cambridge University Press.
Spearing, A. C. and J. E. Spearing, (1979) *The Reeve's Prologue and Tale with*

the Cook's Prologue and the Fragment of his Tale. Cambridge: Cambridge University Press.
Spearing, A. C. (1987) *Readings in Medieval Poetry*. Cambridge: Cambridge University Press.
Spitzer, L. (1948), "Linguisitics and Literary History," *Leo Spitzer: Representative Essays*, edited by A. K. Forcione, H. Lindenberger and M. Sutherland. Stanford: Stanford University Press, 1988.
Steadman, J. M. (1961) "Chaucer's "Desert of Libye," Venus, and Jove," *Modern Language Notes* 76, 196-201.
Stevenson, K. G. (1978) *The Structure of Chaucer's House of Fame*. Michigan: University Microfilms.
Sudo, J. (1967) "A Preliminary Note on the Langauge and Style of Chaucer's *Book of the Duchess*," *Kobe Gaidai Ronso*. Vol. 18, No. 4, 1-28.
Sukagawa, S. (1967) "Kobun ni miru ME no Togohou — Chaucer to sono Jidai wo Chushin ni," *Metropolitan* 12, 56-62.
Tajima, M., ed. (1998) *A Bibliography of English Language Studies in Japan 1900-1996*. Tokyo: Nan'un-do.
Tajiri, M. (1989) "Variation of Word Order in the Manuscripts of the *Canterbury Tales*," *Osaka Gaikokugo Daigaku Ronshu* 2, 39-52.
Takahashi, H. (1991) "Why not 'this Criseyde'?" *Language and Style in English Literature: Essays in Honour of Michio Masui*, edited by M. Kawai. Hiroshima: The English Research Association of Hiroshima. 374-91.
Tatlock, J. S. P. and A. G. Kennedy (l963) *A Concordance to the Complete Works of Geoffrey Chaucer and to the Romaunt of the Rose*. Gloucester, Mass.: Peter Smith.
Taylor, Davis. (1969) *Style and Character in Chaucer's Troilus*. Michigan: Unpublished PhD Dissertation.
Ten Brink, Bernhard Aegidius Konrad. (1969, rpt of 1901) *The Language and Metre of Chaucer*, 2nd ed. revised by Friedlich Kluge, translated by M. Bentinck Smith. New York: Greenwood Press.
Thiebaux, Marcelle. (1974) *The Stag of Love: The Chase in Medieval Literature*. Ithaca and London: Cornell University Press.
Tilley, M. P. (l950) *A Dictionary of the Proverbs in England*. Michigan: The University of Michigan Press.
Tillyard, E. M. W. (1943) *The Elizabethan World Picture*. London: Chatto & Windus.
Tisdale, Charles P. R. (1973) "Boethian "Hert-Huntyng": the Elegiac Pattern of *The Book of the Duchess*," *American Benedictine Review* 24, 365-80.
Tolkien, J. R. R. (1934) "Chaucer as a Philologist: *The Reeve's Tale*," Transactions of the Philological Society, 1-70.
Toyama, S. (1982) "'Watashi' no Mondai," *Eigo Seinen* (*The Rising*

Generation) Vol. CXXVIII, No. 5, Tokyo: Kenkyusha, 335.
Traugott, E. C. (1972) *A History of English Syntax*. New York: Holt, Rinehart and Winston.
Traversi, D. (1977) *Chaucer: the Earlier Poetry*. Newark: University of Delaware Press.
Traversi, D. (1983) *The Canterbury Tales: A Reading*. London: The Bodley Head.
Tripp, R. P. Jr., (1976) "On the Continuity of English Poetry between *Beowulf* and Chaucer," *POETICA* Vol.6, 1-21.
Tsuru, H. (1962) "'Koushaku Fujin no Sho' Kenkyu(I)," *Kassui Ronbunshu* 5, 1-6.
Tsuru, H. (1965) "'Koushaku Fujin no Sho' niokeru Nagusame," *Academia* 45.46, 59-75.
Uemura, R. (1956) "Characteristics of the Impersonal Constructions," *Hiroshima Studies in English Language and Literature*, (The English Literary Association of Hiroshima University), Vol. 3, No. 1, 82-92.
Utley, Frances Mae. (1974) *The Hunt as Structural Paradigm in The Book of the Duchess*. Michigan: Unpublished PhD Dissertation.
Wesse E. Walter. (1950) *Word-order as a Factor of Style in Chaucer's Poetry*. Michigan: Unpublished PhD Dissertation.
Whiting, B. J. (1934) *Chaucer's Use of Proverbs*. Cambridge: Harvard University Press.
Whitmore, S. M. E. (1972) *Medieval English Domestic Life and Amusements in the Works of Chaucer*. New York: Cooper Square Publishers, Inc.
Whittock, T. (1968) *A Reading of the Canterbury Tales*. London: Cambridge University Press.
Wilson, G. R. (1972) "The Anatomy of Compassion: Chaucer's *Book of Duchess*," *Texas Studies in Literature and Language* XIV. 3, 381-88.
Wimsatt, James I. (1967) "The Apotheosis of Blanche in *The Book of the Duchess*," *Journal of English and Germanic Philology* 66, 26-44.
Wimsatt, James I. (1970) *Allegory and Mirror: Tradition and Structure in Middle English Literature*. New York: Pegasus.
Windeatt, B. A. ed. (1982) *Chaucer's Dream Poetry: Sources and Analogues*. London: Brewer.
Windeatt, B. A., ed. (1984), *Troilus and Criseyde: A new edition of 'The Book of Troilus'*. London and New York: Longman.
Winny, J. ed. (1966) *The Clerk's Prologue and Tale: from the Canterbury Tales by Geoffrey Chaucer*. Cambridge: Cambridge University Press.
Winny, J. (1973) *Chaucer's Dream-Poems*. London: Chatto and Windus.
Wrenn, C. L. (1967) "On the Continuity of English Poetry," *A Study of Old English Literature*. New York: Harrap.
Wyler, S. (1944) *Die Adjective des mittelenglischen Schönheitsfeldes unter*

besonderen Berucksichtigung Chaucers. Diss. Zurich, Biel: Graphische Anstalt Schuler.

Wynne-Davies, M. ed. (1992) *The Tales of the Clerk and the Wife of Bath.* London: Routledge.

INDEX

A

Absolon 46, 47
accessories 139, 142
Achille 62
adjective 14, 30, 34-35, 37, 53-54, 57-61, 65-67, 76-78, 96, 102, 120, 124, 126-127, 129-132, 136-137, 139, 141, 143-144, 147-149, 154-157, 165, 167-169, 171, 175, 180-181, 190, 192, 194, 207, 214, 224; adjectives 8, 9, 57, 66, 71, 96-97, 100, 102-103, 117-134, 136-137, 152, 154, 159, 166, 168, 171, 173, 182-183, 190, 196, 210, 222-225
adjective-noun collocations 119
adverb 14, 30, 80, 89, 101, 104, 192, 194, 210, 214, 230; adverbs 100-101
adverse 180
Aeneas 27
Aeolus 36
al 96
Alayn 89
Alcyone 12-16, 20, 23
alderlevest 127
Aleyn 82, 88-89, 91-93, 115
Alison 45-47
allas 107-108, 116
alliteration 162
alliterative effect 91; alliterative expression 64; alliterative expressions 59, 76, 115; alliterative phrase 66, 77; alliterative verse 79
allye 65

almyghty 167-168, 174-175, 182, 224
ambivalent values 38
amyable 117
anaphora 233; anaphoric 107
Anglo-French 111
animals 154, 163
Antenor 151, 204
Antigone 96, 103
antithesis 19
antithetical description 72; antithetical expressions 11; antithetical keywords 7, 25, 220; antithetical presentation 38; antithetical values 36
Apollo 32
Arcite 43-44, 47-48, 74, 171, 184, 186, 188
arms 139-140
Arrathoon, L. A. 72, 114
art 32, 36
Artemis 177
ascetic 226
astrological expression 158; astrological expressions 157
astrology 45, 111
astronomy 111
atanes 89
auctoritee 38, 39, 220
audience 6, 12, 65, 68, 82-83, 85, 87, 130, 134-135, 167, 201, 213, 219, 227-228, 233
auditory sense 29
aungelik 140
auntre 84
autonomy 199

247

Aventure 37
aventure 178, 180, 181
awn 86

B
Bachelard, G. 75
Bachus 232
Baird-Lange, L. Y. 214
Baldeswelle 114; Bawdeswell 83; Bawdswell 114
Baugh, A. C. 14, 69, 147, 186
Baum, P. F. 12, 68, 219
bawdy words 107
bay 141; baye 142
bayard 142
bed 13, 45, 82, 91-93, 203; bedde 92; beds 115
bed-chamber 45, 46
Bedfordshire 86
befal 200; byfalle 204
Belial 41
bemes 154
benigne 173, 188
Bennett, J. A. W. 36, 72-73, 83, 115
Benson, L. D. 6, 68, 114, 139, 146-147, 166, 185-186, 191-192, 215
bente 157
Beowulf 122, 158, 168, 182, 184
Beowulf, the king 122
best 104; beste 103, 122-123
betide 200
bifel 202
bird 157, 164, 232-233; birds 16, 164
Black Knight 12-13, 17, 19-20, 23, 71
blak 139, 140, 154, 223; blake 140, 158-159
Blake, N. F. 80, 83-85, 87, 95, 114-115
Blake, William 117
blew 162, 165, 223; blewe 142
blisful 143, 159, 167-168, 171, 173-174, 182, 224
blood 18, 65, 67, 78, 113, 174, 222

blynde 150
Bobbe-up-and-doun 228, 230-231
body 11-13, 15, 18, 20, 22, 24, 40, 42-43, 56
Boethius 44, 180
Boitani, P. 70, 72
Bole 154
Bollnow, O. F. 75
Book of the Duchess, The 6-7, 11-13, 24, 68, 70-71, 219
book-production 3
bor 127, 163-166, 223; boor 164
Brewer, D. S. 74, 76, 140, 142, 163, 166, 179, 184-188, 216
Brewer, L. E. 185-188
bright 128-129, 154-155; brighte 125-126, 154; bryght 127; bryghte 155
British isles 87
broche 142, 205
Brook, G. L. 115
brother 119
broun 139
bryd 233
Buckinghamshire 87
bucolic level of speech 93
burlesque scene 46
burlesque sense 45
Burnley, D. 3-4, 78, 95, 206, 216

C
Calcas 147, 151, 173
Calkas 105, 113
Cambridge 63, 82, 87, 221; Cambridge students 8; Cambridge University 82
camus 65, 67
Cannon, C. 3
Canon's Yeoman's Prologue and Tale, The 190
Canterbury 230
Canterbury Tales, The 2, 6-7, 9, 39,

40, 43, 47, 62, 73, 76, 79, 83, 97,
117, 120, 152, 160, 182, 189, 201,
207, 209, 213-214, 216-217, 220-
221, 226-227, 230-231
capel 84
cas 178, 180, 181
Cassandre 145, 165; Cassandre's speech 177-178
caste 158
cat 232, 233
certes 100, 101
charitable 117
Chaucer, Geoffrey v-vi, 1-10, 14, 24-25, 39, 40-42, 45, 47-48, 52, 62, 65, 67, 70, 72-74, 76, 79, 80, 82, 84-85, 87-91, 95, 97, 106, 112-114, 116-120, 122, 125, 130-131, 134, 152, 161, 165-166, 168, 173, 183, 189, 191, 194, 196-197, 199-201, 203, 206-207, 214, 216-217, 219, 220-227, 231, 233-234; Chaucer's English vi, 3, 8, 79, 222, 225; Chaucer's language 1-4, 6, 110, 113, 219; Chaucerian 3, 6, 214, 226
chaumbre 55, 135, 138
chaunce 178, 180-181
Chiappelli, C. P. 73
Christ 167; Crist 169
Christian 40, 41, 42, 166, 188; Christians 168, 175; Christian God 167-168, 170, 175, 182-183, 187-188, 224-225; Christian god 188
Christianity 167, 183, 187, 224
Christmas 175
Cinthia 177, 182, 224
city speech 222
classic mythology 171
classical words 42
clauses 189, 206
Clemen, W. 70
Clerk of Oxenford 211

Clerk's Tale, The 9, 112, 189, 190, 191, 192, 195, 194, 207, 209, 211, 213, 216, 225, 226
closet 75
clothes 139, 140
Coates, J. 96, 98, 102, 107
Coghill, N. 69-70
cohesion 5
Cokkow 233
colde 58, 137
collocation 14, 102, 119, 121, 124, 131; collocations v, 5, 6, 8-10, 104, 117, 219, 222
colloquial English 87; colloquial language 96; colloquial speech 2, 102
communicative activities 4
complex expression 34
complex word 216
composite nature 33
compound word 12, 219
computer programme 6
conjunction 100; conjunctions 100
constellacioun 158
contentio 184
contractions 84
contradictory nature 34; contradictory values 34, 36, 38
contrastive techniques 38
Cook, the 228, 230-233
Cook's Tale, The 231
Cooper, J. C. 68
coordinate clauses 99; coordinate sentences 100
Copland, M. 80, 114
corage 192-193, 211
Correale, R. M. 39, 73
correspondence 142, 146
cote-armure 205
countrefete 228, 229
country speech 222
courtier 219

courtly 222; courtly games 142, 147
courtly love 21, 22, 49, 51; courtly manners and customs 134-135, 152; courtly society 113, 222; courtly speech 98
courtship 16
cradel 93
craft 31, 32, 33, 34, 35, 71
creative reading 4
creature 125, 129, 131
Criseyde 8, 49-63, 75, 79, 95-110, 112-113, 116-133, 135-148, 150, 153-154, 156-160, 162-166, 168-176, 178-184, 187-188, 201-207, 220, 222-225; *Criseyde* (vocative) 125-126; Criseyde's language 95, 100, 113, 222; Criseyde's letter 116; Criseyde's speech 100, 101, 102, 105, 112; Criseyde's verbosity 112; Criseyde-Antenor hostage exchange 95
crow 229, 231-233; *crowe* 229, 233
cruel 159, 174-175, 180, 182-183, 224
cuckold 233
cuckoo 233
Cuddon, J. A. 76
Cupid 167, 171, 173-174, 179, 182, 188, 224
curteis 117
customs 135, 148-149, 150, 152; customs and society 134, 135, 148

D

daf 84
data-based text 95
daunce 142, 147
Davenport, W. A. 73
Davis, N. 2, 4, 76, 215
day 154, 158, 159, 160
dede 162
deere 126, 128-29
Deiphebus 51

Delany, S. 72-73
Delasanta, R. 12, 68-69
delicious 143
demonstrarive pronoun 23
Denver University v
viderivatives 25, 27-29, 70, 72, 110, 192
derke 138
descriptive 3
destyne 178
devoir 110
devoure 78
dialect 83, 85, 94, 113, 222; dialects v, 5-6, 8, 10, 82, 89, 94, 219, 222; dialect speech 82
dialectal pronunciations 90; dialectal words 90
dialectology 3
Diana 171, 177-178, 182, 188, 224
Dido 27
Diomede 62, 105, 117-118, 120, 133, 140-141, 151, 163, 165-166, 173, 176, 204-205
disconsolat 58, 137
discourse 4
discreet 195, 196, 215, 225
disparage 67
dispitous 159
divine 170
dog 17, 71; *dogs* 17
Donaldson, E. T. 14, 69, 192, 214
dore 41, 45, 71, 138; *dores* 56, 58, 137
double entendre 11, 63
double meaning 229, 233
double-faced 11, 33, 38, 64, 66
draf-sak 92; *draf-sek* 84
dredful 181
driue 84
Durham 83

E

East Midland 81-83, 114
East Riding 86
Edwards, R. R. 71
egle 28-29, 31, 37, 163, 164, 166, 223
Eliason, N. E. 2, 76, 115
Ellesmere MS. 207
Elliott, R. W. V. 2, 4, 81, 113-114, 200, 206, 216
ellipsis 98
Elmer, W. 215
embroidered 139
Emelye 43-44, 47-48, 171, 184, 186
emotional adjectives 57
England 83, 113, 167, 222
English Research Association of Hiroshima, The vi
ensaumple 149
envious 159
epistemic clause 21
erme 14
ernest 231
erratik 157
esement 91
Essex 86
estat 104, 105
estatlich 117
eternal 170
etymology 14
Europe 74
everyday speech 30
experience 20, 26, 31, 70, 89, 121, 125, 139, 184
Experiencer 198
experimental use 34
eyen 22, 42, 61
eyr 59

F

fabliau 74, 85, 115; *fabliaux* 107
fair 67, 125, 135, 140, 180; *faire* 128; *feir* 67
fal 198, 200
fals 6-7, 11, 25-29, 31, 34-38, 72, 219, 220; *false* 148, 150
falsly 27
fame 25, 32, 35-36, 38, 106, 186
Fame, the goddess 32, 34, 36, 37, 72
faukoun 54
female characters 218
feminine style 99
ferfulleste 129, 131
ferli 84
Fichte, J. O. 69, 71
fierse 175
figurative 111
Finlayson, J. 71
Firth, J. R. 118, 184
Fitzpatrick, L. J. 73
flor 37
fo 125, 132, 183
folt 84
fonne 84
Forcione, A. K. 10
forlost 131
formal language 98
forms 83, 84
forshapen 164
Fortune, the goddess 54, 62, 72, 109, 167, 175, 178-181, 183, 188, 206, 224, 226
fra 86, 88
frame 52, 75
framework 118
fre 120
fredom 120
French 2, 80, 84, 110
frend 119
fresh 34, 54, 119; *fressh* 120; *fressh as is the month of May, as* 117, 120; *fresshe* 119, 162, 165, 223
Fukumoto, H. vi
Furies 109

G
ga 90
Gaaf, van der 196, 215
gallantry 7, 39
game 231
gar 84
garden 75; *gardyn* 74
gas 88
Gellrich, J. M. 71
gemme 142
General Prologue, The 9, 67, 77, 83, 97, 117, 120, 152, 160-162, 201, 207, 209, 213, 226, 230-231
gentil 54, 117, 123
gentileste 103, 104, 122
Gestalt 130
glade 37
gladly 9, 211, 213, 226
glas 77; *glass* 72
God 166, 168-170, 180, 182, 183, 187, 209, 221, 223-225, 231; *god* 166-167, 170, 175, 187
Goffin, R. C. 73
gold 33, 38; *gold-tressed* 166, 223; *gold-ytressed* 155
good 180, 186; *goode* 117, 119, 120; *goodlieste* 96, 103; *goodly* 110, 125, 180; *goodnesse* 195
Gordon, I. L. 184
Gothic 53, 74
Gower, John 3, 142
grammar v, 3, 6, 10, 96-97, 189; grammatical 5, 84, 189, 207, 226, 230; grammatical expressions 6, 9, 10, 219, 225
graphemics 3
Greece 95, 108, 116, 141, 148, 188; Greek 42, 55, 58, 61, 110; Greek camp 59, 60, 131, 136, 160, 176; Greeks 54, 176, 177, 178, 204
greeting 15
greipen 84

gret 165; *grete* 186
grey 77; *greye* 77
Griselda 9, 112, 189-196, 208-209, 211-226
Gruber, L. C. vi, 39, 187

H
hail 84
halles 59
Hamel, M. 39, 73
Hanning, R. W. 72
hap 200, 204
hardy 120, 123
harp 142
hart 12, 13, 16, 17, 19, 24, 71; *hert* 12, 16, 17, 23; *hart-hunting* 23; *hert-huntyng* 12, 24, 68, 219
Hart, W. M. 77, 115
Havely, N. R. 36, 70, 72
Heaven 221
Hector 105, 123, 203, 204
hede 12, 13
heigh 59, 175; *heighe* 168, 173, 174
helm 141
Hengwrt MS. 81, 84-85, 207
Heorot 158
hepen 84
heping 84
here 29
herte 6-7, 11-24, 40, 42-44, 55, 57, 62, 70, 119, 125, 128-129, 219
hertely 14
hertes line 48-49, 51, 62-63, 74-75, 221
Hertfordshire 87
hete 33
heteronomy 199
hethen 87
heven 62
hevenyssh 130
Hill, J. M. 68
Hiroshima University v, vi

Hoad, T. v
holy 167-168, 182, 224; *hooly* 78
honour 104, 105, 106, 113; *honure* 105
hope 84
Horaste 150
Host 39
hou 87
hougat 84
hous 6-7, 45-46, 56-57, 62, 71, 74-75, 116, 135-137, 220
House of Fame, The 6-7, 11, 24-25, 27-28, 30-33, 35-36, 38-39, 72, 106, 186, 219-220
house of love, the 48, 51, 52, 53, 54, 55, 59, 60, 61, 62, 74, 221
House of Rumour 37
Howard, E. J. 184
howgates 88
hows 52
Hudson, W. H. 152, 186
Humanistic 40
huntyng 16
Huppe, B. F. 69
Hussey, S. S. 72
hyperbolical terms 125
hypertextually 10
hypocritical nature 8, 63, 65, 68, 82, 221; hypocritical vocabulary 6, 11, 94, 222
hypotaxis 99, 100
hypothetical situation 190
hyt 18

I
ice 33
ik 81, 83, 88, 114
il 84
Imahayashi, O. vi
imell 84
Imeneus 109
imperative 90

impersonal "it" 199
impersonal construction 2, 201, 202; impersonal constructions 6, 9, 75, 196-200, 203, 206, 215, 225-226; impersonal and negative constructions 9-10; impersonal "it" 199; impersonal speech 110; impersonal verb 204; impersonal verbs 197-198, 200, 216
inconsistent structure 7
inferior 81, 221
inflections 84
infortuned 131
inorganic 11
insomnia 12, 13, 24, 219
integrated 2, 4; integrated technique of poetry 34
intellectual class 8, 63, 83, 221-222
intellectual inferiority 80
intensive adjectives 102
intensive adverb 96; intensive adverbs 96, 100
inter-sentential 4
interjection 107-108, 116; interjections 107
interrogative 98, 99
intra-sentential 4
Isenor, N. 71
Ito, E. 215
iwis 100, 101; *iwys* 101; *ywis* 96, 101; *ywys* 96, 101

J
Japan Society for Medieval English Studies vi
Jespersen, O. 102, 215
Jimura, A. vi, 71, 74, 116, 185, 216
John 45, 82, 87-93
joie 59-60, 102, 158
Jordan, R. M. 68, 74
Jove 109, 167, 170-171, 174-175, 180,

182, 187-188, 224
Judeo-Christian 42
Juno 14-15, 109, 178
Jupiter 187

K
Kawai, M. v, 107
Kawasaki, T. 75
Keisuisha Publishing Co., Ltd. vi
Kennedy, A. G. 73, 216
Kerkhof, J. 1, 2
key-expression 109
keyword 7, 12-13, 26, 28-29, 35, 43, 68, 70; keywords 1, 5-6, 11, 25-29, 32, 67, 71, 105
Kimura, I. vi
Kittredge, G. L. 18, 69, 184
Klaeber, Fr. 184
Knight, the 117, 120
Knight's Tale, The 7, 43, 45, 47, 62, 73, 134, 166, 171, 186-188, 220
knotte 185
knotteles 60, 136, 149
knyght 119, 121, 122, 123, 125
Kökeritz, H. 12, 22, 68-69, 219
Koonce, B. G. 70
Kubouchi, T. v
kunnynge 33
Kuya, T. 214
kynde 28-31, 71
kyndely 28

L
labyrinth 53
lady 125-127, 129, 234
Lakoff, R. 96, 100, 102
lame 144
Langland, William 3
language of Chaucer, the 1-4
language of Criseyde, the 79, 95, 96
language study 4
language use 3

lape 84
Late Mediaeval English 85
Latin 110-112, 187
Latin proverbium 112
Latona 109
laurer-crowned 155
Le Dit de la Panthere d'Amours 72
Legend of Good Women, The 73, 76
lemman 228-229, 233-234
lerne 31
lerned 230
lewed 149, 230
lexical 230; lexical point of view 85
Leyerle, J. 68, 71
light 172
Lindenberger, H. 10
linguistic community 94; linguistic innovation 3; linguistic joke 80
linguistic reality 87; linguistic theories 196
litel bok 146
literacy 96, 110
literary and linguistic 4
Livre de Melibee et de Dame Prudence 7, 39
loathly hags 130
logic 234
London 83-87, 114; London dialect 87, 90, 94, 222; London English 79; London spellings 97
lord 119
Louens, Renaud de 39
love 219
lovere 119
low social status 80
Lucina 177
lust 228
lusty 162, 165, 223, 228
lynage 67, 195
lyoun 120
lystes 134

M

Machine Readable Texts of Chaucer Project 216
macroscopic approach 5
makeles 140
male characters 218
man 119, 123, 124, 125
Man of Law's Tale, The 191
Manciple, the 227-228, 230-233
Manciple's Prologue and Tale, The 227, 234
Manciple's Prologue, The 228, 230, 231-232
Manciple's Tale, The 228, 231-232
Manly, J. M. 2
Mann, J. 72
Manning, S. 69
mannyssh 130, 207
manuscript 3; manuscripts 84, 85, 146
market-betere 64
Mars 109
Marte 167, 171, 175-176, 182, 188, 224
Masui, M. v, 1, 4, 38, 43, 67-69, 73-74, 76, 78, 113, 120, 146, 166, 186-187, 202, 215, 216
Matsuo, M. 6, 214
McIntosh, A. 85, 115
MED 13, 14, 52-54, 60, 64-66, 70-71, 75-77, 131, 142, 145, 157-158, 185, 191-192, 195
Melibee 40
Melibeus 40, 41, 42
men's speech 99, 107
Mercurie 109
Metamorphoses 163
mete 48
mewe 52, 53, 75
microscopic approach 5
Middle Ages, the 107, 139, 166, 168
middle class 94

Middle English 8, 16, 81, 94-96, 100, 110, 160, 189, 196, 206, 215; Middle English Dialects 83; Middle English period 107
Middlesex 86
Midlands 81
Miller, the 8, 63-65, 67-68, 78, 82-83, 87-89, 91-94, 221, 222
Miller's Tales, The 7, 45, 47, 62, 220
Milton, John 41
Minerva 177; Minerve 109
Minnis, A. J. 70
Missouri Valley College vi
miri 160, 186
modal verb 90
Modern English 196, 199
monologue 102
moon 154; *moone* 154, 155
morphemes 10, 189, 206
Morpheus 15
morphology 3
morwe 158
Mosse, F. 206
moste 96
multi-layered meanings 227
Muscatine, C. 43, 74, 77, 80, 114, 125, 133, 184
music 142-143
musical terms 143
muwe 54, 75
my deere herte 128
myghty 167, 168, 182; *myghty God* 168
mynde 12
mythology 174, 231

N

na 90
Nakajima, F. 10
Nakao, T. 197, 215
Nakao, Y. v, 214
Nakatani, K. v, 43, 73

namore 216; *namoore* 216
name 104, 106
namo 216
narration 219, 227; narrations 234
narrative parts 100; narrative structure 5, 233; narrative structures 49, 189; narrative stylistics 4, 6, 219, 227, 234; narrative techniques 227; narratives 11
narrator 9, 56, 63-68, 74-75, 81, 83, 86, 96, 100, 103, 105-106, 120-123, 135, 138, 142, 144-145, 148, 153, 160, 162, 167, 172, 175-176, 179, 180, 183, 200-201, 207, 212-213, 219, 221, 225-226, 233-234
nat 216
native words and phrases 2
natural objects 154, 155, 165
Nature 18, 203
nature 152-153, 155, 157, 160-163, 165-166, 198, 202
naught 216
nay 212, 216
ne 216
nece 125, 128
negatives 9, 206-207, 211-212, 216-218, 226; negative affix 216; negative expression 212; negative expressions 6, 9, 189, 206-209, 211-213, 226; negative prefix 189, 196, 207, 225; negation 195;
neither 216
Neptunus 109
never 216; *nevere* 216
New Testamant, The 42
newe 35-37, 127, 181, 223
newe tydynge 219
Nicholas 45, 47
night 158, 160; *nyght* 154
nightingale 163
noght 216; *nought* 216

Noah 45, 47
noble 60, 62, 65, 67-68, 119-121, 136, 220-221
nolde 216
non-violent language 109
noon 216
nor 216
Norfolk 83, 86, 87, 114
normal inanimate noun 18
North country speech 80
Northern 82, 83, 114
northern colouring 82
northern dialect 8, 63, 68, 79-85, 87-91, 94, 221, 222; northern dialects 83-85, 88-89, 97, 101, 221
northern feature 84; northern features 89; northern form 81, 86, 94, 114; northern forms 86, 88; northern pronunciation 90; northern speech 80, 82
Northumberland 83, 87
Northumbria 83
Norwich 83
nothing 216; *nothyng* 216
noun 13-14, 18, 21, 35, 66, 75-77, 102, 104-106, 109-110, 120-125, 128-129, 131-133, 138-139, 166, 170, 182, 192, 194-195, 207, 222, 224, 230; nouns 6, 8-9, 14, 57, 60, 76, 100, 102, 104, 118-119, 125, 134-135, 137, 141-142, 148, 154, 223-224; noun phrase 230
ny 216

O
o 107
oath 109; oaths 108, 109
obeisance 195
objective expression 199
observaunce 148, 149; *observaunces* 149
Odin 41

OED 13, 52-53, 60, 64-66, 70-72, 75-77, 81, 92, 96, 107, 111-112, 126, 128, 130-131, 136-139, 141-144, 147, 150, 152, 156-159, 162, 164, 167, 169, 171, 173-178, 180, 185-188, 190-191, 194-195, 207, 228, 230
Ohno, H. vi
Old English vi, 14, 39, 101, 111, 168, 182, 185, 196, 224
Old French 111, 169, 182, 224
Old Norse 111
Old Testament, The 42
olde 34, 35, 37, 148, 149; *olde bokes* 143, 145
omnipotens 187
opposite values 31
ordal 110
organic 12, 219; organic function 71; organic relationship 9; organic unities 5; organic unity 11
Otsuka, T. 10
Ovid 163
Oxford v, vi, 45

P
pagan god 167; pagan gods 166, 169, 171, 182-183, 223-224
pair 84
paired alliterated verbs 91
palais 75, 76; *paleis* 56
Palamon 43, 44, 47, 48, 171, 186, 188
paleography 3
palestral 147
paleys 57, 135-138
palinode 76
Palladium 171, 176, 182, 201, 224
Pallas 109, 182, 224; Pallas Athena 176
Pandarus 8, 48-54, 56, 60-63, 75-76, 95, 98, 101-106, 108-109, 112-113, 119, 121-126, 128-129, 138-144, 146-147, 149-50, 155, 157-159, 164, 168-170, 174-176, 178-181, 183-184, 188, 201-202, 220-222, 224; Pandarus's speech 102, 126, 181
Paradise Lost 41
parataxis 99, 100
parentheses 103
Parlament of Fowls, The 73, 143
parrot 229, 232
Parson's Prologue and Tale, The 227
Parson's Prologue, The 79
paved 139
Pearcy, R. J. 80, 114
Pearsall, D. 77
pecok 64
peert 66; *peert as a pye* 66
pejorative meaning 112, 234
Perotheus 44
perpetual prisoun 43
personal construction 199; personal constructions 200
personal noun 199
personal pronoun 199
personification 135
Phebus 155-156, 166, 204, 223, 228-229, 231-233
Phillips, H. 18, 69-70
philological 3
philological circle 5
Philological Society 83
philological studies v
philologist 80
Philomela 164
philosophy 234; philosophic eye 63; philosophic speech 44
phonology 3; phonological 84
phrases 189, 206
physical adjectives 138; physical love 62, 63; physical sense 138
physiology 18
piled 65

pilgrim 7, 39, 63, 219
pilgrimage 161, 234
Pilgrims 230
plants 154, 165
playful words 41, 42
plesaunt 117
pley 147
poet-pilgrim 41
poetic name 177; poetic persona 7, 39; poetic technique 31; poetic techniques 227
polysemic words and phrases 227
prefix 10, 111, 141
preposition 86
prescience 167, 169, 170
present indicative 88
Present-day English 101, 194
Prior, S. P. 69
Prioress 117
Prioresse, the 67, 77, 97
prisoun 43, 44, 45, 73, 74
pronominal form 114
pronoun 18-19, 23, 71, 81, 86, 88, 105, 114, 121
pronunciation 87, 96-97
proper noun 40, 89, 109, 119, 121, 230
proper words 41
protagonists 182
proud 64, 66, 67
proverb 90, 91, 231, 234; proverbs 90, 115; proverbial expression 159, 231; proverbial expressions 115; proverbial legalistic terms 91; proverbial statements 90
Providence 183, 225
Prudence 40, 41, 42
psychological aspects 198; psychological effect 67; psychological mental processes 199
pun 22
purveiaunce 169; *purveyanunce*
183, 224; *purveyaunce* 167, 170
pye 66

Q
quasi-adverb 136
queen 228
queynt 139

R
'real' subject 200
rakel 232
rakle 159
readers 65
recurrent adjective 30, 58, 59, 78, 140; recurrent expression 143; recurrent expressions 43; recurrent negatives 210; recurrent word 59, 120; recurrent words 5; recurring sounds 162
rede 162, 165, 223
reed 66
Reeve, the 8, 63-64, 68, 81-83, 86, 221
Reeve's Prologue and Tale, The 7-8, 63, 79-80, 85, 94, 97, 221-222
Reeve's Prologue, The 81-82, 88
Reeve's Tale, The 7, 11, 67-68, 78, 82-83, 87, 94, 221-222
regional and social dialects 9; regional and social varieties 8
regional dialect 9; regional dialects 6, 8, 79, 94
rein 154; *reyn* 154, 156, 165, 223
Reiss, E. 24, 69
repetition 98; repetitions 5
retracciouns 76
rhetoric 111; rhetorical device 233; rhetorical point of view 43
rhyme word 78, 106, 131; rhyme words 1, 68, 76, 121, 122, 123
rhyming adverbs 67; rhyming couplet 67; rhyming pair 59; rhym-

ing position 124; rhyming tag
    59
richesse 195
Rickert, E. 2
righte 126, 127; *rite* 148
Robertson, Jr., D. W. 69, 74, 115
Robinson, F. N. 2-3, 166, 216
Roman 42; Roman mythology 173, 177
Romance languages 111
Romaunt of the Rose, The 69, 73, 77, 191
rook 72
Rooney, A. 68
Roscow, G. H. 3, 206
rural dialect 97
rustic speech 88
ryng 142

S
sad 190-196, 212, 214, 225
sadly 193-194, 214
sadnesse 194
St. Peter's College v
sal 86, 90
Salmon, V. 2, 95
Samuels, M. L. 3, 94
samyt 139
Sandved, A. O. 3, 206
Sarpedoun 143
Sasaki, F. 70, 72
satirical poem 7
sauf 105
Sawada, M. vi
say 86
sayn 86
Scandinavian 41, 84
Schlauch, M. 1-2, 4, 95
Schnuttgen, H. 214
Scot-Macnab, D. 69
Scotland 101
scribe 3, 89; scribes 85, 94

season 161
secre 53, 138
see 29, 154
sel 84
self-mocking, satirical poem 39
sely 91
semantic 5; semantic features 197; semantically related words 26
semelieste 228, 229
sentence 32; sentences 189, 206
serious words 42
sey 86
Seys 12-16, 20
shal 90
shame 106
she-wolf 232, 233
sheeld 141
Shigeo, H. 74
Shirley, C. G. 104
Shoaf, R. A. 69
Shomura, T. 74
signpost 82
sikerly 101; *sikirly* 101
simile 36; similes 66, 117
Simpson College vi
Sir Gawain and Green Knight 79
Sir Orfeo 160, 185, 186
Sir Thopas 39
Sisam, K. 185-186
Skeat, W. W. 166, 185, 216
skilled words 41
slep 48
slik 84
slouthe 102
slydynge 60, 62, 105, 184; *slydynge corage* 184; *slydynge of corage* 60, 74, 120, 131, 133, 135, 136, 205, 216
Smith, J. J. 3, 94
smoterlich 66
social activities 5; social dialect 9, 222; social dialects 6, 79; so-

cial inferiority 80
society 150, 151, 166
sociolinguistic 1, 5, 8, 94
sonne 154, 155, 187
sonnet 96
Sophia 40-42
sorwe 48, 158
sorwful 119, 124, 129, 131, 164, 181
sory 181
soth 6-7, 11, 25-29, 31, 33, 35, 37-39, 70, 72, 219-220
sothe 64
sothfast 169
soule 55
sound 30
sounds 83
southerners 83
sovereyne 170
Spearing, A. C. 65, 71-72, 77, 83, 115
Spearing, J. E. 77, 115
speech 29-30, 58, 63, 87-89, 91, 93, 97-98, 100-101, 105-107, 112, 127, 129, 173, 192, 195, 204-205, 209, 211-212, 229, 231, 233
spelling 87
spiritual love 63
Spitzer, L. 5, 10
spoken language 99
Squire, the 117, 120
standard language 79
statistical data 2
Steadman, J. M. 71
stede 141, 142
sterre 154
Stevenson, K. G. 70
stew 52
stidefast 191
stormy 190, 196, 225
straunge 146
strengthe 120
strong verbs 84
stronge 165

structure 7
structure of love 50
style 3; style of the language 5; styles 116
stylistic 5-6, 9; stylistic study 1; stylistics 5
subjective expression 199
subjectless constructions 196
subordinate sentences 100
Sudo, J. 116
Suffolk 87
superior class 94
superlative 96, 102-103, 121-124, 126, 229; superlatives 103
supernatural 178, 226
surface text 29
Sutherland, M. 10
Suzuki, S. 214
swain 84
swalowe 163, 164
swear words 107
swearing 96, 107, 172
sweete 152; *swete* 127, 128, 132
swerd 141
swilk 86
swoote 152
symbolic expression 45; symbolic meaning 56; symbolical departure 55
symbolism 7, 40-41, 62, 220
Symkyn 63, 65-67
synchronic 1
synonyms 5, 12-13; synonymous words 178
syntax 3; syntactic 189, 196, 198, 206-207, 226; syntactic aspect 197; syntactical unit 14; syntactical units 5
Sypherd, W. O. 70

T
Tabard 182

taboo language 96
Takahashi, H. v
Takeshima, T. v
tale 144
Tale of Melibee, The 7, 39-40, 56, 62, 220
Tale of Sir Thopas, The 7, 39
Tanaka, T. v.
Tatlock, J. S. P. 73, 216
Taylor, D. 98, 100, 104, 110, 123, 153, 161-162, 184, 186-187
technique 234; technique of language 31; technique of poetry 32
tendre 152; *tendre-herted* 131
tene 102
term of address 16
Teseida 76
text 2-6, 11, 15, 25, 147, 186, 216, 219; texts 4-6, 80, 84, 189-190, 194, 206-207, 216; textlinguistic 4, 5; textual comparison 6; textual criticism 3; textual structure v, 6, 9-10, 11, 219
Thebes 43
theek 81
Theseus, Duke 43
thi nece 129
Thiebaux, M 69
thoght 12; *thoughte* 199
thriftieste 103
til 84, 86, 88
Tilley, M. P. 75
Tillyard, E. M. W. 143, 185
Tisdale, C. P. R. 68, 69
Tokyo University v
Tolkien, J. R. R. 80, 83-85, 114-115
town 135, 136
Toyama, S. 200, 216
trappe 53; *trappe-dore* 53, 138
Traugott, E. C. 196, 215
Traversi, D. 73, 80, 114

trew 196, 225; *trewe* 35, 70, 72, 120-121, 123, 129, 194-195, 212; *trewelich* 100; *treweliche* 100; *trewely* 70, 72, 96, 100-101
Tripp, Jr., R. P. vi, 73, 160, 186
Troie 59, 60
Troie town 136
Troilus 8, 21, 48-63, 70, 74-76, 95, 98-109, 112-113, 116-129, 131-133, 135-151, 153, 155, 157-160, 162-168, 170-184, 187-188, 195, 201-205, 207, 220-225; *Troilus* (vocative) 119, 121, 124; Troilus's speech 101, 170, 182
Troilus and Criseyde 3, 5-9, 11, 39, 47-49, 62-63, 70, 72-73, 95, 107, 116-118, 125, 134-135, 151-153, 158, 160, 165-166, 170-171, 173, 177, 195-197, 200, 206-207, 220-223, 225-226
Trojans 49, 54, 149, 176, 204
trouthe 120, 195
Troy 54, 56, 59-60, 95, 105-106, 116, 136, 141, 148-149, 151, 176, 178, 180, 201, 204-205
truth 194
tulle 84
twa 86
twaie 86, 115
two-faced 94, 222
tydynge 37; *tydynges* 30-31, 36-38, 70
tymbur 52, 75

U
Ueda, Y. v
Ueki, K. v
Uemura, R. 215
uncerteyn 189
undergraduates' language 84
undigne 189
undiscreet 9, 189, 190, 225

unfamous 186
unkynde 207
unlyk 189
unnethe 189
unnethes 189
unreste 189, 190
unsad 9, 189-190, 196, 225; *unsadde* 212
unsely 180
untressed 189, 190
untrewe 9, 125, 127, 129, 189-190, 225
University of Oxford v
"un"-words 9, 91, 189-191, 196, 212, 214, 225
unworthy 189
upper class 8, 83, 95, 102, 110, 222
usage 148, 149

V
value words vi, 6
variant spellings 110
variants 25, 27-29, 72, 101
variation 8
variety 3
Veer 162
Venus 28, 109, 143, 156, 162, 167, 171-173, 182, 188, 224
verb 14, 22, 29, 72, 88, 132, 158, 198-200, 215, 229-230; verbs 14, 18, 105, 197-198, 200
verb of motion 90
verbal inflections 88, 89
verbal nouns 110
verbosity 96, 112
verray 102, 167, 169, 182; *verrey* 102
vers 144; *verse* 142, 143
versification 143
vileynye 207
visual sense 29; visual simile 57
vocabulary 3, 8, 83-84, 95-96, 111, 222

vocative 119
vulgar 234; vulgar words 107

W
wagges 88
walles 59, 60, 61
Walter 9, 189, 192-193, 195-196, 208-209, 211-213, 215, 226
Wanderer, The 39
wanges 84
Warwickshire 87
wel-willy 188
well-balanced sense of style 214, 226
werk 75, 76, 86; *werkes* 84
West Riding 86
whilk 86, 89
White 12-13, 21
white 155, 162, 165, 223
Whiting, B. J. 115
Whitmore, S. M. E. 75
Whittock, T. 74, 77, 116
Wife of Bath, the 112; wyf of Bath, the 213, 226
Wife of Bath's Tale, The 130
wight 84, 119, 122-125, 129, 131, 132
wikke 186
wikked speche 116
willyngly 210
Wilson, G. R. 69
Wimsatt, J. I. 69, 71
Windeatt, B. A. 72, 76
Winny, J. 196, 210, 215, 218
wise 117, 119-120
woful 119, 120, 124, 129, 131
wofulleste 103, 131, 124
women's language 5-6, 8-9, 95-96, 100, 102, 113, 222
women's speech 8, 94-96, 99, 107
wommanysshe 96
Woolner, K. 71
wordplay 7, 11-12, 19, 22-23, 219, 227

words 189, 206
words of wisdom 42
Wordsworth, William 185
world 150
worse 186
worthy 117, 119, 121; *worthi* 119, 120; *worthiest* 122; *worthieste* 103, 104
wrecched 152
Wrenn, C. L. 187
wretched 150
Wyler, S. 77
wynd 59, 154, 156
wyndow 37, 43, 44, 45, 46, 47, 54, 61; *wyndowes* 40, 42
wynter 162

Y
yate 61
yates 49
yen 77
yogh 86
yon 76, 84
yond 61
yonder 59
yong 117, 120; *yonge* 152
Yorkshire 83